# Seizing Jurisdiction

by

J H Mack

TELEMACHUS PRESS

Cover designed by Telemachus Press, LLC

Cover art used with permission from Melanie Pouch

Publishing Services by Telemachus Press, LLC
7652 Sawmill Road
Suite 304
Dublin, Ohio 43016
http://www.telemachuspress.com

ISBN: 978-1-951744-29-8 (eBook)
ISBN: 978-1-951744-30-4 (Paperback)

Version 2022.12.21

# Dedication

To my wife who read it every time it was revised. Bless her patience!

To Sarah, Liz, and Pic who said it was good enough to finish, before I did.

To my friend, Jimmy Hipp, my first sounding board, Rest in Peace.

# Table of Contents

# Seizing Jurisdiction

# Chapter 1

THE INFORMANT HAD called late in the afternoon. "Pier 29, 2 a.m. The *Snowman* will be there for a cocaine shipment." Detective Spencer Baldwin rolled down the window of the borrowed pick-up truck to let in the cool spring air, and he put the night vision binoculars onto the seat. Dressed in faded jeans and a denim shirt, he took off his Braves cap, rubbed the stubble on his face, and ran his fingers through his dark brown hair before tugging the cap back into place. His partner, Hiram Meadors, dressed similarly in jeans and a tee shirt, picked them up and continued scanning the water from their vantage point on the service street to the pier.

The Snowman was a drug smuggler operating in the Savannah area. The coastal seaport, with its direct access to the Atlantic Ocean via the Savannah River and the surrounding rural area, was perfect for a drug smuggling operation. There were so many small boats, salt marsh creeks, and remote backcountry airstrips, it was impossible to cover it all. The Snowman's personal supervision was rare, and Spencer hoped that tonight he'd finally catch the bastard. He'd become an obsession.

"Do you think he'll show this time?" Meadors spoke without taking his eyes off the water.

"I hope so. We've been chasing him long enough," said Spencer. "All of the arrests we've made for the past couple of months must be having an effect on his operation, but I can't tell if we've even slowed him down."

"We keep getting calls from the informant though," Meadors replied without shifting his gaze from the water. "I wonder why he keeps running the risk. Ever since the first phone call and the bust we made at Groom's field, the calls have been steady."

Spencer nodded.

"Well, he's driven by something, that's for sure, because this guy is obviously dangerous. Everybody we've arrested and questioned has disappeared."

Meadors put down the binoculars and looked at Spencer.

"I tell you what's even stranger. Every time that sucker calls, all we get is the name of the place, the cargo, and the time. We've gotten nothing substantial we can use to track the Snowman down, and then like you said, everyone we arrest and question disappears later."

"You're right," said Spencer. "He hasn't given us anything but delivery information."

"He's never been wrong though," Meadors reminded him.

Spencer nodded in agreement and checked his watch; it was ten minutes past two but too early to be worried. The smugglers had been late before. He shifted his lean frame in the seat in an effort to get more comfortable and Meadors did the same. Their earpieces crackled, breaking the silence.

"We got lights on the water moving toward the pier and headlights coming from the north end."

Spencer acknowledged and reminded everybody to wait for his signal. He pulled his weapon free from its holster and checked the action. Meadors followed suit, popping the slide. He looked at Spencer, "Showtime." A 30-foot boat with twin inboard engines and no markings slowly approached the pier. The boat's engines changed pitch and created a muted roar as it went into reverse to stop the forward momentum, and two men jumped out to tie it off.

"Shit, they're loaded for bear," said Spencer as he watched the men with Uzis slung across their backs begin to moor the boat.

"So are the guys in the car," said Meadors, handing the binoculars over.

Spencer surveyed them. "Yep, they got shotguns."

When the twin engines on the boat cut out and silence returned, the crew moored the boat and began to off-load duffel bags of cargo onto the pier. Once on shore, they began to load the car.

Spencer gave the signal and the police net closed in silently and fast. With the element of surprise, the bust went down without a shot fired, and afterwards the cuffed suspects sat sullenly on the pier. There were five duffel bags. Upon opening, they found them packed with marijuana.

Meadors closed his notebook and walked up to Spencer.

"I'm guessing these bags of dope weigh about seven hundred pounds total."

Spencer's face reflected his frustration. There was no cocaine and no Snowman. The informant had been wrong.

The shrimp boat, Mary Lou, out of Beaufort, sat anchored and unseen in the river. In the wheelhouse of the darkened boat, Carl Powers scowled as he watched the pier through binoculars. Tall with blonde hair, light features, and an athletic build that enhanced his *Esquire* appearance, he cursed softly. He had an informer.

That damn cop Baldwin had been there every time, and now everything was in jeopardy. He'd eliminated everyone arrested as a precautionary measure. The marsh was a great place to bury your dead.

As he watched the pier, a Coast Guard patrol boat hit them with a spotlight. Powers didn't move but continued to watch while the captain stepped out of the wheelhouse. The patrol boat's officer wanted to know why they'd anchored in the river without lights on for identification. The captain told him they were having generator problems and were trying to fix it. The young lieutenant ordered them to put up a battery-operated light or he'd escort them into the harbor.

The captain played his role perfectly. "I've forgotten more about handling a boat than your young ass will ever learn."

The officer kept his cool and calmly repeated his order. Two men, armed with M-1s, flanked him on the side rail.

The captain continued to cuss the officer and ordered his deckhands to, "put up the damn light for the *'lootenant'*." The patrol boat moved away, maintaining a watch on the shrimp boat to be sure they complied and to keep the water lane safe.

Powers let the binoculars hang from the strap around his neck and smirked when the captain gave the finger as a salute in the general direction of the patrol boat before entering the wheelhouse. Powers looked at him and said, "I've seen enough. Let's go."

The captain leaned back out the door and said to the man watching the patrol boat from the deck, "Pull up the anchor and let's go."

The engines started with a belch of diesel smoke. The shrimp boat headed down river and the patrol boat followed. They turned toward Beaufort after entering the sound, and the patrol boat turned back up the river toward base.

At his private dock, Powers watched the shrimp boat turn around in the wide creek and head back toward the Intra-Coastal Waterway. As the boat headed into deeper water, he walked up the short gravel path through the thin line of trees from the dock and crossed the wide lawn to the restored plantation house. He skirted the pool deck, entered the house through the French doors, and patted the dogs on the head as he went to the bar. He fixed a drink and decided to drive back to Savannah.

From the car, Carl called Rupert, the aging caretaker, to tell him he was leaving. He'd stayed on when Carl bought the property several years ago, and Carl was glad to have him, although he'd been reluctant at first. However, Rupert had turned a blind eye and deaf ear to Carl's activities, and he'd been helpful during the restoration process.

Approaching the gate, he slowed down and eased through the opening flanked by the big stone columns, leaned out the window, and entered the code on the pole-mounted keypad to close the gate. He pulled the Jaguar out onto the road and quickly shifted through the gears. He was speeding down Highway 17 when the blue light appeared in his rearview mirror. He pulled onto the shoulder, got out, leaned against the Jag, and waited for the patrol car.

The Sheriff, Sam Miller, pulled up and saw the "*Shrimp1*" license tag. He swallowed hard, got out of the car, and looked sheepish.

"I'm sorry, Mr. Powers. I didn't recognize the car in the dark, but you were speeding. Better me than the regular highway patrol though. They'd give you a ticket."

"That's OK, Sam, you're just doing your job."

"Thank you, Mr. Powers. I'd appreciate it if you slowed down to the speed limit though. It's getting late. Lots of deer and other animals stirring; wouldn't want you to get into an accident."

Powers smiled. "You're right, I'll slow down."

"Good night, Mr. Powers, and drive careful now."

Sheriff Miller got into his car and sighed in relief. Mr. Powers had helped keep him in office by supporting his campaign at election time. He watched Powers get into the car and roll off the shoulder onto the pavement. The car accelerated and the tires squealed as he shifted gears and picked up speed. He watched it disappear, too fast, into the night.

Dawn was breaking as Powers crossed the Savannah River Bridge. Deciding he was tired and needed rest, he called his long-time administrative assistant, Jeanette LaCrosse, and left a message for her to handle his morning appointments. LaCrosse had been with him from the beginning of the company and, most recently, she had assumed the role of running the daily operations. She was tough as nails and all business. From the beginning, she had been protective of his time and his schedule, and she guarded access to him like a pit bull.

Spencer was pissed, and his mood reflected it as he brooded through breakfast at his desk. Not only had he been up all night processing paperwork, the information on the bust had been wrong and that had never happened before. He wondered if it was a simple mistake by the informant or if he was misled on purpose.

He was sure of one thing—he needed some time to talk to the prisoners before they hit the street and disappeared, if the pattern held true. He decided to take it up with Captain Drake. The Captain was a veteran cop and a salty son-of-a-bitch who didn't take any crap. He backed his men if they thought they were right, but you'd better watch your ass if you were wrong because he'd chew it off if you screwed up and made him look bad.

Spencer tapped on the door and Drake looked up.

"Come on in, Spencer. I hear we got some bad information last night."

"It wasn't all bad, Captain, we still made a good bust. I'm not sure what happened or what went wrong, if anything, but I need some time and your help to keep the prisoners wrapped in red tape. It'd give me more time and maybe I can get something new. I might even be able to scare one into talking if he doesn't know what might happen to him."

Captain Drake tapped his pencil on the desk.

"OK, but you'll need to work fast," said Drake as he reached for the phone.

"Thanks, Captain," Spencer said, and he walked out.

Spencer decided it was time for the scary side of Meadors. Meadors was an ex-marine and a two-tour veteran of Afghanistan. He was also a physical specimen. He was six-four and his body rippled with muscles. Even though Spencer was six feet and had a lean, muscular build as well, he felt like a dwarf standing next to him. Meadors was a good partner, but he was a crazy bastard who would break the rules to get results. Spencer found him in the squad room.

"How'd you like to scare the crap out of some redneck?"

Meadors flashed a huge smile. "Just close the door and give me some time."

Vernon Faris was a carbon copy of everyone else they had arrested. He was in his late thirties and the epitome of a low country redneck, rawboned, ugly and weathered from hard work and hard drinking. He took one look at the malice evident on Meadors' face and looked back to Spencer for reassurance as they walked into the room and sat down. He didn't get it.

"Mr. Faris," Spencer began, "do you know what's happened to everyone we've arrested who was connected to the Snowman?"

"No. What?"

"Vernon, do you mind if I call you Vernon?"

"No."

"Good! Well … Vernon, they've all just vanished. Within a week of talking to us they disappeared."

"What happened to them?" Vernon asked, warily.

"We aren't sure. Would you like a cigarette?"

"Yeah."

Spencer opened the envelope containing Vernon's effects. He pulled out a smashed pack and lighter, slid them across the table, and waited for Vernon to light up and take a drag, then continued.

"Every time we arrest and question somebody about the Snowman they disappear. We usually follow them around for a couple of days, but eventually we stopped. Priorities you know. Anyway, after we quit, they vanish. No one we've questioned is still around. My guess is they're probably dead."

Spencer let his words sink in. "Vernon, I can arrange to keep you somewhere nice and safe if you can give me information I can use."

"I don't know nothing," he said without conviction.

"Vernon, haven't you been listening to me?" Spencer asked with fake concern. "It doesn't matter. You're a marked man just for being arrested. The Snowman isn't going to take any chances on what you might or might not have told me."

"I don't believe you, and besides, you ain't got no proof." Vernon said defiantly.

"That's true, but I'd say he covers his tracks with murder rather than relocation. That'd be too risky and expensive. Murder is easier and leaves no loose ends," Spencer said in a matter-of fact-tone.

A pre-arranged knock came, and the door opened.

"Sarge, you got a phone call."

"OK, I'll be right there."

Spencer looked at Vernon. "I'll be right back. In the meantime, you should think about what I've said."

"Yeah, sure," Vernon said.

Meadors grinned at Vernon. He shifted in his chair and tried to be cool, but it wasn't successful.

"What's the matter redneck, you scared of me?"

"Hell no," Vernon replied weakly.

"You should be. I could kick your ass, and nobody around here would give a damn."

"You wouldn't dare touch me!"

Meadors grinned again and moved quickly. In seconds, he'd pinned Vernon by his scrawny neck against the wall. Vernon tried to call out but knew no one would hear him. The fire alarm began to ring in the hallway, drowning out his yell for help.

"Listen, you country-ass cracker. I'm going to tear you apart and throw you into the dumpster for the rats if you don't tell my partner what he wants to know."

Vernon squealed, "I don't know nothing. I just do as I'm told!" Meadors squeezed tighter and pushed him higher up the wall.

"Who tells you what to do?"

Vernon, gasping for air, said, "Jake, Jake Sweet."

"Where is he?"

"You got him locked up downstairs. You busted him last night too."

"That's much better, Vernon. Now, you'd better cooperate with my partner when he gets back."

Vernon nodded in the affirmative, and Meadors released his grip. He fell to the floor, sucking in huge gulps of air and rubbing his throat.

"You black son-of-a bitch! You almost killed me."

"Believe me, Vernon, if I was going to kill you, you'd have been dead a long time ago."

The fire alarm stopped, and Spencer returned.

"Sorry about that, Vernon, some asshole in holding tripped the alarm and that freezes the elevators. I couldn't get back until they turned it off. Here, I brought you some coffee."

He slid the cup across the table along with the pack of cigarettes and the lighter. "Now, Vernon, tell me about last night."

Vernon was very cooperative after that, but he didn't tell them anything they hadn't heard before except that Jake Sweet was the leader of his own delivery gang for the Snowman. The others they interrogated corroborated Vernon's story. Jake Sweet was the boss, and he was the key to the puzzle. They saved him for last.

Sweet was a hard case, and he wasn't going to let them scare him, so he made sure they knew it.

"I'm Klan, boy," he said with emphasis on the boy as he sat down looking at Meadors. "You can scare that worthless git Vernon and the others but not me. You two mess with me, and I'll see you end up in the swamp with a rope around your neck."

Meadors started to get up, but Spencer grabbed him by the arm, holding him down.

Sweet sneered. "That's right, boy, control yourself. You just need to be put in your place."

Meadors said through thinned lips, "I suppose you think you're the one to do it."

Before Sweet could answer, Spencer cut in and told Meadors to leave.

Sweet smiled at Meadors. "I'll be seeing you."

"I'll be waiting."

Spencer turned and looked at Sweet with contempt. "You're awfully sure of yourself, Mr. Sweet. How come?"

Sweet smirked. "I might know a bit more than the others, but it has a price."

Spencer looked at him with level eyes. "It has to be good information and prove to be true; no deals until then; if it turns out to be true, you'll need protection."

Sweet snorted. "If you were protecting the ones before me forget it. You can't protect shit. I'm safer on my home ground with the Klan around me."

Spencer didn't show any emotion at this statement, but it was obvious Sweet knew something about the disappearances of the others. "They weren't under our protection because they didn't tell us anything. They claimed they didn't know who the Snowman was. How do you know so much? You aren't much more than a delivery boy."

"That may be true, but I've made a lot of deliveries, and I've learned some interesting things."

"I need details."

"OK. How about an address?"

Back in his cell, Sweet thought fast. He knew Baldwin couldn't keep him safe, and the address would be useless once they checked it out. They'd have to put him on the street after he made bail, and then he was going to have to be cautious. He made a phone call, left a message and felt better, but he was still worried. That crazy bastard, Baxter, would still probably try to kill him, regardless of what he'd said on the phone.

Spencer and Meadors checked out the address while Sweet brainstormed in his cell. It was a local company's seafood warehouse complex. There were about twenty warehouses inside the fenced compound with multiple gates in and out. Coastal Seafood Inc. was on the large sign in the air over the complex and stenciled on the buildings. The address was a dead end.

Back at the jail, Spencer met with Sweet again.

"Your address is worthless unless you can give me something else. You know I won't cut a deal or protect you if you don't play square with me. What's the deal on the address and Coastal Seafood?"

"I met some guys there for a pick-up about a month ago."

"Who were they?" Spencer asked.

"I don't know, just some guys."

"How many?"

"A couple."

Spencer lost patience. "I need details, or I'll lock your butt up on every charge I can imagine, and bail won't be an option. Right now, all you're facing is a dope charge."

"OK! OK! There were two," Sweet said as if he was surrendering. "One of them met me on the street, got into the truck, and showed me where to go. I pulled into one of the warehouses. I don't know which number. They loaded the truck with about ten, heavy cardboard boxes sealed with tape. One was a skinny little freak that could barely carry a box. The other one was a big man, mean looking mother, and he teased the other one about carrying the heavy loads. I didn't touch a box. Once loaded, the little one gave me a map. I met a plane at an airstrip and got paid in cash, by mail, like always."

Spencer pressed for more. "Where was the landing strip?"

"Some farmer's airstrip out in the sticks."

"Do you remember the farmer's name?"

"You're kidding," Sweet said sarcastically. "I followed the map, delivered the goods, and went home."

Spencer stared at Jake. "How long did it take you to get there?"

Sweet, wary, wrinkled his brow.

"I guess about an hour; took me about that long to get home, too."

Spencer changed tactics, now that Sweet had unknowingly given him a search area. "You got paid by mail. How'd the cash come?"

"Same as always, wrapped in newspaper, packed in a cardboard box, and addressed to me, no return address."

"You've got a lot of details, but so far nothing that will save your ass. You made a phone call. Who did you call?"

"None of your business. That's private still, ain't it?" Sweet said with contempt. "You going to let me go now?"

"It's against my better judgment, but your bail's posted. I've a feeling you'll be dead soon. I just hope you last more than a few days. It'd be a first."

Sweet sneered. "Don't worry about me; I can take care of myself."

Spencer sent Sweet back to his cell, met with Meadors and the Captain, and they laid out a plan of action. They'd begin snooping around Coastal Seafood and let desk people review the search radius for airfields. Meadors would take charge of the detail that would follow Sweet. They hoped he'd make a move and contact somebody to help him out of his predicament.

Meadors and the Captain set up the detail while Sweet was being processed out, and he was waiting on the sidewalk when Sweet was released.

"What you want, boy?"

Meadors smiled. "I'll be watching you, redneck. Just be careful you don't get yourself killed."

Sweet flipped Meadors the finger. "Fuck you." Then he got into a late model, maroon Thunderbird.

Meadors copied the tag number, went to his car, and called it in. The tag belonged to the brother, Vincent Sweet, but it was for a different car. The detail following Sweet had instructions to be obvious, and they radioed their progress as they followed them around.

Sweet's brother, Vincent, was driving.

"Jake, we got a tail, couple of darkie cops in a blue Ford. What do you want to do?"

"Fuck them. Let's go home and get drunk."

He opened a beer he fished out of the grocery sack, giving it to Vincent, then got another one, opened it, and took a huge drink.

"Let's call the boys in when we get home and make some plans. I need to be sure Baxter doesn't kill me before I get the chance to leave town."

Vincent nodded and headed for home.

The car tailing the Sweets followed them onto a narrow-track dirt road and stopped on the road at the mailbox with the number 19 and the name, Sweet, painted in a crude hand. They watched them park in front of a rundown farmhouse. Tires and junk cars littered the yard, and an abandoned barn close to the house was falling down. The Sweet brothers got out of the car, glanced in their direction, and went inside. The detail reported to Meadors the suspects had returned home and gave him the address. Meadors told them to hang around until dark and leave. He knew they'd spot the detail and was counting on it. Sweet's arrogance would write them off because of their color, and he was going to take advantage of it. He was going to scare the hell out of Jake Sweet.

# Chapter 2

ALISHEEN DELANEY WAS Irish in name and looked damn good for someone in her mid-thirties, according to Spencer. She spoke with a sweet southern drawl and had a fearful temper. She owned a restaurant, the She Crab, on River Street. It had a grand view of the Savannah River and was famous for its seafood. Alisheen greeted every customer with a warm smile and a happy, "Welcome to the She Crab!"

She surveyed the Tuesday night crowd as she walked around. It was only six o'clock, but the place was already full, and the line of people waiting for a table was out the door. She hoped to see Spencer soon. He'd broken their date last night, saying something had come up, and she hadn't heard from him since. Alisheen pulled up short as she entered the bar, looking for Spencer and greeting customers. On a stool sat Carl Powers. He saw her, and she smiled at him.

Carl and Alisheen met by accident a few weeks before, when he was riding on the delivery truck. Carl rode the trucks occasionally to keep in touch with his customers and to maintain a relationship with his drivers to get a feel for their challenges on the job. Alisheen was working in the kitchen that day and received the order. Even though they were on time and the order was correct, Alisheen voiced her displeasure with their service. She ignored him and began a tirade against the regular driver.

"It's about damn time you showed up," Alisheen said with deep sarcasm. "I guess if the order is right too it will be my lucky day."

As she went over the delivery slip and checked the unloaded boxes, she said with mock surprise, "Two miracles in one day, I don't think my poor heart can take it."

The driver looked sheepish, ducked his head, and continued to unload the truck while Alisheen continued.

"If I could meet Mr. Powers face-to-face, I'd give him a piece of my mind. He sits in his air-conditioned office on his fat butt, no doubt, while I'm in this hot-ass kitchen working mine off, and my whole day is screwed because you can't get here on time with the correct order. He needs to pay better attention to one of his best customers, or he can kiss my business goodbye, and you can tell him I said so."

Alisheen noticed the other driver was watching her intently and with an amused look on his face.

"I've never seen you before, are you new? Do you think I'm funny?" she asked with a sarcastic tone.

Carl smiled and bowed slightly.

"No ma'am," said Carl. "I've been around for quite a long time. I'm Carl Powers, the owner of Coastal Seafood."

Alisheen turned forty different shades of red, and the driver ran to the back of the truck, out of sight, howling with laughter. Powers extended his hand in greeting with a look of sincerity. Now red-faced and embarrassed, she stammered in an effort to make an apology after failing to find a place to hide. She shook his hand and managed to ask him to stay and have lunch on the house. He accepted and sent the driver, who was still giggling, on the rest of his route. From that day on, he was a regular in the She Crab and a friend.

As Alisheen walked toward his seat, she smiled inwardly. He was a handsome man, 40-ish, and his cool, confident manner was evident. He drained his beer as she sat down and waved at Mickey, the bartender, to bring another one.

She put her arms around him in a brief hug and said, "Hello, Carl!"

"Hello, Alisheen, you're gorgeous as always."

"Thank you," she laughed. "You're in early tonight. I usually don't see you until later."

"I had a late start today and missed lunch. I was hungry. Would you care to join me?"

"Thanks, but no, I've got to keep moving. Customers you know."

"Alisheen, you're amazing. How about you and I go out sometime?" Carl casually asked.

"Like on a date?" she asked, surprised.

"Well, yes," he paused. "We could ride over to my plantation in South Carolina, take the plane to Atlanta, and see a play or a concert. Let's have some fun and do something different out of Savannah. Let's get away from it all." The look of enthusiasm and sincerity on Carl's face was evident, and Alisheen was flattered that he'd asked her out.

"I don't know. I do date somebody seriously, but I'll think about it."

Carl laughed. "Well, at least that wasn't no."

Alisheen smiled and kissed him on the cheek. "I'll see you," and moved off through the crowd.

Carl watched her walk away. She was dressed in blue jeans and a She Crab tee shirt. The starched, long-sleeve white shirt she wore as a cover up, with the sleeves rolled up and the tails knotted at the waist, set off her figure. She didn't wear too much make-up, and her flowing red hair, pulled back and tied loosely at the nape of the neck with a thin ribbon, accentuated her face. She was beautiful. He confessed inwardly that since he'd met her he wanted her to be more than a friend. She liked him and that was a start.

As Alisheen started to exit the bar and enter the main room, Spencer came in the door off the street. She waved at him as their eyes met, then smiled and shook her fist at him. He instantly looked sheepish and knew he was in trouble for not calling. They kissed and embraced, and she led him to the opposite end of the bar from Powers, where they sat down. Mickey brought Spencer a bowl of boiled shrimp and a Corona.

"Hey, Spencer, how's it hanging man?" Mickey asked with a smile.

"OK, Mickey. Thanks. How're you doing?"

"I'm doing OK, I guess, although it's hard to make a living on what she pays me. You think you can talk her into giving me a raise?"

Alisheen broke up the conversation with a laugh. "You can forget the raise, Mickey, you're overpaid anyway. I just keep you around because I feel sorry for you."

"Thanks, boss, I appreciate that," Mickey said with mock sincerity. "You need anything else Spencer, or you, boss?"

Spencer shook his head no because he had a mouth full, and Alisheen said, "No, Mickey, thanks though," then she turned to Spencer. "Well, who'd you stand me up for this time?" she asked with a hint of frustration.

"I'm sorry, Al. We had a bust go down last night from a tip, and I barely had time to pull it together."

With a look of concern Alisheen said, "Everything go OK?"

Spencer frowned. "Yes and no, it was a good bust but not what or who we were hoping for."

"Anybody get hurt?"

"No, it went down clean."

"Thank God for that."

"Shrimp is good," mumbled Spencer, his mouth full.

"You want anything else, Spencer?" Alisheen asked as she slid off the stool.

He grinned mischievously. "Yeah, but I don't think I can get it here."

Alisheen laughed. "Hold that thought. I own the place you know, maybe I can arrange it."

Spencer chuckled.

She kissed him on the lips. "Eat a good supper. I'll check on you later."

Spencer watched her as she walked through the crowded room, passing from the bar into the dining room, greeting customers as she went. She moved with grace and poise through the crowd. He loved her with all of his heart, and he desperately wanted to ask her to marry him. Most recently, she'd started hinting around the subject again by reminding him they had been dating over three years now, and she would like to get married on the beach. As usual that rolled into the question of how long to wait before they tried to start a family. They weren't getting any younger, she'd reminded him.

The topic of marriage and children always made him uncomfortable, and he tried to change the subject, which started the usual argument over why he couldn't commit to her. Ashamed, Spencer simply argued, they were still in their thirties and had time, but he was unable to tell her the truth. He loved her dearly and knew she could get on with her life if he was killed in the line of duty, but he couldn't have children while he was a street cop. He'd grown up without a dad, and he wasn't going to let any children they would have suffer the same fate.

A teenager high on meth had robbed a convenience store. His dad was on patrol and answered the alarm. The suspect was armed, and he emptied the gun at the patrol car as it pulled up. His father was killed before he even got out of the car. He'd vowed then that he'd be a cop like his dad. His vow had become his passion. He worked tirelessly to keep drugs off the street, and he'd risen quickly through the ranks. So far, he'd been unable to share these fears with her. His memories were painful, and their arguments dredged up old feelings of hate and guilt. He assumed she would disregard his fears as silly, given how rational she was, but it would only make things worse. He wanted to keep things going until he earned a promotion to a desk job. Right now, he knew that as long as he was on the street there was no way he could marry her. He sighed and felt a little bit of the old sadness come over him. He sipped his beer and turned to watch the ballgame.

~~~~

Carl saw Alisheen greet Spencer and recognized him as the cop he'd seen on the pier. He kept his emotions in check and maintained his demeanor. He watched them for a few moments then forced himself to look away. Carl grabbed the server as she went by and gave her a $100 bill to cover his tab.

He left the bar, exiting into the dining room, and barged into Mickey, who was coming back from delivering drinks to a table and carrying a bowl of boiled shrimp.

"Excuse me, Mickey, I got an urgent call," Carl said, and he quickly made his way out to the street.

Mickey, delivering the shrimp to a table by the window, watched Powers walk the length of the sidewalk, get into his Jag parked outside the bar entrance, and drive away. Alisheen saw Mickey staring out the window and asked him why he wasn't behind the bar.

"I was wondering why a person would go through the restaurant from the bar and leave out the other door to get to his car, when it's parked right outside this door?"

"Go back to the bar please, Mickey, it's very busy," Alisheen said, as if she hadn't heard him.

He went back to the bar muttering out loud that people who do crazy stuff like that usually got something to hide and can't be trusted.

Carl left the She Crab and headed for his office. It was an older two-story building located on the river at the edge of the business district. He parked beside the steps that led up to the second floor entrance and noticed the lights were on in the building. He didn't see any other cars in the lot so he was cautious. He quietly entered, went down the short hall that led to the large open area, and burst out of the hallway, scaring the hell out of Jeanette LaCrosse. She gave a frightened yelp of "OH!" and dropped the files in her hands.

"I'm sorry, Miss LaCrosse," Carl said. "I thought it was a prowler. I didn't see your car outside."

Flustered, she said, "My car is in the shop so I took a cab. I was just going to be here a short while, and I lost track of time." Slightly out of breath, she gathered herself together and began hastily to pick up the scattered papers.

Carl moved to help her, but she waved him off. "That's OK, Mr. Powers. I can handle this, and besides, I know what order it's all in. You don't, so just let me do it."

Carl chuckled. "You're right. I'd just get it messed up, and you'd have to straighten it out anyway. I am sorry though."

She shooed him away with an "it's all right, I've got it look," so he went into his office and quietly closed the door. He went to the bar in the corner and poured some scotch, neat. Sitting down at his desk, he turned his chair to look out the large window with a view of the river. The smuggling business had made him rich beyond his dreams. If he quit now, he couldn't spend it all if he tried, but he knew he wouldn't quit. He thrived on wealth and power, and most importantly, the thrill of taking the risk. He needed it to survive, to feel alive.

He reflected on how he felt when he recognized Baldwin. His blood had gone cold, but it wasn't with fear, it was exhilaration. It was his primal urge to compete and beat him at the game. He looked at his football memorabilia from Georgia and remembered how his athletic fame had opened doors for him in the community he now owned. They all wanted to be friends with the famous Carl Powers. It'd been too easy.

Jeanette heard the door close, breathed a little easier, and finished the mundane paperwork without much thought. She wanted to be sure her excuse for being there looked legitimate, but she'd been there to make the phone call to Atlanta and finish the flash drive. She decided she could leave and put everything away, locking her desk and the files. She knocked on the office door and entered with his acknowledgement.

"I'm leaving now, Mr. Powers."

"Goodnight, Miss LaCrosse. I'm sorry for startling you."

"It's OK, Mr. Powers. Will you be here in the morning?"

"I think so, but I'll call if I change my mind. How's my appointment schedule?"

"It's pretty light, nothing I can't handle until your 11:00 o'clock meeting with Mr. Jenkins of Sun Diesel."

Knowing his calendar off the top of her head was her trademark, and she was proud of her recall ability.

Carl reflected for a moment at the mention of the name. "OK, I'll be here for that. I don't want to miss him."

"Well, goodnight then," she said as she turned to leave.

"Goodnight, Miss LaCrosse," he said looking back out the window. "You can leave the door open."

Jeanette had already called the cab, and she waited impatiently. It arrived in a few minutes, and she went out and got into the back. After giving the driver her address, she settled back into the seat and opened her purse.

She took the flash drive out, and looking at it with a smug smile, said to herself, "I've got you now."

Carl finished thinking through his plan for discovering more about Baldwin. It was simple. He'd be more aggressive with his intentions for Alisheen, in an effort to get her to talk about him, hoping she'd reveal something he could use. If he could get her to talk about him freely, it'd be easy to find out more about the man causing him so much grief. He decided to go home and get some sleep. It'd turned out to be an interesting day after a long night. As he drove home, he thought it odd that through all the years of working together, he still referred to Jeanette LaCrosse as Miss, and she still called him, Mr. Powers.

~~~~

Meadors arrived home, went straight into the bedroom, and opening the closet door, carefully pulled the Marine trunk out, placing it on the bed. He spun the combination lock with practiced ease and opened the lid, looking down on a display of sorts, of the awards and medals from Afghanistan, and he lifted the Recon patch from the center.

He looked at the photograph of his squad and recalled their names, remembering the dead and those who'd survived the second tour. Damn few of them, he mused. He saluted the picture and rubbed the patch with his thumb for the magic and luck it'd brought him in the past. He changed into his camo, went to the closet again, and carefully unwrapped his sniper rifle. He returned to the trunk, found the silencer, and screwed it on. He put the scope on the mounts, sighted the rifle, and pulled the trigger, smiling at the lack of sound, and slid the assembled rifle carefully into the carrying case. He packed a small backpack with a camo hood and night vision goggles, and then he put on a blue police jacket to cover the fact that he was fully dressed in camouflage. He picked up the rifle case, shouldered the pack, and headed out the door. He was going to scare the hell out of Jake Sweet.

Meadors drove to the truck stop that marked the turn onto the dirt road that led to the Sweet's farmhouse about a mile away. He parked on the edge of the vast parking lot, swarming with cars and trucks off the interstate. The large trailers hid him from view of the restaurant entrance and fuel pumps. He quickly grabbed the gear from the back seat and left the perimeter of the lights entering the adjacent field. He shed the jacket, put on the hood and goggles, and placed the rifle sling over his shoulder. After a quick bearing on his gear to find it when he returned, he crossed the road into the woods.

After a short hike, he found the house the surveillance team had described with the old cars in the yard. He made his way to the road and read the name "Sweet" on the mailbox. He crossed the road and scouted around for a good firing position. He couldn't believe his luck. A deer stand overlooked the fields and the farmhouse. After climbing into the stand, he calculated the range to the house with the night scope and settled in to wait for the opportune moment.

Soon enough, three cars came rolling down the road and turned into the drive that led to the house. Meadors counted eight people get out and go inside. In minutes, Jake Sweet came out, leading them all onto the porch with a beer in his hand and a cigarette in his mouth. He sat down on the porch, under the light, and the rest of them followed suit or leaned against the wall, listening to him talk.

Meadors looked through the scope at the large head of Jake Sweet, bathed in the glow of the bare bulb on the screen porch, and checked the range again. He wanted to be sure. If he wounded him that would be better, but the shot was too far, and he couldn't risk killing him by accident. He wanted to scare him into talking; they needed information, and they were going to get it.

Jake, Vincent, and the rest of the boys were drinking beer and passing a joint and a bottle around. Meadors took one last look at Jake's head and targeted the bottle on the table in front of him. Jake was reaching for the bottle when it exploded in his face, cutting him with flying glass. Everyone froze, then the porch light went out with a loud pop, scattering more glass. All hell broke loose. They were all flat on their faces, cussing and screaming like crazy, and during the chaos, Meadors put two more rounds into the windows that looked out onto the porch.

Meadors ceased fire, quickly climbed out of the deer stand, and used his night goggles to quickly navigate his way through the woods and back to the car.

After recovering his gear from the field, he decided he was hungry. He pulled around the parked trailers he'd used for cover, then found a front row space by the restaurant and went in. He sat down in a booth and ordered, recalling the scene on the porch. He chuckled as he pictured it in his mind and smiled all the way through his meal.

~ ~ ~ ~

While Meadors was eating a hearty meal at the truck stop, Jake Sweet's boys were combing the woods, armed with guns and flashlights, looking for the shooter. Jake was in the house staying away from the windows and being careful not to walk in front of any lights that could outline him to anyone outside.

Vincent came in and lit a cigarette.

"Jake," said Vincent with a plea, "We got enough money to get out of here. Let's just go and don't risk it."

"No, I ain't going until I get me a decent payoff for not talking to the cops. I can protect myself with the boys helping out and being on the lookout for the Snowman's hitman." Jake said with defiance.

"Damn, Jake" yelled Vincent angrily. "You mean like tonight? They'd better do a lot better job, or you're going to end up dead for sure. You never should have called him and tried to make a deal."

"You dumb ass Vincent, this is an opportunity for a big score," Jake said with sarcasm, "I left him a message saying I was leaving town and he'd never see me again, but I needed some traveling money to be gone for a long time. When he pays off, we'll be set." Jake, Vincent, and the boys planned all night after that. He just hoped it would be enough.

A satellite hook-up had forwarded Jake's call from jail that morning, through an untraceable relay system, to a residential phone where he left his message. Ian Baxter listened to the message, then, dialing through the relay, placed a call to Coastal Seafood. He made an appointment to meet with Mr. Powers the next morning at 11:00 under the guise of Mr. Jenkins with Sun Diesel Company. Sun Diesel serviced the Coastal trucks and fishing fleet. He was going to be in the area and wanted to go over some service contracts with Mr. Powers. Miss LaCrosse made the appointment. As Ian Baxter, the head of the Snowman's security hung up, he smiled. He was looking forward to contract negotiations tomorrow regarding Mr. Sweet.

~~~~

Benjamin Whitley was the head of D.E.A., southeast branch located in Atlanta. The phone call he'd received earlier that evening worried him. Somebody in Savannah was endangering the operation, and it would go down the tubes if he couldn't stop it. Heads would roll, and his would be the first one. He dreaded the fact he was now going to have to call Mr. Chambers in

Washington. He dialed the number to Clifton Chamber's private line. He answered on the first ring.

"Mr. Chambers?" Whitley said hesitantly.

"Yes, what do you have so far?" The tone of frustration was evident.

"The second informer called again this evening with another offer to expose the Snowman if we're willing to meet the conditions."

Chambers vented his displeasure, and Whitley held the phone away from his ear.

Before he could begin again Whitley said, "I know perfectly well what's at stake, sir. After all it was partly my proposal."

Chambers started ranting again.

Whitley was finally able to say, "I don't know, but I'm going to send a team to Savannah as soon as I can."

"Fix it now, whatever it takes damn it!" shouted Chambers, and he hung up.

Whitley exhaled. "That was fun," and rang his secretary who had stayed late per his request. "I want a meeting with Skip Fitzgerald and his team first thing in the morning, and I don't give a damn where they are or what they're doing."

"Yes, sir," she replied as she began to dial furiously.

Skip Fitzgerald and his team assembled in the conference room the next morning after the demand to appear the night before. Whitley walked in, tossed a file folder onto the table, and sat down.

"Gentleman, we've gotten another call from the second informer in Savannah. We can't afford to have this second unknown person jeopardize an ongoing investigation. Skip, I want you and your team in Savannah as soon as possible, and I want answers. We know the locals have been busting the Snowman crews now for a couple of months so either our first informer is giving them information or it's the new caller. Have you heard any more from our man?" Whitley asked, looking directly at him.

Agent Skip Fitzgerald, in charge of the Savannah operation and the only person that had had contact with the first informer, shook his head.

"No, sir, I haven't gotten anything from him for a couple of months, which coincides with when the locals started making busts. Bo Biggers calls me if he hears anything. He files a weekly report, but the locals are keeping the busts out of the press."

Whitley rubbed his temples. "Make a guess about what's happening."

Fitzgerald said, "I don't know, maybe this second person is in the same sort of position as our first informer, and they don't know about each other. My guess is our original snitch got tired of waiting on us to make a move, and that's why the locals have been getting information."

Fitzgerald's last sentence had a tone of frustration. He looked pointedly at Whitley, wanting his own explanation.

Whitley ignored him. "You're going to have to go down there, find him, and make contact. You must warn him there is somebody else, and he'll have to be careful."

"You know we don't know how to contact him! We never established a procedure because he doesn't want to be contacted. It was too risky for him," Fitzgerald said irritated.

"Well you'd better think of something. Whatever it takes, you get your ass down there and get me some answers."

Whitley stood up, signaling the meeting was over. Without another word, he left the room and went to his office. He sat down, lit a cigar, put the file back into the credenza, and locked it. This plan was the most complex and, at the same time, the simplest plan ever contrived. His offhand comment to Clifton Chambers had put into motion a string of meetings and planning sessions that had gone from outlandish, to doable, to an order to get it done. The concept was so obvious and simple it was a wonder that no one had tried it before. The past attempts to control drug traffic into the States focused on the cartels and dealers, this plan revolved around the smugglers.

He sighed. "I've got to be crazy." The Snowman was their first target. They needed him and his organization intact, and they weren't arresting anybody until they were ready to put the plan into action. Now the locals were making arrests but so far had done very little damage if they were getting the same information. It could still work, but this second person could screw up everything. He needed to keep this second informer off guard until they could eliminate this new threat to the operation.

Whitley called Chambers later that morning to report. Whitley outlined the results of the meeting. He listened to the instructions and said, "Yes, sir, I understand."

He called his secretary. "Find Blackwell and have him come and see me as soon as possible."

Disgusted, he hung up the phone. He didn't like Blackwell very much. He was a cold-blooded bastard whose line of work was distasteful to Whitley but, as they say, "Somebody's got to do it."

Skip Fitzgerald knew things were bad; he just didn't know how much. Preparing for the drive to Savannah in the afternoon, he called and made a room reservation and began to pack his clothes. He went back to the very beginning in his mind to see if he could pull out a clue.

The man had walked into the Atlanta offices that morning and asked to speak to an agent saying, "He might have some information that'd be useful."

Fitzgerald had been walking through the lobby, and overhearing the conversation with the desk attendant, he offered his services to the visitor.

The man handed him an envelope and said, "Look at this. If you're interested contact me to discuss the details." Then he said, "Thanks," and walked out.

Fitzgerald went immediately to his office and loaded the flash drive. A narrative describing the Snowman and his organization, with sufficient detail to give it credibility, unfolded on the screen before him. At the end, there was a procedure and a phone number to call, if the D.E.A. was interested.

Fitzgerald then met with Whitley in his office and gave him the flash drive. Fitzgerald left his office, and Whitley called Mr. Chambers in Washington. After a few weeks, Fitzgerald received a strange set of orders. He was to make contact with the informant per the instructions, start an investigation, and maintain a top-secret file. If he identified the Snowman, he was not to make an arrest without approval from Washington. When Fitzgerald asked why, Whitley told him it was not necessary for him to know, but to follow instructions.

Fitzgerald knew a reprimand when he heard one and followed orders, but he didn't like it. He contacted the informant per the instructions, and they met in a secluded park on the north side of Atlanta. The rules were simple.

"I'll send you a flash drive whenever I feel it's safe to do so. Never attempt to find me or contact me. If you do, I'll end it and disappear. There'll be no more meetings between us."

The informant walked off and disappeared into the park. Even though Fitzgerald had a keen eye for details, the informant's description he provided wasn't much help. He was a slender white male dressed in jeans, and the light blue jacket he wore was zipped up to the neck. A solid blue baseball cap was pulled down low onto his forehead, but it could not hide the blonde hair around his ears. He wore dark sunglasses to cover his eyes. He was under six feet and somewhere in his 30s. There were no distinguishing marks or tattoos. He was about as average looking as you could get. So basically, they had nothing to use from that one encounter to help them find him. Since then he'd been following orders and collecting information.

~~~~

Skip went to the fridge and got a beer. His mind shifted gears back to the present, and he thought about what they did know. "Crap, we don't know a damn thing, except for the fact the informant was in Savannah. How in the hell were they going to find him and make contact?"

~~~~

Clifton Chambers sat in his office looking out the window over Washington as the sun was beginning to set. The city was beautiful at sunset and Chambers liked it here, but everything he worked for could be gone in a matter of hours. He was going to meet with Isaac Henry, the head of D.E.A., and it wasn't going to be pleasant.

Chambers was running this operation without Henry's knowledge, and it was going to hit the fan when he found out. He'd taken a risk and moved ahead without approval, wanting to demonstrate he could be bold and decisive. He wanted to prove himself as an "out-of-the-box" thinker and be rewarded for his moxie. He'd hoped to have the details wrapped up before he approached Henry. Now he had to tell him everything before it was ready to go, and he was going to be lucky if he wasn't arrested, much less, still have a job after it was over.

He continued to gaze out at Washington as the sun faded away to dark, and the city turned itself on to greet the night. The phone rang and he answered it quickly. He hated the sound of a ringing telephone.

"He'll see you now."

He finished the drink he'd been nursing in a big gulp, picked up the file, and walked down the hall to the Director's office. He entered the outer office, and the secretary waved him through to Henry's office without slowing down. Isaac Henry was an old bald-headed son-of-a bitch with a temperament like a junkyard dog. He was also cunning and perceptive enough to have survived the politics of several administrations to keep his post for over twenty years.

Isaac Henry looked up from his desk and said, "Close the door, Clifton. Tell me all about the Savannah project—from the beginning."

# Chapter 3

ALISHEEN AND SPENCER walked up the stairs to her loft apartment in a refurbished warehouse on the water. Once inside, Spencer grabbed a beer from the fridge and headed for the rocking chairs on the deck. He flipped on the ceiling fan to keep the bugs away, then he settled into one of the chairs facing the river.

She put some light jazz on the stereo and took a shower. The mellow sounds drifted out through the open windows onto the deck. Alisheen appeared with damp red hair and wrapped up in a fluffy white bathrobe. She looked sexy as hell, and Spencer smiled appreciatively.

"What are you looking at?" she said with an air of aloofness.

"Only the best ass in Savannah," Spencer replied with mock seriousness. She laughed and Spencer pulled her to the rocking chair as she sat on his lap.

"You flatter me, sir," and she kissed him long and deep.

Alisheen rested her head on his shoulder as they listened to the music.

"It certainly is beautiful tonight," she said.

Spencer said, "Uh-huh."

Alisheen got the feeling he wasn't listening, so she decided to test him. "I think I'll paint my butt green so we can go downtown, OK?"

Spencer replied, "Whatever color you want is fine with me."

She slapped him on the head.

"Ouch, that hurt."

"Well pay attention to me," Alisheen said, and she kissed his head where she'd slapped him.

"I'm sorry. I was thinking about this smuggling case. Our information was accurate until last night, and then it was wrong. Something is going on, but I don't know what, and I don't like it."

"Can you tell me more about it?"

"I really can't tell you much more; you might be a spy or something. You're not a spy are you?" Spencer said with a gleam in his eye.

"No, but I'll let you torture me to see if I am, OK?" she said with a half-smile matching Spencer's tone.

"Mmmm, sounds good to me," Spencer said, hugging her close and caressing her hair and neck. With a serious tone he said, "We have to find a way to get somebody we arrested last night to talk because we need information. The rules have changed, and I don't have a copy."

"Spencer, is this dangerous?" Alisheen asked quietly.

"Yes, honey, it is, but you know me, I'll be careful. I know you hate it, Alisheen, but it's what I do and, for now, we'll just have to deal with it."

"I know," she sighed. "I'll just keep the bad thoughts away until they do call me," she said with an effort to be cheerful.

"That's my girl," he said as he hugged her again. "Come on, let's dance." Spencer led her off the deck into the living area of the apartment.

The lights were off, but the dim light filtering through the open window from the docks and street below was enough. They kissed tenderly, and Alisheen slowly undressed him. He opened her robe, slid his hands underneath, and caressed her naked body. She led him to the bedroom and pulled him onto the bed. They aroused each other tenderly and made love.

Alisheen drifted off to sleep, and Spencer looked at her soft features in the dim light. She was beautiful. He felt a touch of sadness as he looked at her, and he wasn't sure why. Their lovemaking seemed to have a sense of urgency lately that hadn't been there before. It felt as if they were trying to create a memory that was going to have to last forever because of some unforeseen event in the future they were dreading.

Unable to go to sleep, Spencer got out of bed and quietly went to the kitchen. He poured a large glass of milk and raided the cookie box. Vanilla Wafers, he loved them. He went out to the deck, sat in a rocking chair, and munched on his snack. He looked at the river and watched the dark water roll by on its way out to sea.

Alisheen woke to the sounds of the dock activity and the noise of the busy river coming through the window. She missed Spencer and found him asleep in a rocking chair on the deck with an empty box of Vanilla Wafers on his lap.

"Gross," she thought. He woke up as she looked down at him and grinned sheepishly.

"The whole box, Spencer?" she said in an accusing tone but with a smile.

"Yep, the whole box."

"Unbelievable," she said. "Come on. Let's take a run and go to the Dixie for breakfast. I'll have to keep you exercising, or you'll get fat as a pig on those cookies," she said with a big smile.

They finished their run, then showered, dressed, and went to the Dixie. Breakfast at the Dixie was low country style; shrimp and grits, eggs on the side, biscuits, orange marmalade, and a steaming cup of coffee. It was great food and, Dixie, who owned the diner and gave it his name, was a good friend. Dixie also weighed 300-pounds, was queer as they came, and he made no effort to disguise it.

"My friends, how are you?" yelled Dixie with loud dramatic flair, announcing their entrance as they came in the door. He waved them to a booth, pointed to a server to get them coffee, and said, "I'm so glad to see you. Give me a few minutes and I'll be with you."

Dixie soon made his way to their booth and asked them how things were going.

Alisheen spoke. "Things are going great, Dixie, how about you?"

Dixie heaved a great sigh. "Same as always, just working myself to death. What will you have this morning?"

Alisheen smiled at the "business is great" answer Dixie always gave. Spencer grinned and sipped his coffee.

Spencer put his coffee down. "A ham biscuit and a bowl of grits for me and the 'Low-Country' breakfast for Alisheen."

Dixie clucked his tongue into his teeth. "Eating Vanilla Wafers again Spencer? You always order that to make up for your gluttonous ways," Dixie said with a mocking tone, and he walked away chuckling.

As Dixie served them, he said, "How are things at the She Crab, Alisheen?"

"Business is great, and we're already seeing the spring crowds, so it should be a great season. I don't see much of you though. How come you don't come see me anymore?" she asked brightly.

"I know, I know," said Dixie with a tone of exasperation and martyrdom. "Things have been so busy here too that it seems I don't do anything but work."

Dixie focused on Spencer with a solid stare and said with bite in his voice, "Spencer, when are you going to marry this woman? You're going to lose her if you keep messing around and wasting time. Get on with it, man!"

Spencer gave Dixie a go-to-hell look, and Alisheen looked out of the window.

With a devious look on his face, Dixie said, "Have a nice day and y'all come back soon," then he walked off.

Spencer began to mutter about that asshole doing that on purpose, and Alisheen stopped him.

"Spencer, it's OK, and I'm not upset, but it's a question that you've been unwilling to answer," she said pointedly. "We won't discuss it right now, Spencer, and ruin our brief time together this morning, but promise me that soon we will?"

Reluctantly he said, "I promise," and he proceeded to eat his breakfast.

After they finished, Spencer dropped her off at the restaurant and waved goodbye. She waved and turned to go inside. As he passed the alley to the back of the restaurant, he noticed a Coastal Seafood truck parked in the delivery zone.

~~~~

Jake Sweet was hung over. Getting up, he went into the bathroom, threw up, and felt better. He went into the kitchen, grabbed a beer out of the fridge, and opening it with a crack, took a big gulp.

He went to Vincent's room and yelled at him. "Get up boy, we got things to do today!"

Vincent rolled over, looked at him, mumbled an obscenity, and snuggled deeper into the worn out bedding. Jake went to the front room and peered through the shot-out windows.

He cursed as he sat down on the couch and turned on the television, flipping the channels with the remote until he found some cartoons.

He yelled, "Come on, Vincent, get your ass out of bed."

Vincent appeared in the hallway and walked across the room to the fridge in the corner. He reached in, grabbed a bottle of orange juice, and lit a cigarette.

"Damn, Jake, how can you drink a beer this early in the morning?"

"Because I'm a man, piss-ant. Hurry up and let's go get us some breakfast."

The brothers nervously exited the house, anticipating a gunshot but none came. They got into the Thunderbird and rode down to the truck stop, where the blue Ford from the day before was waiting for them.

"Where in the hell were they last night while that son-of-a-bitch was shooting at us?" said Jake. Ignoring them, they parked, went inside, and ate. After finishing, they went out to the car. The blue Ford was nowhere in sight, and all four tires on the Thunderbird were flat.

"Damn those bastards," spat Jake, "they slashed our tires."

"I guess we walk," said Vincent.

After arranging for the truck stop mechanic to replace the tires, they walked down the narrow dirt road back toward the farmhouse. As they walked, a pickup truck came barreling down the road behind them. They looked back when they heard it coming and moved to the side of the road by the ditch. The truck veered toward them at a high rate of speed.

"Son of a-bitch is going to run over us! JUMP!" yelled Jake, and the two brothers dove headfirst into the ditch filled with muddy water.

Meadors began laughing when he looked into the rear-view mirror and saw the Sweet boys pop up out of the ditch, wringing wet, dirty, and spitting mud from their mouths.

"You bastard!" yelled Jake at the rapidly disappearing truck. "You won't get me that easy."

They crawled out of the ditch and hurried back to the house. When they got back, Jake went immediately to the phone and called the number he had to contact Baxter, but there was no answer.

"Damn," he swore and slammed down the receiver. "Call up everybody and get them on the lookout for that truck, and call Vernon. Tell him to get over to the truck stop and pick up the car. I got to pack and get out of here, money or no money."

While Jake's kin and the Klan were gathering for protection and looking for the truck, Meadors arrived at his apartment, returned the truck keys to his friend, and thanked him for letting him borrow the truck again so he could haul some stuff for his sister. When he arrived at the police station, Spencer was waiting on him with a worried look on his face.

"Where've you been? You're late."

"Let's go outside and get some coffee at the cart," Meadors suggested.

After they got their coffee, Meadors told the tale from last night and this morning. Spencer was at first angry with Meadors, since he hadn't cleared it with him, but by the time Meadors described their appearance in the ditch, he was laughing.

"Holy smoke, you damn fool," Spencer said with humor.

"Do you realize what could happen if they identified you, or worse, caught you? They could sue us, we'd be out of a job, or you'd be dead."

Meadors said with defiance, "You're right, Spencer, but I had to do something. We're stuck, and scaring the hell out him was the only thing I knew to do. I figured the odds were in my favor. There's no way that scum bag is going to figure out it was me. He doesn't think us *boys* got the balls or brains to pull something like that off. I know it was wrong, but I'd do it again if I thought it would help."

Spencer knew it was a done deal now, so he could only hope for the best.

"Well, let's go call him and see if it worked."

They went to Spencer's office and closed the door. Spencer dialed the number from the file on his desk listing Jake Sweet's information.

Vincent answered with a rude, "Yeah?"

"This is Detective Baldwin. I was wondering if Jake was around this morning. I'd like to talk to him to see if he's remembered anything that might be useful."

Spencer heard Vincent yell, "Jake, it's that cop, Baldwin, from yesterday. He wants to talk to you."

"What the hell does he want?" Spencer heard Jake say with a sneer.

"You, damn it. He wants to talk to you," Vincent said.

Spencer heard the receiver changing hands then Jake spoke, "Yeah, what do you want?"

Spencer replied in a cheery tone, "Good morning, Mr. Sweet, I trust you slept well and are still safe and sound?"

"Good morning my ass. I almost got it shot off last night and run over this morning no thanks to those damn fools you gave me for protection."

Spencer smiled at Meadors, giving him a thumb's up. "I'm sorry, Mr. Sweet, would you like to file a report?"

"Hell no."

Spencer said, "We aren't providing you any protection, and no one is assigned to follow you around. You gave us nothing we considered useful, and you said you didn't need our protection."

It was quiet for a full minute before Sweet spoke.

"What do you mean there ain't nobody following me? I saw 'em."

"I don't have anyone following you, Jake. I told you before the only thing I'd do was take you into custody. I don't have the manpower to cover you." Spencer let it sink in some more, then began to reel Jake in. "Jake, you better be careful, you may be running out of time. If I were you, I'd reconsider my offer."

There was silence on the other end, then a click and a dial tone.

Spencer looked at Meadors. "He's scared all right, he's thinking about what's going on. Let's just hope he takes us up on it before it's too late."

At precisely five to eleven that same morning, Ian Baxter, presenting as Mr. Jenkins of Sun Diesel, arrived for his meeting with Carl Powers.

"Mr. Powers, it's good to see you again," said Baxter, smiling.

Carl extended his hand in greeting. "It's good to see you too. I understand we have some new contracts you want me to look over?"

He signaled to the new girl, working as his administrative assistant under the watchful eye of Miss LaCrosse. "Will you please close the door and see that we aren't disturbed?"

"Yes, sir," she said as she backed out of the office and softly closed the door.

Ian pointedly said, "We need to renegotiate a service contract, Mr. Powers."

Carl took the slip of paper with the name written on it and read it. "Just a formality, isn't it?"

"Yes, sir. I'll take care of the details."

"Yes, please do. I won't need anything final, just give me a call when it's done," Carl said without emotion.

"I will, sir," Ian said with a hint of a smile. "Is there anything else I need to do?"

"No, but let's be sure there are no surprises later," Carl said with emphasis.

He stood up, signaling the meeting was over, and Ian left. Carl waited for a few minutes then peeked out his door and said he was going to lunch at the She Crab. He went down the back stairs to the parking lot and, looking up as he got into his car, noticed Miss LaCrosse looking down at him from the window. She smiled at him and waved goodbye.

Ian fiddled with the CD on the dash to find his favorite song, "Highway to Hell," and cranked it up as he drove, humming the tune. Their conversations were always the same, with no names ever mentioned, just basic talk about contracts and details. He laughed as he burned the slip of paper with Jake Sweet's name on it in the ashtray.

~~~~

As Alisheen surveyed the early lunch crowd, Carl Powers came in the front door. She met him with a hug and escorted him to a booth.

"What're you doing here?" Alisheen asked since he rarely came in for lunch.

"I'm hungry," he said simply. "Will you join me?"

To his surprise she said, "I will. I'm hungry too. What'll you have?" Before he could answer she said, "Never mind, I'll fix you a surprise. Do you want a beer?"

"No, I want a Coke with crushed ice."

Alisheen smiled in agreement and brought him a large glass of crushed ice and a pitcher of Coke. She fixed two tremendous bacon cheeseburgers with extra crispy onion rings on the side and returned to the booth. She sat down, filled her glass with Coke, and took a sip.

Carl stared at the plates amazed. "Wow, this is absolutely fantastic. These works of art aren't on the menu. I know because I would've spotted them a long time ago."

Alisheen smiled. "I know the cook so I can get what I want out of the kitchen. Besides, I was thinking of adding some variety to the menu and experimenting today, so you're the guinea pig."

They ate in silence for a few minutes, then Carl asked, "How come the special treatment?"

"I don't really know. I like you and wanted something different to eat, that's all. You're the lucky winner today."

"I thought you dated someone seriously. I don't want him seeking me out because I got a lunch date with his girlfriend."

Alisheen, with a full mouth, looked at him, paused then swallowed. "I do, but I'm mad at him so just shut-up and eat."

Powers went silent at the rebuke and began to think his plan wasn't going to go very far when she started talking.

"Carl, if you'd been dating somebody for a long time, you know, and doing the things people do that love each other, and they wouldn't ask you to marry them, what would you do?"

Stunned, Powers was unable to hide his look of surprise. This was beyond his imagination, and he wanted to be cautious.

"Well." he said after a few moments. "Is this a hypothetical question or reality?"

Alisheen sighed, looked away, and focused on filling her glass again. "Reality, I guess."

"Do I get to think about it for a while?"

She suddenly acted as if she came to her own conclusion and said, "No, just forget it. Forget I asked. I was just wondering, that's all."

Powers said, "If you say so, but I'll be glad to talk about it. You caught me off guard, that's all."

"Let's finish up and talk about something else. If you're lucky I'll make you an ice cream sundae."

"You're on," and they finished their meal.

Carl polished off a sundae and settled into the comfort of the booth with a cup of coffee. Alisheen cleared away the dishes and came back to sit with him.

Carl said, "Alisheen, I'd like to get to know you better, but if you're dating somebody I understand. I'd like to know more about him though so I can size up my competition."

Alisheen, surprised by the bold statement, recovered and said, "He's a Detective with the Savannah Police, Carl, and his name's Spencer Baldwin. He heads up the narcotics division."

"Narcotics, sounds dangerous."

Alisheen frowned. "It is, and he plays it down for my sake, but I'm not fooled. I worry about him. Sometimes he breaks dates at the last minute because something comes up, and then I won't see him for a couple of days, then he appears. It drives me crazy."

"Well, if it continues, I'm just going to have to press harder for your hand."

Alisheen was surprised. "Carl, you've never expressed these feelings before, why now?"

"I'm a shameless opportunist. I've always wanted to tell you I have feelings for you. It seemed to be a good time to throw my hat into the ring, so to speak."

She looked at him strangely. "You never cease to amaze me, Mr. Powers."

Carl lifted his cup and smiled at her over the rim. She got up from the table pondering his words and went back to work. Carl left after a second cup of coffee and kissed Alisheen lightly on the cheek on the way out. That was a first too. She admitted to herself she liked it, but his sudden openness and advances toward her were puzzling.

Mickey witnessed the kiss, didn't like it, and said so.

"Alisheen, I don't trust that guy."

"It's none of your business, Mickey, but why not?"

"I smell a rat in a polo shirt."

Alisheen reflected on Mickey's advice and admitted that something about Carl was different, but she didn't have any reason to believe he wasn't sincere. Yet she'd be cautious. Besides, she still loved Spencer very much and Carl was just a friend, but today he admitted he wanted more.

"A shameless opportunist." That's what he'd called himself.

# Chapter 4

SKIP ARRIVED IN Savannah at 6:00 p.m., checked into the Hilton DeSoto, arranged for a conference room for in the morning, and went to bed. At 7:00 a.m. the next morning, he distributed the artist's sketch of the informant, hoping to find their man with dumb luck to avoid asking questions and arousing suspicion.

Afterwards, Fitzgerald called the head of the local branch in Savannah, Bo Biggers. With a deep southern drawl, Bo answered the phone with frustration.

"Savannah D.E.A. This is Bo Biggers, can I help you?"

"Damn, I'm glad I'm not trying to get anything important from you; you sound pissed-off."

"Skip, is that you? Damn it, you know I hate answering telephones. Peggy is out sick, and I'm stuck in the office. How in the hell are you, and what're you doing in Savannah? I take it this isn't a social visit."

"You're right, and I'm going to give you an excuse to get out of the office. Find a temp to answer the phone as soon as you can and haul your ass over here to the Hilton DeSoto, room 212."

"What's going on?"

"I'll tell you when you get here," Skip said and hung up.

Bo arrived within an hour of Fitzgerald's call.

Bo said light-heartedly, "I got here as fast as I could. Now would you mind telling me what's going on?"

"This is serious, Bo, and I don't have time for your southern boy bullshit."

Skip walked to the seating area in the suite, sat down and poured coffee, gesturing for Bo to join him.

"What can you tell me about the Snowman, and I mean beyond what you've been sending me in the reports? Have you done any digging at all?"

Bo rubbed his chin. "Skip, I don't know anything beyond what I've been sending you. All I do know is that he's in Savannah. What in the hell is going on?"

Skip sighed. "Somebody else has called Whitley offering information on the Snowman and his operation."

"Damn!" was all Bo said since he immediately knew what the repercussions of two informants meant. The Snowman could go underground and be lost with his organization leaking like a sieve.

Skip continued, "That's not the best part. I got to find the informant we've been working with and warn him."

"Tell me about Spencer Baldwin."

"He's head of narcotics for the locals, a square guy. I see him around sometime. Why?"

"Well, from your reports we know he's been busting the Snowman. Where's he getting his information?"

Bo said, "I don't know. I don't know him except socially. I assume he's getting his information from the same source. The busts seemed to tally with what we're getting, so it makes sense, but I don't think he's any closer to finding out the identity of the Snowman than we are, and he's been working the case hard. There's been nothing in the paper either. They're definitely keeping a low profile."

Skip said, "I'm not sure there is anything else we can do until we get a break. Just help me find our man."

Skip stood to end the meeting, and Bo left after committing his local agents to the operation. Skip hung the "Do Not Disturb" sign, called the front desk to hold his calls, and spread the file of papers around him on the floor. Then he went through them one by one hoping to find a clue to the man he was looking for.

~~~~

Bo was thinking hard as he drove back to his office. How in the hell were they going to find this guy in Savannah? To top it off it was early spring and the town was crawling with tourists and the spring break college crowd. They were crazy as hell in Washington. All he had was a generic sketch, basic details, and no idea where to start. Deciding he was hungry, he headed for the She Crab. He could slam a fried oyster sandwich and fries down, with some sweet tea, and think about it. He always thought better on a full stomach, and it showed for he was overweight by more than a few pounds.

~~~~

The tables were filling up with the early lunch crowd, so he sat at the bar, ordered, and watched the sports channel on the television. His order arrived and he began to eat. Out of the corner of his eye, he noticed two men walk in and settle into seats at the bar. He looked at them, nodded in their direction as they sat down, and they gave a slight nod in return. Bo looked back at the television and resumed eating his lunch. Something was familiar about one of them, so he casually looked back in their direction, then back at the television with a shrug, thinking, "Where have I seen that guy before?" Then it hit him. The man they were looking for was sitting at the bar drinking a beer two seats down from him! He had come in wearing a baseball hat and sunglasses. He was a dead ringer for the sketch and the physical description he had matched up. He couldn't believe his luck. Bo was excited, but he forced himself to eat the rest of his lunch calmly and deliberately as he eavesdropped on their conversation. They were discussing the ball game on the television. He finished his lunch, paid the tab, and went out into the street. Once outside, he hurried to his car and quickly dialed Skip's hotel. The hotel operator told him Mr. Fitzgerald was not currently receiving calls, and they'd be glad to give him a message. Bo exploded, "Listen here, sonny boy, you put my call through now, damn it, or I'm coming down there to shove that phone up your ass. It's an emergency." The operator, shaken by the threat, quickly put him through. Skip heard the phone ringing and couldn't believe it, especially after he'd left strict instructions not to be disturbed. Muttering, he answered the phone in a bad temper. "Whoever this is, it'd better be good or I'm going to kill you."

"Skip, you are without a doubt the luckiest bastard I know."

"Biggers?" asked Skip, shaking his head. "What in the hell is going on, and why am I so damn lucky?"

"Guess who I just had lunch with?" Bo asked, ignoring the threat.

"Out with it man before I fire your ass for bothering me."

"I had lunch with him," Bo said with emphasis on the last word.

"Him who?" Skip yelled impatiently.

"I'm pretty sure I just had lunch with the guy we're looking for, the informer."

Skip was silent for so long that Bo thought he'd lost the connection.

"Skip, are you still there?"

"Yes, yes I am. Bo you follow him and don't let him out of your sight. After you know who he is and how to find him again, come to the hotel and report."

Bo took up vigilance, full of excitement and pleased at his luck. After a short wait, the informer and his lunch companion exited the She Crab and turned right in the direction of the docks. He eased out of the car, put on his sunglasses, and followed them from the opposite side of the street. The traffic was light, and they weren't in a hurry.

After a couple of blocks, they turned toward the water and the industrial area of the dockyards. Bo continued straight and, from around the corner, peeked down the street in their direction. They turned through a gate in a high chain link fence into the warehouse yards of Coastal Seafood Inc. Bo walked past the gate, pausing long enough to light a cigarette, and then continued walking toward the water. They'd stopped beside a black BMW continuing their conversation. He continued down the street to the first corner and turned out of sight.

He took off his coat and sunglasses, hoping the quick change in appearance would be enough to fool the casual observer, and he walked back toward the gate. As he approached, the black BMW exited the gate, paused to check the traffic, and headed back toward downtown. Bo decided to take a risk. He walked up to the front door of the building and read on the glass door as he entered that it was the main office of the Coastal Seafood distribution center. He hung around the desk of the small waiting area hoping someone would spot him. He heard the flush of a toilet in the back. Shortly, a pretty woman entered the room and, upon seeing him, reddened with embarrassment. It was obvious she'd flushed the toilet.

"May I help you?" she asked flustered.

Bo smiled at her and with his best southern manners said, "Why, I hope so, ma'am. I'm looking for a job. You wouldn't be hiring drivers, would you?" He flashed his smile at her again, and she smiled back, taken in by his charm.

"Well, we don't typically take applications here, but I do happen to have a blank one you could fill out. Applications are usually taken at the corporate office, but I suppose I could make an exception this time."

"I'd appreciate it if you'd do that for me, ma'am. It'd be a blessing."

She smiled again, nodded primly, and passed a clipboard with an application on it over the counter to him with a pen. He nodded his thanks, sat down, and as he filled out the application, he looked around the office. He noticed the row of pictures on the wall and, looking closer, realized they were "Employee of the Month" pictures. The trucking manager's picture was his man. Andrew Jackson "A.J." Guilford. Pleased with his discovery, Bo quickly finished filling in the application with bogus information. He stood up, thanked the woman again for her help, and reminded her that she truly was a blessing to him.

As he came out of the Coastal gate, Bo used his cell phone to call Skip and brief him.

"Fitzgerald."

"Skip, this is Bo. His name is A. J. Guilford. He's the trucking manager for Coastal Seafood."

"Bo, where are you?"

"Outside of Coastal Seafood on my cell."

"Get your ass over here and report." He paused for a second and said, "Nice work," then hung up.

~~~~

Ian Baxter parked at the apartment complex away from the other cars and carefully covered the BMW with a tarp before going inside. Once inside, he noticed the blinking light as he walked by the answering machine, but the timer was very short so he didn't check the message. The directional microphones he had placed around the Coastal yards for security picked up all kinds of conversations. When they were that short, it was typically a whore checking in with her pimp or a street dealer arranging a meet. He'd check it later. First, he had important business to take care of. He needed to call Jake Sweet and make an appointment.

Ian enjoyed his work. He'd known Powers for a long time. Powers had first seen him almost beat a man to death in a bare-knuckle fight and had approached him afterward. He'd said he enjoyed watching him work, then pulled a large money clip out of his pocket, rolled off five grand, and handed it to him.

"Would you like to work for me and give this up?"

Ian, always impressed by money and power, wanted both. He sensed an opportunity to have what he envied and craved.

"Yes," he said simply.

Powers said, "Good, I'll be in touch." Then he turned and walked away.

Approximately two weeks later, Ian received a call from a company called Sun Diesel. They asked if he was Mr. Jenkins and was he still looking for a job. If so, would he be interested in working for Sun Diesel?

Ian had never heard of Sun Diesel or the name Jenkins but playing a hunch said, "Yes, I'm seeking employment. How did you get my information?"

"Mr. Powers submitted your name to us for a sales opening. He specifically requested you and said he wanted you exclusively for his account."

Within two weeks, Ian was in Savannah and employed by Sun Diesel. He'd been Mr. Jenkins with Sun Diesel for several months, enjoying his new life, when the call came. Mr. Powers wanted to meet with him regarding some contracts he'd been reviewing.

The meeting day came and Powers was all business but very cordial. After reviewing the contracts, Powers suggested a walk. As they walked, Powers admitted that he'd been watching him work to be sure he was the right man for the job he had in mind for him. Now it was time to move forward. He led them to the dockyards and ended the walk at the outer edge of one of the Coastal docks. There was no one in sight.

Powers looked out over the water. "Ian, I'm a drug smuggler as well as a very successful businessman. I own Savannah and nothing comes in or out without my help. However; I need a man with your, shall we say, ability, to be the head of my security. I need an enforcer who can take care of things for me. Are you willing to be that man?"

Ian looked out over the water, matching Powers' stare across the river, to nowhere in particular.

"Work for me and have more money than you can spend and the kind of power that will make men afraid of you, or you can fall off this pier and disappear forever."

Ian looked down for the first time at a garbage barge tied to the pier below and then at Powers who had a gun aimed at his chest.

He pulled his sunglasses from his pocket, placed them on his face, and turned looking back at the water. "When do I start?"

Powers handed him a sheet of paper. "Right now."

From that day on, Ian took care of the Snowman's security. From the beginning, he'd set up an extensive security system, including the directional microphone system covering the yards around the warehouse complex, to protect the operation. Powers had directed him to "take care" of anyone that could have any information that could lead to Coastal, so he'd taken him at his word.

Killing people didn't bother him, and he'd learned to be quick and efficient. He'd been a bit apprehensive about the very first kill because it'd been a woman, but she was just a hooker on the docks in the wrong place at the wrong time. The shock effect on the Snowman crews served its purpose and erased any doubts about him. They feared him.

Snapping out of reminiscing, Ian picked up the phone and called Sweet, dialing the number through the satellite hook-up, and waited with a yawn.

"Hello," said the voice with caution.

"Mr. Sweet, I have your money."

Jake replied with a surly, "OK, now what?"

"Providing you agree never to return as promised, we're willing to let you get out of town. I'm authorized to terminate your contract and help you leave."

Ian smiled, knowing what terminating the contract would mean for him. "Do you still agree?"

"Yeah, I agree. I just want to get the hell out of here. Have you called those spooks off that are trying to kill me?"

Ian, puzzled by the question, wondered what he was talking about so he responded carefully, "What do you mean, Mr. Sweet?"

Jake answered impatiently.

"You damn good and well know what I mean. Those damn fools that shot up my house last night and damn near ran me over this morning. You call those guys off, or I'll go to the cops."

Ian paused, thought, and said, "I'll call them off. Have you got a pencil and paper?"

"Wait a damn minute." After a few seconds Jake said, "OK, I got it."

Ian gave Jake the details and asked if he understood.

"I understand," said Jake and he broke the connection.

Ian hung up. He reprogrammed the satellite to roam for available numbers to use, went to the fridge, and got out a bottle of water. He sat down on the sofa and began to think about the conversation. *Who was trying to kill Sweet? It could prove to be very useful later. Maybe, whoever it was would do his work for him.* He decided to take a nap and set the alarm on his watch. He sprawled out on the sofa and plumping the pillows behind his head, continued to ignore the blinking light on the machine.

~~~~

Bo was so excited when Skip opened the door; he almost knocked him down as he entered.

"Damn it, I'm sorry Skip," Bo said, catching him by the arm. "I'm just so damn glad we lucked out."

Skip straightened himself up and said, "OK, no harm done; tell me about it."

Bo explained he'd gotten hungry and decided to go to the She Crab for an early lunch, and while he was at the bar, two men came in and sat down. He recognized the informer after a few minutes and set up outside after he'd called Skip. He detailed how he'd followed them to the Coastal warehouse complex and saw the other man leave in a black BMW. Then he related the bit with the fake job application and finding the informer's picture and name on the wall.

Skip was quiet for a moment. "What do you know about Coastal Seafood?"

"Man, they're famous. I can't believe you've never heard of them. The owner, Carl Powers, is a former All-American from Georgia. He started the business and it's huge. Fortune 1000, not to mention the money he gives to charity and other causes. He sits on half a dozen boards. He could be the next Governor if he wanted to."

Skip pursed his lips thinking. "Let's do some digging around on Coastal and Powers. Someone in Coastal is a part of this, maybe even Powers. On the other hand, somebody could be using them without their knowledge. Bo, let's do this on the sly. We don't want to alert anyone that we're looking around."

Bo nodded. "Anything else?"

"No. We'll go with what we got for now. Put Guilford under surveillance, and get me what you can on Coastal. Thanks, Bo. I'll brief my guys and send them your way."

Bo left more calmly than he came, and Skip made a few notes to keep things straight in his head before proceeding to the conference room to meet with his team.

"We've been extremely fortunate today. The man we've been sent here to find has been found."

The startled looks on the faces around the table changed into multiple questions, and they all started talking at once. Fitzgerald raised his hand to quiet them.

"Bo ate an early lunch in a restaurant called the She Crab and found him by accident," Skip said with a grin, drawing smiles from the ones in the room that knew of Bo's affection for food.

"As luck would have it, the man walked in with a friend and sat at the bar to eat. Bo recognized him, tailed him, and identified him as the trucking manager for Coastal Seafood. Our informer's name is A.J. Guilford. We're going to coordinate with the local agency. Bo will be teaming you up with his agents that know the territory so you don't get lost. You'll report to him and he'll bring everything to me. I need to know Guilford's pattern, and we need to pick a spot to approach him. We caught our break. Dinner is on me tonight!"

Skip dismissed the men, went back to his room, and placed a call to the Savannah Police Department. It was time to find out what he could about Spencer Baldwin.

"Carol Naster, please," he said after the operator answered.

"Just a moment. I'll ring Sergeant Naster for you."

Carol was ex-D.E.A., and now she was a Detective Sergeant with the Savannah police working homicide. He recognized her voice when she answered.

"Sergeant Naster. How can I help you?"

"Carol? It's Skip Fitzgerald. How are you?"

"Skip? It's been a while. I knew I'd hear from somebody in your office sooner or later, but I figured it would be Bo, not the man himself. After that weasel Whitley called me two months ago asking questions, I knew something would be coming my way. It was just a matter of time. It's about the Snowman, isn't it?"

"What do you know about him?" asked Skip.

"Not much, just what I've gotten from the grapevine," Carol replied.

Skip spoke with a serious tone. "Carol, can we meet tonight and talk?"

"OK, dinner at my place around 7:30. How about that?"

"Sounds great," he said with relief.

Carol gave him the address, directions, and her cell phone number just in case, then hung up after a quick goodbye. She liked Skip and knew he was higher up in the D.E.A. than when she was there. After Carol hung up, she admitted to herself that she was looking forward to seeing him again.

Spencer had been contemplating the Coastal Seafood truck parked at the She Crab all day. He walked out into the squad room, found Meadors at his desk, and sat down.

"What do we know about Coastal Seafood?"

"Nothing except what we know from their reputation, and Mr. Humanitarian, Carl Powers, runs it," Meadors said.

"Let's see what else we can find out about him and the company."

"How do you want to start?"

"The usual and nothing more than what is on the surface for now. I want basic information—phone records, bank records, customer lists, a visit to look over the premises, to get a look at the people and the operation. I want to know what we might be dealing with. Let's set up a detail to watch the docks, too."

Meadors finished taking notes. "Have you heard anything from Jake Sweet?"

"Not a damn word."

"Do you think he bought it, Spencer?"

"I hope so for his sake and ours. He knows more than he's telling us that's for sure."

Meadors got up to start the background investigation, and Spencer went back into his office. As he sat down, he decided he'd ask Alisheen about Coastal tonight. She might know something about them beyond their reputation. He tried to work for a while longer but couldn't concentrate. He decided to go to the She Crab and convince Alisheen to go out to eat, instead of the usual routine.

At the She Crab he found her in the kitchen sampling a dessert.

He said with a mocking tone from behind her, "You keep that up and you're gonna have to run more to keep your butt from getting fat."

Surprised by his early appearance and obviously glad to see him, she laughed. "Ha! That's coming from a man who'll eat a whole box of cookies in one sitting."

"Touché," said Spencer smiling back at her and kissing her on the cheek at the same time. "Let's get out of here."

Alisheen looked at him as if he was crazy. "Tonight? I can't go out! I've a business to run, and besides, it's Friday night. You know that's my busiest night of the week."

Spencer looked stern. "I don't care what night it is. We've both been working hard, and we're going out. Your staff can take care of things and will do a great job. Let's go."

"Spencer, I just can't," she said, but he heard the waver in her voice.

"Come on, Alisheen, everything will be fine. Just tell them you're going and it's theirs for tonight."

"Where are we going?" she asked, further weakening.

"That's not important."

"What if they need me?"

"They won't." He grabbed her by the elbow, escorted her out the back door, closed it behind him, and blocked it, daring her to try to go back in.

She smiled at him giving in. "OK, you win and I'm hungry too. Will you tell me where we're going now?"

Spencer smiled. "Pizza at Genoa's and then a movie."

"Thank goodness. What took you so long to get me out of there?"

They both laughed and hurried to the car for a long overdue date. The pizza at Genoa's was hand tossed with the works, and a cold beer perfectly quenched the spicy fire of the pizza.

"Hmmm, pizza and beer, it's the best," sighed Spencer as he finished off another large slice.

Alisheen raised her eyebrows, "What about my oysters and beer?"

Spencer laughed and said, "OK, pizza and beer, a second best."

"That's better," she said, smiling. She looked at him for a moment and said with a serious tone, "Spencer, I want to talk about this morning at the Dixie."

Alisheen was calm but spoke with frustration, "I don't know why you can't commit to marrying me. You won't tell me the real reason. I love you. But, I think we've been together long enough to do something, either get married or seriously consider seeing other people."

Spencer was stunned. "What exactly are you saying?"

Alisheen quickly blurted, "I'm saying that if marriage isn't an option for us, soon, then I need to see other people. I want a husband, kids, house, yard, cats, dogs; the whole enchilada. I'm not getting any younger and neither are you."

"Alisheen," pleaded Spencer. "This is not something I wanted to discuss while I'm trying to make things up to you on a date."

"When are we going to discuss it, Spencer? Why can't you tell me the real reason, the truth?"

"Alisheen," Spencer began, and she cut him off.

"I'm not going to talk about it anymore tonight, you just think about what I've said."

Spencer sulked while they ate, and Alisheen made an effort to be pleasant and make the evening better. He cheered up after a while and they chose a movie. It was a good one, a thriller with a surprise ending. Spencer thought he figured it out about halfway through and leaned over to tell Alisheen.

"I am a Detective you know," he whispered after she shushed him for telling the ending, but he was wrong and Alisheen made fun of him on the ride back to the loft. He hesitated getting out of the car and followed her slowly as she walked up the stairs to the door.

"Are you going to stay tonight?"

"I wasn't sure if I was welcome or not," said Spencer with a hopeful look.

"You're welcome. All I'm asking you to do is to consider the future, our future, and determine what it's going to be. In the meantime, I've two boxes of Vanilla Wafers for you."

He broke into a broad grin, grabbed her, kissed her and followed her upstairs.

~~~~

Isaac Henry sat with his back to the large window with a bird's eye view of Pennsylvania Avenue and the White House, and he listened to Clifton Chambers describe the Savannah operation. As he listened to the details of the outrageous scheme unfold, he thought this crazy plan might have some merit. Chambers finished and nervously waited for the blast that was sure to come. Henry folded his hands as if in prayer and bowed his head for a moment. He then turned his chair around and looked out the window.

He spoke calmly. "Clifton, pour us drinks and let me ask some questions."

Chambers jumped out of his chair as if it was on fire and hurried to the bar in the corner. He poured two liberal drinks of single malt scotch whiskey, neat. The Director didn't drink anything else. He then walked over to the desk, placing one on the leather-bound pad on the desktop. Henry turned around after a few minutes, picked up the drink, and continued turning around in his chair to face the window again in a continuous motion. After what seemed like hours to Chambers, he spoke.

"Clifton, do you know what could happen if the press ever got wind of this, much less Congress? The D.E.A. would be dismantled and those responsible would end up in jail for drug trafficking and racketeering."

He turned around again, his face calm, and fixed his eyes on Chambers. "Just what in the hell did you think you were doing, and why do you think this will work?"

Chambers wasn't caught off guard by the question, but the calm that surrounded it. He'd expected an explosion.

"Mr. Henry, we've been fighting a losing proposition since the day we officially started the war on drugs. By controlling quantity and quality through an agreement with the smugglers as our 'representative' so to speak, we can negotiate trade arrangements with the cartels. The money we make we spend against those that don't participate in the trade agreement. I predict the cartels will police themselves to protect the arrangement. We manage the supply and purity and use our money to develop programs that will reduce drug use in the States. It's a win-win situation for everybody, though it's a bit unorthodox."

Henry sputtered, "Unorthodox? You're damn right it's unorthodox. It's illegal as hell and suicide if you, and I do emphasize you here, Clifton, get caught."

Henry leaned back in his chair and with a wild look in his eye said, "It's just crazy enough to work too. Have Whitley here in the morning. We'll go through the plan with a fine-tooth comb and beat out every detail until I'm satisfied. I want this Savannah situation cleaned up, and I want the Snowman."

Isaac Henry looked down at his calendar and then up at Chambers.

"Be here at 9:00 a.m. and we'll have breakfast with Whitley. I'll see you in the morning."

Henry dismissed him by turning his chair around and looking out the window.

Chambers shook his head in disbelief. He'd thought for sure it was over, and now he was running a sanctioned operation.

"I'm in it now." He dialed Whitley's number muttering, "Unbelievable."

Whitley had been waiting for the phone to ring. He hesitated, because he knew it was Chambers.

"Whitley."

"Get on a plane to Washington tonight. We're meeting in the morning with Mr. Henry at 9:00 a.m. for breakfast," then he hung up without giving him any more information for the summons.

Benjamin Whitley was a basket case. A meeting with Director Henry couldn't be good given the current situation. He was going to have a lot of explaining to do. He called his wife, told her he had to go to Washington tonight for an urgent meeting in the morning, and asked her to pack him a few things and a suit for tomorrow. He'd be by later to pick up his kit and kiss her goodbye. Then he booked a ticket on the late flight out of Atlanta. He unlocked the credenza, pulled out the file with the details on the Savannah operation, and began to make notes.

# Chapter 5

SPENCER WOKE UP late the next morning, and Alisheen's side of the bed was empty. He got up, went to the bathroom, and headed for the kitchen, making a half-hearted attempt to close his old robe. He found a fresh pot of coffee, poured a cup, and then went out onto the deck.

A note on the rocking chair read, "Gone for a run, back in a while. Love, Al." Spencer yawned and scratched himself, then sat in the chair and drank his coffee watching the morning traffic on the river. It was going to be a beautiful spring day. Since it was Saturday, he was on his second cup of coffee thinking about a round of golf when Alisheen returned.

"Hey sleepyhead," she greeted him with a cheerful smile and a kiss.

"Hey yourself. Why didn't you wake me up to run?"

"You were cute asleep, and I felt like running alone and doing some thinking. Besides, you just slow me down and I wanted to run fast."

Spencer snorted.

She said, "I've planned the rest of the day for us."

"There goes my golf outing," sighed Spencer, obviously not enthusiastic.

"Well, would you rather play golf or go to the beach and spend the day looking at me in my hot new swimsuit?"

"Golf," said Spencer in as serious a tone as he could muster.

Alisheen looked at him for a moment, then realized he was kidding, but she kept up the act, talking to him as a parent would to a small child. "Well too bad. You're going to the beach with me so get cleaned up and dressed while I fix us lunch."

Spencer silently finished his coffee and proceeded to shower, shave, and get dressed. Then he went into the kitchen, where Alisheen instructed him to load up the car while she got ready. She soon appeared from the bedroom and indeed looked very sexy in a black one-piece strapless swimsuit. Her red hair was on top of her head in a neat braid of some kind and her sunglasses were on her forehead.

Spencer grabbed her from behind and kissed the back of her exposed neck. "Let's forget the beach."

"Oh no, I'm going to tease you all day, so you'll be willing to grant my smallest request tonight."

Spencer feigned a wounded expression and laughed. "Your wish will be my command."

They went into the bright, warm sun and got into the car. Spencer's personal car was a sleek, "62," black, convertible "Stingray" which was in cherry condition. They arrived at the beach, and Spencer parked away from other vehicles, as was his custom. Finding a suitable spot, they placed the chairs in the sand and settled onto the beach, soaking up the warm sun. Spencer placed the cooler in a convenient spot, popped a beer, checked his cell, and surveyed the beach.

Alisheen said, "Do you have to have the phone on?"

"Yes, you know I do. I have to be able to be reached in case there is an emergency. I'll put it on vibrate."

She looked at him over the top of her sunglasses. "If it goes off, vibrate or not, I'm going to throw it into the water," she said with a determined look on her face. She resumed thumbing her magazine.

Spencer just grunted, found the binoculars in the beach bag, and pulled them out. He adjusted them and scanned the numerous shrimp boats on the water.

"Son-of-a-bitch, Coastal Seafood."

Alisheen looked up with a start and an unexplainable feeling of guilt.

She recovered and acting disinterested said, "What did you say, Spencer?"

"All those shrimp boats belong to Coastal Seafood. They must be a pretty big outfit."

She recovered from her initial shock, and relieved Spencer hadn't noticed, calmly said, "Oh?"

"Yeah, they've got a huge warehouse complex on the docks, and there was a truck at your place the other day, wasn't there?"

"I suppose so," she said casually. "They are my biggest supplier."

Alisheen saw an opportunity to needle Spencer and took advantage of it. "I believe they're the biggest wholesale distributor in the southeast," she said with arrogance.

Spencer rose to the bait, "Oh really?"

"Yes," she replied with a matter-of-fact tone.

"How come you know so much about them?" asked Spencer with suspicion.

Alisheen was beginning to enjoy herself. "Well, I do know the owner, Carl Powers. He comes in and eats at the She Crab a good bit."

"Hmmm," said Spencer. "Just how well do you know him?"

She was enjoying herself so much she didn't notice Spencer threw his own bait into the conversation. She took it hook, line, and sinker and became defensive and defiant. "I know him well enough to call him Carl, personally fix him lunch, and to be asked out!"

With furrowed eyes Spencer said, "What did you say when he asked you out?"

Alisheen closed her magazine abruptly, leaned forward, and looked him the eye. "I told him I had a fat-headed boyfriend, who frustrates the hell out of me, eats Vanilla Wafers like a pig, snores like a rhino, and those were his good points."

She had enjoyed telling him off and decided to make him squirm some more. "I also told him if he could come up with a good enough reason to convince me to dump you and go out with him instead, I'd consider it."

She looked away and pretended to be angry, roughly turning the pages of her magazine and trying to keep from laughing. Spencer looked like a wounded puppy. She began to think she'd gone too far when he sprayed her with ice-cold beer. Spencer burst out laughing and took off running down the beach, diving into the surf. She jumped up, screaming at him, and chased him into the water. He waited for her and when she caught up with him, they embraced and kissed deeply, tasting the salt water on the others' lips and tongues. They kissed again and became aroused.

"This is a very serious situation," Spencer said with a mocking tone.

"And what do you suggest?" said Alisheen, raising her eyebrows.

"We must explore the dunes."

Alisheen rubbed her body against Spencer. A frown of concern appeared on her face. "This is serious. I agree the dunes are the only option, and we should go exploring."

They exited the water laughing and, grabbing towels, headed down the beach until it was empty. They turned toward the dunes and Spencer led the way, holding her hand and picking his way through the saw grass and sea oats, following a faint trail. In seclusion under the dappled shade of the pine trees, they spread the towels and sat down next to each other.

Spencer started to speak, but Alisheen shushed him with a kiss and pushed him onto his back. She sat across his waist and, reaching up, let her damp, flowing red hair down. It shined with brilliance in the sunlight that beamed through the trees. He reached up and caressed her face and lips with his fingertips. She sighed with pleasure then lay down on the towel next to him.

They aroused each other in silence and made love slowly, until the passion and sensuality of the experience overcame them, and they held each other close. Afterwards, Alisheen lay next to him cradling her head in the crook of his arm, and Spencer stroked her hair.

Alisheen said, "Spencer, I love you."

Spencer kissed her head and said, "I love you, too."

Alisheen waited for a moment and said, "Spencer, I need for you to tell me the truth about why you won't talk seriously about getting married. Is it my career?"

Spencer looked at her face. It was full of love but reflected the hurt and resentment she felt not knowing the truth.

"Alisheen," Spencer pleaded, "please don't do this now."

She sat up quickly with tears beginning to stream down her face. She was hurt and angry.

Alisheen stood up, put on her suit, and began to walk away with determination.

Spencer shouted at her as he pulled his suit on, "Alisheen, wait!"

She turned and faced him with fury. "No, Spencer, I can't wait anymore. I'm going home. Don't call; and stay away from me. I need time to think about my future." With that she turned and ran away, sobbing.

Spencer followed Alisheen trying to talk to her, but she wouldn't listen. She packed up her beach bag, stormed to the parking lot, and left in a taxi, ignoring his plea to stop and talk to him. Spencer went home and tried to call her several times, but all he got was her voicemail.

Pissed-off, Spencer went to the station and tried to work, but all he could think of was Alisheen. He absent-mindedly thumbed through the small pile of phone messages on his desk. He sat up with a start, grabbed the phone, and called Meadors.

"What's up, Spencer, and what in the hell are you doing working on Saturday?"

"Never mind that. I got a call from Vincent Sweet. He wants to talk."

"I'm on my way." While Meadors was making his way to the police station, Spencer called Vincent.

He answered before the first ring was through. "Hello?"

"Vincent, this is Detective Baldwin. I got a message here that says you want to talk to me."

Vincent sounded anxious. "Yeah, I got to talk to you right away."

Spencer said, "Come down to the station, Vincent. There aren't many people around. You won't be seen."

Vincent scoffed. "Hell no, I'm no damn fool. I'm not coming down there. Do you know where the Shady Pines truck stop is on the interstate?"

"I know it. It's about ten miles south of here."

"Yeah, that's it. There's an old road behind the truck stop. It leads to some backwater off the river. Jake and me got a cabin down there. Come down the road 'til it turns to dirt, take the left fork when the road splits, the cabin is in the trees at the end of the road. You'll see it easy enough."

Spencer had been writing the directions down, and checking his watch, looked at Meadors as he came in. "See you in an hour."

"One hour," Vincent said, and the line went dead.

They grabbed body armor, extra rounds, and were on their way. Locating the exit, they followed directions and soon could see the cabin in the trees at the end of the road. They were deep in the woods and apprehensive as the daylight faded and the woods became dim. They stopped the car short, put on the body armor, and then pulled their weapons in case there was a trap. The taillights of the Thunderbird reflected in their headlights as they pulled up behind it and parked. Lights were on inside the cabin. Spencer and Meadors opened their doors, and using them as shields, called out to the cabin. A dim light flickered on the porch. Vincent came out with a rifle in his hands, and Spencer identified himself.

Vincent peered at them in the gloom then lowered his rifle. "Y'all come on in," then he turned and went back inside.

The cabin was small but surprisingly neat considering the characteristics of the owners.

Vincent could tell they were surprised. "I'm not a slob like Jake. I try to keep things a little bit nice."

Spencer looked around the room as Meadors explored the rest of the cabin.

Satisfied it was empty, Spencer said, "What do you want to talk about, Vincent?"

His answer shocked them. "I want you to arrest Jake."

"Why?" Spencer asked surprised.

"He's going to get killed if he ain't careful."

They sat down at the small table in the kitchen area.

Spencer asked, "How is it going to happen?"

Without hesitation Vincent said, "Jake had a number to call for trouble situations. He called it to cut a deal. Everything is set for tonight. He's supposed to meet the contact, pick up the money, and thumb a ride to the train station, where he'll hop a train and leave town. He said he'll call me to let me know where he ends up, and then I could sell everything and join him, but I don't think he'll get through this night alive unless you arrest him."

"Where do you think he is now?"

Vincent grunted. "Hell, if I knew that I wouldn't be talking to you. I checked all the usual places he hangs out, and I got his boys out looking for him, but ain't nobody seen him."

"OK, Vincent, you got a deal. Tell me what you know about all of this starting with why you didn't get busted the other night," Spencer said, leaning back in his chair.

Vincent lit a cigarette. "I got a full-time job at the sawmill. I only help Jake if he needs it, but he don't like for me to do it. He tries to keep me out of it if he can."

Their faces reflected surprise at this information. They'd assumed Vincent was in it up to his eyeballs. Spencer prodded him with another question.

"Vincent? What's Coastal Seafood got to do with it?"

"Jake sometimes picks stuff up at the docks or the warehouses."

"What does Jake know about the drug smuggling operation?" asked Meadors.

Vincent looked at him as if he hadn't seen him until then. "I'm not sure what he knows, but he's been doing it a long time. He probably knows more than he's told me, but like I said he keeps me out of it. Usually, Vernon picks him up for the runs and brings him back."

"Vernon!" exclaimed Meadors.

Vincent laughed. "You sure scared the hell out of him, but he's more scared of what Jake would do to him if he talked."

Spencer said, "How does Jake get his instructions?"

Vincent exhaled and looked at Spencer. "He usually gets a phone call and then tells me he's going out." Cash in the mail, wrapped up tight, and shipped to him third class. Looks like a box of checks but the money count is always right.

"For somebody that smuggles drugs, Jake doesn't have much to show for his effort," Meadors said.

Vincent looked at Meadors as if he was stupid. "I convinced Jake the cops would notice he's got too much money if he started to spend it around so he gives most of it to me. My boss helped me out. I told him I inherited some money from relatives and didn't know what to do with it. He took me to his bank and told them to take care of me. What about finding Jake?"

Spencer said, "You keep looking for him. I'll call the station and have them issue a warrant for his arrest."

Spencer paused then said, "We'll do our best to find him."

Vincent finished the cigarette and exhaled. "I hope so, or he'll be dead before morning."

The next morning, Carol was reflecting on the previous evening with Skip Fitzgerald. Their dinner was pleasant as they'd caught up with each other, and she'd considered asking him to stay the night until he revealed the motive behind the visit. She'd listened in silence as the request unfolded. At first, she staunchly refused his proposal and was somewhat angered by it, but he continued to talk and offered her a slick D.E.A. desk job. She could name her price, stay in Savannah, or go wherever she wanted to. He made it all sound good. She calmed down and told him she'd think it over and call him in the morning.

After thinking all night, Carol had decided to help. She could use the money and it wasn't illegal. She dialed the number and extension he gave her.

"Fitzgerald!"

"Skip, its Carol. I decided to take you up on your offer. I only have one condition."

"What's that?"

"Promise me Spencer Baldwin will be told everything if it becomes necessary, and there will be no attempt to cover it up by you or anybody else, if the situation goes bad."

Skip without hesitation replied, "Carol you've got my word on that, and you know my word is good."

Carol replied with sarcasm, "It's not you I'm worried about. It's those sneaky bastards you work for."

"What do you want me to do first?"

She heard an audible sigh of relief. "Find out what Baldwin knows about the Snowman, look at the files if you can, listen to squad room gossip, rumor, any scrap of information will be helpful. I need to find out what he knows so I can figure out what to do next."

"I'll call you when I know something," and she hung up.

She got a notepad and pen, fixed another cup of coffee, and put on headphones to block out the phone. She sat on the couch, documented her conversation with Fitzgerald, and made plans for her undercover role.

By the time they got back to the station it was late at night. Meadors volunteered to stay and see if anything developed so Spencer went home.

Out of habit, he flicked on the TV and realized he was hungry as he channel surfed. He went to the kitchen and found baloney, bread, and a fresh bag of potato chips. He made a couple of sandwiches and took them and the chips back to the couch along with a beer. He found an old movie to watch and tried not to think of Alisheen.

"Damn it!" he swore, expressing the thoughts swirling around in his head. She was right. He had to tell her.

As he grew up and watched his friends with their fathers, he felt the loss. The biggest blow came at school when the annual corny father-son field day occurred on his thirteenth birthday. His Mom had his uncle take him, and he had a good time, but it wasn't the same. He remembered crying that night in his room, hoping his Mom wouldn't hear. He didn't want to hurt her feelings or his uncle's, but the rage and the emptiness he felt after that day were the lowest points of his young life. Tired, Spencer went to bed.

Alisheen had been heartsick all day. She was so mad at Spencer. She'd hoped to wheedle it out of him that morning by trying to force the issue, but she'd miscalculated her emotions and lost it. Alone in her loft, Alisheen missed Spencer. It hit her hard. She got angry all over again and made a useless effort to hold back her tears. She went onto the deck to get some fresh air and to clear her head.

She sat in one of the rocking chairs and hugged her knees. As she rocked, she thought maybe now was the time to accept Carl's offer for a date out of town. It might do her some good, and a change of scenery would be nice. With a new determination, she went to bed.

It was past midnight when the eighteen-wheeler with the Coastal Seafood logo on the side pulled into the rest area on the I-95 northbound side. Jake Sweet had hitched a ride earlier to the rest area, and he had waited since dark for the truck. He looked around anxiously for Vernon. He was supposed to be there to back him up, and he hadn't showed.

"Damn fool is probably lost."

The truck stopped per the pre-arranged plans, and the driver got out and went into the restrooms. Jake patted the gun in his waistband for reassurance, warily walked out to the truck, and climbed into the cab. Ian was in the sleeper compartment and greeted Jake after he closed the door.

"Well, Mr. Sweet, I see you made it OK."

Jake sneered. "Yeah, I made it; you got my money?"

Ian smiled disarmingly. "Of course I do, and you'll get it in due time."

Jake was instantly suspicious. "Give me my money now or I'm of here. The deal was to give me the money when I got into the truck. Now you got the money or not?"

As he spoke, he pulled the pistol and pointed it at Ian.

"There's no need for that, Jake. I have the money. I think we should get out of the rest area first so there are no people around to see you get out of the truck with a briefcase."

Jake waved the gun at him. "I don't care if anybody sees me. I'm outta here after this. I told you that's the way it's going to be. I got a ride coming any minute now. I figured you might try to pull a fast one. I ain't no newcomer to this game; now give me the damn money or I shoot."

Ian very slowly reached behind him, grabbed the briefcase, and placed it on his lap, opening it so Jake could see the money.

"Here you are, Jake. Just like I said, one hundred thousand dollars in twenties and fifties like you asked for."

Jake relaxed at the sight of the cash and lowered the pistol. He reached to close the case and pull it onto his lap when suddenly the driver side door of the cab opened without warning. With Sweet's attention diverted toward the door, Ian had the opening he needed and quickly pointed the gun hidden behind the briefcase's upraised top. Jake realized what was happening and began to curse as Ian raised his gun. The curse died on his lips as Ian shot him twice in the chest. Then, in the head for good measure. The silencer made no noise and the attempt at an enraged scream from Sweet was lost in the idling noise of the truck's diesel engine.

A.J. finished climbing into the driver's seat and closed the door. He pushed the body down onto the floor, put the truck into gear, and began to roll forward, gaining speed as he entered the on ramp to the interstate.

Ian leaned forward through the curtain of the sleeper. "Did anybody see anything back there?"

A.J. ignored the question. "Damn it Ian, you got blood all over the place, and that stuff is a bitch to get out even with bleach. I'm going to have to make up a story and get the interior replaced. I can't let blood evidence hang around. I thought you were going to kill him later on the roadside, not in the truck."

Ian looked at him with contempt. "I had to shoot him. He was carrying a gun. The crazy bastard might have shot me. You shut up and drive. Let's get rid of the body in a different place this time. Keep going north and take the exit I tell you to."

A.J. followed directions and soon began to chuckle.

"What's so funny?" Ian asked.

"I was thinking about you of all people calling this guy crazy."

"Just keep your mouth shut and drive."

They took the exit Baxter indicated and soon the truck disappeared in the darkness and back roads of Georgia. They pulled onto a dirt-logging road and followed it until Ian directed A.J. to stop and cut off the engine. He reached over Sweet's body and opened the door. The body fell out and hit the ground with a thud.

Ian said, "Get your ass out and help me carry him down to the water."

A.J. jumped out and they carried Sweet down to the creek that flowed out into the vast marsh.

"How in the hell did you find this spot?" A.J. asked.

"I look at maps and ride around looking for places like this for just such an occasion," said Ian with a teaching tone. "It pays to know your territory like any good salesman."

They both laughed and Ian said, "Go back to the truck and get the concrete blocks and the rope so this guy doesn't turn into a floater before the marsh rots him."

A.J. hurried back to the truck and soon returned with the blocks and the rope. They tied the rope around Sweet's feet, binding them together, leaving a trailing end, and then tied the blocks to the free end.

"Let's go get the boat," said Ian.

In the back of the rig was a small johnboat with an electric motor and a set of oars. After a couple of trips the boat was ready, and they put Sweet's body into the boat, and A.J. pushed them out into the creek with an oar while Ian readied the motor. Hunched down in the front, A.J. alternated shining the large flashlight on the banks and in front so Ian could navigate. After traveling a short distance, the current picked up speed as the creek connected into a larger one that flowed toward the distant intra-coastal waterway.

"This looks like a good spot. We'll go around the bend where the creeks meet and into the deeper water," said Ian.

A.J. nodded in agreement, and Ian guided the john boat around the bend and up the creek a couple of hundred yards into deeper water. Ian held the boat steady with the motor, and A.J. slipped the blocks of concrete over the side, but he couldn't lift Sweet's large body. Ian had to let the boat drift to help A.J. and, with a final push and a small splash, Sweet was gone. Ian resumed his post at the motor and guided them back to their landing spot. They beached the boat and broke down the equipment, hauling it all to the truck with practiced efficiency.

Ian said, "Let's get the hell home. I'm bushed." A.J. got into the cab and fired up the diesel with Ian settled back in the sleeper with his eyes closed.

~~~~

The body of Jake Sweet wavered with the current along the bottom of the creek. The spot would turn out to be a bad one. When Ian left the motor to help with the body, they'd drifted back toward the bend in the creek and the oyster bed that had formed there on the slower waterside. The current swayed the lifeless body back and forth against the small oyster bed. Soon, the line holding Jake Sweet down was cut clean by the sharp edge of oyster shells, and the body floated down the creek toward the open water.

Vernon drove up the entrance ramp to the rest stop as the Coastal truck was going down the ramp on the other side. He parked and walked to the last shelter at the far end of the picnic area expecting to see Jake sitting there smoking a cigarette and mad as hell because he was late. He didn't find him there, so he checked the bathroom. Not finding him there, Vernon became worried and frantically searched the grounds, calling out Jake's name. Desperate, he searched the women's bathroom and scared the crap out of some old women who screamed. His search producing nothing, he drove back to Savannah as fast as he could.

It was late Sunday morning when Spencer woke up. He sleepily focused on the digital clock and was instantly awake when he realized how late it was.

He cursed and jumped out of bed, hurrying into the bathroom. After a shower, he dressed quickly and hurried into the kitchen to make coffee. Spencer went through the cupboard and found an older jar of instant. As he prepared the instant coffee, he thought Alisheen's coffee sure would taste good.

He frowned, recalling yesterday's event, and thought about calling her. He sipped the coffee and made a face. It was too strong. He dumped the coffee in the sink and rinsed out the cup. As he checked his weapon and prepared to leave, the phone rang. It was Meadors.

"Spencer?"

"Yeah, I overslept. I'll be there in 15 minutes to relieve you. Sorry."

"No big deal but you might want to hurry anyway, you got a visitor this morning."

"A visitor? Who, it's not Jake, is it?"

"No, but you're close. Vernon Faris!"

"Damn."

"Big as life and waiting for you in your office," Meadors said, laughing.

"I'm on my way."

Alisheen woke up convinced she made the right decision the night before. She dialed the number he'd given her and waited for an answer.

"Hello?"

She hesitated then said, "Carl, this is Alisheen."

"Well, this is certainly a pleasant surprise. What's the occasion?"

She began to cry a little, and Carl sensed something was wrong. "Alisheen, what's the matter?"

Alisheen stammered, "C-Carl?"

"Alisheen, what's wrong? Are you in trouble? Are you hurt? Where are you? Are you alright?"

She was sobbing as she answered and blurted out, "Will you take me away for a few days?"

The silence on the other end seemed endless.

In a moment, Carl said, "Of course. I'll send my limo right away to pick you up, and we can talk about it some more."

Alisheen, calmer now that she'd asked the question, stopped crying.

"No, don't do that. Call me later this afternoon. I'll have gotten my act together by then."

"Alisheen, what's happened?"

"I don't want talk about it right now."

"OK, I'll call you this afternoon. Where will you be?"

"I'll be at my loft. Just call me back at this cell number," she said with a surreal sound to her voice.

She looked at her reflection in the mirror on the dresser across the room.

She felt lost. She called Spencer's apartment but hung up before he could have answered. She called her general manager and best friend, Emily, at the restaurant, and told her she was going to be gone for a few days.

"Alisheen, what's going on?" Emily asked. "Do you want me to come over?"

"Nothing, I just need to get away for a few days. I'm exhausted and need a break. I haven't told Spencer so if he calls looking for me just tell him I went to a food show in Atlanta. He won't know the difference and will think I told him I was going and he just forgot."

Emily said, "Alisheen, what in the hell is going on? You've never been to a food show in your life. What's happened, what's wrong?"

"Emily, you're my best friend so please don't ask any more questions. Just cover for me and keep things going while I'm gone. OK ?"

Emily sighed and resigned herself to the request. "You're the boss. I'll take care of everything. Call me if you need me. I'll be here."

"You're a love, Emily. Thanks and I'll call you later. Bye."

"Bye, Alisheen, be careful."

"I will, Emily," and she hung up.

~~~~

Carl didn't know what'd happened and didn't care, but whatever had happened, it was enough to get her to take him up on his offer. He was pleased and immediately began to plan a trip, and then it hit him. This opportunity would draw unnecessary attention to him with Baldwin after the Snowman. His demeanor clouded a bit, but he decided it was worth the risk.

He brightened at this thought and decided to have a drink to celebrate, so he poured a brandy. He had to get things in order and make preparations. He called the garage and told them to get his limo ready for this afternoon. He then called his pilot and told him to prepare to fly out this evening on short notice to Atlanta. He wasn't going to give Alisheen a chance to think or make any decisions. Last, he called Miss LaCrosse and told her to book reservations and find concert and theatre tickets in Atlanta and New York.

"Will you be traveling alone, Mr. Powers?"

"No, I will have a companion. Be sure you make hotel reservations for two; a suite with two bedrooms, one filled with flowers, champagne, and chilled strawberries with dark chocolate sauce, ready for our arrival."

"How long will you be gone sir?"

"I'm not sure, but you'll know where I'll be if you need me."

"Will there be anything else, Mr. Powers?"

"No, thanks, that's all," and he hung up.

Jeannette gently replaced the receiver in its cradle and pursed her lips. It was the only indication of her fury, because the man she loved was going off with another woman.

"Soon, Carl darling, soon, you will be all mine."

# Chapter 6

"I ALREADY TOLD you what the plan was," yelled Vernon. "I was supposed to be at the rest stop by midnight and meet Jake at the picnic shelter. I was late. I got there about 15 minutes after. I searched the rest area and the bathrooms; scared the hell out of people looking through the cracks in the toilet stalls to see if he was in one of them—disgusting damn faggots—and some woman screamed at me like I was going to rape her. I looked everywhere and he wasn't there. If I didn't find him, I was supposed to come straight to you and tell you what I know."

Baldwin looked at the door as it opened, and Meadors entered the room smiling. "His story checks out. The rest stop attendant on duty filed a complaint about a pervert going through the bathrooms last night."

Vernon cursed under his breath at the description.

"Spencer, we also caught a break. The rest stop is a big target for tagging, and they installed cameras about a month ago. The attendant on duty says last night's video is still intact and being held for the police per policy."

"That is a break," said Spencer. "Let's go."

Spencer turned to Vernon. "Go find Vincent and meet us there in an hour."

Vernon promised he'd bring Vincent and left.

"Meadors, anything from the APB we put out on Jake?"

Meadors shook his head. "No. We got all forms of transportation covered, but he hasn't shown anywhere."

Spencer said grimly, "I'm afraid Mr. Sweet is no longer with us."

They arrived at the rest stop, met the attendant and his supervisor, and waited for Vernon and Vincent to arrive.

"That's him! That's the damn creep that was peeping in the toilets last night. Good job officers. I'll be glad to testify against him," the attendant said proudly, pointing at Vernon as they walked up.

"Thank you, sir." Spencer smiled. "We appreciate your willingness to testify, but right now we're looking into another case this man is involved with."

The attendant was disappointed. "OK, but I'll be glad to testify. I want to do my civic duty."

Spencer, with sincerity, said, "Thank you. We'll look around a bit while you get the video ready."

The attendant swelled with pride at the chance to help again and hurried toward the small office where the security equipment was located.

Vincent asked, "You think Jake is dead, Baldwin?"

"I honestly don't know, but I'll be straight with you. I think it's a possibility if he wasn't here to meet Vernon and he hasn't shown up yet."

Vincent paled and said to Vernon with contempt, "You tell them everything you know, you hear?"

Vernon nodded his head in the affirmative, scared of Vincent.

Spencer turned to Vernon. "Show me where you were supposed to meet Jake last night."

Vernon said, "Follow me," and led them to the last picnic shelter. "I was supposed to meet him here."

Spencer looked around, concluding it was the farthest one away from the road and the bathrooms. Late at night, it'd be remote and away from the traffic that would use the rest stop.

"Jake was here alright," said Vincent.

"How do you know?" asked Spencer.

"Look at all of those cigarette butts in a pile! Unfiltered Camels are Jake's brand. He's a chain-smoker. I'll bet these are his."

Spencer motioned for the CSI officer to pick up a few for fingerprinting. "We can tell if he was here or not from these." They scanned the area, increasing the pattern of the search, but found no other traces.

"Let's go look at the video," said Spencer.

The cameras on the building covered the parking lot, the bathrooms, and the shelters in the immediate vicinity. The attendant put the disc into the machine and punched the play button. Within seconds, they were looking at last night's recording. At the eight o'clock time marker, an eighteen-wheeler pulled into the truck stop. After it parked in the spaces designated for the big rigs, the driver and passenger got out. The passenger was Jake Sweet. He strolled into the bathrooms, appeared again after a few minutes, and then disappeared into the darkness, headed for the shelter out of range of the camera lens.

"Well at least we know he made it this far," said Meadors.

"I told you so!" snapped Vernon.

"Quiet!" said Spencer tersely.

"He must be in the shelter smoking and waiting," said Spencer, "but who is he waiting for?"

At the 11:45 marker, a truck rolled into the rest area and parked in one of the designated slots, but it parked as far away from the building as it could get.

"Must be going to get some sleep," said Vincent.

They watched the driver get out and head into the bathrooms. He wore a sweatshirt with the hood pulled up over his head, and he kept his face down, as if he was cold, but hidden from the camera.

"That's odd, I wonder if he's doing that on purpose because he knows the camera is there or if he's just huddled down because he's cold."

"It was warm last night," said Meadors.

No one offered any other comment, and the picture continued. After a few minutes, Jake emerged from the darkness, stopped, and carefully looked around. Then he slowly walked across the parking lot to the truck and climbed into the passenger side of the cab. Vernon started to speak, but Spencer quickly silenced him again. They continued to watch the truck, the dim outline of Jake visible in the window of the cab. A few minutes later, the hooded driver emerged from the bathroom and walked out to the truck. He went to the trailer end of the truck and walked around it out of sight.

He obviously opened the driver's side door of the cab a few minutes later because the light inside the truck came on and Jake was clearly visible. At the same instant the light came on, they could see Jake's body jerk up and back then slump down into the seat. The driver leaned over, pushed him down to the floor, and then the cab light went out. They watched in stunned silence as the truck shifted into gear and began to roll forward toward the interstate.

Within minutes, Vernon's car came into view and they watched him park and disappear from view as he headed for the shelter where Jake was supposed to be waiting. They watched him frantically search the property and the restrooms then get into his car and drive away.

The attendant reached over and stopped the video. "That's all of it."

Meadors looked at Vincent, who was trembling with fury and looking at Vernon with malice.

Spencer suddenly said, "Son-of-a-bitch, rewind it, rewind it!"

The attendant quickly rewound the video, and after a few moments Spencer loudly said, "Stop! Stop it there and start it again."

As they watched the scene again, he said, "Freeze it, right there. Look at the name on the cab door. Do you see what I see?"

Meadors closely examined the still frame then said with a low whistle, "Coastal Seafood Company."

It was late that afternoon when the lab verified the shot had come from the sleeper compartment of the truck and not from the driver. They were unable to read any of the identification numbers on the cab or trailer, due to the angle and distance, so they were unable to identify the actual truck unless they examined every Coastal truck for blood evidence, and they were scattered all over the southeast. It was a big job and would draw a lot of attention to Coastal. Spencer didn't want to go that far yet.

It was a good break, but if they went straight to Coastal and began asking questions, they could drive the Snowman underground and never catch him. It was better to wait, keep Coastal under surveillance, and investigate on the sly. It was hard to convince Vincent it was for the best, but he'd agreed for now, to let them handle it with the promise they'd keep him informed.

After Vincent left, Spencer was in his office reviewing notes and the video again when the lab technician arrived.

"Spencer, we got a lucky break that's going to help you a lot."

Spencer looked at him with interest.

"We kept enlarging the picture with the computer, and we got a fair picture of the driver. He was under the dome light of the cab with the hood off when he pushed the body to the floor. It's a little fuzzy, but I think it's good enough for an ID."

Spencer called out to Meadors and thanked the technician as he left the squad room. He examined the picture and handed it to Meadors, who gave it back with a shake of his head after looking at it closely.

Spencer tapped the picture and looked at Meadors. "I've seen him. He eats at the She Crab all the time. I don't know his name, but if we set up surveillance I know we can make him."

They went to Captain Drake's office and proposed the plan.

"I don't want an arrest or anybody to make contact. There's too much at stake. This information does not go out of this room. We have a chance to put a major smuggler and a murderer out of business, and this is our only link. Spencer, please arrange for an undercover team to be in place in the restaurant. You know the owner so you should be able to arrange it without any problems."

Spencer briefly made a face at the mention of his knowing the owner and nodded his head.

"Let's set it up," Drake said.

As they left Meadors said, "Spencer, why'd you make that face when the Captain mentioned Alisheen? What's wrong?"

"We had a huge fight yesterday morning. She is really pissed off at me right now, and she won't talk to me."

"What happened? I was wondering why you were here Saturday afternoon instead of with Alisheen."

"She started talking about getting married, and I told her I didn't want to discuss it right then. We'd gone off behind the dunes ..." Spencer caught himself and with anger on his face said, "I don't have to explain my personal life to you."

Spencer stomped into his office closing the door behind him. Undaunted, Meadors followed behind him. Spencer stared at him across the desk, but Meadors didn't budge. Finally, Spencer slumped back in his chair and threw his pencil onto the desk with a sigh.

"I'm sorry, damn it."

Meadors sat down. "Tell me what happened."

"We had another fight only this was one of the worst we've ever had. She took a taxi home from the beach and wouldn't even look at me, much less talk to me. I haven't spoken to her since."

"Spencer, why won't you marry her?"

Spencer flushed with surprise and anger. "That's none of your business."

"Look, Spencer, I'm your friend, and I'd do anything for you or Alisheen for that matter."

"Well, you marry her then," Spencer said hotly, "Maybe that will make her happy."

"I'm just trying to help," said Meadors remaining calm. "Maybe I can give you a new perspective or something."

Spencer calmed down and, somewhat embarrassed, said, "It's just something very personal from the past and I'm not comfortable sharing it with anybody. It hurts too much."

Meadors snorted, "That's the worst excuse I've ever heard, and I thought I'd used them all to stay single. I've never had anyone like Alisheen to love. You're a lucky man to have someone love you as much as she does." Meadors, angry now, stood up and leaned across the desk. "You don't think anybody else has ever had it bad or been hurt? Give me and the rest of the people around you a little more credit than that, especially Alisheen. Move on Spencer, as they say, get over it. Because I'll tell you one thing you self-righteous bastard, if you lose Alisheen, the emptiness you feel now will never be filled."

Spencer was speechless. That was the most Meadors had said to him about anything. Before he could recover, Meadors turned on his heel, opened the door, and walked out of the office. Spencer sat in his chair looking out of the window until long after dark.

~~~~

Late Sunday afternoon, Mike Reed and his son, David, in a small motorboat, cruised down the main channel of the creek. It was the first day of the private shrimping season. Mike slowed the boat, turned out of the main channel, and entered a smaller creek. He wound his way up the creek, advancing into the marsh a few hundred yards until he found a straight section of water.

"Let's put the bait poles out here son. The tide will be turning in a while and going back out, but we should be able to catch our limit before the water gets too shallow." After they had placed the ten poles into the muddy bottom, they threw the bait into the water by the poles to attract the shrimp, and then they anchored and fished while they waited on the tide to change.

After a while they decided the tide had changed enough, and it was time to start shrimping.

Mike said, "OK, son, I'll cruise the poles and you cast the net. We'll switch after a couple of runs."

David set himself in the bow and cast the net in the direction of the first pole. After it settled to the bottom, he pulled up the net filled with shrimp.

"Man look at all of the shrimp!" said David to his father with excitement. "You sure picked a good spot."

"Let's hope it keeps up," said his father. "It'd be nice to get a limit first time out."

After dumping the net into the bucket, they guessed there were six or seven quarts of shrimp.

Over the next hour, they shrimped and though it slacked off a little, the catch was still very good. After a while, they took a break and ate the sandwiches they'd brought with them, then switched places. As they turned to start another run against the current, something bumped into the side of the boat startling both of them. At first, Mike thought they'd run aground but a quick assessment of the bank told him that wasn't the case. As he turned to look at his son, he realized David was pointing at the water with his flashlight and screaming. He looked down from his vantage point on the bow and saw the waterlogged and decaying body of Jake Sweet bumping against the side of the boat.

The Coast Guard had reacted quickly to the emergency call on the marine radio from the Reeds and found them in shock. The body had drifted down the creek, and the rope around the feet had hung up on the exposed banks of the creek during low tide. The crabs and fish had done a job on the corpse, feasting on the exposed soft tissue. The recovery crew for the Coast Guard provided medical attention to the Reeds, and they detailed a crew to take the boat back to the marina while a police detail escorted the Reeds home.

The coroner's crew placed the body into a body bag and transported it to the hospital where they logged it into the morgue for autopsy. On Monday morning, the medical examiner came in, briefly examined the body, and declared it a John Doe, death by gunshot. It'd be Thursday morning before Spencer found out.

~~~~

Sunday afternoon, Alisheen, expecting a call from Carl, answered the door to find him standing there. She was surprised, and embarrassed because she'd been crying all day.

"Carl, you were supposed to call first. I look terrible. I haven't even put any make-up on, and I'm dressed in these ratty jeans and a t-shirt."

Powers smiled. "A true southern lady to the core, embarrassed with no make-up on regardless of the circumstances, and besides, you look just fine. Alisheen, I'm here to take you away, and I won't take no for an answer."

Alisheen turned and walked into the apartment with Carl following.

"Carl, I just can't leave, although I've put someone in charge just in case. I haven't packed any clothes or made any other arrangements."

Powers smiled. "I figured you'd say that, but it doesn't matter. I'll take care of what you might need so go pack the bare essentials."

Alisheen didn't have the will to resist his forceful nature. She packed a few things in a bag, washed her face, brushed her hair, tied it back with a scarf, and put on a trace of make-up. She collected her purse with wallet, cell phone, and keys, made a list of things for Emily to do, and left a note on the neighbor's door. She thought about calling Spencer but decided against it. She called her best friend and general manager, Emily, from the limo, told her she was on her way out of town and she'd left her a note in the kitchen.

"How long will you be gone?" Emily asked, attempting to get information.

"I don't really know."

"Where are you going? How will I get in touch with you if I need to?"

"Just call my cell, and I'll call you when I get to wherever I'm going."

"Alisheen, what's going on?" Emily pressed.

Alisheen looked at Carl. "Emily, I'm fine. I just need a break. Bye."

She ended the call, and Carl reached over and took the cell from her, turning it off.

"No more business now."

Alisheen looked at him, took her sunglasses out of her purse, put them on, and looked out at the city as it went by barely noticing it was a beautiful afternoon. She slumped in her seat, put her head back, and closed her eyes. A tear rolled down her cheek, and she turned away from Carl, wiping it away. She opened her eyes at the sound of planes; they were at the airport.

They drove straight to the private hangars after the guard at the gate waved them in. At the hangar, the driver flashed his runway pass and drove directly to the jet sitting on the runway fueled and ready. In minutes, they were on board and in the air. The flight attendant appeared with champagne and snacks, and disappeared. Carl poured a glass for Alisheen, handed it to her, and poured another.

"Carl, I'm very impressed, but where are we going?"

Carl looked at her with a broad smile.

"I told you once before that I'm a shameless opportunist. I assumed I'd only have one chance to show you what life with me could be like, so I'm pulling out all of the stops. Tonight, dinner and rest at the Atlanta Ritz-Carlton in one of their penthouse suites. Tomorrow will be shopping, with lunch thrown in, then dinner and box seats at the Atlanta symphony. The next day will be more of the same except for the entertainment. In the evening, the 'Phantom of the Opera' opens at the Fox."

"Box seats?" asked Alisheen with a smile.

"Of course," said Carl, returning her smile. "Then we fly to New York for more of the same. When you're ready, we'll come back to South Carolina, and if you're up for it we'll go to the plantation."

Alisheen was exhausted. She finished the champagne, placed the glass on the table, put her seat back as far as it would go, and blew Carl a kiss.

"Wake me when we get to Fantasy Land," she said softly and closed her eyes.

Carl got up, covered her with a blanket, turned off the cabin lights, and pulled down the shades. He leaned over and softly kissed the top her head. "Your wish is my command."

He sat down, poured himself another glass of champagne, toasted the air, and drained it.

~~~~

Monday morning Carol was at her desk looking at the backlog of cases that needed follow-up or filing. She hadn't heard from Skip since the weekend and wondered what was going on. With a sigh, she reviewed the morning faxes from the medical examiner's office, reporting possible homicides. There were four.

Her partner, Jack Cooley, came in and sat down placing the coffee he'd brought her on the desk.

"Anything from the medical examiner's office?" he asked.

She picked up the coffee with a nod of thanks and pointed at the faxes.

"The reports from this morning; there are only four."

He picked up the pile and leafed through them.

"Do you want to go down there this morning?"

"No, you go. I have to get some of this paperwork caught up. Just let me know what you find out, and we'll prioritize after that."

"OK, I'll see you later. Oh, by the way …" Jack said.

Carol looked at him expectantly.

"You know the paperwork never gets caught up," he laughed.

Carol looked disgusted and gave him the finger.

Jack hated this part of his job the most. He liked working homicide, but the initial shock of seeing the body, especially when it was torn-up, and the smell, was something he couldn't get used to. Once he got past the first look he was usually OK, but it always sickened him. He arrived at the hospital and took the stairs down to the morgue. Doc Fenton was there.

"Crap," he said to himself.

Doc was always cracking jokes about the dead bodies. He was gross and took particular delight in trying to make Jack puke with his commentary. He saw him coming through the door and smiled.

"Please Doc, no jokes today. Give me a break for a change you sick bastard," which is what Jack always asked and was always ignored.

Doc said, "I got a body here you're going to like. The Coast Guard fished it out of one of the marsh creeks Sunday night. The crabs and fish did a job on the places not covered with clothes."

He walked over to the table and flipped the cover off the body without ceremony, exposing the upper half. The skin in places looked like the frayed bottoms of cut-off blue jeans, where the crabs had been feasting. Jack, instantly repulsed by the scene, found it hard to control the bile rising from his stomach.

Doc Fenton, with a smirk, said, "Looks like linguini doesn't it?" and began to laugh hard and loud.

That was all Jack could take, and he rushed out of the room sick to his stomach.

He returned a few minutes later. "Doc, one of these days I'm going to puke on you! You're such an asshole. Don't you have any respect for the dead, you damn ghoul."

Doc ignored the tirade as usual. "Do you want to hear my findings or not?"

Jack had sufficiently recovered to look at the body and nodded.

"The preliminary finding on the cause of death was by gunshot, two as a matter of fact, to the chest at close range."

"Any ID?"

"Not yet, so I've left him labeled as a John Doe. I was going to examine the rest of him after you got here."

Jack nodded and the medical examiner uncovered the rest of the body. The rope tied around the feet fell over the end of the table.

Doc said, "Looks like somebody didn't want him found. He was probably weighted down with something to make him sink, but the rope got cut somehow."

"Any ideas how?"

Doc shrugged. "It could've been anything. It was a clean cut though by looking at the frayed end of the rope. The ends frayed but equal across the cut. It could have been a gator, oyster reef; who knows."

"How long has he been dead?" Cooley asked as he moved in closer to the table.

"I would guess 24–48 hours by the condition of the body. The marsh does a number on a body in a hurry. The creek critters do more damage than time does though. Any longer and there usually isn't enough to identify them except for the dental records if we find those. In this case we're lucky enough to have a few fingers still intact enough to get a partial set of prints."

Jack shivered at the thought and Fenton continued.

"I'm going to examine the skull and brain, then the body." Cooley stepped back as Fenton moved behind the head. He skillfully and quickly used the saw to cut away the top portion of the skull to examine the brain mass.

"Damn, I missed this due to the condition of the face on the outside. Look at this!"

Cooley moved in, prepared for another of Fenton's jokes, but looking at the brain in the doctor's hands, he saw the bullet lodged in the tissue.

"This looks like a professional hit, Jack, two shots in the chest and one in the head. Whoever did it was making damn sure this guy was dead." Cooley nodded in agreement, walked over to the phone, and called Carol.

"You better forget those files for a while and get down here." Carol didn't ask any questions.

Jack was outside waiting for her when she arrived.

"I thought I'd get some fresh air and brief you on the body before you see it. It's pretty ugly."

Carol looked at him with thanks in her eyes. "I appreciate the heads up. Let's go and get it over with."

When they arrived downstairs, Doc Fenton was all business.

"Carol, this looks like a mob hit or something like that. This isn't your typical street shooting. Whoever did this was a pro and shot him at close range. I've sent the bullets to ballistics for you already."

Carol examined the rope with a gloved hand. "Any chance of finding fingerprints on this?"

Doc replied, "I doubt it, but we can send it to the lab and see what they find."

"What about this guy's prints? You get any?"

Doc nodded. "Yeah, we were able to get a couple of partials and two full single finger prints from one of his hands. The rest were too waterlogged or half eaten to be of any use. They went to the lab for ID about half an hour ago. You should have something on him if he has a record soon enough, but it's going to take some time due to the damage."

Carol casually covered up the body and motioned for them to go.

"Thanks, Doc!" said Carol as they began to leave.

Once outside Carol said, "Let's go back to the station and browse through the recent "Missing Persons" reports, maybe this guy is in there. We might get lucky and ID him from a mug shot before the prints come back."

Jack nodded and began to walk toward his car.

"Hey Jack," said Carol with a smile as he turned around, "want to go and get something to eat?"

"Very funny, Naster, very funny."

# Chapter 7

IT WAS LATE Monday afternoon when Skip and Bo met in Skip's room.

"OK, Bo, what do we have so far?"

"Skip, this Guilford dude hasn't done anything but work since we started to follow him. He left in a Coastal truck Saturday night, but we quit following him after he hit the interstate. He got back to his house late on Sunday night and went to work today. Except for eating lunch at a hotdog stand by the docks, he hasn't left his office. As of this minute, he's working."

Fitzgerald frowned. "Where did he go in the truck?"

"We don't know. He drove to the interstate and headed north. They followed him but turned back after a few miles, assuming he was on a long haul."

Fitzgerald frowned deeper.

"We probably screwed up not following him in the truck. He may have been making a drug run. From now on stay with him wherever he goes. I don't care if he drives to Cleveland, stay with him, anything else?"

Bo shook his head. "No."

"What about the restaurant where you saw him for first contact? Maybe a crowded place is our best option. It'd give him less cause to be alarmed and take a chance at running on us. In a crowd it'd be easier to blend in."

Bo thought for a minute. "The She Crab just might work, but we don't know when he goes, how frequently, or when he goes alone. The day I saw him he had company."

Skip said, "OK, keep watching him and look for other opportunities where we might get to him. I'll go to the She Crab and see what I can find out."

Bo said, "They'll know him. The bartender greeted him like he knew him pretty well."

"OK, I'll start there and go this afternoon to check it out. Find a secure, out of the way place for us to meet, somewhere off the beaten path. I also need a bio on Baldwin, outside of the police background. I need to know him, what makes him tick. I need a good evaluation from you to see if I can trust him if I have to."

"Anything else?"

"No, just get back to me as soon as you can."

After Bo left, Skip left an update message for Whitley on his voicemail. He changed into something casual, got his rental car, and followed the hotel concierge's directions to She Crab.

Blackwell removed the headphones and took a sip of the drink he nursed. The bugs in Fitzgerald's room were easy enough to plant with the short-staffed housekeeping crew. They left doors open all over the place, so he just slipped in, planted the bugs, and slipped back out. He knew everything Fitzgerald knew about the informer. All he had to do now was patiently wait for him to find the other one. Blackwell was used to waiting. He turned on the television and poured another drink.

~~~~

Skip hoped the She Crab would be crowded so he could blend in, and he wasn't disappointed. It was packed. He discovered there'd be a short wait for a table, or he could go straight into the bar. Since the bar was where he wanted to be anyway, he accepted, thanked the hostess, and found an empty stool. Mickey moved quickly to offer him service.

"Welcome to the She Crab. What can I get for you?"

Skip said, "How about a Corona with a lime and a menu?"

"You got it," and Mickey handed him a menu and went to get the beer. He came back quickly with the beer and a frozen mug.

"Man, that looks great," Skip said appreciatively.

Mickey poured the beer. "It's the only way I'm allowed to serve it. Cold beer in a frozen mug every time. Have you decided on any food yet?"

"It's my first time here. What's good?"

"That's easy," said Mickey with a laugh and a wave of his hand. "Everything on the menu has been personally tested by me, and it's all good. For a beginner, I suggest the 'She Crab Sampler'. It's a mixture of the house favorites. You get some raw oysters, boiled shrimp served chilled, and then a combination of fried or broiled seafood. You can pick from any of the fresh fish we got in today, or shrimp, scallops, oysters, fries, baked potato, salad bar, etc."

Mickey finished with his enthusiastic description and Skip, with a chuckle, said, "You make it sound terrific. How can I resist? Let me have the 'Sampler'."

After they'd gotten the details of the order resolved, Skip drank his Corona and surveyed the crowd, hoping to spot his man. Mickey resumed his duties and attended to the other customers but watched the new customer with interest as he worked. He had to be a cop, but he wasn't from around here. He was sure though. He could recognize one anywhere. He'd had enough experience with the other side of the law that he could tell. The haircut, the clothes, the seemingly casual way he surveyed the crowd, probably a damn fed, he thought.

*At least he ain't hunting me.*

The order was ready, and Mickey delivered it. "You want anything else?"

The stranger said, "You've been watching me, how come?"

Mickey was surprised but recovered quickly. "You're a new customer, and I'm just making sure you get good service. The boss insists on it."

Skip said, "Is she here tonight?"

"No!" Mickey said quickly. "She's out of town for a few days. I'm sorry if I offended you."

Skip said, "Look, I'll be square with you because I need some help. Here's my card."

Mickey took the extended card, read it, and his face turned ashen.

"Look, Mister, I been out of the game for almost three years. I'm clean. I don't want any trouble."

"Relax," Skip said. "You're not in any trouble with me, and if you're clean, that's OK by me. I'm trying to find somebody. If you cooperate I'll make it worth your while, but it has to be confidential. All I want is a phone call if he comes in. I'm not going to arrest him, but I do need to talk to him in private. I don't want to scare him off. So what do you say, will you help me?"

"How do I know you're telling me the truth? I spotted you for a fed but never figured D.E.A. What's the deal?"

Skip pulled the picture of A.J. out of his pocket and showed it to Mickey.

"You ever see this guy around here?"

Mickey said with disgust. "That's A.J. Guilford. He's a low-life. I wouldn't trust him as far as I could throw him. He comes in all the time acting like a big shot and throwing large cash tips around. Hell, it's the only way he can get anybody to associate with him, except for that scary fucker he runs with."

Skip perked up at this piece of information. "Who exactly are you talking about?"

"The guy A.J. hangs out with all the time, Mr. Jenkins," Mickey said with a snort. "At least that's what he calls himself now, as a sales guy for some engine company or something like that. They eat in here all the time. His real name is Ian Baxter. He used to be a bare-knuckle fighter on the underground circuit. I recognized him from my gambling days. He's a bad dude, and he damn near killed a couple of guys in the ring. He's definitely someone to steer clear of."

Skip said, "Does A.J. ever come in here alone?"

"All of the time; he's the trucking manager for Coastal Seafood. Their warehouses are just over and down a couple of blocks from here. But, like I said, I wouldn't trust the bastard."

Skip said, "Mickey, I need your help. Will you call me if he comes in by himself?"

"Yeah, I will. I don't give a rat's ass about him anyway. Are you sure I won't get into any trouble?"

"Mickey, you're not doing anything illegal so you're in the clear."

"What about the restaurant? I don't want any trouble for Alisheen. I owe her a lot."

"Nothing will happen here, I promise. Keep the card, the number where you can reach me is on the back."

Mickey nodded, walked away, and Skip ate his "Sampler." When he finished, he called Mickey over and placed two one-hundred-dollar bills on the bar. "Your dinner suggestion and conversation were perfect, keep the change."

~~~~

Alisheen woke to sunlight peeping around the drawn curtains of the hotel window and focused on her surroundings. When they had arrived last night the limo had brought them straight to the hotel. The room was full of fresh flowers, chilled champagne, and strawberries dipped in chocolate, and were accompanied by an assortment of cheeses, crackers, and fruits.

They snacked for a while and had a late dinner. After the tribulations of the day, Carl insisted she get some sleep and go to bed. She was pleased that he'd gotten a suite and hadn't assumed they'd be sleeping together, and gratefully agreed.

She looked at the digital clock on the bedside table. It was close to nine, which was late for her. She got up, put on the fluffy robe provided by the hotel, walked over to the window, and opened the curtains. The city of Atlanta spread out beneath her, and she marveled at the view. It was a beautiful spring day, and she felt relaxed. She thought about calling Spencer, but she decided to call the restaurant instead.

As she dialed the number, there was a light knock on the door. "Come in," she replied as the phone at the She Crab began to ring. Carl entered the room and was about to speak when the ringing phone was answered. She held her finger to her lips to signal quiet. Carl nodded and backed out of the room, leaving the double doors open to the suite.

"Emily, it's me. How is everything?"

"Alisheen, how are you? Where are you? You sound much better than yesterday."

"I'm better. How was last night?"

"We did just fine, no problems. No one believes you actually went to a food show either. Where are you, and what should I tell them?"

She decided she was going to have to tell Emily something, and said, "I'm in Atlanta, but don't tell anybody more than that. I'm at a food show as far as you know. I've got my cell, but if there's an emergency, you can leave a message at the Ritz-Carlton."

"What in the world are you doing there?" asked Emily surprised.

"I'm taking a much needed vacation," she replied cheerfully.

"Ah ha, I get it. You're not alone are you, and if I miss my guess, you're not with Spencer either. OK girl spit it out. Who're you with?" Emily demanded.

Alisheen looked at Carl, who was setting up the breakfast table, and smiled, "My version of a fairy god-mother."

Carl made a face.

"Emily, we're going to New York in a couple of days. I'll call and let you know which hotel."

"Alisheen, I hope you know what you're doing."

"I hope I do too."

"Well, have fun with your fairy god-mother," laughed Emily, "and be careful."

"I will, and thanks for caring and covering for me. You're a good friend. Bye for now."

Alisheen had sat on the bed during the call. She got up, adjusted her robe, and walked out to the sitting room. She sat down at the table across from Carl who was reading the paper and sipping coffee. He put the paper down and poured her a glass of orange juice.

"A fairy godmother, huh. Why not Prince Charming?" he asked with a laugh.

"This way I keep her guessing," Alisheen said with a bright smile.

"It's good to see you smiling after yesterday. I thought I was going to have to hire a clown to cheer you up."

Alisheen's face clouded. "I want to clear up all that with you this morning before we begin our excursion together. You may not want to after we talk."

Carl sipped his coffee and began eating. Alisheen took a sip of the orange juice, bit into a blueberry muffin, and mustered her courage.

"I want to tell you how yesterday came about and why I called you. Spencer and I had a fight—a big one—and I couldn't think of anything else to do but get away. I called you hoping you'd get me out of town, although I didn't expect anything like this, and I'm very grateful. Now that I'm here, I'm not sure what's next. I still love Spencer, but if the things I want from life aren't going to happen with him, then I need to see other people and do other things. I called you out of desperation, fear, hope, and reasons that I can't even begin to sort out, much less put into words. I just hope you won't think I'm terrible to have used you like this. If you want to go back to Savannah, I'll understand."

Alisheen picked up her orange juice and nervously waited for his answer. Carl sat without expression and continued to eat. Alisheen waited a few minutes more in deafening silence and became inpatient.

"Well, aren't you going to say anything?"

"You want some coffee?"

"That's not funny. Please answer me before I go crazy."

Carl put down his fork and held her gaze.

"Alisheen, the reasons you have or think you have for calling me don't matter, and I know you still care about Spencer. However, I think that if you decide to turn to somebody else to fulfill your dreams it should be me. I told you before that I'm an opportunist. I don't expect anything from you nor will I ask you to do anything for me in return. My only wish is for you to forget your troubles, share some adventures with me, have some fun, and for us to learn more about each other. All we know is the relationship we've had through business. Let's find out about the rest. In short, I expect you to have a good time, relax, and enjoy yourself. We may find out we can't stand each other after a few days, but in the meantime, I intend to finish my breakfast and go shopping. You can do what you want, but tonight is the symphony and dinner, so if you're staying, you'll need to buy something appropriate."

Alisheen looked at him with grateful eyes. "What time do we leave?"

"As soon as you are ready."

She smiled and began eating her breakfast.

When Alisheen was ready, they left the hotel, crossed over to Lenox Square, and stopped inside the entrance.

Carl said, "Your money is no good here, so don't worry about paying for anything."

As Alisheen began to protest, he cut her off and handed her a debit card.

"There is no negotiation on the subject. This card is loaded with five thousand dollars." Alisheen's mouth flew open in shock. "Carl, are you crazy?"

Carl ignored her and said, "You won't have any trouble using that, but if somebody questions it call me. I've some shopping to do as well. It's ten. Let's meet back here around two and have a late lunch. Have fun," he said with a laugh and walked off, leaving her in disbelief.

Over the next four hours, Alisheen was in pure heaven. She bought lingerie, cosmetics, evening clothes, casual clothes, accessories, shoes, and jewelry. Suddenly, she remembered to check the time. It was almost time to meet Carl for lunch.

"Where are all of the bags?" asked Carl with a slight case of panic, thinking she'd refused to buy anything. "I thought for sure you'd be loaded down."

"I've been spending as instructed, so you can get that look of panic off your face," she laughed. "Some things needed altering, and the stores deliver for guests of the hotel. Carl, it was the most fun I've had in a long while," and she kissed him on the lips. The kiss lingered a moment as he responded, and then he abruptly broke it off.

"I'm sorry, Alisheen. I shouldn't have done that, but you were so happy and excited it just happened."

She looked at him in amazement.

"Carl, it's OK. I kissed you. I'm no prude and we're adults. I'll tell you if I think it's going too fast. There'll be feelings for me to sort out, but that's my call. Right now I'm hungry," and she led the way toward a hot dog cart in the mall. "Four dogs, please, with sauerkraut, chili, and mustard, two beers, and I'm buying," she laughed brightly.

When they returned to the suite Carl said, "It's getting late, we should get ready. The limo will be here in about an hour to pick us up."

"An hour!" screeched Alisheen. "Carl, you're kidding. I can't possibly be ready in an hour."

Alisheen frantically searched through the pile for the things she would need and hurried off to the bedroom. Carl chuckled, picked up the phone, and called the concierge, telling them to have the limo ready in an hour and a half, then went into his room to get dressed.

"Alisheen, it's time to go," and he looked out the window impatiently.

From behind him he heard, "I'm ready."

She was dressed simply but elegantly with a strapless black evening gown and just a hint of make-up. Her red hair was styled on top of her head in an elegant fashion that held cascading curls. She looked stunning.

"Good things are definitely worth waiting for. You're beautiful."

"Thank you, kind sir," Alisheen said with a curtsy. "You look dashing in your tux. Carl, this is wonderful. I haven't been out like this in a long time."

Holding his arm out for her to hold onto, he escorted her to the elevator; reaching the lobby, they were quickly ushered into the waiting limo.

They ate a dinner Carl had pre-ordered and arrived in the box as the house lights dimmed. By the end of the evening Alisheen felt like she owned the world and said so to Carl.

"My dear all you have to do is ask."

# Chapter 8

TUESDAY MORNING JACK said, "Bingo. I got an ID on our stiff in the morgue."

Carol walked over to Jack's desk and reached for the file.

"Jake Sweet, nice guy. Arrested for everything from DUI to drug trafficking. Damn, did you see this? Narcotics busted him last week. He was out on bail and had an APB issued for him over the weekend."

"Who busted him?" Jack asked.

"Spencer Baldwin," Carol said. "Jack," she paused, "let's not go straight to Spencer yet. I want to do a little digging around first. Let's see if we can come up with something we can use for our cause before we tell narcotics."

"OK by me, what do you want to do first?"

"He's got a rap sheet a mile long, and there're plenty of underground sources we can talk to. Let's check it out."

"Your call, you're the boss, only let's not hold out on Spencer too long. I know you're interested because of the drug angle and probable hit, but remember we're working homicide, not narcotics."

"I'll remember and don't worry. I'll definitely talk to him in a day or so."

They spent the rest of the day tapping their sources for information on Jake Sweet but didn't find out much. If he'd been up to something, nobody was talking. Later that afternoon, the Coroner's office called to confirm what Jack had found out already. The John Doe in the morgue was Jake Sweet.

"OK, now that it's official we should contact the next of kin, but I want to finish poking around before we do."

"Carol, I sure hope you know what you're doing because if you don't, we could get into big trouble."

"Jack, you worry too much about the rules. Besides, all we have to say is we didn't pick up on the drug part of it until we got into the investigation. Let's keep digging."

They worked late into the evening, calling it quits when they'd learned nothing new. Wednesday morning and into the noon hour still left them without any new information.

"Carol, we're getting nowhere."

"I know. I can't believe no one out there knows anything about Sweet. Is there anybody we haven't thought of? Anybody we haven't talked to yet?"

Jack scratched his head. "Benny! We haven't talked to Benny! He's our last shot."

~~~~

They found Benny panhandling on River Street where the tourists get off the buses after their ride through the historic district. Jack eased up behind him, putting him in an arm-lock. He smiled, flashing his badge to the tourist Benny was trying to wheedle money out of, and then none too gently escorted him around the corner and out of sight. They ducked into a short alley, and he bounced Benny off the alley wall and into the side of a dumpster.

"I told you to stay away from that bus stop. You're going to give the city a bad name."

Benny rubbed his shoulder and arm and whined at Jack. "Hey man take it easy. I ain't got medical you know. I have to make a living."

Jack forced Benny back against the dumpster.

"I need some information, Benny."

Benny defiantly said, "Screw you, I ain't got nothing to say to you."

Jack cuffed his head. "I'm not asking the questions. Sergeant Naster is."

Benny rubbed his head and looked at Carol as she leaned against the alley wall.

"Easy, Jack. Are you OK, Benny?" Benny nodded.

"There's something in it for you if you cooperate. All I want to know is what you can tell me about a guy named Jake Sweet."

Benny looked nervous. Jack looked at Carol.

"I think you scared him with that question."

Benny said in a scared tone, "Hey, there ain't nothing to tell. I don't know the guy."

Carol snorted with disgust. "That's bullshit. You better tell me what you know, or I'm going to let Jack kick your ass."

Jack pressed Benny harder against the dumpster, and he whined at Carol. "Look, a guy can get killed talking about Jake and anybody he does business with."

Carol perked up with interest. "Why, Benny? What makes him different?"

"It's not him so much as who he works for. He plays for keeps. Why are you checking up on Sweet anyway?"

The reason came to Benny as soon as he asked the question, and he tried to run. Jack reached out quickly, grabbed him, and threw him back hard against the dumpster, then punched him in the gut. Benny gave a loud grunt as his breath left him. He groaned and gasped for air, sinking to a sitting position.

"Answer her!"

Carol calmly said, "That's enough, Jack."

He backed away but remained between Benny and escape to the street. Carol stooped down next to Benny, fished a cigarette from a pack she pulled out of her coat pocket, and gave it to him, holding a match. Gratefully Benny took the cigarette, lit it, and inhaled deeply.

"Thanks, you're OK."

Carol smiled briefly. "I'm glad you think so, now tell me what you know."

Benny took another drag off the cigarette, exhaled, and leaned back against the dumpster.

"Somebody popped Sweet, didn't they? That's why you're asking about him aren't you?"

Carol nodded.

"Good riddance to that mother. He was a mean bastard. He was real big in the Klan you know and a drug runner."

"We knew about the drugs but not the Klan," Carol said.

Benny laughed because he knew something they didn't.

"Hell, he was their leader. There's a whole bunch of them. They'd kill me if they found out I talked to you about Sweet, but since he's dead I guess it don't matter now."

"Is that why you tried to run?" asked Jack.

Benny nodded. "That's part of it; the guy he works for is the real reason, but if Jake's dead and you know about the drugs, then you know about the Snowman."

Carol and Jack exchanged questioning looks.

Carol said, "We know a little. What else can you tell us?"

Benny was conned by the question. "The Snowman is the biggest smuggler around. Nothing goes in or out of Savannah without his say so. He's a killer; and so is the guy that works for him. They've been getting busted lately. That's why that crazy bastard that works for him has been down here asking questions about an informer. Rumor says he killed everyone that was arrested. I'll bet Sweet was busted, or he was the leak, and now he's dead. That's why you're asking questions, isn't it?"

Carol ignored the question. "Tell me about the crazy bastard down here asking questions."

Benny shook his head. "Some guy named Baxter. He put it out on the street that there was big money if anyone could help him with his problem. Maybe somebody did and that's what got Sweet killed."

Carol continued, "What else can you tell me about Sweet and the Snowman?"

"Sweet was always picking up stuff down here on the docks and throwing his weight around. I sleep outside a lot you know, but if I can sleep inside, I do. I got a friend at the Coastal Seafood warehouse lot who'll let me in sometimes to sleep in a truck that's down for maintenance when he's working the night shift. I get in the sleeper of the cab, and he wakes me in the morning. I haven't seen him in a while though. I don't know if he's still working there or not."

Jack said, "Come on, Benny. You're stalling."

"I was sleeping in a warehouse one night and heard a bunch of noise. I could see what was going on from the window of the sleeper. Sweet and a couple of guys were loading boxes into a pick-up truck. They were talking about the Snowman."

"What did they say?" Carol asked.

"They were talking about how they couldn't wait to get paid because they needed the money, and they were guessing about who he was."

"Well?" asked Carol impatiently.

"One of the guys said they bet on Gilly. Jake slapped him and told him to shut-up. They finished loading the truck and left."

"Did you recognize anyone else?" Jack asked.

"No, I'd never seen them before. That's all I know, I swear."

Carol pulled a hundred dollar bill out of her pocket, rolled it up tight, slid it into the cigarette pack, and then dropped it in Benny's lap.

"You let us know if anything else hits the street."

Benny nodded, "Yeah, sure."

They left him and entered the street.

Jack said, "You think he's telling the truth?"

Carol looked grim. "I know he is," and without explanation kept on walking.

Jack grabbed her sleeve, turning her around with frustration.

"How do you know he's telling the truth?"

"I'll tell you later. Just trust me for a while and believe me when I say I can't tell you yet."

Carol pulled her sleeve from his grip and resumed walking to the car.

By the time they got back to the precinct, Carol had convinced Jack to calm down and listen to reason.

"Right now all I can tell you is I've been told some things in confidence by an outside source."

"Carol, what in the hell is going on? I'm your partner, damn it."

"All I can tell you is that it's on a federal level."

Jack said with an accusing tone, "You've been contacted by some of your old friends from the D.E.A. You're working for them on the sly and feeding them information, aren't you?"

"Yes and no. I'm not working for them, but they did ask for my help. Will you keep it a secret?"

"OK, I can be stupid a bit longer, but don't go too far."

Carol smiled at him. "Thanks, Jack, you're a sweetheart."

That night Carol met with Skip at his hotel. She told him about the visit to the morgue and the information from Benny. He was pleased.

"Carol, that's great work. You've confirmed a few things. I'd bet Benny's Gilly is A.J. Guilford, the trucking manager at Coastal Seaford and our informant. The guy offering money around town for information is probably Ian Baxter."

"Who's he?"

"We think he's running security for the Snowman. He's usually with our informer so it makes it harder for us to get to him. You can read the file on him when I get it. He served time in the federal system, so we should have it soon. For now, let's focus on Guilford and Sweet's murder. I want you to go to Baldwin tomorrow and tell him what you know. Try to join forces by focusing on the angle that you're involved via the homicide. With your D.E.A. background and the homicide, you might get in the door."

"What about my partner? He's covering my back, and I need to bring him in."

"Tell him whatever you want. I'll leave that up to you. If you think you can trust him, tell him. He could be a good ally."

After they finished trading notes and information, Carol left. On the way home, she called Jack's cell phone, even though it was after eleven. She needed to get square with him in the morning. He sleepily answered the phone.

"Jack? Meet me at Eddie's Coffee Wagon outside the precinct in the morning for breakfast. I'll tell you what's going on before we break the news to Spencer."

"What changed your mind?"

"I trust my partner. See you around seven?"

"OK, and you're buying since you woke me up."

"See you bright and early," Carol said and she broke the connection.

~~~~

On a bench outside the station the next morning, Carol outlined for Jack what Skip had asked her to do. Jack listened without interruption, but his face betrayed his astonishment.

"Carol, this is incredible."

"I know, but everything Fitzgerald knew was confirmed by Benny."

Jack became worried.

"I'm not sure I want to be there when you tell Spencer what you know. This could blow up in your face, our faces, big time. Are you sure you know how Spencer will react?"

Carol sipped her coffee.

"No, and you're right. It could blow up and we'll get hit with the blast. If it does, I'll take the hit because you were following orders. It could be good for both us Jack."

Jack didn't say anything. It was obvious he was worried. After they were inside, Carol called Spencer from her desk. Jack sat, massaging his forehead and temples as if warding off a headache.

He looked out from beneath his hands as Carol said, "Spencer, this is Carol Naster in homicide. I need to ask you about Jake Sweet."

"What do you know about Jake Sweet?"

"We got his body in the morgue on Monday. We made a positive identification from his prints on file. We noticed in his file yesterday he'd been busted by you so we were just trying to get some information."

Carol held her breath, and Jack looked at the floor.

"Did you say you got his body in the morgue on Monday?" Spencer asked.

Carol replied, "Yes, but the coroner didn't ID him until Tuesday afternoon."

"Today is Thursday. Why are you just now calling me? We've had an APB out on him since the weekend."

"I know Spencer that's why I'm calling. We just figured it out from the file ourselves. We've been out asking questions and doing background work and haven't been in the office. We noticed it last night, and that's why I'm calling you this morning. I assumed you want to know he's dead, and you'd want to work with homicide."

Jack rubbed his temples harder.

"You'd better come to my office," Spencer said.

"We're on our way." Carol hung up and grinned at Jack. He didn't share her enthusiasm.

Spencer hung up and looked at Meadors. "We got a problem."

Before Carol and Jack made it upstairs, Spencer filled in Meadors and asked the Captain to join them. They appeared and Meadors motioned them into Spencer's office.

"Get your butts in here!" The loud order from Captain Drake boomed from Spencer's office, and all eyes looked at them. Jack followed Carol into the office and the door closed behind them. Spencer was sitting in a chair against the wall. Meadors remained standing next to the door he'd closed, and the Captain had taken over Spencer's desk, but he wasn't sitting. He pointed at the two vacant chairs in front of him and came around the desk to stand in front of them.

"OK, you two hotshots better tell me what in the hell is going on, or you'll both be out of a job."

Jack was nervous, but Carol remained calm.

"We want in on the investigation."

Jack winced.

Drake exploded.

"You don't negotiate with me, Sergeant, and I'm using the term temporarily. I'm the damn boss around here. You will tell us what you know about Jake Sweet, or I swear to the heavens above you'll be out on your ass. Do I make myself clear?"

Carol remained calm in the storm.

"Crystal, Captain. But I'd like to remind you that there's been a homicide, and that also makes it our case."

Jack looked at Carol with a plea in his eyes as if to say, "Please leave me out of this!" Drake was reloading for a new tirade when Spencer spoke up.

"Captain, if I might say something here. Carol and Jack have done some exceptional work, and I could use their help. We're thin and Carol has D.E.A. experience, which could be useful. I don't think it's a bad idea to work this from both angles. If I'm guessing right, these cases are connected. If the Snowman's not directly responsible for Sweet's murder, then he had a hand in it."

Carol smiled, Jack was relieved, and Meadors was enjoying the show because Drake looked like he was going to explode. He was mad as hell, and it was obvious. He was straightening paper clips and then breaking them into pieces. After a few more paper clips and a walk around the room, Drake stopped and faced them.

"Well, Detectives, for the moment anyway, welcome to the team, and I'll expect a report from somebody by the end of the day outlining what in the hell is going on around here."

Captain Drake left the room and moments later was heard laughing in the hall.

Jack looked at Carol.

"Carol, you've got the biggest balls I've ever seen." The room burst out laughing, and everyone relaxed until Spencer asked a question.

"What about Jake Sweet?"

Carol looked at Spencer, stood up, moved to the wall, and turned to face the room.

"Jack went to the morgue Monday morning where he was promptly assaulted by Doc Fenton."

Meadors interrupted. "I hate that guy and his sick jokes."

Jack nodded appreciatively.

Carol said, "Yeah, he does his best to gross Jack out. The autopsy, at first look, showed two shots to the chest, close range. When he opened the head, there was another bullet lodged in the brain. He missed it on the visual examination due to the damage done to the body by the marsh and its inhabitants. A rope, tied around the feet, probably to a weight to keep the body down, had been cut by something, probably oyster shells. It floated in the creeks until it bumped into a father and son on a shrimping outing that scared the hell out of them. That was on Sunday night. The coroner looked at it Monday and declared it a John Doe, death by gunshot, which we get automatically. We identified it as Jake Sweet's body on Tuesday. We took Wednesday to poke around and see what we could find—then we contacted you this morning."

"A caveat, Spencer, is that Jack wasn't exactly a willing party to delay talking to you after we found out you'd busted him last week. I convinced him to wait because I wanted to see what we could find out first. Yesterday we talked to one guy who knew about Jake Sweet, drug smuggler, Klan leader, and Snowman delivery boy."

"Damn, what did you find out? We've been working the streets trying to turn up something on him."

"That's the way it was for us until we talked to our source, Benny, yesterday. He may know more than he's telling. He was scared but rather happy about the demise of Mr. Sweet. He sleeps around the docks mostly, but occasionally he takes advantage of the opportunity to sneak into a warehouse to get warm or out of the weather. He saw Sweet one night loading a truck. He heard some names thrown around."

"What names have you got?" Spencer asked.

"Our source said the people loading the truck were speculating about the identity of the Snowman. They threw the name Gilly around, but Sweet told them to shut up. It turns out, after some checking around, that Gilly is probably A.J. Guilford, who works at Coastal as the trucking manager. I don't have anything else on him. There is also a guy named Baxter throwing money around trying to find out about a leak."

That was too much for Spencer. "Son-of-a-bitch!"

"Carol, we've had an informant passing us information about the Snowman from the beginning. That's how this whole thing got started. The fact that there's an informant is top secret. Only three people know about it, and now you're telling me it's on the damn street! I want your source in here on the sly. If we can encourage him to spy for us full-time, we may get lucky, especially if he can sneak around the Coastal warehouses. Jack, I want you to arrest him and bring him in as soon as you can. Meadors, call Vincent Sweet and let him bury his brother. Carol, we're going to the movies."

After Carol and Spencer reviewed the video from the truck stop, he filled her in on the history of the Snowman investigation.

"We've kept the fact that there's an informer a secret to help protect him. The Snowman is extremely dangerous. If he identifies him, he's dead, so we've never acknowledged his help. We've never gotten any information to help us identify the Snowman though, just cargo times and delivery places."

"Where does Coastal Seafood fit into the picture?"

"We don't know. We think the warehouses are a holding point for the drugs, but that's just a guess. We don't have any proof. Whoever's in charge has distanced himself far enough from the operation to protect his identity.

That's why Sweet's body turning up is so big. Everyone we've questioned has dropped out of sight, probably in the same manner as Sweet. His body is the first lead we've had that's turned up dead."

"Why can't it be a woman?" asked Carol with a smile.

"You sound like Alisheen," Spencer said, then frowned, realizing he hadn't talked to Alisheen since Saturday's blowup.

Carol noticed. "I'm sorry. I didn't mean to bring up a sore subject."

"You didn't. I'm just having a few problems with my relationship these days and I'd forgotten about it. I tend to lose focus when I get deep into a case. The other part of my life tends to suffer."

Carol said sympathetically, "I understand. I quit the D.E.A. for some of the very same reasons. If you ever need a woman's perspective, I'll be glad to listen."

"Thanks, I'll keep it in mind. Where do you think we should go from here?"

Carol thought for a moment. "Our ultimate goal is to identify and bust the Snowman, but we've no idea who he or she may be," she said smiling.

Spencer smiled back.

"I think we should concentrate on Benny. He'd do anything for a few bucks, but he's scared, so he'll be hard to convince. But Jack and I can handle that."

Carol said, "Spencer, Benny said something that's been buzzing around in my head, and it finally hit me. If Sweet was the local leader of the Klan, and they were running drugs for the Snowman, then there're three questions. First, will the Klan continue to run drugs now that Sweet is dead, or will they be out for revenge? Second, if the Klan does continue to run drugs then who'll take Jake's place? Third, if it's not them, then who?"

"I know how to get answers to the first two, but the last one I don't have a clue. Let's go see Vincent."

Vincent was leaving the morgue when Carol and Spencer tracked him down. They were waiting outside when he came out with Meadors.

"Vincent, I'm sorry about Jake. I wish we'd found him in time. If he'd cooperated with us from the beginning things might've been different."

Vincent didn't say anything but looked at Carol, then Spencer, with a questioning look.

"Vincent this is Detective Naster with homicide. We were hoping you'd come down to the station and talk."

Vincent took a drag off his cigarette then flipped the butt into the gutter and exhaled.

"Baldwin, have you seen what those bastards did to my brother?"

"No, I haven't Vincent."

Carol said, "Mr. Sweet, I have. I'd like to bring the people responsible for your brother's death to justice, but I need your help."

Vincent said with contempt, "Lady, no offense, but my deal is with Baldwin."

Spencer said, "Vincent, the lady is OK. Anything you'd say to me you can say to her."

Vincent said, "I got some things to do. Come out to the farm tomorrow morning."

Spencer said, "Vincent, don't do anything stupid. Trust us and let us handle it."

Vincent shrugged, walked to his car, and drove away.

"You want me to tail him, Spencer?" Meadors asked.

"No. We'll wait and see what he says tomorrow."

Jack knew where to find Benny. He waited for him at the bus stop where he'd found him the day before. He saw Benny coming down the street and eased back into the shadows of a doorway. Benny, focused on his objective, didn't see him. The bus came to rest at the designated end of the tour. The doors opened and Benny began to move forward. Jack grabbed him from behind, placed him in handcuffs, and escorted him to the unmarked police car.

"Hey, Jack, what in the hell is going on? I ain't done nothing man!"

"You're under arrest for possession Benny."

He palmed some joints and made a show of going through Benny's ratty coat pocket, producing the joints in his open hand.

"I never saw those before! They're not mine! This is a frame job! What's going on? Why you rousting me?"

Jack told him to watch his head as he shoved him into the back seat of the police car, with Benny protesting loudly.

"Come on, Cooley," Benny whined after Jack got into the car. "I don't do no drugs and you know it. What's the score?"

"I'm busting you for possession, but if you cooperate I can get you on the streets in a couple of days."

"Screw you man. I ain't no squealer!"

"That's a laugh; you'd sell your own mother out to the highest bidder. Now shut up or I'll stop the car and come back there and beat the crap out of you."

Benny was silent the rest of the way to the police station where he was booked. Jack went to report to Carol and Spencer.

"I planted some joints on him and busted him, but it's flimsy as hell."

"He doesn't know that though," Spencer said. "We'll let him think about it for a day or so, and then go to work on him. First thing tomorrow, Carol and I will go see Vincent. Jack, go and see the family that found Sweet's body and see if they can remember anything else. Meadors, go down to the She Crab and place a working surveillance crew in there."

Spencer went into his office and closed the door. He picked up the phone and called Alisheen's cell phone, got her voicemail and hung up. He then called the She Crab.

Expecting Alisheen's voice, he was surprised when Emily answered, "She Crab, this is Emily. How can I help you?"

"Emily, this is Spencer. Is Alisheen there?"

"No, Spencer, she isn't. She left town and went to a food show in Atlanta on Monday."

"A food show?" Spencer said doubtfully. "When will she be back?"

"I'm not sure, Spencer. She said she might stay a few days and take a short vacation. Do you want me to give her a message if she calls?"

Spencer was disgusted.

"Well tell her I called, and to call me. Thanks, Emily."

"OK, bye Spencer," and Emily hung up feeling guilty.

Spencer wondered, "Where in the hell could she be?"

~~~~

Alisheen turned from the window of the jet as the plane made it's decent into New York.

"Oh, Carl, I've never been to New York before. It's huge." When she turned back to the window, she thought, "*I need to call Spencer.*"

# Chapter 9

FRIDAY MORNING ALISHEEN picked at her breakfast with something on her mind. The night before, they'd gone out on the town after dinner, visited some of the clubs in the city, and returned to the Plaza early in the morning. She had gotten a little drunk and when they returned to the suite she'd grabbed Carl and kissed him with affection.

He responded at first but decided it'd be better to put her to bed. He picked her up and carried her to the bedroom, gently placing her on the bed. She looked up at him expecting him to stay, but instead he leaned down and kissed her forehead.

"Good night, Alisheen. Go to sleep and we'll talk in the morning."

Then he covered her with a blanket and turned out the lights as he closed the door.

Alisheen slept late the next morning. When she opened her eyes, she remembered the events of the night before, had a headache, and felt like an idiot. Carl, as usual, was up reading the paper and drinking his coffee. She walked over to the breakfast cart, served a plate, then sat at the table and poured coffee. Carl folded the paper, looked at his watch, and picked up his cup. He spoke to her, breaking the silence.

"You'll be absolutely worthless when you get back to Savannah. All you've done is sleep late, eat, and play. I hope you haven't ruined your work ethic."

She didn't respond, but feigned interest in eating.

Then she blurted out, "Carl, I'm sorry about last night. I was a little bit drunk and ..."

Carl cut her off. "Alisheen, I want you to consider calling Spencer today."

She was surprised and angered. "Why do you want me to call Spencer and what about last night?"

"You haven't spoken to Spencer since Saturday. Last night was potentially embarrassing for us both. I've no doubt we would've regretted it this morning, and I wasn't going to bed with a silly-ass schoolgirl with a buzz. Call Spencer and tell him whatever you want but call him. I'm going to the stock exchange. I'll be back around noon so you have the rest of the morning to yourself."

Alisheen said hotly, "You can't talk to me like that!"

Carl replied calmly. "I will as long as you act like a child. You told me in Atlanta we were adults. Well, it's time to be a responsible adult. As for Spencer, if you don't call him, I'll consider doing it myself."

Carl finished his coffee, stood up, walked around the table, and kissed Alisheen's cheek. With firmness he said, "Call Spencer."

She heard the elevator call bell, the doors opening and closing, and he was gone.

She seethed as she ate her breakfast. "Who in the hell is he calling a silly-assed schoolgirl?" Pouring a fresh cup of coffee, she went into the bedroom.

She checked the time and sat on the bed. Carl's words echoed in her mind. It dawned on her why Carl was different. He'd orchestrated their time together since they'd left Savannah. She admitted that she didn't mind because for once she wasn't responsible for planning everything.

She wondered what would happen if she took control and rearranged their schedule. Would he go along?

"I wonder how he'd like that." Damn, she was plotting revenge. She was acting like a child. He was right though, she owed Spencer a phone call, but she wouldn't tell him she was with someone. She'd do that later, in person. She'd tell him where she was, and she'd just needed some time away.

She went into the bathroom, ran a hot bubble bath in the oversized tub, and wrapped her hair in a towel. She eased into the hot water, put her head back, and placed a warm washcloth over her eyes. The steam from the fragrant water entered her nose, and she inhaled the subtle scent. The warm cloth on her eyes felt good, and her headache was almost gone. She slid farther down into the water submerging her body and tried to relax.

When she felt better, Alisheen decided to call Spencer. She sat up and reached for the phone in the convenient cubbyhole beside the tub and dialed Spencer's apartment. The cell phone rang until the voicemail picked up.

"Spencer, it's me, I'm OK. I'm in New York at the Plaza Hotel. I needed to get away and take a vacation so I ended up in New York. I'll explain everything when I get back."

She then called the police station. He was probably there anyway since it was Friday morning.

The police operator answered the call, "Savannah Police Department, how may I direct your call?"

"Detective Baldwin please."

The voice on the other end took her by surprise.

"Narcotics, this is Detective Naster, how can I help you?"

"Oh," said Alisheen surprised, "I was expecting Spencer. This is Alisheen Delaney. May I speak to Spencer please?"

Carol knew the name. After her brief conversation with Spencer had irritated him, she'd grape-vined enough information to know Alisheen was Spencer's girlfriend and they were having problems.

"Alisheen, this is Carol Naster. I'm new to the department and was looking for some files on Spencer's desk. He's out right now; can I give him a message?"

Alisheen was jealous that a woman was working at Spencer's desk.

"Yes," she said flatly. "Tell him I called and left a message on his phone."

"Is there anything else?"

Alisheen hesitated. "Detective Naster, is Spencer all right? I mean is he being careful? Is he OK?"

"He's fine, Alisheen," Carol said, hurting her feelings without knowing it. "Is there anything else?"

"No, just give him the message please." Alisheen hid her emotion.

"Goodbye, Alisheen. Nice talking with you."

Alisheen angrily pushed the phone to the floor.

"Well, if he's OK and seems fine to his new co-worker then he's obviously not given our situation a whole lot of thought."

Angry again with Spencer, she picked up the phone and called the restaurant.

"Thanks for calling the She Crab, this is Emily. How can I help you?"

"You sound chipper. It's good to hear a familiar voice."

"Alisheen, thank goodness," Emily said anxiously.

"Emily, what's the matter?" Alisheen said, sitting up quickly, sloshing water everywhere.

"Oh nothing. I just got cops in here busing tables, that's all."

"What?" yelled Alisheen, "Emily, what in the hell is going on?"

"Meadors came in this morning and said that the police were looking for somebody that frequents the restaurant so two of them started working this morning. They're experienced though. I told them that if they quit being cops, I could use them here."

Alisheen asked, still in shock, "Who're they looking for?"

"Meadors showed me a picture, and I recognized him but didn't say anything."

"Who is it?"

"It seems that prick A.J Guilford has been a bad boy. I couldn't turn Meadors down and besides, he said he'd just get a court order if I said no. I was pissed-off about that but told him to go ahead. He promised they'd be helpful, and he was true to his word. They're not going to cause any trouble in the restaurant. They just want to identify him and keep an eye on him. Did I do the right thing?" Emily asked with a plea.

"You did the right thing, Emily. With this going on I'll be back Monday. Does Spencer know about this?"

"I'm sure he does. Meadors said Spencer sent him to get the surveillance arranged."

Alisheen was furious. "I'll deal with this when I get back. You just keep things as normal as possible. You're doing a great job. Thanks, Emily."

"You're welcome and I'll see you Monday," Emily said with relief and hung up.

Alisheen was furious.

"That son-of-a-bitch, he can't run roughshod over my people and threaten them with a court order. I'll throw them out on their ass. As for you, Mr. Powers, I'll show you who's a silly-assed schoolgirl."

She quickly finished her bath, dressed, then organized and packed the clothes she wouldn't need for the rest of the trip. Then she called the Concierge and had them send someone to the room.

When the bellman arrived she said, "Please put these bags on a plane to Savannah today and have them delivered to the address on this business card by Monday." She then looked at him pointedly and said, "Understand?" The bellman nodded nervously and said, "Yes, ma'am."

She was beginning to feel like her old self and decided to do what she wanted to do for a change. She left Carl a note, "Gone Out!" She checked her watch, noted it was 11:30, and decided four hours would be enough, and then added, "Back by 4, Al."

Downstairs, she went to the Concierge's desk. "Please get me a cab that won't jerk me around."

The flustered Concierge went to the cabstand and opened a door and spoke to the driver, "Be straight, Sid, or I'll kick your ass, and you won't be allowed back at my stand."

Sid nodded with understanding and leaning over said to Alisheen, "Where to, Miss?"

"Fifth Avenue, please," Alisheen said firmly.

Sid said, "Whatever you say, Miss!" and in minutes, Alisheen was standing in front of Saks.

Carl returned to the hotel and found her note. He noticed some of her bags were missing and called the Concierge, who related the story of the bags and the taxi, fearing he was in trouble. Carl assured him he wasn't and thanked him for his help.

Carl hung up laughing. "Look out, New York, I think she's back," then called his office.

Miss LaCrosse answered, "Coastal Seafood, Mr. Power's office."

"Miss LaCrosse? How're things going?"

"Just fine, Mr. Powers. I hope the arrangements I made were satisfactory?"

"Excellent, Miss LaCrosse, I wanted to let you know I'll be back soon. I'll probably go to the plantation so you can reach me there. Are there any messages for me?"

"Yes, Mr. Powers. One from Mr. Jenkins about the new contract. The labor issue has been resolved."

"That's good news. Goodbye, then."

"Yes sir," said Jeanette, and she hung up. "Soon, you ungrateful bastard, you'll be taking me on lavish trips instead of whores."

She decided to take an early lunch and call it a day. After she arrived home, Jeanette locked the doors, closed the curtains, and went into her bedroom.

She opened the closet and took off her clothes, carefully hanging them up, then stripped bare and dropped her underwear and bra into the hamper. She walked to the full-length mirror and examined her naked body with a critical eye. She was forty-nine years old, fairly attractive, but still single. She'd done nothing but work for Carl Powers and had put her life into Coastal Seafood. She didn't know when she'd fallen in love with him, but for years now she'd wanted him.

After all, she was as responsible for the success of Coastal Seafood as he was, but that'd never seemed to come out. He was the big success story and took all of the credit. He was the one with all the fame and the money while she worked nights and weekends to make it all happen. It was time for him to pay her back, and she wasn't going to be satisfied with just anything. She didn't want accolades and money; she wanted his love and devotion to her for the rest of his life.

She left the mirror and opened the bottom drawer of the dresser. She took out the snow-white lingerie and carefully put it on, relishing the feel. When she finished she put on the matching robe and went to the dressing table. She sat down, turned on the lights around the mirror, and carefully touched up her make-up. She walked to the other bedroom and opened the closet where she kept her wedding gown carefully preserved for her big day. She dressed, fastening the buttons on the sleeves with practiced ease. She put on her high heels, wedding jewelry, and wrapped her hair up in a tight bun, pinning it in place. She went to the mirror and watched herself put on the crowning glory of the veil.

She pulled the thin white covering over her face and exhaled deeply, realizing she'd been holding her breath. She went back to the closet and pulled the long white flower box off the shelf. Inside was the carefully wrapped silk flower bridal bouquet she'd constructed. She walked into the living room, lit the candelabras that flanked the fireplace, and turned on her wedding music. She began to stride gracefully as if she was going down the aisle in a promenade to marry Carl Powers. Her eyes glazed over with madness as she circled the room.

Alisheen spent the day shopping and returned to the suite at 4:15 with a few bags on her arms and the rest shipped home. Carl was watching a game on television, sipping a beer, and munching on some nuts.

"Well, I see you've been out on the town. Where've you been?"

"I went shopping, had lunch, and explored Fifth Ave. I've gotten my act together as they say."

"I'm glad. I've been getting a little bored with your company. You're no fun as a pushover."

Alisheen walked over to the couch where he was lying down and kneeled on the floor next to him. She leaned over and kissed him with passion. He responded and she crawled up onto the couch beside him.

She kissed him again and whispered in his ear, "I'm no silly-ass schoolgirl either."

Alisheen stood up, reached for Carl's hand, and led him into the darkening bedroom. She pushed him into a sitting position on the bed and stood in front of him in the dim light. She unbuttoned and removed her blouse, unzipped her jeans, pushed them down over her hips, and let them slide to the floor around her ankles. Then she stepped free from the pile of clothes and stood in front of Carl.

He stood up and began to unbutton his shirt, and she reached to help him. They hugged and kissed pressing their bodies together and laid down on the bed. Alisheen pushed Carl onto his back and she spread her body over his like a cat and kissed him again. Their foreplay became more intense. She was still on top of Carl when she suddenly stopped and put her head down on his chest. He realized she was crying, and he held her without speaking.

Her body shook gently as she cried. After a while, she was still and Carl knew she'd fallen asleep in his arms.

"Someday, Alisheen, we will." He slowly eased her off him, and he covered her up, got dressed, and left her to her dreams.

Alisheen woke up suddenly alert. She was under the blanket and realized Carl had left her. The afternoon had passed into night, and she looked at the clock. It was almost eight. She got up, dressed, and made herself presentable. She went into the living area but didn't find Carl. She knocked on the door to his room and cracking open the door heard water running. He was in the shower.

Alisheen fixed a pitcher of martinis with Stoli vodka, Carl's favorite. She poured one for her and then for him. She steeled herself and carried them into his bathroom. He was wrapped in a towel and holding a razor.

"Your martini, sir, just the way you like it," she announced. She kissed him on the lips and handed him his martini.

"Thanks for understanding. I guess I wasn't ready after all."

He sipped the martini.

"Perfect. Alisheen, I think you're ready for the world. The fact that you took control is a good indication. I won't tell you that I wasn't disappointed because I was, but our time will come if it's meant to be."

She kissed him again. "Carl, I want to go home tomorrow. Emily needs me. There are things that need my attention at the restaurant."

"Is everything all right?"

Alisheen caught herself. She knew A.J. worked for Carl. Until she got back and had all of the facts, it was best not to say anything.

"Nothing really, it's been very busy and she's tired, that's all. I've neglected my work long enough."

"Well, if we're going home, then we'd better have a big night tonight. Go put on your best dress or whatever you have left, and I'll see what the hotel can find for us in the way of entertainment."

"I don't want to change. Let's do something simple."

"I'll compromise. I'll go casual if you can find something casual."

"That sounds like a challenge."

She left Carl to finish dressing and picked up the phone. As he finished, she returned with another martini and a face that resembled the look of the cat after he ate the canary.

"I've done quite well for us, if I may say so."

"What're we doing?"

"It's a surprise. I'll tell you in the limo after we eat."

They were in the lobby waiting for the limo when Carl said, "Alisheen, let's go back to the plantation in Beaufort instead of Savannah. We can spend the weekend there and drive over on Monday morning. It's close enough for business but far enough away to be away. If you decide you need an extra day or so we can stay there as long as you want."

The limo arrived and Alisheen gave the driver the address.

They rode in silence for a few minutes.

Carl said, "You didn't answer me about the plantation."

"Can it wait? I'm not sure yet."

"I guess so. Where are we going to eat?"

As he asked the question Alisheen leaned forward and said, "Up here driver."

The limo pulled over to the curb and Carl followed Alisheen out of the limo and onto the street. They were standing in front of a McDonalds. Carl was in disbelief.

"You're kidding."

"Nope, I want a quarter-pounder with cheese and large fries. What will you have? I'm buying."

Alisheen walked into McDonalds laughing gleefully, leaving Carl standing on the sidewalk. He began to laugh and followed her inside. The rest of the night was enjoyable. She'd gotten the names of some blues and jazz clubs in the area, found Buddy Guy was playing in one of them, and managed to get seats up close. Carl was impressed by her resourcefulness.

On the way back to the hotel Alisheen said, "Carl, the plantation does sound nice."

"You'll love it."

~~~~

Carol gave Spencer the message from Alisheen that morning, and before they left, he checked his voicemail. She watched him listen to the message and saw his anger rise as he listened.

He slammed the cell phone down on the desk. "Let's go."

Carol drove them out to the farmhouse following a brooding Spencer's directions. After they turned off the main road Spencer said, "Here's the turn off for the farmhouse." As they pulled up to the house they could see Vincent standing on the screened porch fanning himself with a newspaper.

As they stepped onto the porch he said, "I told you yesterday, I got nothing to say to you as long as she is here."

"Vincent," Spencer said with frustration, "Detective Naster is trying to find Jake's killer."

Vincent grinned. "Couldn't take that colored boy no more, huh? Well, at least with her you can get laid."

Before Spencer could react, Carol moved quickly. With a solid fist, she hit Vincent with a powerful punch. She broke his nose with the blow and hit him again before he could recover. Spencer grabbed her from behind and dragged her off the porch as she cussed Vincent and before she could hit him again. Vincent's nose was bleeding freely and his cheek and eye were already starting to swell from the second blow.

"She broke my damn nose! She's crazy!" yelled Vincent, holding his nose and trying to stop the blood. "I'm going to kick her ass!"

"Try it, redneck, and I'll finish what I started," Carol yelled, held back by Spencer. Spencer fought the urge to let her go because she'd probably beat the hell out of him.

"Vincent, you'd better go inside."

Spencer waited for him to go inside before he turned to Carol.

"Damn, Carol, have you lost your mind? What in the hell were you thinking?"

"I couldn't stand there and let him imply I was a whore. I'm not sorry I hit him."

"You did more than that. You broke his nose and blacked his eye. Get in the car!"

She got in the car, slamming the door, and Spencer got in behind the wheel.

He sat for a moment then burst out laughing and began to chuckle.

"Holy smoke, all this time I've been worrying about Meadors kicking somebody's ass, and it turned out to be you. Where in the hell did you learn to punch like that?"

Carol smiled. "Marine Corps. They offered boxing lessons and a women's boxing league. I took them and was base champion in my division two years running before I was transferred."

"Damn," said Spencer with another laugh at Vincent's misfortune. "You and Meadors were both Marines. He'll be happy to hear another Marine kicked Vincent's butt for him. I'm going back in. You stay here until I call you."

Spencer tried to erase the mirth from his face before leaving the car. He walked up to the house, knocked, warily opened the door, and entered. Vincent was on the sofa with a bag of frozen vegetables on his nose. Spencer was inwardly wishing for a camera.

"Baldwin, you going to pay to get my nose fixed? That damn bitch broke it. She's crazy."

Spencer bit his tongue to keep from laughing.

"You better be glad I stopped her when I did, or she'd have kicked your butt some more. She's an ex-Marine boxing champ and besides, you deserved it. She stopped you from being disrespectful to a lady."

"Lady my ass. She hits like a mule … and I been kicked by some of them too."

Spencer suppressed his laugh, turning it into a small chuckle.

"Vincent, are you going to talk to us, or are we going to do this all over again?"

"You got to promise me you won't tell anybody what she did to me. I'd sue the police, but I'd be too embarrassed in court to tell the truth. I'll say I fell down when I was drunk."

"You got a deal and send me the bill for the nose."

Vincent began to mellow a little bit and when Carol came in, she apologized. He did the same, saying he was sorry for "fergittin" his manners.

"I know who to call if I need help in a fight."

Carol smiled. "Anytime, Vincent, anytime."

Spencer recapped for Vincent the information that Carol and Jack had uncovered, except the part about the Snowman and their informer, and explained the reason for the visit.

"Vincent, is the Klan going to be out for revenge, or are they going to continue to make drug runs for the Snowman?"

Vincent said, "Some of them will probably keep smuggling and figure Jake got his because he was careless. A few of them were very tight with Jake though. I can't promise they won't be out for blood. He was my only family, you know. I'll be looking for justice too. I can promise you that."

"Vincent, you'll have to be patient and trust us," Carol said, "or Jake's killer and the Snowman will disappear, and we'll have nothing. Right now, the Snowman doesn't know about the video or that we found Jake's body. We need to keep it that way."

"She's right," said Spencer. "Interference from you will only make things worse."

Vincent didn't respond, so Spencer asked another question.

"Vincent, who's going to lead the Klan now?"

"I don't know. We'll vote on it soon enough I guess." Vincent shifted the bag of frozen vegetables on his face.

"An outsider approached Jake in the beginning. He was in the Klan and some of the boys were interested in easy money. Jake was voted the leader after the money started rolling in. Most of them had been out of work for a while or farmed so they all needed money."

"Who else around here has the clout to gather the resources to take up smuggling?" Carol asked.

"Jake was the only one I know, but that doesn't mean there ain't somebody else. He knew lots of people and could get just about anything done. Most of the folks around here have been letting him use their land. They take the money and don't pay any attention because it keeps their bills paid. I don't know who is in and who isn't. They don't talk about it."

Carol said, "Vincent, you've got to convince them to let us handle this and keep what we know a secret. I don't want to be tripping over anybody."

"I'll tell them but don't know if it will do much good."

"Give me some time, Vincent, and I'll get him for you."

~~~~

Friday afternoon A.J. went to the She Crab to eat some oysters and drink a couple of beers before going home. The schedule was light and Ian was out of town. He strolled in the door, ignored Emily, and went into the bar. Hiding his contempt, Mickey walked over and greeted A.J.

"Well, look who's here. What can I get you?"

"Let me have a dozen raw and a Bud, and don't forget the horseradish this time."

A.J. spoke with arrogance and it was all Mickey could do to keep from reaching across the bar and smacking him.

He forced a smile. "Right away, and I won't forget this time."

Mickey put A.J.'s order in his pocket, told the other bartender he was going to the bathroom, and went outside to call Fitzgerald from his cell.

"Hello?" Mickey recognized Fitzgerald's voice.

"This is Mickey."

"I'm listening."

"Your friend is here by himself."

"How much longer will he be there?"

"As long as you need him here, His order got lost in my pocket."

"Give me twenty minutes."

"You got it."

On his way through the kitchen, Mickey gave the order to the kid shucking the oysters. "There's no hurry with this one." He nodded with understanding, and Mickey went back out to the bar and over to A.J.

"It'll take a few more minutes than usual. The kid shucking the oysters had to get a fresh basket and still has to wash them down."

A.J. started to grumble a little and Mickey said, "Have a beer on the house since you have to wait?"

A.J. brightened up. "I'll take another Bud."

Mickey served the beer and talked to A.J., watching the door to the street until he saw Fitzgerald enter.

"I better get to work. You want anything else?"

"No."

Mickey walked to the end of the bar and began to clean glasses.

Skip asked A.J. if he could sit next to him so he could see the television better. A.J., without looking, nodded at the stool. Skip sat down and ordered from the other bartender while Mickey kept his distance. He saw A.J. look at Fitzgerald, do a double take, and go white as a sheet with recognition. He attempted to leave, but Fitzgerald quickly grabbed his arm and spoke tersely. A.J. shook his head in a short nod and took a piece of paper from Fitzgerald.

Fitzgerald spoke to him again, then got up, grabbed his beer and walked into the restaurant, leaving A.J. at the bar. The other bartender went into the kitchen, and Mickey walked over to A.J.

"You OK, man? You look like you're going to be sick."

He was in shock from seeing Fitzgerald and didn't hear him.

Mickey kept the smug grin he felt off his face as he realized that Fitzgerald had scared the hell out of him. He finally heard Mickey's voice.

"I, I, I'm fine."

A.J. looked around to see who might have seen him with Fitzgerald. There was a man bussing tables but no one else.

He said, "Give me my tab. I got to get going."

Quickly paying the tab, he left without eating. Mickey ate the oysters and resisted the urge to call Fitzgerald and thank him for the entertainment.

A.J. was in a panic. His first thought was to run like hell, but it was too late now. They'd found him. He knew Powers was suspicious of a leak. Ian told him, so for the last two months he'd only made a couple of calls, the last one being the other night when he'd overheard Carl might be at the dock. He knew it was a chance to get him busted, so he'd phoned in the tip. The feds didn't start an investigation after his Atlanta visit, and he'd grown frustrated with their lack of interest. In desperation, he'd called the local police and gotten results, but they'd been unable to identify Carl as the Snowman.

"*The Snowman, that's a laugh,*" thought A.J. as he hurried back to the warehouse. "*He's more like a damn reptile, even worse. He was a cold-blooded bastard that wouldn't hesitate to kill. He was as dangerous as a shark. That's what they ought to call him, The Shark, a big fucking great white, like Jaws.*"

He entered the office and his secretary looked up at him with a questioning look. "I thought you were going home?"

"I am," said A.J. quickly. "But I needed to check a couple of things first. Why don't you go on home?"

"Thanks, my husband and I are supposed to go out to dinner so it will be nice to get home early."

A.J. shut the door and locked it. He sat down and stared out the window. His mind was spinning, and he couldn't think of a way out except to run or commit suicide.

"I'm dead if Ian finds out. I might as well save myself some pain and get it over with."

With resolve, he left the office and drove home. On the way, he vividly remembered his shock as he recognized Fitzgerald and received his warning.

"You're in danger; we need to meet tomorrow night."

He'd taken the piece of paper offered to him and realized he hadn't even looked at it.

Fitzgerald had said, "Meet me here tomorrow night at 10:00. I'm leaving now, finish your food, and follow your normal routine."

A.J. pulled the slip of paper out of his pants pocket at the next light. Neatly printed were the words "Lighthouse Park." The car behind him beeped its horn, and he quickly accelerated through the intersection. He checked to see if it followed him. It did. They were watching him.

A.J. arrived at his house, pulled into the garage, and watched the car following him drive by, then he closed the door. He entered the house, locking the deadbolt and putting the chain on the door for good measure. He passed through the kitchen, took a bottle of scotch out of the cabinet, grabbed a glass, went to the bedroom, and turned on the television. He poured a generous shot and took a gulp, choking with the fierce burn of the booze. He went to the dresser and opened the drawer, taking the nine-millimeter out from under the pile of socks and underwear. He crawled on the bed, placed the gun beside him, and flipped through channels, sipping the scotch. He put the drink down and picked up the gun.

A.J. clumsily released the clip, checking to be sure it was loaded. After a couple of tries, he finally secured the clip back in the magazine. He turned it over in his hands, trying to remember how to jack a round into the chamber. He made a failed attempt but finally released the slide lock, and he pulled it back hard enough to load the round. All he had to do now was get drunk. He sipped the scotch for a while, watching the tube and occasionally looking over at the gun. He decided he was ready.

He picked up the gun and put the barrel in his mouth. He sat there for a few moments with his finger on the safety and began to cry. He pulled the gun out and carefully put it down. Crying like a baby, he curled up on the bed and sobbed himself to sleep with the knowledge that he was going to die soon enough. There was no need for him to hurry things along.

~~~~

The busboy finished cleaning off the table and walked over to Mickey.

"Who was that guy at the bar? Did he get some bad food or something?"

Mickey dunked a glass into the rinse sink with a laugh. "No, he didn't get any bad food. I'd say bad news is more like it."

"Who was he?"

"A.J. Guilford, and with some luck his name will soon be changed to 'mud'."

"Where does he work? I've seen him before throwing money around, but it doesn't seem to do him much good. I wonder if I could buddy up to him and get in on some cash?"

"Don't bother," said Mickey. "He's a prick."

"Oh well, I thought it'd be worth a try."

He shrugged his shoulders, picked up his bin of dirty dishes, entered the kitchen, dropped the dishes off at the dirty dish table, and took off his apron. He went into the dining room and signaled his partner who was crossing the room with an order for the kitchen.

"I've made him. We can go."

"Great, I'll turn this in."

He disappeared into the kitchen then came back out. Together they sought out Emily working the cash register.

"Miss Mackey, we have what we need so we'll get out of your hair. We just want to thank you for cooperating with the police."

Emily looked relieved. "I can't say I'm sorry to see you go. Alisheen will be back Monday and she'd have a conniption if you were still here."

Skip met with Bo back in his room.

"The pass went off quick and smooth. Unless Guilford panics and runs, he'll be at the park tomorrow night. I want him covered, obviously, so he doesn't try. How soon can we get him covered?"

Bo said, "It's done. They picked him up when he left you at the restaurant."

"That's good news. Everybody knows the drill for tomorrow night. I want the park secure. There may be others around, but we can't worry about that. Let's keep him safe until we can get our arms around this thing. He's all we got."

Bo opened his briefcase on the table and pulled out two folders. He handed them to Skip without satisfaction.

"What's the matter?"

"Skip, I can't find anything on Coastal except for what's public knowledge. If anything illegal is going on, it's buried deep and well protected. There isn't even a suggestion that something might be going on there."

"That's not the news I was hoping for but tell me what you do have."

"Carl Powers is the owner, and he's a legend if you're a Georgia Bulldog fan. He's the prototype small town boy made good. He grew up a local shrimper's son and worked the boats as a kid. He went to Georgia on a scholarship, 2nd team All-American, was drafted into the pros, played a year, hurt his knee, and came home to start a business. He bought a few shrimp boats, and the rest is history. Except for a few select friends that are shareholders, he owns it all. He is also the most eligible man in town but has no steady girlfriend. He owns this town and has important friends all over the State. He could run for Governor and be a shoe-in. Skip, everybody, and I mean everybody, loves him."

"What else?" Skip asked, closing his eyes and leaning back in the chair.

"His company sponsors public events and social work. Schools, art festivals, they donate tons of food to the shelters and the missions. Hell, he even goes and cooks sometimes on the holidays. His parents are still living. He's currently traveling but expected back soon. That's the story I got from his office today. He bought and restored an old plantation in South Carolina near Beaufort, and he spends a lot of time there. Beyond the public eye I got nothing else, Skip. The guy is a handsome version of Mr. Clean."

"Where does A.J. Guilford fit into this picture?" asked Skip, scratching his head. "How did he get involved with Powers? It sounds to me like there's no way they could've crossed paths."

"I can answer that one. Believe it or not, they were roommates in college for a year."

Skip looked at Bo amazed.

"Yeah, it's hard to believe, isn't it? A.J. came looking for a job, and Powers hired him. When Coastal started distribution, he became the trucking manager. A.J. is single, an arrogant asshole, and nobody likes him. There's speculation, of course, that he wouldn't be in his position if he and Powers weren't friends."

"Are they? I wonder if A.J. knows something about Powers that forced him to give him a job," Skip speculated.

"I doubt it," replied Bo. "Powers wouldn't be intimidated by a little prick like A.J. I'm guessing Powers felt sorry for him."

"Why would A.J. rat him out then? It makes no sense to bite the hand that feeds you."

"Skip, A.J. hasn't said Powers or Coastal is involved. Maybe he's trying to protect him."

"That doesn't make any sense either. If Powers is in danger, A.J. would tell him, and I think Carl Powers can deal with any threat. A.J. is going to have to give us some answers tomorrow night. Tell me about Baldwin."

"He's a first-class cop, and I'd personally vouch for him. He comes from a small town north of here, and his mother is still there. A kid high on drugs killed his father, a beat cop, when he was young, and his mother raised him. He joined the police force after college and worked his way up to Detective Sergeant in the shortest time on record. He's been head of narcotics for two years and is up for lieutenant next time around. If he stays with law enforcement and plays his political cards right, he can make Captain. He has citations for public service, bravery, and being wounded in the line of duty. You can count on him. You want to meet him?"

"No, not yet. We'll let Carol be our source of information for now. Keep digging around on Powers, there must be something else. He's too good to be true."

"OK, I'll keep trying to find some dirt."

Bo left and Skip took a Coke out of the mini bar. He opened it, picked up the folders, and sat down on the sofa to commit them to memory.

Blackwell took off the headphones, turned off the tape machine, and smiled. He poured another bourbon, downed it, rubbed his lips, and dialed the cell.

"Yes?"

"I just wanted to let you know things are progressing nicely."

"That's good news, keep me informed."

"Will do," Blackwell said and hung up.

Whitley put the cell back into the holder on his belt and looked at his wife who was glaring at him.

"Sorry, honey, it was business." She put down her fork with deliberation.

"You promised, Ben, especially since you just got back from your trip to Washington."

"I'm sorry," he said. "No more tonight, I promise," and he turned off the cell phone.

# Chapter 10

SATURDAY FITZGERALD WOKE up late after a long night. He took a shower, dressed, and called Whitley. He heard Whitley's muffled voice over the receiver speaking to someone, and then his voice was loud and clear as he removed his hand.

"Skip, what's going on in Savannah?" asked Whitley with a jovial voice, which was certainly different from before.

"It's fine, Ben. We'll make contact tonight if everything goes as planned."

"Excellent. I've been forwarding your reports to Mr. Chambers and Mr. Henry, keeping them informed of your progress."

Skip was surprised but pleased that the case was getting attention from the head of the D.E.A.

"Skip, I want you in Washington Monday afternoon to meet with Mr. Henry. He has given this case a top priority, and he wants to discuss it with us."

Fitzgerald was astonished and now a little bit angry. He didn't need interference from a politician and said so.

Whitley firmly said, "That's a directive from the head of the D.E.A. Be here Monday," and the connection was broken.

"Kiss my ass!" Skip said to the silent receiver, and he slammed it down.

~~~~

That morning, Spencer and Carol were sitting in Spencer's office and preparing to question Benny when Meadors knocked on the door and entered.

"Spencer, the guys at the restaurant reported in this morning. They made our man yesterday, and one of them witnessed a strong arm on him at the restaurant. His hunch is something is about to go down. He said the guy left in a hurry afterwards, and he looked like he'd seen a ghost."

Spencer said, "Get them in here and let's have it." Detectives Cooper and Bridges walked into the room a few minutes later, and Spencer directed them to a couple of chairs with a quick wave.

"I hear you guys have done a good job. Give me your report."

Detective Cooper had witnessed the scene.

"Sergeant, I was working the detail with Detective Bridges yesterday afternoon when I recognized our suspect. He ordered, the bartender went into the kitchen, and the suspect sat there drinking a beer. Not long afterwards, a man came in and sat down next to him. Later, I got from the bartender that our suspects name is A.J. Guilford, and he works for Coastal Seafood as the trucking manager. Guilford recognized whoever sat down next to him, but he wasn't expecting him because he was surprised as hell and he tried to run, but the man grabbed his arm and held him in his seat. He spoke to him and handed him a piece of paper, then went into the next room. He paid a tab for food he didn't eat and left. As a side to all of this, the bartender seemed to know something more about what'd happened, but I didn't press him on it. I then got with Detective Bridges, and we thanked Miss Mackey for her cooperation. She said we did a fine job but that the owner, who gets back on Monday, will be glad we're gone."

Spencer reddened at the mention of Alisheen.

"Thanks guys, you've gotten us a big break."

Spencer looked at Meadors. "We need a detail on Guilford."

Detective Bridges spoke up. "Sergeant, we'd like to stay with him since we found him."

Spencer said, "You got it."

The junior grade detectives left with Meadors, who was threatening to kill them if they screwed up.

Spencer's mood had darkened with the mention of Alisheen's return, and he started to brood. He knew she wouldn't be happy about cops in her place, and he'd hear about it, regardless if she weren't speaking to him or not.

Carol said, "Spencer, what's next?"

Spencer, still in a fog thinking about Alisheen, didn't respond.

He turned and looked at her with a blank expression on his face. "What did you say?"

"Good grief, Spencer," said Carol with exasperation. "One mere mention of Alisheen, and you're in deep space."

Spencer reddened a bit and said, "I'm sorry, it's just a bad situation, and I haven't heard from her."

He closed his eyes and exhaled deeply in an effort to relax and clear his mind. The last of the conversation with Cooper and Bridges came to his mind, and he chuckled as the picture of Meadors threatening them with death popped in. Suddenly, he bolted upright startling Carol.

"Son-of-a-bitch! Carol, do you realize what that detective said?"

Carol was still recovering from the curse and the surprise. "No, Spencer, damn it. And you scared me to death. I thought you were having a heart attack or something."

Spencer apologized. "I'm sorry I startled you, but don't you see?"

Carol, puzzled, said, "See what? What's so important?"

"Detective Cooper said the bartender took the order into the kitchen."

"So what?"

"There's a pass-through window from the bar to the kitchen. Why would he carry it into the kitchen when all he had to do is stick it through the window?"

"Spencer, I don't get it, what's the big deal? It's not a big break."

"It is if you put it into the perspective of the events he described. Look at it from another angle. The bartender leaves and goes into the kitchen with the order. The unknown man appears a short time later, scares the hell out of Guilford, and passes him a message of some kind. The bartender made a phone call!" Spencer said emphatically.

"Maybe he was followed," Carol said, unconvinced.

"I doubt it. The detective also said the bartender seemed to know more than he was telling."

Carol shook her head, still not convinced.

"I don't know, Spencer. What do you want to do?"

"I'm going to the She Crab and talk to the bartender. I want you and Jack to interrogate Benny. After I get through at the She Crab, we'll meet and review with the team."

Carol nodded in agreement and picked up the phone to call Jack and have Benny brought to the interrogation room. Spencer left for the She Crab, and Carol stopped in the squad room, spoke to Meadors, and briefed him on the plan of action that Spencer had outlined.

Meadors made a few notes, started to walk away, but turned back to Carol and said with a big smile, "I wish I'd seen you kick that redneck's ass. *Semper Fi.*"

Carol smiled at him and gave him a short salute.

She found Jack waiting outside one of the interrogation rooms, and she could see through the glass that Benny was sweating it out inside. She stood by the window for a few minutes without speaking, staring at Benny. Without speaking to Jack about their possible strategy to interrogate Benny, she suddenly turned on her heel and burst into the room with Jack trailing and trying to utter a protest.

Benny was startled when the door opened suddenly.

Carol said, "Benny, I'm in a really bad mood so I suggest you cooperate."

"Come on, Sergeant Naster, you know I ain't done nothing. This is a frame up, and I want a lawyer. I ain't talking!"

Carol walked over to Benny and put her finger in his face.

"Listen, you little bastard. I want to know everything you can tell me about Coastal Seafood, the deceased Mr. Sweet, A.J. Guilford, and anything else you can think of."

Benny said, "I want a lawyer! I know my rights!"

Carol leaned forward on the table and said with malice, "Talk, you weasel!" Then she grabbed him by the shirt and shook him vigorously before she realized what she was doing and abruptly let him go.

Benny, surprised and terrified by her actions, was defeated. He turned his head, and dejected he slunk down in his chair. With defeat in his tone said, "OK, OK, I'll tell you what I know."

Carol looked at Jack with a face drained by her emotional outburst and sat down at the table across from Benny. Jack was pale, surprised by her actions, but remained silent and supported her with a brief smile. She then lit two cigarettes, handed one to Benny, and sat across from him smoking the other one in silence. Finally, in a calm soft tone she said, "What do you know about Coastal Seafood, and don't lie to me. I know you know who A.J. Guilford is."

Benny was scared now and looked away, swallowing hard. He took a drag off the cigarette and shifted in his seat.

"Like I told you before, I sleep in the warehouses sometimes. One night I saw Sweet loading a truck with some of his boys. They were talking about who the Snowman probably was, and Jake told them to shut-up or they could get into trouble."

"What else?" Carol said, taking out another cigarette and tossing it onto the table in front of him?

"They loaded up the trucks and left. I seen Sweet come back in, and somebody stepped out of the shadows and spoke to him."

"Was it Guilford?"

"I don't think it was him. This guy was taller; Guilford is short compared to this guy."

"Was it Baxter?"

"No, I would've knowed if it was him. Like I told you before, I've seen him around asking questions on the docks, so I'm sure it wasn't him."

"Could you recognize him if you saw him again?"

"I don't know; I might be able to."

"What else can you tell me about Baxter?"

"Not much, except he's the Snowman's muscle. That's all I know."

"Why did you lie about who Guilford was?" Carol asked with a threatening tone. "You knew who I was talking about."

"I was scared to tell. Guilford's one of the Snowman's top guys, and Baxter would kill me if he knew I was talking to you about the Snowman."

"How do you know Guilford is one of the top guys?" asked Jack from the wall.

"My friend let me into a warehouse one night. It was cold and a truck was open. I climbed in the sleeper to get warm. The vent on the sleeper was open, and I heard voices. I moved so I could see out the vent. Baxter and Guilford came around the front of the truck and stopped underneath, and I heard them talking about a delivery for the Snowman. Baxter told him he'd better be careful. The Snowman was watching things real close with the leak, and he was sure it was one of his lieutenants. Guilford denied it was him, so I assumed he is one."

"What else can you tell me about Guilford?" asked Carol.

"I don't know nothing else; I swear."

"Jake Sweet?" Carol asked, standing up and pacing the room.

"I told you everything about him too."

"What about the smuggling?" Carol asked.

"The only thing I know is that the shrimp boats bring the goods into port. They pick the stuff up out in the ocean."

"How do you know?" asked Jack.

"I got friends that work on the boats sometimes. They told me." Carol moved next to Benny, and he cringed.

She leaned on the table again. "OK, Benny, here's the deal. You're going to be our eyes and ears down there. If you can get me identification on the Snowman, I'll put you on easy street in the Fed's "Witness Protection Program." I want to know when they move, what they do, and who's involved. We got a deal?"

Benny sat up and looked at Jack, who nodded in agreement.

He looked back at Carol with a renewed sense of courage. "You got another pack of cigarettes?"

Carol smirked and handed Benny a pack of unopened Marlboros.

Benny shoved them into his pocket. "You got a deal."

~~~~

Spencer strolled into the She Crab before the happy hour with a casual wave at Emily.

She gave him a hug. "She's not back, Spencer."

"I know."

Emily said hesitantly, "I hope you guys work everything out."

"Thanks, Emily. Is Mickey here?"

Emily was surprised. "He's in the bar. Is everything alright?"

"Yeah," said Spencer with reassurance. "I haven't talked to him in a while, and I was going to drink a beer. No trouble."

Emily looked relieved. Spencer patted her on the shoulder and went into the bar, sitting on the stools reserved for Alisheen.

Mickey cruised up to him in a matter of seconds and greeted Spencer with a handshake.

"What're you doing here on a Saturday afternoon?"

Spencer gave Mickey a serious look and didn't respond right away.

"Spencer, is there a problem? Am I in trouble?"

"No, Mickey, you're not in trouble, I just need some information. Bring me a Corona and we'll talk."

Mickey made the trip to the cooler, came back with the beer, and poured it in the mug. Spencer took a sip and put the beer down. Mickey licked his lips nervously.

"I want you to tell me everything that happened yesterday afternoon with A.J. Guilford."

Mickey gulped hard.

"Mickey, you aren't dealing again, are you?"

Mickey jumped like he'd been poked with a pin.

"Oh, man, hell no. Spencer, I swear man, I'm clean."

"Then you better tell me everything that happened."

Spencer picked up his beer and Mickey said quietly, "All I did was call the D.E.A. guy. I swear Spencer, that's all I did."

Spencer was floored.

"What D.E.A. guy?" he asked with disbelief.

"Look, Spencer, I figured you knew all about it."

"I don't know what in the hell you're talking about."

"A few days ago, a guy from D.E.A. comes in and flashes some ID and a badge. He says he needs help and promises me some cash if I call him when that prick A.J. comes in."

"Why was he looking for A.J.?"

"I don't know. Honestly man, he didn't tell me anything like that. He just said that A.J. would be surprised to see him, and boy was he ever. He looked like a ghost had sat down next to him. I bet he damn near pissed in his pants," Mickey said, laughing.

"OK, what then?"

"The guy asked me to call him if A.J. came in alone. He came in yesterday afternoon by himself, so I called him and told him he was here. He showed up later, talked to A.J., and left."

"Mickey, how do you know for sure this guy was a fed?"

"He had ID like I said, and he gave me a business card with his number on it. Besides, he dressed like one. You can always spot one a mile away if you know what to look for," Mickey said with a grin.

"I still got his card if you want to see it?"

"Let me have it," Spencer said.

Mickey fished into his apron pocket, took out the ragged looking card, and handed it to Spencer. He read it with slight anger and spoke to Mickey.

"If this guy shows up again, you call me. I want to meet him."

"Spencer, I didn't do anything wrong, did I?"

"No, just let me know if he comes back in."

Spencer finished the beer, slid off the stool, and put a twenty on the counter.

"Thanks for the information."

"OK, Spencer, and I'll call you man, I swear."

Spencer began to walk away but suddenly turned back.

"Mickey, how do you tell?"

"Tell what?" asked Mickey, puzzled.

"You know, how can you spot a cop?"

Mickey laughed and pointed at Spencer's feet.

"Dorky shoes, man, dorky shoes," and Mickey walked away laughing.

Spencer grinned, sighed and left the She Crab. It'd been a long day. He drove back to the police station and walked directly into Captain Drake's office unannounced and closed the door behind him. Captain Drake looked up but didn't speak until Spencer had sat down.

"This must be important if you're here on Saturday. I closed the door, because I'm not really here. I came in to be alone and get some paperwork done."

"Captain, you won't believe what I found out today."

Drake sighed and put down his pencil.

"OK, Spencer, I'll be in for you. What is it?"

Before Spencer was done with the details, Captain Drake was on the phone to D.E.A. in Atlanta.

"This is Captain Drake with the Savannah Police Department. Put me through to Ben Whitley's house."

After a short wait, Drake was connected to Whitley.

"How're you, Sam? This call is certainly a surprise."

"Don't you give me that crap, Ben; we just saw each other two weeks ago at the conference. I want to know what in the hell you got going on in my city. I found out today you got a crew down here, and I don't know about it. What's going on?"

Whitley said in a soothing voice, "Now, Sam, let me explain."

"You better explain, you son-of-a bitch. I don't like it when you sneak into my town."

Whitley became angry. "If you'll shut-up for a minute, I'll tell you."

Drake went silent and Spencer watched with curiosity as his facial expression changed from anger to disbelief while Whitley instructed them not to make an arrest without approval from his office, and that this was a "personal request" from Mr. Henry in Washington.

"Are you out of your mind, Ben? That's way out of line!"

Whitley replied with force, "Sam, this is a D.E.A. request and has top priority. I'll give you the rest of the details when and if you need to know. I've asked you to cooperate. I don't need your approval. If your department interferes, you'll be under investigation so fast that you'll be up to your ass in alligators. You got me?"

Drake responded with a "Go to hell!" and slammed the phone down.

Spencer looked at Drake expectantly.

"Spencer, I have to meet with the Commissioner, which can't happen until Monday morning. For now, we've been asked to make no arrests and to continue to gather information."

"What?" Spencer leaped from his chair.

"You heard me. Make no arrest but continue the investigation."

"Why?"

"I can't tell you why because I don't know. The request was to cooperate. My guess is the D.E.A. has something going on we could mess up if we make an arrest. Do you understand?"

Spencer shook his head in defiant understanding and walked out of the office slamming the door behind him. Frustrated at this new development, he entered the squad room with fury and gathered the team.

"We have a new directive as of right now. We are to continue the investigation but make no arrests."

Everyone was surprised and immediately started asking questions. Spencer raised his hand for silence.

"All I can tell you is this comes from the Captain who got it from D.E.A. in Atlanta."

Carol sucked in her breath through her teeth, but it went unnoticed.

Spencer changed the subject and tried to refocus the group.

"Carol, how'd it go with Benny?"

"Fine. He had some more information to share, and I persuaded him to cooperate."

Jack nodded in affirmation.

"He confirmed that he lied about Guilford and admitted that Baxter is the Snowman's enforcer. He also overheard a conversation between Guilford and Baxter, who warned him the Snowman knew about the informer. Benny may have also seen the Snowman talking to Sweet, but they were in the shadows, so he didn't get a good look. He might be able to identify him if he saw him again, but he wasn't sure."

Spencer then addressed Jack.

"Jack, what did you learn from the family that found the body in the creek?"

"Not much, they were shrimping in the creeks, and the body was floating with the tide when it bumped into the side of the boat. The Coast Guard is backtracking some of the smaller creeks during low tide. They lead to the bigger one where they found the body, hoping to come up with whatever might have been holding the body down, but it's like looking for a needle in a haystack. There're numerous backwater inlets and logging roads all over that area. The body could've been dropped anywhere."

Spencer looked at Meadors. "What have you found out?"

Meadors, without enthusiasm, said, "Spencer, this guy and Coastal are as clean as a whistle. Carl Powers, all around nice guy, college football hero, eligible bachelor with tons of money, who is known for his good works and community service. He owns most of his company's stock, except some private issues of stock to persons unknown. The stock and the company are worth a fortune. His company owns the boats, the docks, trucks, warehouses, everything he needs for an independent operation. It's an ideal set up if you were going to smuggle anything, but it's so big, with so many employees and visibility, that it'd be tough to keep it a secret."

Carol interrupted. "It's not a secret! Benny said the boats pick up stuff out at sea. All of them have done it at some time or another. I'm guessing there's a significant fear of retribution. Somebody squeals and messes up the gravy train for the rest of them, and they'll be shark bait. Benny says he knows guys down on the boats, and they told him about it."

"It sounds reasonable enough," said Spencer. "Is there anything else Meadors?"

"I almost forgot. He owns a plantation over in South Carolina near Beaufort. I haven't done anything with that yet."

Spencer was quiet for a minute.

"Meadors, you stick with Guilford. Carol, I want you to bird dog Benny and talk to Vincent again. He knows more than he's telling us. Jack, you go to Beaufort tomorrow and nose around the town and the plantation to see what you can find out. Take some pictures and get a layout if you can. I know it's in South Carolina, but if we have to cross the river and need help, I'd like to have some background. I'm guessing Powers is popular in Beaufort, too, but it'll help us to know the climate that surrounds him. I'm going to get back with the Captain."

Spencer was worrying about the interference from the Feds. He buzzed Captain Drake's office and discovered he'd gone to an emergency meeting with the Commissioner. The afternoon progressed quickly, and the day ended with no news from the Captain.

~~~~

Ian returned from his road trip tired and hungry. He fixed a drink, went out onto the deck, and felt the breeze. It was cool and a nice evening, so he decided to grill a steak. He thought about calling up a whore for some company but decided he was too tired.

Noticing the blinking lights on the dual answering machines, he pushed play on the one for his business and personal calls and walked out to the deck to light the grill. There was nothing new except for routine calls. He walked back inside and reset the machine, then punched play on the machine that recorded the directional microphones in the Coastal yard. As he leaned forward to reset the machine, he heard a voice say "Skip, this is Biggers. I know who it is, a guy named A.J. Guilford."

Ian froze when he heard A.J.'s name and missed the rest of the conversation because he was shocked. He re-played the message, listening carefully, reset the machine, and sat back in the chair thinking. He prepared his dinner as he ran the conversation over again in his mind. "Who were Biggers and Skip? What in the hell was A.J. up to?"

On a hunch, he opened up his laptop and Googled the residential listings for Biggers. There were only two. He copied the addresses into his notebook and decided to check them out on Monday.

~~~~

Alisheen and Carl touched down at the Savannah airport early Saturday afternoon. They hopped into the waiting Jag, and Carl took the by-pass around the city, crossing the bridge over the river into South Carolina. He phoned the plantation, and Rupert picked it up after a few rings.

"Rupert, this is Carl."

"Yessir, I know," replied Rupert with a matter-of-fact tone.

Carl smiled. "I'm on my way to the house. Are you cooking anything tonight?"

"No, sir. I ain't planned to, but I can if you want."

"I've got some company with me for tonight and maybe an extra day or two. Call Annie and see if she can come over to help put a shrimp boil together for us by the pool, and we'll eat together."

"Yessir, I will, sir, and I'll call Annie now. How long before you get here, Mr. Carl?"

"About 45 minutes I guess, we've already crossed the bridge."

"OK. I'll start to get things ready for your company."

Without a goodbye, Rupert hung up the phone. Carl laughed and looked at Alisheen.

"Old Rupert's eyes are going to pop out when he sees you. He's been after me to get married for years, and Annie, the housekeeper and cook, is just as bad. They're great people and have been taking care of the plantation for a long time. Rupert's ancestors were slaves on the plantation, and his people have always been there. He's the last one, though; all of his children have grown up and moved away."

Alisheen looked at the low country scenery as it passed by. The top was down, and the afternoon was warm.

"Carl, this is a great idea. I must confess I wasn't quite ready to go back, and I'm looking forward to seeing the plantation and meeting Rupert and Annie. They sound great."

Carl smiled at her and focused on the road as he accelerated the Jag. Alisheen turned her head again to view the scenery and brushed a wisp of hair off her face. Carl looked at her out of the corner of his eye from behind his sunglasses and inwardly felt a surge of emotion. He turned his head and focused on the road. After passing through Beaufort, he began to slow the Jag down with a series of down shifts, and finally he turned off the main road.

After passing through the iron-gate between two large stone columns, Carl made sure the gate closed behind them. He drove down the dirt road, deep in the shadows and through the woods. They turned a corner and as the woods began to thin out Alisheen caught her first glimpse of the house.

"Carl, it's absolutely beautiful!"

"I've fully restored it and added some modern conveniences, like air conditioning, and completely overhauled the kitchen. I didn't want to change it too much, but I did want it to be comfortable year-round. Rupert grumbled about it some until he got a taste of air conditioning; now he's spoiled," Carl said laughing.

He stopped the car and tooted the horn. The door opened and two big black Labrador retrievers bounded out to greet them. Alisheen was a little startled by them and Carl yelled, "Sit!" The dogs stopped instantly and sat down, looking at her with their tongues hanging out and panting. Before Alisheen could speak, Rupert trudged out of the house admonishing the dogs.

"I told you dogs to be nice to Mr. Carl's comp'ny. You apologize to her for scaring her so."

The dogs looked at Alisheen as if they were waiting for forgiveness.

She laughed merrily. "You're forgiven. I was not expecting such a large greeting."

Rupert smiled at Alisheen with a broad-toothed smile.

"Welcome, Miss. Mr. Carl's manners are shameful. I'm Rupert. Annie's in the house fixing up some snacks for us while we wait for the sun to get right in the back. If'n we don't, the skeeters will eat us alive."

Alisheen laughed with glee and with a sideways glance at Carl said, "I'm Alisheen, and I agree with you about his manners. They're shameful."

"Mr. Carl, you bring the bags in and put them upstairs. I'll take Miss Alisheen and escort her around the house. Hurry up now so we can visit on the patio."

Rupert held his arm for Alisheen and, with a wave over her shoulder, she left Carl standing there with a smile. Rupert showed her the downstairs rooms ending in the kitchen where Annie, the housekeeper and cook, was busily preparing a variety of snacks. Annie took charge the minute they walked into the kitchen. Annie appeared to be in her early sixties. She was tall, slim, and light skinned with a broad smile. She moved with practiced efficiency, and it was obvious she had boundless energy.

"Rupert, you let this lady get herself refreshed after riding with Mr. Carl in that car with no roof on it. Lordy mercy, you ain't got good sense. Now Miss, you follow Rupert, he'll show you where your room is. There is a bathroom off your bedroom, and I laid out some fresh towels for you. Rupert, you go tell Mr. Carl to hurry up with those bags, and then you two get on the patio and get to cooking the sausages and the corn. I got it all on a tray in the big fridge. Now, Miss, when you're ready, you come see Annie in the kitchen, and we'll be introduced proper."

Without wasting a motion, she turned her back to them and went back to her work.

Rupert grinned at her and said, "Follow me, Miss Alisheen," and he led her through a short back hallway and up a narrow staircase.

"These steps were the ones the slaves had to use to stay out of sight of the company in the old days."

"Carl told me your family has lived here for a long time."

"Yes, ma'am," said Rupert with pride. "We been taking care of Blue Creek Plantation since it was built in 1832."

"Blue Creek?"

"Yes, ma'am. The big creek that runs along the back of the property is named Blue Creek. It's because of all the blue crabs that are in it. They say there were so many crabs in the creek back then that the water looked blue from the color of their shells. It's still good crabbing out there if you'd like to try it later."

They arrived at the top of the narrow stair, onto a small landing, and exited through a small door, entering a large spacious hall. Rupert held the door for Alisheen and closed it behind her.

"Looks like a closet door, don' it? It used to be open, but Mr. Carl closed it off to help with the drafts that blow in the winter."

Rupert led Alisheen down the hall, and they met Carl coming out of her room.

"I put your bags on the bed. Rupert giving you the tour?" Rupert answered for her.

"Just bits and pieces, Mr. Carl. I'll save the rest for you. Annie says to hurry and to start cooking the boil. Everything is ready in the big fridge. Miss Alisheen is going back to the kitchen to meet up with Annie."

Carl laughed. "I dare not disobey Annie, nor should you. Can you find your way back downstairs?"

"Yes, I can, and I want to see if I can help Annie."

Carl smiled at the thought. "Well, good luck with that idea anyway. I'll see you in a little bit."

Carl and Rupert disappeared down the stairs. Alisheen entered her room and found it beautifully decorated and traditionally southern. She looked out the window and saw the water in the distance, sparkling with the diamond lights of the afternoon sun. She looked down. A wide flagged stone patio ran the length of the house, bordering a large swimming pool and hot tub under a trellis. A guesthouse was at one end of the pool and a smaller structure housed the outdoor bar and grill. Alisheen saw Carl working with Rupert, who was pointing a finger and giving directions.

She took in the expansive lawn that ran from the pool to the manicured row of azaleas which fronted the tree line of old oaks and pines bordering the creek. A graveled walkway from the wide lawn entered the tree line to a dock, and she could see the top of a large mast from a sailboat gently swaying back and forth above the treetops. Alisheen was content, something she hadn't felt in a while, and it felt good.

The sun was beginning to set so she quickly freshened up and changed clothes. She appeared in the kitchen "refreshed," as Annie had described.

Annie greeted her with a smile. "I'm Annie, Miss."

"I'm Alisheen, and please don't call me Miss, you and Rupert both."

Annie laughed. "It's habit with me and Rupert, Miss, but you can help. I've got a tray ready full of shrimp and things that Mr. Carl likes if you'll take it out there for me."

Alisheen said, "How about letting me make some cocktail sauce?"

"That would be nice, Miss. I haven't made any yet to go out to the patio."

She found an apron and poked through the well-stocked cabinets and pantry with some direction from Annie. She quickly put the sauce together and asked Annie for her approval.

"Oh Miss Alisheen, that's better than mine."

Alisheen blushed. "I doubt that, but I'll take the compliment."

She carried the sauce and snack tray out to the patio. Rupert and Carl had started the boil, and the sausage was already in the pot. Carl got Alisheen a beer, and they began to snack off the tray.

"Annie has changed her dipping sauce, Mr. Carl," said Rupert. "It's different from her usual. It's got some hot to it."

Carl tasted it.

"It's Alisheen's, Rupert."

Annie came out a few minutes later, and Carl couldn't resist the opportunity. He made a big show of dipping a boiled shrimp into the sauce and, at the same time, bragging to Alisheen that Annie's sauce was the best.

He popped the shrimp into his mouth, made a few exaggerated chewing motions, and swallowed with a frown on his face, making a retching noise.

"Annie, this is terrible! It's awful. It's the worst thing I've ever tasted. I can't believe you would serve something like this. Throw it out immediately."

Annie's face masked with horror and embarrassment as she tried to shush Mr. Carl and save Alisheen's feelings. Powers continued to berate her and the quality of the sauce, while she continued to make every effort to get him to "hush-up." Unable to keep it up, he began to laugh at Annie's predicament. Rupert was holding his side and whooping with loud wails of laughter, and Alisheen was trying not to laugh too hard because Annie was making such an effort to keep Carl from hurting her feelings.

Annie stopped in mid-sentence, realizing the joke was on her, and broke into a broad grin. She grabbed Carl by the arm, threatening to "spank him like a young'n," and started a laughing tirade against him for "playing tricks on an old woman like that and scaring her half to death." Annie poked the boiling sausage, pronounced it done, and to put in the corn.

"Rupert, you come on to the kitchen now and get the shrimp. It'll be time for them soon enough." Annie looked at Carl and shook her finger at him, having the last word, then went back into the house.

Rupert checked the sausage for himself. "Seems about right, I guess," then followed Annie.

The sun was beginning to set over the trees and the creek.

"Carl, this is absolutely wonderful, and I can't thank you enough."

Alisheen put down her beer and faced Carl, putting her arms around his neck. She kissed him lightly on the lips and then with passion.

The kiss broke. "Carl, I'm beginning to have some strong feelings for you, but I still have a lot to sort out about Spencer. I know I still care for him, but if things don't work out …"

Carl looked at Alisheen with affection and held her face.

"I told you I'll be here."

Alisheen hugged and kissed him again.

She broke the kiss as Rupert walked up saying, "It sure is a pretty sunset."

They broke the embrace, laughed, and agreed with Rupert that it indeed was a pretty sunset. Annie appeared and took over the supervision of the boil. Carl and Alisheen insisted that Annie and Rupert eat with them, and Rupert entertained Alisheen through dinner and into the evening with stories of the plantation and his ancestors.

Rupert finished telling a story about his father then said, "It's after nine, Mr. Carl. I'm going to let the dogs in and go to bed."

Annie had already left for the evening. Rupert went into the house and Carl stood up and stretched.

"You want anything else?"

Alisheen stood and arched backward. "I don't think so. It's been a long day. I think I'll go to bed too."

She kissed him on the cheek and turned to go into the house.

"Alisheen," Carl said suddenly.

She turned and faced him. "Yes?"

"I hope for my sake that you and Spencer don't work things out."

She came back and embraced him, then kissed him again. She broke the kiss and looked into his eyes. She saw the affection there and that he'd meant what he said.

"We'll see," then she turned and went into the house.

Carl went inside, found the cognac, and poured a generous amount into a crystal tumbler. He took a Cuban cigar out of the humidor, expertly clipped the end, and flipped the top closed. He went back out to the patio. He sipped the cognac, then lit the cigar and smelled the aroma. He was falling for her, but Spencer Baldwin was in the way.

Baldwin was screwing up his business and now his personal life. Maybe it was time to have him killed in the line of duty. If Alisheen went back to him, he'd think about it and conveniently be there to pick up the pieces. There was no rush.

He heard Rupert open the door behind him and come out onto the patio.

"The dogs are settled down in the hall, Mr. Carl, so I'll see you in the morning."

"Good-night, Rupert, and thanks for your help tonight. You made Alisheen feel very welcome. I appreciate it."

"Yes, sir. Miss Alisheen is awful nice, Mr. Carl."

"Yes, she is."

Carl felt like Rupert was hinting around so he said, "Is there anything else, Rupert?"

"No, sir, I just think a nice lady like that could get a man to change his ways. She deserves a man she can trust. That's all I'm saying. Goodnight, Mr. Carl." Rupert turned to go inside.

Carl sipped his cognac, looked at the lengthening ash of his cigar, and said, "Rupert?"

"Yes, sir?" Rupert said, turning to look back at him.

"You might be right. It's a possibility I hadn't really considered."

Rupert smiled, nodded, and headed into the house. Carl's eyes followed him into the house. The lights went out downstairs, but a small lamp was on in the den. He turned around in the chair. He wasn't sure how much Rupert knew, but he was sure he knew enough. Carl finished his drink and sat in the dark, watching the glow of the lengthening cigar ash.

# Chapter 11

SPENCER HAD GONE home after the team had dispersed that afternoon, thinking about his situation with Alisheen. He was thinking about what to do for dinner when his cell phone rang.

He looked at the number and answered. It was Meadors.

"Spencer?"

"Yeah, what's the matter?"

"A.J. is on the move. The men tailing him called in. They need some help. He's evidently taking a roundabout route in case he's being tailed, and it's getting dark."

"Where are you now?"

"I'm in the car and on my way to help."

"OK, I'll call Carol. We'll use her car and be able to help as soon as we can get there. We can coordinate the tail on the fly. Where is A.J. now?"

"He's on Main in heavy traffic heading north."

"Tell those guys not to lose him until we can set up a screen around them. That way if he turns off quickly or runs a light, we'll have him covered."

"Got it," said Meadors.

Spencer called Carol and told her to pick him up at headquarters. When she arrived, he got into her car and filled her in on the way. He then called Meadows on his cell phone.

"OK, we're on the way. Let's all stay on cell phones to maintain contact. The radio handsets could give us away." Meadors acknowledged, and they hurried to join the team following A.J.

In minutes, they were downtown and in communication with Cooper, who was, for the moment, behind A.J., who then ran a red light and turned left across traffic. Cooper relayed the tactic and Meadors picked him up, following him to the expressway. A.J. took the exit ramp into a residential area with Meadors behind him and Spencer and Carol in pursuit. From the bottom of the ramp, A.J. turned left. Meadors continued straight, leaving Carol and Spencer to follow.

Carol was at the wheel and Spencer had ducked down in the back seat so she appeared to be alone. It was unlikely A.J. would think a woman was following him. Spencer listened to her narrative, while she pretended to talk on her cell.

"He's still going straight on Mason Drive."

A car appeared behind Carol.

"Meadors is back and behind me now."

Carol continued to follow A.J. He turned onto a residential street and suddenly pulled over to the curb across from Lighthouse Park. Carol drove past him, talking into her cell phone with enthusiasm, faking a laugh, and telling Spencer and Meadors what'd happened. Carol put the cell phone on speaker and Spencer told Meadors to park around the corner and follow A.J. if he went into the park. Meadors passed A.J., who was sitting in the car looking around and checking his watch. He was waiting.

Meadors had turned at the next corner and stopped the car once he was out of sight. He walked back to the corner, staying in the shadows until he could see A.J., then called the rest of the detail and they all stopped within a few blocks to wait. Meadors checked his watch and settled in to wait until A.J. made a move.

A.J. had taken extra measures to avoid the tail. He congratulated himself on the red-light trick. He'd seen that on television and thought it was cool. He'd become suspicious of the woman, but she was alone and paid him no attention after he parked, and she drove by talking on her cell phone, the dumb broad. A.J. waited to see if any other cars came around the corner. The car with the black dude had gone past, turned down a street up ahead, and kept going. No other cars appeared and A.J. felt safe as he waited. Checking his watch, he realized it was almost 10:00 p.m. It was time to go.

He nervously checked the gun in his waistband and got out of the car, crossed the street into the small park, and followed the concrete path to the playground area. No one was around. He checked his watch again; he was early. He patted the gun again for security and moved into the shadows to wait.

Meadors was about to move out of the shadows and cross the street when headlights appeared and pulled into the curb on the opposite side of the street from A.J.'s car. He saw two men get out of the car, look up and down the street, then enter the park. He turned the cell phone off and crossed the street, entering the park, working his way in the direction A.J. and the men had taken. Soon he could see a shabby playground in need of repair. In the dim light of the playground, Meadors saw three men. He recognized A.J., but the other two had their backs to him. He moved to get a better look, and was stunned as he recognized Bo Biggers. The other man he didn't know, but he committed the face to memory.

"Was this the Snowman?"

A.J.'s voice was getting louder, and he was agitated.

Meadors heard, "I don't know who," and something about, "not being able to wait any longer."

After more argument, A.J. left. Biggers and the other man remained talking, and then walked toward the park exit. Meadors debated on what to do and decided to go the opposite way, walk around the park, and back to the car. As he exited the park, he heard a voice say, "Don't move, put your hands on your head, and kneel down."

Meadors complied while he was trying to think of what to do next. Two men appeared and while one covered him with a gun, the other handcuffed him.

"We found somebody leaving the park sir."

"Bring him back into the park."

"OK. Let's go."

Meadors was considering some type of action to escape when two more men appeared. He hoped Spencer and the rest of them were close enough to save his ass.

"Un-cuff him," said Skip Fitzgerald as he looked Meadors up and down.

Biggers came into view and cursed. "Damn, Skip, it's Detective Meadors, narcotics division of the Savannah police, and I'm betting Spencer Baldwin isn't too far away. What in the hell are you doing here?" asked Bo in an angry tone.

"I was following A.J and found out he has some strange friends with guns," Meadors said with sarcasm.

"What are you implying?" Biggers asked hotly.

"I'm implying I might have found a dirty cop."

"Fuck you, Meadors!"

"Take it easy, Bo," said Skip. "I'm sure that once we explain to the detective he'll understand."

"Try me," said Meadors.

Skip reached into his coat pocket and pulled out an ID and a business card. He turned on a small flashlight and held it for Meadors to read by.

"This will do for a start."

Meadors took the offered ID and business card, and Fitzgerald held the light. He examined each one closely, then handed them back.

"This still doesn't explain what you're doing here, nor does it convince me that you are who you say you are."

Skip smiled. "I don't blame you for having some doubt, it's only natural. I'd be surprised if I got a reaction that was much different. Come with me to my hotel and I'll tell you what you need to know. Bo can drive your car and follow us back to the hotel. You'll ride with me."

Meadors decided if they were going to kill him, they'd have done it already.

Meadors tossed his keys to Biggers and said, "It's the black Ford Explorer around the corner from yours."

"Can I contact my people?"

"No, not yet; I'm going to have to meet with Spencer now that you've found A.J. Guilford, and us. Right now, we need to get out of this park. There has been enough activity tonight and I don't want the neighbors calling the rest of your police force down here."

They escorted Meadors to the car and one of them opened the door to the front seat, while Fitzgerald got in to drive. At the hotel, Skip told Meadors the complete story, beginning with the day A.J. Guilford walked into his office and ending with Fitzgerald describing his meeting with Mickey.

"You can understand why we don't want any arrests made. We're trying to identify the Snowman and his network. We feel an arrest would jeopardize Guilford and we'd lose the network."

Meadors said, "How come you know so much about our case? Outside of a couple of details, you know the whole file."

"I'm not proud of it but I recruited Carol Naster to help me. I needed information and to know if you were going to make an arrest, so I could stop you. She is ex-D.E.A. and used to work for me. She owed me a favor."

Meadors swore under his breath, "Damn!"

"Don't come down on her too hard. She cut a deal for herself, that's true, but she made me promise that I'd contact Baldwin when it was time. She did her best to serve us both. Actually, we were working quite nicely together. Your team turned up solid information that confirmed our guesswork. The murder of Jake Sweet was news to us, and it served a purpose. It pulled Coastal into the picture even more and now we're sure it's involved on some level."

Meadors still had a look of skepticism on his face.

"I better get back to the station. They'll be worried about what happened to me."

He stood up to leave, and Skip stood and extended his hand.

Meadors took it. "So, you'll be calling Spencer now?"

"Yes. I'll contact him as soon as I talk to my boss in Atlanta, to let him know what's happened, and to find out what he wants us to do next."

Skip opened the door for Meadors.

"Good-night, Agent Fitzgerald. I'll tell Spencer to expect your call."

Fitzgerald laughed. "Call me Skip. Since we'll be working together from this point forward there is no reason for us not to be on a first name basis."

Meadors half smiled. "OK, Skip then."

"Do you have a first name?"

Meadors grinned wide and looked around.

"My first name is Hiram, but if you ever call me that in front of other people, I'll kill you."

With a big grin on his face, Meadors turned toward the elevators with Fitzgerald laughing as he closed the door.

Blackwell had heard every word and smiled as he took the headphones off and stubbed out his cigarette. He removed the tape from the machine, dated it, and put it in the briefcase, then put in a blank tape and reset it to record.

~~~~

Carol had continued straight on the street after passing Guilford.

"What should I do?"

"Keep going straight until he's out of sight, and then we'll take up a position and wait for Meadors to contact us."

Soon, Carol stopped the car.

Spencer sat up and stretched. "Turn around and park, then we'll switch places."

They parked, switched places, and waited in silence. Spencer tried Meadors on the cell but got no response.

"He's probably in close and turned it off."

The other details were in the area now and reported in. Spencer told them to stay vigilant and keep radio silence until somebody spotted A.J. or they heard from Meadors. There was no word from Meadors for the next hour, and Spencer became nervous.

Spencer said to Carol, "Let's go in. I'm worried."

She nodded in agreement and Spencer directed all units to move in. They converged at the playground.

"Well?" asked Spencer.

"Nothing sir."

"OK, let's fan out and search. Carol, let's go to where A.J. parked the car."

They exited onto the street; it was empty.

"I want everyone back in the cars looking for Meadors' car. He parked close if he went into the park." They spread out, searching in an increasing perimeter. Six blocks out from the park, there was still no sign of either car and no signal from Meadors.

"Maybe his cell died," said Carol. "You know he'd respond if he could, and he's not going to lose Guilford. Spencer, he's OK. Don't worry."

Spencer said, "Damn, we needed more people to cover all the streets. I hope you're right. I guess we'd better get back to the station in case he calls in."

They told the group to break off the search then went back to the station, putting the patrol units on alert to keep an eye open for the two cars, then waited for some news. It was after midnight when Meadors reported in to say that he was OK and headed for the station. Carol and Spencer breathed a sigh of relief and relayed the news. When he entered the squad room, Spencer immediately began to ask questions.

"What in the hell happened and where've you been all of this time?"

Meadors sipped his coffee and sat back in his chair.

"I've been with Skip Fitzgerald of the D.E.A."

"How in the hell do you know about him? I just found out about him from Mickey this afternoon. I haven't told anyone about him except Drake."

Meadors looked at Carol. "Why don't you ask her?"

~~~~

Jack arrived in Beaufort early Sunday morning armed with fishing tackle and a camera with a telescopic lens in his gear bag. He parked the car and strolled into the bait shop and marina office.

"Got any boats for rent?" Jack asked the whiskered old man behind the counter. "Yep," the man said without looking up from his newspaper.

"I want to do some fishing. You got any tips on bait or where to go?"

The man, annoyed by the early morning visitor, didn't look up. "Wrong time of the month, tides wrong, and the moon ain't right either."

Jack persisted. "Well, I got some time off and want to give it a try. Will you rent to me?"

The man looked at him pointedly. "Can you handle a boat?"

"Yes, sir."

The old man looked him up and down. "I can help you with the boat and the bait, but where won't matter."

Jack grinned. "I'll take my chances."

Once Jack was fueled and ready to go, he asked about plantations in the area.

"We got a lot of them around. Yankees mostly visit them, damn fools, and most of them you have to drive to. There're a few on the water with public docks for boat tours and the private ones will be marked."

"I didn't know there were any private ones around," Jack said.

The marina owner had warmed up to Jack and his money and had become talkative. "Yeah, we got a few, but Blue Creek Plantation is the biggest."

"Sounds interesting, is there any way I can see it? I'd love to get some pictures of a real plantation house."

"I doubt it. You can see it from Blue Creek though. There's a tree line but you can see the back of the house well enough."

"How do I get to Blue Creek?"

The old timer smiled. "I'll have to sell you a map."

On the map he showed Jack how to get to Blue Creek. "Once you're in the creek, you ain't got to worry about the tide changing on you. It's a big deep-water creek and the shrimp boats run in and out of the bottom half of the creek all of the time."

Jack's interest was piqued at the mention of the shrimp boat depth, and he asked the question he already had the answer to.

"Who owns the plantation?"

"Fellow named Carl Powers. He comes into town when he's here and eats down at the café sometimes. Knows everybody and everybody knows him. Keeps his boat here in storage and buys stuff from me time to time to fish, nice fellow. His daddy was a shrimper and so is he, but he owns the boats now instead of working on them. Local folks like him because he hasn't forgotten his roots."

Jack started the engine. The old timer looked at him and said, "Moon's wrong you know," and with that he pushed the boat away from the dock.

Jack grinned, put on his life jacket, and headed up the creek toward the sound. When he reached open water, he slowed down to a cruise and scanned the water traffic. There were sailboats in a regatta and some barges moving up the waterway, but not much else. He looked over his own craft with a closer inspection. It was a 16-foot Boston whaler with a center console and an 85 hp Evinrude motor. There was plenty of storage, extra life jackets, and a fire extinguisher. The gas tanks were full, so he was in good shape for an all-day expedition. He cut the engine and rigged his poles to fish, watching the water traffic to be sure he stayed out of the way.

After his poles were ready, he stored his gear in the big dry box, which doubled as a bench across the back, and set out for Blue Creek following the map. Jack found the entrance to the big creek easily and turned in. The scenery changed to fields and woods, but the creek remained wide as it ran inland and away from the sound. Jack soon saw docks of homes built on the creek and he knew he was getting close to the plantation, according to the directions. He put the boat into a slow and steady trolling speed, dropped his lines into the water, got the camera ready, and continued up the creek.

After a while, he saw a large dock and sailboat as he rounded a turn. He picked up the camera and took a couple of pictures. The name on the sailboat was "Po Boy" and Jack flipped a finger at the boat's name. The house was easy to see from the creek despite the tree line. It was huge. He could see the swimming pool and the large patio area through the lens of the camera. He cruised by and decided to continue up the creek and fish for a while, then return later, anchor, and take a few more pictures.

He continued to fish without any luck, and the morning turned into early afternoon. Jack consumed the lunch he'd brought with him and decided to go back down the creek. He anchored diagonally and across the creek from the dock and began to bottom fish. He eased out the camera and took some pictures of the plantation house and grounds. He noticed the dogs running around and made a mental note.

Suddenly, he got a huge strike, and almost dropped the camera into the water as he reacted. He had been bored but relaxed for most of the day and hadn't really expected to catch anything. He fought the fish for several minutes and soon could make out the outline of his catch. It was a huge flounder and its broad flat body seemed to be at least two feet across.

While Jack was struggling with his fish, Alisheen walked onto the dock in her bathing suit with a large scarf tied in a triangle around her hips. She and Carl were going sailing. She saw the man in the small boat and it looked like he had a whale on the end of his line. Alisheen called out to Carl, who was halfway to the dock with Rupert close behind him.

"Carl, come quick!"

Carl and Rupert arrived with anxious looks on their faces.

"What's the matter?" Carl said slightly out of breath.

"Look at that guy fishing. He's got a really big one!" Alisheen said, pointing at the same time.

"He must have hooked a shark or something."

By this time, Annie had arrived carrying the two baskets of food she'd packed for Carl and Alisheen. They stood on the dock and watched Jack fight his fish. He was mortified at first, but the fish was commanding his full attention, so he didn't have a lot of choice.

"Don't let him have any slack!" yelled Carl.

The back of the flounder broke the water, and they all gasped.

Rupert said excitedly, "That's the biggest flounder I ever did see."

They continued to watch. Jack, with all his strength, held the rod with one hand, keeping the flounder on top of the water. He reached for the net swiftly with the other and in one fluid motion scooped the flounder into the net and up into the bottom of the boat, dropping the rod and quickly ensuring the flounder did not flip back over the side.

"Well done," yelled Carl from the dock.

Jack was exhausted and gave a wave of recognition while looking the fish over. It weighed at least fifteen pounds if not more.

Alisheen said, "Carl, invite him for a drink or something; he looks exhausted and very hot."

"He's OK. Besides, we're going sailing."

Alisheen looked at him defiantly and called out to Jack, "Would you like to come over and dock and have a drink? You look like you could use one and a break."

Her invitation exasperated Carl, but she stared him down.

"We have all afternoon and evening. A few minutes of hospitality won't hurt."

Carl gave in grudgingly. "OK, I guess we aren't in that much of a hurry."

Jack flashed a wide smile at the opportunity.

"I don't really need to rest, but I could use a cold drink. I left my cooler at the house this morning, and I ran out of what I bought at the store a while ago."

Carl shouted. "Just tie up on the dock in front of the sailboat."

Cooley stowed the loose gear, pulled up anchor, and started the engine. He idled slowly into position and cut the engine as he gently bumped the dock and hopped out, expertly securing the small boat. He stood up and looked up at the four people on the dock above.

"Thanks a lot," Jack said as he climbed the stairs from the floating dock to the stationary one above. "I sure could use a cold beer."

Carl looked at Rupert and nodded toward the house.

"Follow Rupert to the house, and he'll get you whatever you want."

Extending his hand, Jack said, "I'm Jack Cooley and thanks for the invitation." Carl hesitated then reached out and shook hands.

"I'm Carl Powers, this is Alisheen Delaney, and also Rupert and Annie."

"Nice to meet you all. I won't be long. I see you're going sailing so I won't keep you. A cold drink and a pit stop would be great."

Jack hurried after Rupert, who'd already started toward the house. They walked in silence for a few minutes then Jack said, "It's sure nice of Mr. Powers to let me rest a little bit."

Rupert nodded. "Mr. Carl don't allow folks to come around except now and then for a big party or something."

"Do you think he'd let me take some pictures of the house? It's very beautiful."

"You can ask him; they ain't no harm in that. I suspect he won't though."

Rupert directed him to the bathroom and escorted him to the large den. After getting him a beer from the fridge, they headed back to the dock. Carl was prepping the boat for sailing and Alisheen had spread out a towel on a lounge chair in the sun. Jack admired her from the corner of his eye as he walked up. Carl noticed and cleared his throat.

"Have you gotten everything you need, Mr. Cooley? I trust you will hurry and get that fish out of the sun before it spoils. It would be a shame to waste a catch like that."

"Wow, I hadn't thought of that. I'll need to buy a bigger cooler and a lot of ice to get it home. Thanks again for the short rest and the drink, Mr. Powers. I appreciate it."

He paused for a minute then decided to go for it. "I've got a camera with me. Would you mind if I took some pictures of the outside of the house? I'm a history buff of sorts. It'd be a nice addition to my collection."

Carl hesitated. "I suppose, but only a few shots please. I like my privacy. If it gets out I allowed pictures, I'll be swarmed with requests."

"I'll be discreet and only take a few. I'd be honored if you let me take a picture of you as the owner of the house and, of course, with Miss Delaney."

"I'm not so sure that's a good idea."

"Oh, Carl," said Alisheen cheerfully, "Don't be so camera shy."

"Just one then," Carl said with mounting frustration at the continued inconvenience.

Jack quickly got his camera from the boat.

Carl immediately noticed the telephoto lens and was suspicious. "That's quite a lens Mr. Cooley."

Without looking up from his preparation of the camera Jack said, "I'm a birdwatcher, which was the real purpose of my excursion today. I was hoping to get some shots of birds around the marsh. I was fishing to pass the time while I waited for the sun to go down. Now how about a picture of you two together?"

Alisheen and Carl posed on the dock with the trees and house in the background. Then Jack walked around the grounds followed by Rupert and the dogs, taking several pictures of the house and the entrances.

He finished his survey of the property and asked Rupert how you got to the plantation by land and, "If the front gate was as beautiful as the house."

Rupert said, "No, it's just an iron gate off the road a piece. The main road, 17, goes by the gate, but you can't see it from the road."

Jack smiled and thanked Rupert for his help. Rupert and the dogs escorted him back to the dock.

"Thanks again for everything."

Carl said, "You're welcome, Mr. Cooley," but his impatience and frustration with the nosy stranger came to the surface.

"We're going sailing now. Unless you have any more requests, we'll be off."

Alisheen looked at Carl with surprise and started to speak, but Jack spoke first.

"I'm sorry. I've been rude and delayed your trip. I must hurry now anyway and get this fish home before it spoils. It was careless of me not to be prepared. Again, my thanks."

Jack quickly got into his boat and stowed his camera under the scrutiny of Powers. He started the engine, untied the boat, and pushed the bow off, stepping into the boat as it drifted away from the dock. He scooped some water from the creek and splashed it on the fish in an effort to keep it from drying out, then pushed the throttle forward and eased past the sailboat, giving them a casual wave as he passed by. He was past the dock before accelerating and headed down the creek under full power. When he was out of sight, he opened the dry box lid and fished out the cooler of cold beer he'd placed in there earlier.

He laughed as he popped it open and grinning, said, "Hot damn!"

When Jack arrived back at the marina it was late afternoon. The old man strolled down the dock to meet him.

"I figured you'd be back before now. I told you the moon was wrong." Jack laughed and lifted part of the big fish out of the bottom of the boat.

The old man whistled. "I'll be damned. That's the biggest flounder I've ever seen."

Jack put the rest of the gear on the dock and looked at the man with a smile. "I guess he didn't know the moon was wrong."

The old man cackled. "I guess somebody shoulda told him."

He helped Jack load up his gear and donated a cooler and ice for the trip home. He insisted on taking a picture of Jack and the fish to put up on the bulletin board in the shop with the weight and the measurements of the flounder.

"Nobody will believe me if I ain't got proof."

Jack drove out of town on 17, passed several dirt roads, and decided to start checking them until he found the entrance to the plantation. After several misses, Jack turned onto a dirt road and after a short distance, found the gate. He took several pictures of the gate, noting the fencing with barbed wire tops running off through the woods in both directions, and the keypad for access. He also noticed the electric fence insulators running along the top of the fence.

"Damn fortress."

Jack put the camera away and backed down the lane and out onto the highway. As he pulled out and headed for Savannah, a sheriff's patrol car pulled up behind him and turned on his lights. Jack pulled over and got out, meeting Sheriff Miller with a pistol pointed at Jack. He was nervous, but the pistol didn't waver.

"Mister, keep your hands where I can see them. Who're you, and what're you doing poking around the entrance to Mr. Power's plantation?"

Jack smiled as disarmingly as possible.

"If you'll allow me to get my ID Sheriff, I'll be glad to tell you. I'm with the Savannah Police Department. I was just taking a leak. I've been fishing all day, and I'll admit I've had a couple of beers this afternoon."

The gun never wavered. "Get the ID, put it on the hood of my car, and then step back from the car, keeping your hands where I can see them."

Jack did as instructed. Sheriff Miller picked up the wallet, went through it completely, and then tossed it back onto the hood.

"Mr. Cooley, you should know better than to drink and drive, but you look OK to me. If you were just taking a leak, how come you went in and out of a couple of roads?"

"Can I put my hands down now?"

The Sheriff holstered his pistol but kept a wary eye and his distance from Jack. "Yeah, I guess so."

Jack dropped his hands and slowly retrieved his wallet from the hood of the patrol car.

"I was just looking for a more private spot, that's all. I didn't want to be seen from the road. The one I came out of had the most cover."

Sam Miller relaxed a little bit more. "Mr. Powers don't like people snooping around his gate. I got suspicious after I saw you go in and out of a couple of roads from my spot where I set up my radar."

"I'm glad I wasn't speeding."

The sheriff relaxed, determining that Jack was harmless. Jack sensed an opportunity for information.

"I was noticing that gate though. It's a real fortress."

Sam Miller nodded his head in agreement. "Mr. Powers used to get a lot of tourists trying to see the place so he put up the fence. He's a nice fella though, and he has friends here. He even supports my election every four years."

"What does he do?" Jack asked, shaking out a cigarette and offering one to the Sheriff.

Sam Miller leaned against the patrol car and took the offered cigarette and light from Jack.

"He owns a big seafood company in Savannah. I'm surprised you ain't heard of him."

Jack laughed. "I guess he and I don't go to the same places."

The Sheriff laughed too. "You're probably right about that."

"Mr. Powers come here a lot?"

"He comes all the time, except during shrimping season. He's busy then, I guess. I know when he's here, though. Rupert or Annie will call me and tell me he's here."

"How come, and who are Rupert and Annie?" Jack asked although he knew the answer.

"Rupert is the caretaker and Annie is the housekeeper. They look after the place. They call me because Mr. Powers drives a black Jag like a bat out of hell. They worry about him getting in a wreck at night, which is usually when he comes and goes. I pull him whenever I can, but I never write him a ticket. It's a game we play. I try and get him to slow down but he doesn't."

Jack stored this information for later use. "Well, Sheriff, I better get back to Savannah."

"Hold on a minute." Jack turned around a little worried.

"Did you catch anything?"

Jack grinned. "Just one," and opening the trunk, lifted the lid off the cooler.

~~~~

"What do you mean, ask Carol?"

Spencer looked at Carol, who sat facing him. She exhaled a long breath that was a combination of relief and exhaustion.

"Skip Fitzgerald is my ex-boss from the D.E.A. He asked me to work my way onto your team and keep him informed. If you were about to make an arrest, I was to notify him so he could stop you. The D.E.A. is also tracking the Snowman through an unknown informant, and there are actually two. Skip told me someone else contacted them offering information on the Snowman under certain conditions. What those conditions are, I don't know. The D.E.A. team came in last week. The concern is that two informers will blow whatever they're working on, and the Snowman will go underground. They were able to identify Guilford from a sketch. They were watching him as we made the connection to Jake's murder and the possible connection to the Snowman. I don't know what else Skip told Meadors, but his orders are coming from Atlanta. I assume that is who Captain Drake talked to yesterday afternoon."

Spencer was stunned and Carol continued.

"Spencer, Skip promised me that he'd contact you when it became necessary. I believed him or I'd never have helped him."

Meadors said, "In Carol's defense, what she's said is true. Everything jives with what Fitzgerald told me, and I confess that I liked him, but I don't like that we were being spied on."

Carol was defensive. "I didn't do anything to hurt this investigation. I made some headway myself and shared it with the team. I've held nothing back."

Spencer eyed her coldly before speaking.

"I trusted you as a loyal and valued member of this team. I made the mistake of counting you as a friend. I guess I was wrong, and it was all a set up."

Carol stood up in anger.

"You're dismissed from this investigation until I talk to Fitzgerald and Captain Drake."

"You can't do that," yelled Carol heatedly.

"I just did. Get out of my office."

Meadors grabbed her firmly by the arm, saying, "Let it go for now" and escorted her out of the office.

"Carol, I'll talk to him. Your temper won't get you anywhere at the moment. Go home and get some rest. I'll call you later."

Seething, Carol stormed out. Meadors walked into Spencer's office and sat down.

"I don't think you need to can her. She's a good cop and didn't give them anything they didn't already know, so there's no harm done. Besides, she didn't keep anything from us."

Spencer was confused and exhausted. He had valued Carol as a team member and a friend, and he felt betrayed.

"My concern now is can we trust her from this point forward. I wonder if Jack knew."

"He did according to Fitzgerald because she's his partner. You got to admire them both for backing each other's play."

"That's great," Spencer said sarcastically. "This is crazy. Who else is working for the feds?"

"Nobody else in our department if that's what you mean, but Bo Biggers was with Fitzgerald last night. They'd arranged to meet Guilford in the park to tell him he was in danger with another informant popping up on the grid."

Spencer shook his head in disbelief, rubbed his eyes and forehead, and leaned back in his chair. He looked at his watch; it was almost four in the morning. It'd been a long night.

"Where is Jack?" Spencer asked as an afterthought.

"He was planning a trip to Beaufort today."

"Do you think we can trust this guy Fitzgerald?"

"He was square with me, and everything he told me matched what Carol told you. I think he's for real."

Spencer said, "Call Carol in the morning and tell her that she's been reinstated to the task force and we'll see if Fitzgerald calls us as promised. It's late. Let's get some rest since it's now Sunday. We'll get the team together Monday afternoon and figure out what in the hell is going on. Also, leave a message in the morning for Jack to come in Monday afternoon, and I'll call the Captain at home in the morning and catch him up." Meadors nodded in agreement and said goodnight. When Spencer went home, he didn't see the tail that picked him up.

# Chapter 12

MONDAY MORNING IAN Baxter parked the BMW down the street from the address he'd written on the note pad. Dressed in jogging clothes, he began to slowly run and check out the neighborhood. The houses were big and the backsides had an excellent view of the marsh. He slowed to a walk and, faking heavy breathing, stopped to watch the landscape crew. He commented it was a shame to be working so early on a Monday. The man that was obviously the boss was eager to talk.

"You're right about that. I hate starting work this early on a Monday, but early spring is our busiest time of year. Everybody wants their yard looking good, and we get a lot of work done when we start early."

"My yard is not as big as this one."

"Well, no job is too small for us. I'd be glad to give you an estimate."

Ian took his card. "Stephen's Lawn Service, can I use this guy here for a reference?"

"Yes, sir, we've been keeping Mr. Biggers' yard for a few years now, and he's never had a complaint."

"It sure is a nice house. I always wonder what people that live in nice houses like this do for a living."

"I think Mr. Biggers works for the government."

Ian smiled. "Well, I better get going, nice talking with you."

He turned around and jogged slowly back down the street, confident that he hadn't aroused any suspicions. He got into his car, put on sunglasses, settled into his seat, and picked up the newspaper. The lawn service left and Ian continued to watch the house.

He was getting sleepy when the front door opened, and a middle-aged man appeared. He walked to the street, retrieved the newspaper, and then looked down the street, fixing his gaze on the black BMW. The instant he'd come out of the house and headed to the mailbox, Ian picked up the small camera on the seat and rapidly clicked off some pictures. He put it down when the man focused on him, decided he was "made," and left. He drove to the nearest CVS and gave them the disk to develop. He drove around and ate a late breakfast while he thought about the next step. After an hour's wait, he retrieved his pictures.

The salesgirl gave him an odd look as he purchased the pictures.

"I hope they came out alright for you. There were only seven pictures on the disk, and they were all the same."

Ian, annoyed, looked at her.

"Private detective," he muttered, and she took on a knowing expression.

Ian left the CVS and, on a hunch, drove downtown to the Federal Building. He entered the building, consulted the directory, smiled, and took the elevator to the fifth floor and the D.E.A. office. A gum-chewing receptionist looked up at him and smiled, obviously pleased to be relieved of her boredom.

"Can I help you?" the girl said in a southern drawl, without pausing between pops of her gum.

"Why, yes," he said in a soft tone. "Is Mr. Biggers here? It's a private matter."

The girl was instantly alert at the mention of the word private.

She lowered her voice to match Ian's tone. "He's not here yet. I started work as a temp last week. I can call him or give him a message for you."

Ian said, "Can you keep a secret?"

She nodded with a furrowed brow and a confidential look.

"I don't really need to see him. I'm just trying to find him. I'm a private detective and his wife hired me to check up on him. She's worried he might be gambling again." He pulled the picture out of his pocket. "I took this at his house this morning. He was going to the mailbox to pick up some winnings. This is Mr. Biggers, isn't it?"

The girl took the picture, and her mouth formed an o-shape in a silent whistle.

"Yep, that's him."

"Don't say anything because Mr. Biggers is an important man, and his wife doesn't want him to lose his job."

"I won't; a gambler, huh? Well, I'll be doggone. I like to play the lottery myself, but I ain't addicted."

"Well, you can't tell anybody like I said, or there'll be trouble for him and you too for talking about your boss. You could get into a lot of trouble."

"Me!" she said in alarm. "I ain't done nothing!"

Ian calmed the girl's fears. "If you be quiet and don't let on what you know everything will be alright."

"I won't tell a soul."

He winked at her, said thanks, and left. Arriving at his apartment, Ian used the satellite relay to call Powers. He was surprised to hear Ian's voice.

"Mr. Powers, I think I found our informant."

Monday afternoon, after clearing away the empty pizza boxes, Spencer began the meeting. He reviewed the details of Meadors' meeting with Fitzgerald but kept Carol's confession a secret.

"I'm pissed off about the feds coming in here and sneaking around behind our backs, but," and he looked in Carol's general direction, "there's no harm done except that they've created an atmosphere of distrust. They were supposed to contact us today, but so far no word. We know from Meadors' meeting that Guilford is the informant, but another one has popped up and the feds are trying to protect him. Does anyone have a comment?"

Carol shifted in her seat and cleared her throat with a nervous grunt.

"Spencer, I know Skip from my Washington days. He's a straight shooter and will be square with us. I'm sure that he's following orders and will tell you what he knows when he contacts you."

Captain Drake had slipped into the back of the room unnoticed and spoke up as Carol finished, surprising the room.

"Before you speculate too much, let me tell you what I know. Special Agent Fitzgerald is operating on orders from Atlanta, and those orders are coming directly from Mr. Isaac Henry."

"I'll be a son-of-a-bitch," Meadors whispered loudly.

Everyone in the room knew the name. Drake turned and addressed Spencer.

"I've spoken with the Commissioner and Ben Whitley in Atlanta several times since you informed me that the D.E.A. was involved. Spencer, you're going to meet with Fitzgerald in his hotel room at the DeSoto Hilton tomorrow morning to discuss the case. Tomorrow afternoon you're both going to catch a plane to Washington to meet with Mr. Henry. All of this comes directly from the Commissioner. Therefore, I suggest that this group get a coherent report together for Mr. Henry. Spencer, you can brief me later."

Drake then turned on his heel and left the room.

"Damn," said Bridges. "Henry is the top dog, Spencer."

Spencer admonished Bridges with an icy tone. "Thank you, Detective. You heard the man. Where are we with the investigation, and who're the players?"

Spencer walked over to the dry-erase board and picked up a marker. Meadors spoke first.

"The most obvious one is Guilford. We have him linked to the murder of Jake Sweet, Coastal Seafood, and the feds. The unknown is the second informant. The feds are sure that Guilford is the informer, but this second one has them spooked for some reason."

Spencer finished writing.

"What else do we have?"

Carol said, "Benny is on the street snooping around. He knows about the Snowman and that the boats bring in the drugs. He's terrified of the Snowman's security guy, Baxter, who's been asking questions and spreading money around for information."

Spencer continued to write, and Meadors spoke again.

"Vincent, Vernon Faris and the Klan will be playing in this game before it's all over. They were smuggling for the Snowman under Jake. Now they'll be out for revenge, or a new leader will step up, and it'll be business as usual. Everyone we busted vanished except Jake Sweet, and he's dead. I'm betting Vernon and Vincent are holding out on us."

Spencer tapped the board. "We got this guy Baxter who is connected to Guilford, and who we think is the Snowman's security. Have we got any information on him yet?"

Meadors said, "I got Cooper and Bridges working on that part; they should be finished soon."

Spencer looked at them. "I'll need it by morning. What about Coastal Seafood?"

Meadors consulted his notebook. "Well, most of us are familiar with them because they're local. It's a big outfit covering most of the southeast coast. They have a good reputation, and the ownership is clean. I'm talking about Carl Powers of course. We know the boats bring goods in and the trucks, which are under Guilford, probably distribute them, but we don't know Guilford's role or motive for being a snitch. I did find out that he and Powers have a past connection. They were college buddies together at Georgia."

"Well, that's something we need to follow up on then," said Spencer.

Spencer completed his summary on the board.

"We got to have more than this; think, damn it."

"Fitzgerald knows what Guilford said in the park and has the details on the second informant."

Carol had blurted this out and looked sheepish.

Spencer said, "I'll press Fitzgerald on those two points when we meet."

Spencer turned to Meadors.

"I want you to interview former and present employees, business partners, anybody that does business with Coastal. Let's get phone records, bank records, anything and everything. Use the Sweet homicide to get you in the door. Carol, you focus on Guilford and Benny. Shake him up some more and get his ear to the ground. Cooper will start on the Baxter angle as soon as we get the file."

He then acknowledged Cooley.

"Jack, I want you to explore their school connection. Take Bridges and go to Georgia in the morning. Look at school transcripts, payment records, any kind of paper trail you can find that could give us a clue to their relationship in college. By the way, you haven't said a word about your trip to Beaufort yesterday."

Jack grinned. "I thought you'd never ask. I got a slideshow in the conference room."

They followed him to the conference room. He dimmed the lights, began to detail the events of the afternoon, and started the slideshow.

"The name of the sailboat is *Po Boy*. I took some pictures from the creek and hooked the fish. After everyone and his brother came down to the dock to watch, a woman invited me over for a drink. I convinced Powers I was a history buff and a bird watcher. He grudgingly let me roam around the place with the caretaker and take pictures. The caretaker, Rupert, lives in the house full time. The housekeeper and cook, Annie, comes and goes as needed when Powers is there. I got pictures of the entrances just in case we go back, but we'll need to bring dog repellant. There are some large Labradors running around, and they trailed us every step. I'm guessing if Rupert said, 'Eat', they would have."

Jack showed the gate pictures and related the details of the meeting with the sheriff.

"The Sheriff seems to be an OK guy, but he was protective of the grounds and gate and admitted that Powers is a contributor to his campaign. So, he has a special set of rules just for him."

Spencer interrupted. "You said Powers is the owner. Did you confirm that?"

"Sorry. I confirmed through the marina owner that Mr. Powers owns the plantation. The Sheriff also confirmed it."

"Jack, is there a picture of Powers?" Spencer said with exasperation.

"I'm coming to those now," he said, quickly changing the slide. "Here's Rupert, the caretaker."

The slide changed. "This is Annie, the cook and occasional housekeeper."

The slide changed again and a picture of Carl Powers at a distance working on the deck of the sailboat appeared.

"That's a shot I took of Powers from the house. I snuck off a frame while I was looking around. I got a better one of him though. It's of him and his lady friend."

The slide changed again, and Spencer saw a scene that tore his heart. There was Alisheen standing on the dock with Carl Powers. She was in a bikini, and Powers had his arm around her with familiarity.

"Some looker huh" Jack said with an appreciative laugh.

Spencer's mind was reeling as he sat, shocked in silence, staring at the screen.

Meadors spoke quietly, "Turn it off, Jack." Cooley complied, still unknowing, and moved to turn the lights back on, but Meadors stopped him and motioned him out. He caught Carol's eye and nodded toward the door.

"OK, everybody, back to the squad room."

As they exited Meadors said, "We'll be in the squad room, Spencer."

In the squad room Jack asked, "What gives Meadors?"

"The girl in the picture is Alisheen Delaney. She is, or was, Spencer's longtime girlfriend. I'm sure him finding out who she's been with for the last few days hit him like a ton of bricks."

"Damn!" Jack swore. "I never would have said those things about her being a looker, and I'd have tried to break it to him some other way instead of a slide show."

"That's OK, Jack. You didn't know," Spencer said as he entered the room.

He went into his office and sat down behind his desk, moving papers around in a vain attempt to be busy.

Meadors said, "Spencer?"

He looked up with the emotion drained from his features.

"Yes?"

"You want to go down to Louie's and get drunk?"

"No."

"Then I'm going to go and get drunk for you then. I'll be there if you change your mind."

Spencer smiled briefly.

"Spencer, I'm sorry man."

Spencer's voice trembled, "Me too, Meadors, me too."

~~~~

The alarm buzzed and Alisheen hit the snooze button forcefully. She was in her own bed and wanted to enjoy it a few more minutes. Dock sounds came through the deck door, and the outline of a freighter cast a profile onto the white curtains that moved gently with the breeze. The alarm buzzed again, and Alisheen cut it off, fully awake.

Carl had brought her home last night, and she smiled as she recalled the scene at the plantation. Annie was begging her to come back soon, with Rupert in the background trying to hush the barking dogs and telling her to come back with or without Mr. Carl. Carl had tried to get her to stay one more night, but claiming the need for an early start, she came home Monday night after dinner.

Alisheen got up and went into the kitchen to make coffee. Spying the box of vanilla wafers she'd bought for Spencer, she frowned. After arriving home last night, she'd checked her voicemail, but aside from a few friends calling to arrange a lunch meeting or to get together for a drink or two, there wasn't much else. She'd call him today but still didn't know what she was going to say to him. Alisheen went into the bathroom, brushed out her hair, and turned on the shower. She stepped in. The steam enveloped her, and the hot water felt good on her back and neck.

She lingered in the shower, thinking about what she'd say to Spencer. Abruptly, she turned off the water, dried off, put on her bathrobe, and put her hair up in a towel. She went to the kitchen, fixed a bagel, grabbed her coffee, and went out onto the deck, and felt the breeze. She sat in a rocker and looked at the water for a minute, then called Spencer. It rang several times and his voicemail picked up.

"Spencer, its Al. I'm back. I'll be at the restaurant today. I missed you. We need to talk. Please call me soon. Bye!"

Alisheen hung up and wondered where he could be at seven in the morning on a Tuesday.

~~~~

Precisely at 7:30, as always, Jeanette LaCrosse entered the executive offices of Coastal Seafood and was surprised to find Carl in his office.

"Mr. Powers? I didn't know you would be in so early today."

"I've got an early meeting with Jenkins this morning."

She became indignant he'd made an appointment without her knowledge. "When did you make the appointment?"

Carl realized she was upset.

"Now, Miss LaCrosse, don't get offended. I'd given Jenkins the number to the plantation when I spent more time on the boats. He still had it, took a chance, and got lucky."

She smiled briefly. "I was just surprised to find you here so early."

Carl said, "I already made coffee, although it isn't very good."

"I'll make a fresh pot."

She went through the small pile of mail on her desk, picked out the newspaper, and handed it to him.

"Here's the paper. I'll bring you a fresh cup of coffee as soon as it's ready."

Carl nodded his thanks and turned to go into his office.

Jeanette said, "It certainly is nice to have you in the office early. It's like old times."

Carl stopped, briefly smiled, and said, "It is, isn't it," then went into his office.

Jeanette dumped out the coffee and started a fresh pot. While she was waiting for the coffee to brew, she made a decision. It would be a bold move and maybe premature, but she decided the timing was right to put her plan into motion.

Carl looked up as she entered the room. She was carrying two mugs of coffee. She surprised him by sitting down in a guest chair after placing the coffee on his desk. Her outfit was a two-piece navy skirt and jacket that was professional and tailored so it fit her slim body perfectly, and her white blouse was crisp, ironed cotton. Her hair and nails were as always perfection, and she always wore just a hint of makeup. In her mind she was the perfect professional executive that ruled her world without question. She crossed her legs demurely and smiled at him over her coffee.

"Mr. Powers," she hesitated then said, "Carl, I think it's high time we call each other by our first names, don't you? We've been working together a long time. I do think we should be professional in front of the employees and clients, but away from them, we can be more casual. What do you think?"

Jeanette raised her mug and inwardly grinned like a cat playing with a mouse. She puckered her lips, blew softly on her coffee, and took a sip. Carl was shocked and missed the look of triumph on her face.

"Jeanette," he said with emphasis, "This is quite a surprise, but I suppose we could be on a first name basis with no problem, and I agree we should keep up appearances in front of staff and clients. You're right; we've been together since the beginning, so it seems fitting."

She pressed her advantage.

"I was hoping we could spend some time together and get to know each other a little better too. We really don't know much about each other outside of the office. Why don't we go to lunch today, my treat, someplace really special to start us off?"

Carl, without thinking, agreed. "I think that's a good idea."

Jeanette bubbled with enthusiasm.

"That's great, Carl. I'll make the arrangements."

She stood up, stretching leisurely, hoping he'd notice. She saw him eyeing her with what she interpreted as admiration.

"I'll let you know when Mr. Jenkins gets here Carl, and I'll let you know shortly about our lunch plans."

She walked out and closed the door behind her. Carl suddenly realized the whole intent of the conversation was to ask him out on a date, and he'd accepted.

He frowned. "No harm in a lunch I suppose."

The efficient sounding voice of Miss LaCrosse sounded over the intercom.

"Mr. Powers? Mr. Jenkins is here."

Carl's thoughts changed to the problem that Ian brought with him.

"Send him in."

"Let's go to the docks," Ian said in a low voice as he approached the desk.

Carl buzzed Miss LaCrosse.

"We're going to the docks."

Without waiting for an answer, Carl motioned for him to follow, and they went out the back entrance and down the steps to the yard. Once outside, they crossed the street and walked the short distance to the docks.

"OK, Ian, who's the snitch?"

"I think it's A.J."

"A.J.!" scoffed Carl. "He doesn't have the balls to cross me."

"Mr. Powers, if you'll hear me out, I think I can convince you."

Ian detailed how he picked up A.J.'s name on the yard microphones, the name Biggers, and how he discovered who Biggers was.

"Maybe they've identified him as a distributor and not an informer," Carl said.

"Maybe, but there's only one way to know for sure, and that's to set a trap."

Powers looked at Ian. "Set the trap. If it catches the rat, I'll want to deal with him personally. Understand?"

Ian shook his head. They walked back to the office and stopped in the parking lot.

"Let me know when you plan to do it. If it's true, we'll take care of it quickly and return to business as usual. I don't want to be shut down much longer."

Ian looked up at the sun as it began to rise higher.

"It's going to be a nice day," and he flipped his cigarette to the ground.

Ian got into the car, backed out of the space, turned toward the entrance gate, and slowed down to pass another car coming in from the street. As he passed the car, he looked directly into the eyes of Detective Meadors. Baxter didn't recognize him, but he knew a cop car when he saw one. He tried to call Powers' cell, but all he got was voicemail. Ian decided it was time to plan for a quick get-away too, just in case.

The receptionist looked up and smiled at Detective Meadors as he approached the desk. Her smile turned into a frown the minute he flashed a badge.

"I'm Detective Meadors, and this is Detective Cooper with the Savannah Police department. Is there someone we can talk to regarding a former employee?"

"I'll call Ms. LaCrosse. You'll have to talk to her," and she picked up the phone and quickly dialed a number.

The girl nervously said, "The police are here. What should I do?"

After listening to instructions, the girl hung up. "Ms. LaCrosse will be with you in a minute. Won't you please have a seat?"

Meadors declined and Cooper sat down. They soon noticed an older, well-dressed, attractive woman approaching from the back of the ground floor office area. She came around the reception desk with an extended hand.

"I'm Jeanette LaCrosse, Mr. Power's Executive Assistant. How may I help you?"

Meadors shook her hand and noticed the firmness of the grip.

"We're following up on a homicide investigation and have reason to believe the victim was a former employee."

Jeanette LaCrosse said without hesitation, "Follow me please," and turned on her heel.

They followed her through a maze of office partitions, stopped at an empty cubicle, and she sat down and picked up the phone.

"Angie, please bring a coffee tray to the small conference room. We'll be there shortly."

She hung up and looked at Meadors, "Name of the employee please?"

"Sweet, Jake Sweet."

The name drew no visible response from her as she typed. After a few moments, the computer screen flashed the message, "No record found."

"I'm afraid there's no active record of an employee by that name. Are you sure of your information?"

Meadors nodded his head.

"Yes, we're quite sure he used to be an employee."

She eyed him suspiciously. "Let's go to the conference room."

They followed her through the maze once again to a small, well-furnished conference room.

"How do you like your coffee detective? I'll be glad to fix it for you."

"Black, please, and thank you," said Meadors.

"And you?" she asked, looking at Cooper as if for the first time.

"Cream and sugar," Cooper said, withering slightly at the look she'd given him.

After serving the coffee, she sat at the head of the conference table, picked up the telephone, dialed, and waited for an answer.

"I need for you to go through the closed files please and look for a file for a Mr. Jake Sweet. Quickly please, two gentlemen are waiting. Thank you," and hung up. "We should have an answer in a little bit. I'll be back shortly."

She stood, and before either of them could move to stand up, she was gone. After a few minutes, she returned and sat back down at the head of the table.

She eyed them coolly. "We have no record of Mr. Sweet working for us that is active or inactive." She looked directly at Meadors. "Why don't you tell me what you're really after, and perhaps we can save some time?"

Meadors shifted in his seat, put his coffee on the table, and leaned forward.

"Mr. Sweet was murdered a few days ago. Our information led us to believe he worked here. We were hoping for some leads from the personnel file."

"Well, that is certainly a good story Detective, but since we've no record of Mr. Sweet, and I think you knew that, what else are you after?"

"We know from phone records that Mr. Sweet placed several calls to this main number. We want to look at your internal transfers to see whom he called. Maybe someone here had a reason to kill Mr. Sweet."

Jeanette replied, "I'm afraid you'll have to get a subpoena for that. Our records are confidential."

She retrieved two business cards from the table behind her, wrote on the back, and handed them to the two detectives.

"I've given you both my card with my direct phone line. On the back, I've written our attorneys' phone number. You'll need to call them if you require anything else that needs a subpoena. If something other than that needs my attention, you may call me. I handle the daily affairs of the company, and this will give you direct access to me should it be necessary. I have a tight schedule so you must excuse me. Good day."

She exited quickly, and they looked at each other with surprise.

"Damn, she's cold!" exclaimed Meadors.

They didn't stick around to finish their coffee but headed back to the station. The only person they found was Carol, and she was on the phone.

"I'll see you in an hour at the cabin," Carol said and hung up.

"Who was that?" Meadors asked.

"It was your friend Vincent wanting to meet with me. How did you guys make out at Coastal?"

Meadors laughed with sarcasm.

"We got stonewalled by the coolest woman I've ever met. She dared us to get a subpoena for the phone records and told us to call their attorney. Besides that, she never even asked how Sweet was murdered and didn't care. She was all business."

"Who was the woman?"

"Her name is Jeanette LaCrosse, and she's the Executive Assistant to Carl Powers. She said she runs the place."

"Do we know anything about her?"

Meadors shook his head in the negative and grunted.

Carol smiled. "I don't want to tell you how to do your job, but …"

"You're right. We need to check her out if she's going to keep us from Coastal and Powers."

Meadors looked at Cooper, who said, "You got it," and left.

Bridges arrived and sat down with excitement.

"We got lucky this morning. It seems our friend, Baxter, spent some time in our federal system of justice. They're faxing a picture and a copy of his file to us this morning."

Cooley came in, poured a cup of coffee, and sat down with a frustrated sigh.

"Who peed on your cornflakes so early this morning?" asked Meadors.

"I looked for Benny early this morning but no dice. He's either skipped town or he's hiding."

Cooley then said to Bridges, "Ready to go to Athens?"

Bridges jumped up with enthusiasm. "Yeah, let's go!"

Cooley looked at Carol and Meadors. "Junior sure is a go-getter, isn't he?" They both laughed.

Bridges was smiling and so eager to go that Cooley sighed. "Damn boy, you're too happy. Come on and I'll even let you drive. You're old enough to drive, aren't you?"

Bridges laughed good-naturedly. "Just barely, old timer."

They exited the room with Meadors and Carol laughing at them as they went down the hall.

Meadors asked Carol, "Spencer at the DeSoto?" She nodded, "Yep, he left about thirty minutes ago. Skip called first thing this morning. I've got to meet Vincent Sweet at his cabin; do you want to go?"

"You bet. I might get to see you kick his butt again."

Carol gave him a dirty look and then smiled. "You just might. Come on, I'll drive."

~~~~

Spencer knocked on the door of the hotel room. It opened immediately and a man extended his hand in a greeting.

"I'm Agent Fitzgerald, but please call me Skip. I'm glad to finally meet you Spencer, although I feel I know you already through Carol. She thinks you're one helluva cop, and I must say from looking at your record, I think she's right."

Fitzgerald finished with a smile that Spencer read as a, "please let's be friends" plea.

Spencer shook his hand, and they sat down.

"Skip, I'll be candid. I'm not too keen on the fact that you were spying on my investigation through Carol, and I don't like that you're more familiar with my record than I am yours. So excuse me if I'm not overjoyed about this deal. I've been trying to nail the Snowman for the past three months. Now you appear on the scene and tell me I can't make an arrest without your say so. That doesn't make me happy."

Spencer finished and spying coffee, got up, poured a cup, and sat back down.

"OK, Spencer," said Skip, "Let's talk about Carol first. She did me a personal favor. I promised her a well-paid desk job after this was over, in the city of her choice, if she'd cooperate. She's seen some ugly stuff working in the field, and I'm sure homicide in Savannah isn't pretty. She deserves it as far as I'm concerned and, in her shoes, I'd do the same thing. As for the Snowman, we were tracking him long before you started, beginning when Guilford strolled into our office. Like you, we've never gotten enough information that would lead to identification without some digging around. Frankly, from the outset, our instructions were not to make an arrest, but to store the information for a grander purpose. What it is though, I don't know, and unless I'm misinformed, you're no closer than I am to figuring out who the Snowman is. However, someone else recently contacted us, offering information on the Snowman and the brass freaked. They didn't want our only solid tie to the Snowman in jeopardy, so we moved in to find him and warn him. We don't have any idea who the second informant is or I'd tell you. Bo found Guilford by pure dumb luck. My orders are to prevent you from making any arrests until we know more about the second informer and what their intentions are."

Spencer loosened his tie and returned to the coffee service.

"Can I warm yours up?"

Skip joined him. "No. I'm particular about my coffee; no one can get it just right but me."

Spencer looked around and with a friendly tone said, "We better get some food up here. We got a long morning in front of us."

Spencer extended his hand. Skip shook it and smiled.

"What kind of doughnuts do you like?"

~~~~

Carol and Meadors arrived at the cabin and knocked on the door. There was no answer, and Carol checked her watch.

"I got 8:30 and Vincent isn't here. What do you want to do?"

Meadors shrugged and motioned to the chairs on the porch. "Let's wait."

After a while, a car drove down the dirt road to the cabin. Carol and Meadors recognized the Thunderbird. They stood on the porch and watched Vernon Faris and three more men get out of the car. Alarmed, they reached for their guns. A voice from the side of the porch said in a drawl, "Leave them guns where they are."

A not-too-friendly face was pointing a double-barreled shotgun. Vernon stepped up onto the porch and faced Carol.

"Vincent sent me to get ya," he said with a confident smirk, "but he can't come."

Indicating the man with the shotgun, Vernon said, "Harry will keep him safe and sound."

Carol looked at Vernon with anger. "The meeting was here. What's the deal?"

"Change of plans that's all. You got a meeting with the Klan Dragon. He wants to talk about a deal."

"Then what?"

"After you talk I'll bring you back here."

Meadors snorted.

"You can't believe that crap. If they separate us, we'll both be in trouble if not dead. If this is on the up and up, why the shotgun and the extra manpower?"

Vernon said with malice, "You stay out of this Meadors. We're just going to a friendly meeting. You keep sticking your nose in Klan business, and you're going to be the subject of one."

This drew guffaws from the men on the ground. Harry, laughing with the rest of them, lowered the shotgun. As he relaxed, Carol moved quickly. She disarmed him with a judo chop to his throat, and Meadors threw Vernon off the porch. When the quick skirmish was over, Carol had the shotgun, and Meadors was holding his pistol. Vernon Faris was in a rage.

He got up from the ground pointing at Harry and shouting, "Help him, damn it."

Harry was on the porch coughing and choking as he gasped for air.

Vernon yelled at Carol, "You could've killed him."

"I didn't hit him hard enough for that, and I don't like strange men pointing shotguns at me, especially early in the morning. It fucks up the rest of the day, and it's not polite. Now, let's start over."

"I got orders to bring you to the Klan meeting to meet with the new Dragon, that's all I know," Vernon said defiantly.

Carol cocked the hammers on the shotgun and pointed it at Vernon.

"I'm going to blow your kneecaps into little pieces if you lie to me again. Who is the new leader of the Klan?"

"Vincent is."

Carol nodded her head.

"Where is the meeting?"

"It's on the farm. There is a small clearing in the woods behind the house. Jake used to grow dope in it. We meet there sometimes."

"OK, Vernon, this is how it's going to go. Detective Meadors and I are going to follow you to the farm. When we get there, I'll ride in with you. Meadors will stay at the house. He'll be in radio contact with the station, agreed?"

Vernon nodded his head. Carol pulled the triggers on the shotgun, firing over his head. The blast from the gun scared the hell out of him and he ducked instinctively.

"You're a damn crazy woman!" yelled Vernon. "What in the hell was that for?"

"I just wanted to be sure I had your attention."

Meadors and Carol waited while they helped Harry, who was in pain and wheezing loudly, to the car.

"I would get some ice on that throat as soon as you can," Carol said. "It will help with the swelling and ease the pain."

They glared at her as they got into the car. After Vernon and his crew were in their car, Meadors and Carol prepared to follow. As Meadors followed the Thunderbird up the dirt road, he began to chuckle and looked at Carol and with a huge grin.

"You know I agree with Vernon."

"What's that?" asked Carol, puzzled.

"You are one crazy white woman."

Carol laughed and threw the shotgun into the back seat. "You haven't seen anything yet."

When they arrived at the farm, Carol got out of the car, and Meadors made a show of contacting the station and relaying their location.

Carol walked up to Vernon's window. "OK, Vernon, these boys, they can walk in. You and I are riding in alone."

The men got out of the car and stepped away as Carol walked around the front, keeping her eye on them.

She got in and said, "Let's go."

Vernon sped off toward the woods, and the others started walking. Meadors watched them disappear down the road and behind a cloud of dust.

He began to wait, one hand resting comfortably on his gun and the other holding the microphone.

In the clearing, Vincent sat on a log surrounded by a group of about twenty men in casual conversation. As the car approached, they spread out in a loose half circle. Vernon stopped the car, and without speaking, got out. Carol surveyed the scene and waited while Vernon went to Vincent. He looked back at the car and pointed in her direction. Carol decided to get out and as she did, Vincent approached her.

She tensed, not knowing what to expect, but relaxed when Vincent said, "I'm sorry about the way Vernon came to get you, Detective Naster. He done wrong, and I told him he was lucky you didn't shoot his dumb ass."

Carol smiled. "I was just making sure we were on equal footing here."

Vincent lit a cigarette then nodded his head. "I suppose you know that I'm elected to take Jake's place. It was unexpected, but it might help us both in the end. We're going to vote on what to do about Jake's killing and if we're going to continue with the drug business. I figured I owe you a chance to speak."

"I appreciate that Vincent," Carol said, following him back to where he'd been sitting. Vincent addressed the group.

"You voted me to be the next leader of the Klan in the county, and I know under Jake some of you smuggled drugs or allowed your trucks and land to be used by Jake, and you got paid cash money. Jake is dead. Now we got to decide what to do."

A voice spoke up from the crowd. "I got paid pretty good letting them use my field to land their plane. What if I want to keep on like that?"

"You can if you want to. I don't want no part of drugs since it got Jake killed. If you do, you do it on your own, or if some of you decide to as a group you can, but you'll do it without support from me."

There was a murmur from the crowd.

Carol raised her hands. "Maybe we can make a deal?"

Vincent said, "What kind of deal?"

"What do you want?" Carol asked.

"I want the name of the guy that killed Jake and where I can find him."

"What are you offering to trade?"

Vincent said, "We talked about it some before you got here. Some of these boys work on the docks and the shrimp boats. We can spy out for you down there and pass along information."

Carol knew a network like that would be invaluable.

"We need a deal before we vote," said Vincent.

"OK," said Carol. "You spy for me and I'll give you an hour head start in front of the cops before they arrest the person that killed Jake. That's the best I can do, and I'll be damn lucky to be able to give you that."

"That ain't enough," Vernon said loudly.

Another voice spoke up.

"No offense Vincent, but I don't mind saying Jake got killed because he was greedy and a snitch, talking to the cops like he did."

This remark drew some angry curses from the crowd, but it also got some support. The unnamed speaker continued.

"I need that money to keep myself going and to feed my family. I don't mind them boys landing in my fields. I get more money out of them than I do trying to make a crop and sell it. I'm sorry Vincent, but I need that money."

Carol spoke, "You'll be empty-handed because when we bust this guy, he'll be out of business and the money stops."

The man looked at her with contempt. "You ain't managed to bust him for a long-time missy. What makes you so sure you will now?"

Vincent said, "You better go."

Carol shook her head and walked toward the car.

She stopped short and turned around. "Have you been contacted since Jake was killed?"

"No," said Vincent.

"Well, I'd consider this. It's quite possible that you no longer have a deal. Voting to continue to smuggle is useless unless he contacts you. I guess you can't count on that money after all."

Carol turned and continued walking to the car and Vernon followed. He drove her back out to the farmhouse and stopped in front of the police car with Meadors still in it, leaving the engine running. After she got out, Vernon quickly turned around and roared off back down the road.

"What happened?" asked Meadors. "I was beginning to get worried."

"Let's get out of here. I'll tell you about it on the way back."

~~~~

Benny lit a cigarette and sat down against the brick wall, looking at the warehouses and yard of Coastal Seafood. He'd spotted Cooley earlier that morning nosing around for him, so he hid out on the docks and managed to stay out of his way. The docks were quiet, and nobody was doing any talking, least ways not around him.

He finished his cigarette, looked into the rising sun, and screened his eyes. It was still early. Maybe he'd go to the church for breakfast. He saw a familiar face walking along the fence at Coastal. It was the old man security guard, Joseph. He'd befriended Benny and occasionally let him into a warehouse to get into the sleeper cab of a truck that was in for service, if it wasn't due to go out the next morning. Benny walked across the street. Joseph saw him coming and slowed his pace.

Benny put his hands and face against the fence. "Can you let me in tonight?"

"No, not tonight," said Joseph. "I'm sorry, but I'll be going off at four this afternoon. I won't be here."

"Well, thanks anyway," Benny said.

Joseph offered Benny a cigarette through the fence and followed with a lighter.

"I go back to nights in a couple of days. Come back then and I'll see if I can help you out."

"Thanks, Joseph."

Joseph gave him a friendly wave and went on with his rounds. Benny waved back and resumed thinking again about breakfast. He saw the black BMW approaching from down the street and recognized the driver. Benny looked down as the car passed him and turn into the entrance of the Coastal yards. Through the fence, he watched the driver get out and enter the office building, then he headed for the church and a meal.

~~~~

After Spencer and Skip had ordered food, Spencer said, "Tell me what happened in the park."

Skip said, "A.J. was scared out of his mind and nervous as hell. I asked him why he was giving the local police information too, and he said, 'The D.E.A. wasn't acting fast enough for him to get what he wanted.' I asked what he wanted, and he said, 'Revenge.' I told him someone else had called our office in Atlanta and offered us information on the Snowman. That scared him some, but he was puzzled at the same time."

"Did he tell you who the Snowman was?"

"No, damn it. He said we had all we were going to get. Spencer, he wants the Snowman busted, but for some reason, he can't or won't give us a name."

Spencer changed the subject.

"What do we have to do to prepare for our trip this afternoon?"

Skip shrugged his shoulders.

"As far as I know we just show up and tell them what we know. We'll meet with Mr. Henry and a couple of other D.E.A. officials."

"What do you think they're holding us back for?"

"I don't have the slightest idea," said Skip.

"Guess then."

"I'm really in the dark, but I'll go out on a limb and assume they want the identity of the Snowman first in case there are repercussions of some sort."

"Repercussions?"

"There could be embarrassing political connections maybe, I don't really know, but it's happened before."

Spencer shook his head. "OK, where do we go from here?"

"I'm not the pushy type, Spencer, so it's still your investigation. I'll put some of my team under your supervision and boost your manpower. The rest of my team will be devoted to Guilford's surveillance and safety. I've already directed Bo to oversee that detail."

"Sounds good," said Spencer. "Carol and Meadors are working a couple of leads, and we have a snitch on the street. Your team can meet with them and give them their assignments. We're also working to identify and find the

Snowman's security, Ian Baxter. He has a reputation, and it's my guess he's responsible for the disappearances including Sweet's murder."

"Mickey told me about him," said Skip.

"He needs more attention from us," said Spencer. "If we can identify him and pick him up, he might be persuaded to turn State's evidence."

"OK then," Skip said, "We fly out this afternoon."

~~~~

Carol and Meadors were discussing the morning's events when Cooper appeared waving a file folder.

"The file on Baxter is here."

He opened it and handed pictures to Carol and Meadors.

"Our friend Mr. Baxter is one mean son-of-a-bitch. He was a bare-knuckle fighter in Virginia, and he was dangerous. He beat two men to death, but the charges didn't stick since it was ruled self-defense. He was also an enforcer for a loansharking and protection syndicate, which got him busted for being an accessory on racketeering charges. I called the prison he was in and talked to the Guard Captain, and he said the file didn't tell the whole story. Baxter's reputation didn't precede him before he was incarcerated."

"Get to the point, Cooper," Carol said impatiently.

"On the very first day, Mr. Baxter crippled a guy for life who tried to be too friendly, if you know what I mean. The Captain told me the prisoners that witnessed it said it was the most brutal thing they'd ever seen. He methodically beat the crap out of him and took great pleasure in inflicting blows and kicks meant to cripple, but not kill. He was successful. The guy ended up in a wheelchair and was released early since he was no longer considered to be a threat to society."

"Why wasn't anything done about it?" asked Carol.

"Well, the guy wasn't exactly a favorite around there so nobody cared. The guards didn't see it, and the prisoners feared the snitch label. There was also an element of self-defense from an attempted rape. He was in a cell by himself after that, and even the gangs didn't mess with him. He was dangerous, even by prisoner standards. No one went near him."

"I've seen this guy before," said Meadors, "but I'm not sure where."

"Well, at least we know he's around. We should be able to find him. Cooper, get some copies of the picture made and distribute them to the traffic units to keep them on the lookout for him. If they spot him, be sure they don't do anything but report it. We don't want to scare him, so he skips out of Savannah."

Cooper left, and Meadors looked at Carol.

"I'm hungry, how about you? You want to eat?"

"Yeah, but it's at my desk. I brought something, on a budget, you know."

Meadors said, "Suit yourself. I'm going down to Louie's for an omelet."

# Chapter 13

ALISHEEN ARRIVED AT the She Crab before everyone else. She wanted to be early to get all the questions about her absence over with so they could get on with business.

"Thank God you're back," Emily said, giving Alisheen a heart-warming hug. "OK, now spill it."

Alisheen closed the door to the office.

"I was on a sight-seeing tour with Carl Powers. Spencer and I had a big fight, and let's just say, I took him up on an offer to get out of town."

Emily was stunned. "Are you serious? How in the hell did that happen?"

"It's a long story. Why don't you come over tonight and I'll tell you everything."

"It's a date, and I'll bring the pizza."

Alisheen changed the subject. "Has Spencer been here?"

Emily shook her head.

"Not except for when he came in looking for Mickey the other day."

Mickey knocked, came in, and interrupted them.

"I'm saved," Mickey said with mock relief as he gave Alisheen a hug and kiss on the cheek. He pointed a finger at Emily.

"This woman is the biggest slave driver; she actually made me work while you were gone. Don't ever do that to me again."

Alisheen laughed. "You'd better be careful. I'm thinking of putting her in charge on a full-time basis."

"Oh, please don't do that," cried Mickey, feinting horror. "I'll be good I swear." He ducked out when Emily threatened him with a fist, then ducked his head back in. "I'm really glad you're back, and by the way, Emily did a great job." Then he was gone again.

"That guy is a lunatic, but he's a great bar manager. I couldn't have done it without him," laughed Emily.

"Why do you think he's my bar manager?" asked Alisheen. "All Mickey needed was a chance, and I've never regretted giving him one."

The rest of the staff was starting to come in so Emily and Alisheen didn't get to talk any more. Everyone was glad to see her but went to work quickly and efficiently after greeting Alisheen with brief hugs. When she couldn't find anything to do in the kitchen, Alisheen went into the bar.

She sat down on her stool and heaved a big sigh. Mickey noting her mood, fixed her a Coke, garnished it with a cherry, and placed it in front of her with ceremony.

"What's this," asked Alisheen?

"It's a Coke," said Mickey.

"Thanks a hell of a lot. I can see that. What's it for?"

Mickey leaned on the polished bar. "You've got something on your mind. You came in here moody as hell and sighed so loud it was heard in the street, now what's the trouble?"

"Is this some bartender trick of the trade to get me to spill my guts so I'll feel better?"

Mickey stood up and crossed his arms.

"It can be a trick if you want it to be, but I'm asking as friend who wants to help."

Unexpectedly, Alisheen broke down in tears. She lifted her chin and wiped her eyes with a bar napkin then blurted out, "I had a big fight with Spencer. I pushed him too hard to tell me why he didn't want to marry me. He avoided it like always, and I exploded on him. I was so upset I asked Carl Powers to take me on a trip, and before I knew it, I was on a private plane to Atlanta. Then we went to New York followed by a trip to his plantation in Beaufort. I thought I could make love with him, but when I tried, all I could think about was Spencer. I love him so much, and he pushed me away. He makes me so mad I just want to slap him silly."

Mickey was obviously in shock from the confession.

Alisheen recognized it. "I'm sorry. I didn't mean to dump on you like that."

Mickey stared at her for a minute and then moved her Coke to the side. He reached behind the bar, got a bottle of tequila, and put salt and lemon on the bar. He got two shot glasses, filled them, and pushed one to Alisheen. He held his up and waited for her to follow suit. Alisheen, puzzled, picked hers up and watched him do the tequila shot. She followed suit, and the golden tequila warmed her insides. Mickey poured another round, and they did the second shot together.

"What happened?" Mickey asked.

Alisheen emotionally recapped the morning on the beach.

"I can't get him to trust me," she said, resting her head on her hands. "How do I reach him Mickey?"

"I've already shown you how."

"How's that?" said Alisheen, lifting her head.

"You missed it, and I thought you were so smart."

Mickey looked at her like a teacher disappointed in a pupil. "Watch."

He poured two more shots, which they toasted and downed together.

"OK, what exactly was I supposed to see," asked Alisheen dryly, "and why are we sitting here drinking my tequila at nine-thirty in the morning?"

"Don't you get it? You need to drink with him."

Mickey leaned against the back counter with satisfaction as if he'd unraveled an ancient mystery. Alisheen looked at him like he was crazy.

"Emily is right, you're a lunatic. You mean to tell me I'm supposed to get Spencer drunk, and then he'll pour out his darkest secrets? That's absolutely nuts."

"Maybe so," said Mickey with smugness, "but it loosened your tongue, and I don't mean get him drunk. When was the last time you two just sat around, watched television, and split a bottle of wine or did shooters for that matter?"

"I don't know," she said defiantly.

"My point exactly, you always have something planned. Stay the hell home one weekend; spend it in bed, in your underwear watching old movies, and share a bottle of something. You have to quit putting Spencer on the defensive. Be his friend first, girlfriend and lover second, you'd be surprised at what people tell me after a couple of drinks because they think I'm their friend. Don't talk about anything serious; just relax. I'm willing to bet you a large raise against no raise this year that if you do it my way, you'll get your answer."

"You're on, Mickey."

She grabbed the Coke, hopped off the stool, and went into the dining room, with a wave over her shoulder as she left. Mickey watched her go with a smile. He fixed a cup of coffee to help fight off the effects of the tequila and relaxed against the bar.

"Easy money."

~~~~

It was 10 o'clock by the time Spencer and Skip had a sensible timeline for discussion.

"I'll be willing to bet that someone in Coastal with the ability to direct and control the transportation side of the business is the Snowman," said Spencer.

"It sure does look that way," Skip said in agreement. "Hell, it could be Guilford trying to throw us off track by diverting suspicion away from him. Powers is clean and well respected. He doesn't have the slightest blemish on his record."

"Not even a traffic ticket," interjected Spencer.

"I wonder what the connection between Powers and Guilford is," Skip said.

Spencer said, "We might know something along that line soon. We found out they were roommates in college. I got two of our guys headed to Athens to see what they can find out. It might be nothing, but it could be the key to unlocking Guilford's lack of motivation to give us a name."

Skip said, "Damn I can't wait to hear about that. What an odd connection."

Spencer checked his watch and stood up to leave. "I'll go by the station on the way home to check in. I'll come back and get you in a couple of hours."

Skip said, "I'll see you then."

They shook hands, and Spencer left and headed for the police station. He found Carol finishing her bagel and startled her when he popped in from the hall.

"Oh!" said Carol with a full mouth.

"Caught you," Spencer laughed.

Carol swallowed and cleared her throat.

"No fair sneaking up on me like that. You could have caused me to miss a crumb or something."

"From the looks of your desktop, I'd say there are several crumbs you missed."

Carol stuck her tongue out at him and swept the crumbs into her trash can.

"How did it go with Skip?"

"Fine, but I think we still have to be cautious. We both agreed it's strange to be told not to make an arrest if we find out who the Snowman is."

"Do you think Henry will tell you what's going on when you meet with him?"

"Skip didn't know. We've gotten some extra help from Skip's detail and the local D.E.A. I told them you and Meadors were directing the investigation, and they should report to you."

Spencer changed the conversation. "So what've you been doing this morning?"

Carol related the events that transpired at the cabin that morning and enthusiastically told Spencer about the deal she'd proposed to Vincent Sweet. Spencer was dismayed.

"Damn, Carol, we can't make deals like that and surrender a suspect over to them. How can we explain what happened?"

"Spencer, I wouldn't give them anything unless we were absolutely sure about who killed Jake Sweet. It could be a huge asset. They work on the docks and the shrimp boats, and if they agree to cut a deal that will help us bust the Snowman, then I'm all for it. Besides, whoever killed Sweet is a murderer. He'd get what he deserves, and it'd be one less case to go to trial."

Spencer was in disbelief.

"Carol, I've overlooked a lot of things, but I've always been a staunch believer in a person's right to due process. I'm not going along with anything like that, and this deal of yours is off."

Carol was angry. "Spencer, we can't afford not to. A network like that at the point of entry is vital to the investigation. Not to mention that if we can form a relationship, there's no telling how successful we might be with future investigations. Who cares if a killer gets what's coming to him? I think Vincent Sweet has a right to avenge his brother's murder."

Spencer's anger went to full boil, and he leaned on Carol's desk.

"Before you say anything else, let me remind you, Detective Naster, that you're a police officer sworn to protect everyone regardless of how you feel about them. You've a duty to protect everyone we arrest until they're proven guilty in a court of law. Your vigilante attitude will no longer be tolerated. You will play this investigation by the book. Am I clear, Detective?"

Carol's eyes were burning with anger and her skin was flushed red, but her voice had no emotion. "Yes."

They stared at each other over the desk for a few seconds until Meadors walked in, breaking off the confrontation. Spencer addressed Meadors with ire.

"Where in the hell have you been?" Meadors knew he was angry but ignored him.

"Cooper and I went to Coastal early this morning and we ran into Powers' Executive Assistant, Jeanette LaCrosse. We're going to have to go around her to get to anything we want. We're checking up on her while we try to justify a warrant for their records. Cooper got the information on Baxter. We put out his picture and have everyone on the street looking for him. Cooley and Bridges are on the way to Athens for background on Powers' and Guilford's college days."

Spencer calmer said, "I'm going home to pack, and then I'm flying with Skip to Washington. You know how to get in touch with me if anything happens while I'm gone. Is there anything else I need to know before I leave?"

A negative nod from Carol and a short "nope" from Meadors were the answers.

"OK, I'll call you this afternoon."

Spencer went into his office, gathered some papers into a briefcase, and left with a brief goodbye.

Carol stood up and slammed her desk with her fist.

"That asshole, he can't talk to me like that. I handed him a waterfront of spies, and he says no to the deal."

"What happened?" asked Meadors.

"I told him about the deal I made with Vincent, and he freaked out on me. He got on his soapbox about the law and due process. I can't believe he thinks that crap is for real."

Meadors rubbed his chin. "I didn't think he'd go for it."

"Why?"

"Carol, Spencer isn't such a goody-goody that he doesn't break the rules. He's even indirectly ordered me to break them to help an investigation, but he won't bargain with people's lives regardless of who, they are or what they've done. He can't stand abuse of authority, and he's let you go farther than I thought he would after your encounter with Vincent. If I were you, I wouldn't push him too much farther."

Meadors sat down and picked up the phone. Carol stared into space, then picked up her purse and keys and left without a word. At his desk, Meadors scanned the picture of Ian Baxter again and then recognized him as the man driving the black BMW that passed him at Coastal that morning.

"Damn, I knew I'd seen him before."

~~~~

Spencer arrived at his apartment and parked the car on the street instead of the garage for convenience. He noticed the plain white car parked across the street with two suited men in it. He laughed and made a mental note to remind Skip he didn't need a tail anymore.

Spencer tossed the suitcase on the bed, noticed the blinking light on his cell phone, and played the message. He froze in his tracks when he heard Alisheen's message saying she was back and for him to call her. Spencer angrily resumed packing.

"I'm not going to call her," he said with indignation. "She's the one that's been out of town with Carl Powers of all people. I don't owe her a phone call or anything else. She left, not me, let her stew awhile. I got work to do."

Spencer finished packing and, going outside, looked for the white car. It was gone. He drove to the hotel and picked up Skip, who piled his suitcase and briefcase into the backseat and got into the front with Spencer. Spencer checked his mirror and pulled out into the traffic.

"We'll be on a company plane so go to the charter gate," said Skip.

"I suppose that since we've agreed to work together that the precautions you took are no longer required?"

Fitzgerald was puzzled. "I'm not sure I know what you're talking about."

Spencer looked disgusted. "Oh hell, come on Skip. I spotted the tail when I left the police station. Don't tell me you're going to deny you've had me followed to make sure I was going to cooperate."

Skip looked at Spencer with alarm.

"What in the hell are you talking about? I haven't assigned anybody to follow you around."

Spencer said with suspicion, "Well, somebody did, and they sure looked like feds. They stood out like sore thumbs. Plain white car, suits, crew cuts; hell man, they looked like they were fresh out of boot camp."

"Spencer, I swear to you I've had no one following you."

Spencer said, "If you're not, who in the hell is?"

~~~~

"Carl, it's time to leave for lunch. I'll meet you outside."

Carl had been pondering the news about A.J., and didn't want to go to lunch with Jeanette anymore. He wanted to see Alisheen at the She Crab.

"Oh well, I'm in it now so I might as well get it over with."

He exited the building and was surprised to see Jeanette driving a sleek white BMW convertible with the top down.

"I thought you had a Chevy or something like that," he said surprised. "When did you get this?"

Jeanette laughed brightly, "I bought it a couple of months ago, but I usually don't drive it to work. It's too dusty and dirty on the docks, but it was a pretty day, so you lucked out Carl."

He winced at her use of his first name, and she noticed.

"What's the matter? Did I say something wrong?"

"No!" Carl said quickly. "I'm just not use to using our first names yet," Jeanette sighed in relief and smiled.

"Get in. I've got a surprise for you."

Carl got in and put on his sunglasses. Jeanette hit the gas, spinning the wheels a little, and sped out of the parking lot.

"It is strange to use our first names," she continued over the muted roar of the engine. "I was thirty-two when I started working with you, and we've spent a lot of time together building Coastal into what it is today."

Carl nodded his head and noticed she took the ramp to cross the bridge.

"Where are we going?"

"Hilton Head! It's a 45-minute ride, but I've cleared your calendar and we're going to my favorite restaurant. I hope you don't mind. I decided since this was our first time out together that we needed to go someplace extra special."

He was agitated but didn't show it. He was hoping to see Alisheen this afternoon and didn't want to be tied-up too long, but he resigned himself to the situation. "That's fine. I really didn't have anything planned this afternoon."

"Great, Carl," yelled Jeanette, and she hit the bridge shifting into fifth gear.

~~~~

Carol slammed her townhouse front door closed with fury. She jerked the refrigerator door open rattling the bottles and containers on the shelves, grabbed a bottle of water, slammed the door, and stomped to the living area, sitting down with a huff. She was convinced the deal would be the difference in the case. Besides, she'd given her word to Vincent, and she needed his trust.

"Damn Spencer, why is he the defender of the faith all of a sudden?"

Carol pondered what to do for a while then picked up the phone and called Vincent.

~~~~

Jeanette never slowed down and kept the BMW in high gear until they reached the island.

"Where are we eating lunch?" Carl asked after they crossed the last bridge to the island.

"The Pelican House. We have a reservation on the veranda over-looking the marsh."

Powers nodded his approval.

"It's an excellent choice. The food is above average, and I do like the view."

Jeanette beamed with pleasure at the praise and was satisfied with her decision to start her plan early. They arrived at the restaurant and, ignoring the parking lot, she drove to the main entrance.

"I get valet service when I come."

A young man emerged from the restaurant and greeted her with enthusiasm.

"Hello, Ms. LaCrosse, I've been waiting for you. Miss Louise told me you were coming. She said to tell you that everything is ready."

"Hello, James, thank you," said Jeanette as she handed him a twenty-dollar bill. "Be sure to put the cover on."

"Yes, ma'am."

Smiling, she looked at Carl and said, "Follow me," and she led him into the restaurant like a queen entering her throne room. Miss Louise was waiting for them and instantly seated them by the window overlooking the marsh.

"Ms. LaCrosse, it's so good to have you with us today. We usually don't get to see you during the week."

"It's nice to be here, thank you." Gesturing with her hand she said, "Louise, this is Mr. Powers."

Carl stood and smiled, "I've dined with you before, but I don't get service like this. I'll have to pry Jeanette's secret from her."

"Ms. LaCrosse is one of my most valued customers. As for you, Mr. Powers, all you'll have to do is let us know you're coming, and we'll be glad to accommodate you."

Carl nodded his head with thanks and sat back down.

Louise continued, "Ginny is your waitress today, and I'm handling the bar for the moment. I have the wine you asked for Ms. LaCrosse. Would you like it now, or would you like to begin with something else and have the wine with your lunch?"

Carl said, "I think I'd like a drink first. I'll take a Stoli."

"Very good, Mr. Powers, and you, Ms. LaCrosse?"

"I'll have the wine please."

Jeanette was inwardly disappointed. She was hoping to control lunch, but Carl had spoken quickly and ordered.

Carl said, "I hope you don't mind that I have a drink instead of the wine, but I prefer wine with food rather than by itself."

"Oh, of course not."

Ginny appeared and after her introduction, described the specials of the day. They requested some time before ordering and she disappeared. Their drinks arrived, and they continued to scan the menu, ignoring each other. Jeanette sipped her wine and stole a look over the top of the menu.

"Carl?" she said casually.

"Yes?"

He put down his menu and picked up his drink as he answered her, and Jeanette knew he'd been waiting for her to speak.

"I'm glad you agreed to have lunch with me. I devote most of my time to work so I don't have the opportunity to meet people and make new friends. Consequently, I don't know many people to call for lunch or dinner. I was hoping, in the future, that we could have lunch or dinner together a couple of times a week. No strings or anything like that, just as friends."

"What's going on, Jeanette? What exactly do you want? Why the sudden need to change things?"

She shook her head as if he was trying to make a big deal out of nothing.

"Nothing really, I just think it's time I was involved in the world outside of the office. I was hoping we could spend enough time together for you to introduce me around to the rich and famous of Savannah, nothing more."

Before Carl could speak, Ginny returned, and they ordered lunch. Jeanette was getting uneasy with the delay and the quick turn of the conversation. Carl sipped his drink and looked at the marsh. He wondered how many bodies he'd buried out there.

"Carl?" her voice broke into his thoughts, and he looked at her. His answer hit her like a cold slap in the face.

"Jeanette, it's not my fault you don't have many friends, nor is it my responsibility or desire to introduce you to mine."

Jeanette maintained her demeanor, yet she was now all business.

"Carl, I'll be direct, since that's what you feel is necessary. I've worked my butt off for Coastal. I've devoted my life to it, to make it a success, but like they say, success has a price, and I've paid the price while you've reaped the benefits. I'm well paid, but some official recognition beyond your Executive Assistant would be nice, and an introduction into Savannah's society as your friend and colleague couldn't hurt either. I want my share of the glory and more, but for now, I'll settle for the glory."

Jeanette picked up her wine. Powers stared at her amused. Ginny served lunch, interrupting them, and Jeanette began to eat, ignoring Carl, who ordered another drink.

She said casually, "I love the marsh view, don't you, Carl?"

He looked at her with an odd smile she couldn't interpret. "I do too," and he began to eat. Jeanette maintained her composure although her insides were in a knot. She'd put the opening statement on the table, though not exactly the way she'd pictured it. Now all she needed was his response. It finally came.

"Jeanette, I'm glad you're all business now, and we're past the bullshit. I was beginning to lose faith in you. I've always appreciated the fact you're cold and calculating. I'd be disappointed if you turned out to be something else. You've an agenda after all. You want what you think should be coming to you. Since we're talking business now and not just making an effort to be friends, I'll be direct. Coastal is a success, and you've played a part, I'll give you that. You want a title, go ahead and pick one. You want to be a social climber, I'll introduce you to some people, but I warn you to be very careful from this point forward. Don't attempt to push yourself too far into my world. You won't like the reception you'll get."

He leaned on the table and said with a warning tone, "Let me remind you of the most important fact. I am Coastal Seafood. I made it, I put it on top, and I keep it there."

Jeanette smiled. "You're going to love the changes, Carl dear. Do you like my suit? It's new."

Powers held her gaze and then smiled. "Jeanette, I like your style, and I do like the suit."

He finished his drink, plucked the wine bottle from the cooler beside the table, poured a glass of wine, and refilled hers. She acknowledged his manners with a nod, and they ate their lunch enjoying the view in silence.

~~~~

When the lunch rush was over, Alisheen and Emily sat down in one of the booths and spread-out papers and notepads to review last week's activity. Alisheen doodled on the pad in front of her while Emily talked about last week. Alisheen interrupted her.

"Emily, I don't feel like doing this right now, and besides, I've decided to let you continue to run the restaurant for me."

Emily was surprised but obviously pleased.

"Thank you, Alisheen, but I'm not sure how the rest of the staff will feel about it."

"They'll love it. You deserve it and a raise too. The place ran without a hitch today and obviously did well last week. I've already looked at the books. I want you to continue. I had fun today not worrying about things."

"I'll take it!"

"Great!" Alisheen said with enthusiasm. "We can get to the details later."

Without looking up from the pad she was writing on, Emily said, "Alisheen, what's going on?"

"What do you mean?" she said, faking bewilderment.

"Come on, you know what I mean. Why this sudden change and the job offer? I'm grateful, but it's just so sudden."

"Emily," Alisheen said and looked around the room, "I've got to do everything I can that'll give me more time to devote to Spencer."

Emily grabbed her arm.

"Alisheen, what's gotten into you? You're not making any sense."

She ignored her.

"Emily, you've a boyfriend, don't you?"

"You know I do. Tom and I are going to be married next fall, but that's still a secret."

Alisheen looked questioningly at Emily. "Are you and Tom friends? I mean, do you sometimes just hang out and do nothing?"

Emily was perplexed.

"I guess we do sometimes. What in the hell are you talking about?"

Alisheen looked at her with misty eyes.

"You and Mickey are the only ones that know the truth about my trip. I learned something. I love Spencer. I must give us another chance. If it fails, it won't be because I didn't try."

Emily said with a serious tone, "Alisheen, exactly what's in that redhead of yours, because I still don't know what you're talking about."

Alisheen continued.

"What do you and Tom do when you hang out? Do you drink, watch movies, do you have interesting conversations?"

Emily sipped her Coke.

"I'm convinced you've lost your mind now."

"It's important, Emily, just play along."

"OK, I'll go along if you promise to clear this up soon."

"Describe a typical weekend together."

"Well, Tom goes to the apartment after work, and he calls me. I finish work and go home. We might watch TV or rent a movie, split a pizza, nothing special, because we're usually tired on Friday nights."

Alisheen interrupted her.

"Do you guys talk about anything special or just small talk?"

"Nothing deep or philosophical if that's what you mean. We just catch up. Whatever pops into our head I guess is the best way to describe it."

"Do you ever sit around and drink?"

Emily was surprised.

"We might have a beer or a glass of wine. Alisheen, this is crazy."

"Please, Emily, I need to know."

"OK."

"Tell me about when you're not working. What do you do?"

"We do something together, not always, but usually. By the end of the day, we're relaxed and we make plans, but we don't always go out. Sometimes we just fix dinner together."

"You don't spend all of your free time together?" Alisheen asked amazed.

"No. We seem to know when the other needs some space, so we respect it."

Emily watched Alisheen as she mulled things over.

"Tell me about a night in."

"If we stay in, we'll decide what to have for dinner. We might go to the grocery, cook together, and clean-up, and since you've an interest in our drinking habits, I'll tell you we'll have a drink or split a bottle of wine."

She nodded as if her understanding was getting clearer by the minute. "What about after dinner?"

"It's kind of like the night before, we just sit around and enjoy being in each other's company."

Alisheen sighed.

"I wish Spencer and I could do that. We're always doing something, filling up every minute like we're afraid we'll miss something. I guess Mickey's right."

"Hold on right there," said Emily with a flash of anger. "What do you mean Mickey is right? What he knows about relationships in a two-word summary is *absolutely nothing*. I can't believe you'd listen to Mickey. His idea of a successful relationship consists of a one-night stand with a condom."

Alisheen giggled, which briefly erased her frown.

"Emily, that's not fair. Mickey's nicer than that."

"Maybe so," Emily said with sarcasm. "What did he say?"

She told her about the morning's tequila shots and Mickey's advice. Emily had a look of disbelief.

"Alisheen," she said like an impatient mother. "Has Spencer ever said, 'Let's hang out in our underwear tonight and drink tequila?'"

"No," she laughed as a mental picture of the scene came to mind.

"Has Spencer ever said, 'Alisheen stop talking to me, so I don't have to talk back?'"

"No," she laughed again.

"Alisheen, Mickey's analogy is very weird, and I can't believe I'm going to say this, but I think he's right in some ways. I think the important part is this—be spontaneous and just let things happen. Did you have fun with Carl by just letting things happen?"

"Yes, I did," she said surprised.

"That's what Mickey's trying to tell you in his twisted way, and I agree with him. The rest of it is just male stupidity."

Emily checked her watch.

"I've got to get things moving for dinner," and she left her alone.

Alisheen closed the books and wiped the tear off her cheek.

~~~~

Ian needed to put some thought into a plan to trap A.J., and it had to be enticing enough to be sure he'd call the cops if he were the leak. Ian was hoping it wasn't A.J. though. He didn't have many friends, and A.J., though he was a pain in the ass, was one of the few friends he did have. He casually strolled into the office and waved at Sarah the secretary.

"A.J. is on the phone. I'll buzz him as soon as he's off. You want some coffee?"

"Yeah, sure, I'll get it though."

Sarah nodded and Ian went to the breakroom. As he finished fixing his coffee, A.J. came in.

He whispered, "What're you doing here?"

Ian said, "We've a shipment to deliver. The Snowman is getting pressure to move some goods or lose business, so he's decided to risk it, and he wants us to handle it."

He looked at A.J. over his cup for a reaction.

"When and where?"

"Monday night through regular channels. I'll call you when I know the details."

"OK, but I don't like it. I can't stop deliveries and hold up trucks from going out without a notice."

"He knows what the problems are, just be ready to move. Be careful, A.J. We don't know who to trust. I'll see you later."

Ian refilled his coffee cup and walked out.

A.J. said loudly, "Let me know soon so I can revise my maintenance schedule." Then he went to his office and closed the door. He sat down with fear and excitement over the news from Ian. With the feds in town, the chances were good they'd catch Powers, and he'd get what he deserved, the bastard.

He thought, with malice. "I'll get you for what you did to me."

Ian drove back to his apartment, feeling uneasy about his own security, especially with the D.E.A. snooping around, in addition to the local cops. In his apartment, he checked the answering machines and re-programmed the satellite, adding A.J.'s house and office.

Ian said to the receiver, "Let the games begin."

# Chapter 14

SPENCER AND SKIP arrived at their hotel in D.C. and checked into their suites. The driver left, saying he would return at "7:00 sharp, sir," and gave Fitzgerald a salute. Fitzgerald sighed and told the young man, "Thank you."

Spencer grinned. "A salute?"

Fitzgerald looked sheepish. "I get it all the time from these young kids. Let's get some rest. I'll call you later."

"Sounds good to me. I'm going to call the office in the meantime."

Spencer entered his suite, slipped off his shoes, and took off his tie. He got a beer from the mini-bar, propped upon the bed, and called Savannah. Carol, waiting on a call from Vincent, picked up quickly. "Detective Naster!"

"Carol? It's me, Spencer."

Carol flushed with guilt and was glad Spencer couldn't see her face.

"Carol, how's everything going? Any news?"

"Yeah, Spencer, everything is OK, nothing new since this morning."

Spencer hesitated then said, "Carol, I'm sorry about this morning, but I hope you understand my reasoning."

Carol said, "I understand. Be careful in Washington and call us when you can."

She heard him sigh with relief, and then he was giving her his hotel room number. She jotted the information on her desk calendar.

Spencer finished by saying, "I'll call you later. Bye."

"Goodbye, Spencer," and she resumed waiting for Vincent's call.

Fitzgerald entered his room, took off his coat, and threw it onto the bed. He opened the curtains, surveyed the view of Washington, then sat down and dialed Whitley's room.

"Hello?"

"Ben? This is Skip."

"Skip, glad you're here. Come over to my room, 412, so you can brief me before tonight," then he hung up.

Skip was beginning to worry. He was getting the feeling that something was going on as he walked to Whitley's suite. Whitley answered his knock and then quickly closed the door behind him. He greeted him with reserve, but Skip could tell he was excited as he sat down.

"OK, Ben, what gives with the cloak and dagger? What's going to happen at the meeting with Chambers and Henry?"

Whitley ignored him and asked about his flight and the comfort of the room.

"The room is fine, and the flight was easy, but you haven't answered my question, Ben."

Whitley tutted him. "All in good time as they say, Skip. Is Baldwin cooperating?"

Fitzgerald was annoyed that Whitley didn't answer his question, and he was wary.

"Yes."

"Good, good, I want to be sure that Baldwin is on our side."

"Were you having him tailed in Savannah?"

Whitley offered liquor and a cigar to Skip, who declined, and continued to ignore his questions. He got up and fixed a drink. Sitting back down, he lit a cigar with an air of victory.

Whitley examined the end of the cigar. "Just some light surveillance. We had to be sure that Baldwin didn't do anything to jeopardize the operation we're about to undertake."

Fitzgerald was angry now, and he stood up and pointed his finger at Whitley.

"What in the hell are you talking about? You better give me some answers, damn it, or I'll make an arrest myself."

Whitley remained in control, but his tone reflected his anger.

"Sit Down, Agent Fitzgerald."

Skip remained standing in defiance and glared at Whitley.

"Just what in the hell are you up to, Ben? Whose back are you pointing the knife at this time?" Whitley brushed off the comment.

"You'll find out tonight at Mr. Henry's house after dinner."

Whitley took a puff of his cigar, sipped his drink, and attempted to ease the tension.

"You'll get all of your questions answered tonight, Skip. Just relax and enjoy the ride."

~~~~

The phone on Carol's desk rang, startling her. She snatched up the receiver in a hurry. "Naster!"

"Have we got a deal?"

Carol recognized Vernon's voice.

"I want to talk to Vincent."

"He ain't talking to you, Detective. All he wants to know is if he has a deal."

Carol was in a bad mood and was about to change her mind when Vincent spoke.

"I'm listening, Detective."

"Vincent, you've got a deal, but I get to dictate the conditions. Otherwise, you get nothing."

There was silence, then Vincent said, "OK, what're the conditions?"

"I'll meet you at the cabin at five," said Carol, and she hung up.

Carol left and went out into the late afternoon sun. She'd committed to giving up Jake Sweet's killer for information to catch the Snowman. Now all she had to do was figure out how to do it.

~~~~

Meadors walked into the She Crab and found Alisheen working in a booth. She smiled brightly as he approached, and she stood and gave him a big hug.

"How are you? I missed you while I was on vacation."

"I missed you too, Alisheen. I haven't been able to get a decent fried seafood platter since you left town."

Emily, working in the room nearby, said, "I heard that!"

Meadors and Alisheen laughed, and they sat down.

"Where's Spencer?" she asked. "Why hasn't he called me? I know he knows I'm back because I've left messages at the apartment and the station."

Meadors' grin turned into a frown. "I don't really know if Spencer knows you're back or not. He's out of town right now, as a matter of fact, but he should be back tomorrow."

She sighed. "You're the worst liar, but thanks for trying to spare my feelings."

"Alisheen, he's out of town I swear," he pleaded. "He's in Washington."

"Washington," she exclaimed, "as in D.C.?"

"Yes, he's there for a meeting."

"It figures," said Alisheen flatly. "He can leave town for business, but he can't find enough time for a trip for fun, but I guess I'm just as guilty too, until recently anyway."

Meadors shifted uncomfortably.

"Is Mickey here? I need to show him a picture."

"He's not in trouble, is he?"

"No," he said quickly. "I just need to see if he recognizes someone we're looking for. We think he comes in a lot and visits the bar."

Alisheen called out, "Emily, is Mickey still here?"

"I'm sure he's still in the back. I'll get him for you."

"No, that's all right," said Meadors. "I'll find him. I got to get moving anyway."

He got up quickly, said goodbye to Alisheen, and headed to the kitchen. She watched him go with a puzzled look. Meadors entered the kitchen and spotted Mickey in the back by the ice machines.

He walked over to him and said, "Mickey, can I see you for a minute?"

"Yeah, sure, what about?" Mickey asked, straightening up from dumping ice into a cooler.

"Let's go out back, OK?"

Mickey shrugged and followed Meadors into the delivery alley. Meadors pulled the picture of Baxter out of his pocket.

"Do you know who this is?"

Mickey nodded his head.

"Yeah, I know him. That's A.J. Guilford's buddy, Ian Baxter, except he goes by the name of Jenkins now. He passes himself off as a rep for some diesel engine company."

"What can you tell me about him?"

Mickey lit a cigarette. "He's bad news. Bare-knuckle fighter, I seen him fight a couple of times. Rumor is he killed a guy in the ring once, did some time. He's an enforcer type."

"Is he legit now as this Jenkins guy? Could he be just hiding his old identity?"

Mickey exhaled and flipped his ash. "I can't say for sure. I know he's in here a lot with that prick A.J. My guess he's legit as a sales rep but works on the side."

"For whom?" asked Meadors with interest.

Mickey shook his head. "Come on man, I don't really know."

"Mickey, you better not be screwing around with me."

"Meadors, I swear I don't know if he's working for anybody or not, but I can tell you this."

"What's that?"

"I'd bet on it."

Alisheen came through the back screen door of the kitchen, interrupting them.

"Is everything alright, Mickey?" she asked, looking at him for reassurance.

He nodded yes, and Meadors said, "Thanks, Mickey."

"No problem, anytime," and he went past them into the kitchen.

Alisheen looked hard at Meadors. "What's going on? What're you not telling me?"

Meadors looked fretful. "Alisheen, I don't think this ..." and she stopped him short.

"Tell me damn it!"

He grabbed her shoulders and held her firmly.

"Alisheen, Spencer knows you were with Carl Powers at the plantation in Beaufort last weekend."

She didn't make a sound, but her emotions screamed inside her head and heart. She collapsed against Meadors and began to shake with quiet sobs.

After a few minutes, she pushed him away from her. Her face was flushed and her cheeks tear-streaked. She wiped them quickly with her hands.

"How?"

"Alisheen, what I'm going to tell you is top secret, and you can't repeat it. It started before your big fight. Carl Powers is a suspect in a drug smuggling case, and we've been keeping tabs on him."

She was stunned. "I can't believe what you're telling me. I've been with this man for a week and have known him for over a year. Carl is well known and connected in Savannah. Now you're telling me he's a drug smuggler. That's preposterous!"

"Alisheen, I know it's hard to believe, but you need to trust Spencer on this."

She retorted with anger.

"Trust Spencer! I don't know if I can trust Spencer at all much less believe this cock and bull story. He certainly doesn't trust me. He isn't willing to commit to anything but work, and he won't share his deep dark secret with me, so don't talk to me about trust. How do I know he hasn't dreamed this whole thing up just to keep me away from Carl?"

"Alisheen, you know Spencer better than that. He wouldn't go that far."

His tone calmed her down.

"You're right I suppose. He doesn't care enough about me to go that far," she replied sadly.

"Alisheen, you're not thinking clearly. You know Spencer wouldn't make this up, that's crazy."

She grew angry as she remembered what put her in Carl's arms to begin with, but her face didn't show it.

"I suppose Spencer wants me to stay away from Carl since he's a suspect?" she asked calmly.

"It's a good idea. Being with him could put you in danger."

Alisheen defiantly looked at Meadors, who realized with dismay he'd said the wrong thing.

"You can tell Spencer for me that I can take care of myself, and I'll associate with whoever I want unless he's going to suspect me of smuggling too. I'll see Carl when and if I want, and it'll be none of his damn business."

Alisheen, trying to keep her emotions under control, turned away, and opening the screen door to the kitchen looked back at Meadors, "I suppose I should thank you for telling me all of this, but I'll handle Carl and Spencer. I'm a big girl."

Meadors grabbed her by the arm with force, surprising her.

"Alisheen, this isn't some damn game. This is real. It's dangerous, and somebody could be hurt or killed."

Meadors released his grip.

"Alisheen, talk to Spencer when he gets back or call him in Washington. He's at the Hilton downtown. Give him a chance. My guess is you'll find a way to get him to tell you want you want to know but let him do it his way."

She was silent then said, "Goodbye, Meadors."

Emily saw Alisheen come back into the kitchen and go straight to her office. Emily followed, alarmed by her appearance.

"Alisheen, are you OK? What's going on? Is Spencer all right?"

Alisheen broke down, "Spencer knows!"

"What!" exclaimed Emily, "How?"

She just shook her head and Emily hugged her. At the same time, Mickey came into the office looking for Emily and was instantly concerned.

"Is she all right?"

"Yes, Mickey. Alisheen felt faint but she's OK. Please get her some water."

Mickey left and quickly returned with the water.

"What happened, Emily?"

"She's all right. She just felt faint," Emily said, trying to explain it away.

"Bullshit. I left her outside with Meadors so he must have told her something."

Emily, exasperated, said, "Mickey, mind your own business and get the bar ready please."

"It is ready, and I'm not leaving until I find out what's going on."

Emily was getting angrier, but Alisheen interrupted her.

"It's OK, Mickey. I'm fine."

She hesitated then said, "Meadors told me Spencer knows I was with Carl Powers."

Mickey's jaw flew open in surprise. "How in the hell did he find out?"

"I can't tell you … either one of you. He just knows."

Emily exploded.

"What do you mean you can't tell us?"

"Because it's confidential police business. Carl Powers may be involved, and you're better off not knowing. As for me, I'll have to deal with it."

Emily fumed silently.

Mickey said, "I told you so, Alisheen."

"What did you tell her?" asked Emily.

Before Alisheen could stop him, he said, "I told her that Carl Powers was a skunk in a polo shirt, and she should stay away from him."

Alisheen's tone was dangerously calm. "It was a rat in a polo shirt, and it's still none of your business. You're guessing that it's because of Carl."

Emily, with a puzzled look, said, "OK, you two, what in the hell are you talking about?"

"Nothing, Emily, Mickey is an alarmist, and he has nothing to go on except speculation."

Talking around Emily as if she wasn't in the room, Mickey said, "If that's so, then how does Spencer know? I bet a few bucks he isn't spying on your new boyfriend for nothing."

Alisheen was furious, and she stood up.

"How dare you speak to me like that! This is my business and my life. You're the one who spent time in jail, not Carl Powers. I suggest you remember that and go back to your job while you still have one."

Mickey turned and walked out of the office. Emily was shocked and angry with Alisheen.

"What in the hell is the matter with you?"

She left quickly to stop Mickey, and Alisheen slammed her office door closed behind her.

~~~~

Spencer tried to rest, but the forthcoming evening with Mr. Henry prevented it. He looked at the clock, saw it was only 4:30 in the afternoon, and groaned. He turned on the television and flipped through the channels until he found a baseball game. He drifted off to sleep with the sportscasters droning in the background. Spencer woke with a start at the sound of the telephone. He scooped up the receiver and said hello with a breathless whisper.

"Spencer, it's Skip. Did I wake you?"

Spencer rubbed his head, cleared his voice, and became alert.

"Yeah, you did. I must have dozed off, what's up?"

"Hell man, we got to be downstairs soon. I thought we could meet and have a drink."

Spencer checked the clock. "OK. I'll be there in 30 minutes."

"See you then," said Skip and he hung up.

Spencer rested on the bed for a moment to shake the cobwebs from his brain, then rolled off and headed for the bathroom. The hot shower and fresh shave revived him, and he got dressed, wondering what the evening would have in store. He dressed casual, per instructions, and buffed his loafers with the courtesy shine kit. He found the key to his room and put it in his pocket. He then checked himself in the mirror before going to Fitzgerald's room.

Knocking, Spencer realized his hands were sweaty. He blew on them and rubbed them together while he waited for the door to open. Skip waved Spencer in and closed the door. He pointed to the mini-bar and sat down while Spencer fixed a drink. Spencer noticed his mood was dark and asked what the matter was.

Skip said, "I'm worried about tonight."

Spencer said, "I'm nervous too."

"No, that's not it. I'm afraid something is going on, and we're caught in the middle."

"What makes you say that?"

"The conversation I had with Whitley this afternoon. He told me Henry had you under surveillance to be sure you didn't try to make an arrest!"

"What? You got to be kidding me."

"No, but I wish I was. Now you know why I'm worried."

"Whitley didn't say anything else?"

"No, just that we'll know the score tonight after dinner."

Spencer sat down and Skip got up to replenish his drink.

He returned and sat back down saying, "I got a bad feeling."

The phone rang. Skip answered, listened for a minute, then nodded and hung up. It was a reminder about the car.

Spencer checked his watch. "Right on time."

~~~~

In the twilight, Carol parked her car and looked around cautiously before starting toward the cabin. The door opened and Vincent walked out.

"Ain't nobody else here."

Carol said, "Let's talk out here. I like the open spaces."

Vincent shrugged his shoulders. "Suit yourself."

He sat on the steps and pulled a pack of cigarettes out of his shirt pocket, shaking one out, and then offered one to Carol. He lit his and tossed her the lighter.

"So what's the deal, Detective? Do I get the guy that killed Jake or not?"

Carol lit her cigarette and tossed the lighter back to Vincent. She took a deep drag and then exhaled.

"OK, Vincent, here's the deal. You guarantee your little group on the docks and boats, passes information to me and only me, until I get the Snowman. When I get a bead on Jake's killer, I'll give you a head start. I've a good idea I know who it is anyway, but for now, it's just a guess. After four hours, he's mine if you haven't found him. The other condition is if the Snowman killed Jake, I can't turn him over. Too many people are involved."

Vincent smoked and blew smoke rings before answering.

"How do I know you're not lying?"

"You don't, but I'm here and you have my word."

Vincent stood up and stuck out his hand.

"OK, Detective, you've got a deal. Let's go inside."

Carol looked around at the gathering darkness, dropped her cigarette to the ground, and followed him into the cabin.

~~~~

The car turned up a long tree lined drive, stopping at a massive house obscured by the trees on the front but open on the back to the ocean. The house was the private residence of Mr. Isaac Henry, Director of the D.E.A. Before the car reached a full stop, Benjamin Whitley rushed out the front door, greeting Spencer before his feet hit the ground.

"Welcome Detective Baldwin," Whitley exclaimed with an outstretched hand.

Spencer took the hand and noticed the rock-hard grip.

"Please call me Spencer. I feel like I know you already sir."

Whitley grinned, obviously pleased to be called sir. "Please Spencer, call me Ben."

With a quick handshake greeting to Fitzgerald, Whitley ushered them inside and led them through the spacious house to the patio. An elderly black man in a white coat was tending bar and took their drink orders. Spencer was surveying the ocean view when a new face appeared at his elbow at the same time the bartender did. Spencer took the drink and the man introduced himself as Clifton Chambers, head of the southeast bureau of the D.E.A.

"Come now, Clifton," said an older voice from behind Spencer, "Let's not be so formal."

Spencer turned to see Isaac Henry speaking as he walked toward the group from the beach below. He was wearing a bathing suit and closing a robe as he approached. Spencer could see he was very fit for his age. The bartender hurried toward him with a drink and saying, "Thank you, Amos," as he accepted the glass.

Henry continued, "I've read your file, Detective, and I must say I'm impressed by your record."

He extended his hand. "I'm Isaac Henry."

He acknowledged the rest of the group.

"Gentlemen, enjoy my hospitality while I change. We'll have some appetizers out here, and then we'll have dinner inside. Amos will take good care of you. Amos, please go ahead and serve the food, I won't be long."

He looked at Spencer. "I hope Amos does as good a job as your friend, Ms. Delaney, and you'll find his cooking to your satisfaction. Gentleman, please excuse me."

He turned and walked into the house, leaving Spencer with his mouth open in disbelief. He was stunned at first then became uneasy. Isaac Henry knew too much about him, and he didn't like it.

"Easy, Spencer, Henry does his homework on everybody," Skip cautioned.

"Well, I don't appreciate being an assignment. Who in the hell does he think he is?"

Skip said simply, "He's Isaac Henry, head of the D.E.A., and he can do what he pleases. Spencer, don't get on a high horse and develop an attitude. Too much is at stake for us."

Spencer hissed, "What in the hell is at stake for you? I guess maybe I had you figured wrong."

Skip bristled.

"Listen up man. I've been square with you from the day we met, and I've busted my tail to be sure you knew it. Yes, I've something at stake. I got twenty years in service and a chance to make the biggest bust of my career, along with you, if you don't let your emotions get in the way. Henry has a file on you, so what! Get over it and cool down."

Spencer relaxed. "You're right, damn it, his comment about Alisheen just got under my skin. Let's have another drink."

As they approached the bar, Whitley came up with his mouth stuffed full of food.

"Hey, you guys look too damn serious. Let's enjoy ourselves a little before we get down to business."

Spencer raised his drink. "I'm for that."

Isaac Henry, observing the patio from his window above, witnessed the tense exchange between Baldwin and Fitzgerald. It was a bad omen for the evening to come. He stepped back from the window and went to shower. He finished quickly, noticed the fresh clothes prepared for him on the bed, and picked up the phone. "I'll be down shortly."

Dressing quickly, he went downstairs and into the study, closing the door. He went to the desk, picked up the receiver, and dialed from memory.

"Hello?"

"It's Henry. I need to speak to him. Is he available?"

"Yes, sir."

In a few minutes, a new voice came on the line.

"Yes?"

"I have them here now. Do you want to move forward?"

After momentary silence, the answer was, "Yes, but understand if it comes down around them, I'll do everything to bury them and you, if necessary, to protect the position I'm in."

Henry said, "I understand. I've taken the necessary steps to insure we're protected if the operation fails and goes public. Chambers is scared and Whitley is a fool. He'll be blamed if necessary."

The voice said, "What about your agent and the police officer?"

Henry replied, "They can be implicated or made to disappear."

The voice answered, "Very well, proceed," and the connection was broken.

Henry lightly hung up. "Thank you, Mr. President."

He left the study by a different door and went out to the patio.

"Gentleman, I think it's time to eat. Amos, please escort our guests to the dining room."

Henry went to the bar, poured a liberal draught of single malt, and brought up the rear.

~~~~

Carol sat across the table from Vincent listening to his story. When he finished he got up, went to the fridge, and pulled out two beers. He put one on the table in front of Carol and opened his. Carol opened hers and lit another cigarette she had mooched from the pack on the table.

"I got the feeling you're holding out on me, Vincent."

"You know what I know, Detective. If I find out anything, I'll give you a call. You got to trust me sooner or later."

Carol stood up and picked up the beer.

"If you double cross me, Vincent, I'll make your life miserable. Call me at this number and leave a message. This is between us so don't call me at the station."

She tossed a card with her cell number on it onto the table and walked out the door. Vincent followed and stood in the doorway. He watched her drive away and then turned back into the cabin, closed the door, and called out, "You can come out now."

Vernon came out of the bedroom where he'd been hiding and grinned.

"I got it on tape if she double crosses you."

"She won't, but it might be useful in the future."

Vernon got a beer and sat down on the ragged couch. He flipped on the small black and white television and adjusted the rabbit ears until he had a slightly fuzzy screen.

"You didn't tell her you know Carl Powers is the Snowman."

Vincent grinned. "I'm saving that for the name of Jake's killer."

Vernon nodded in agreement and Vincent failed to notice the shadow that came over Vernon's face.

~~~~

Spencer finished the fresh key lime pie and sipped his coffee. The others were finishing, and Amos was hovering with the coffee pot. Henry spoke up from the end of the table. He had remained relatively quiet while Whitley and Chambers provided most of the light conversation during dinner. The conversation ceased as he spoke.

"Amos, it was a fine meal as usual."

The group echoed his praise, and Spencer attempted to put Henry off guard. "Amos, I know a redhead who'd love to get your dessert recipe."

Skip looked at Spencer with surprise and Henry laughed.

"Let's go to the library where we can be more comfortable and have a brandy."

Henry rose and the group followed. He led the way down the hall into a large well-furnished library. Faithful Amos appeared with a decanter of brandy and a humidor of cigars, then left. Henry himself served the brandy, and after offering cigars, he took a seat in a high-backed leather chair that sat him up straight. It was a position of command, and the minute he sat down the atmosphere in the room changed. He surveyed the end of his cigar and sampled the brandy, then scanned the room, and cleared his throat.

"Gentleman, what you're about to hear is considered vital to our national security. It is therefore, to be considered top-secret and an act of treason if it leaves this room. If it does find its way out, I'll personally make sure whoever is responsible regrets it."

His words, carefully measured, had the intended effect on the room.

"This matter has been under consideration for some time. It's been decided this case will be under the jurisdiction of the D.E.A. and supervised by Benjamin Whitley, who'll report to Clifton and subsequently me. After we've made a positive identification of the Snowman, all activity will cease except for twenty-four-hour surveillance. Orders will come only from me. Benjamin, give us the details."

Before Whitley could begin, Spencer exploded out of his chair.

"Who in the hell do you think you are? You can't just seize jurisdiction. I've been tracking this son-of-a-bitch for months. I'll arrest him when I please, and you'd better not try to stop me. If you do, I'll go to the papers and blow whatever this little operation of yours is so high you'll never recover."

Spencer stepped towards Henry, but two secret service agents stepped forward from the shadows flanking him.

Spencer remained standing but backed away from Henry with malice. Henry waved him off like a horse at an annoying fly.

Henry said, "Listen very carefully before you say or do anything else. I want no misunderstandings. If anything of what you are about to hear in this room even gets a glimmer in the press, I'll bury you so deep for treason against the State that you'll be an old man or dead before you dig out. Do you get my meaning, Detective?"

Spencer didn't speak but sat down, looking angrily at Skip. Henry noticed.

"Agent Fitzgerald didn't have any knowledge of this Detective. He was under orders to prevent you from making an arrest, and I insured those orders by having you followed. I needed to be sure that you didn't screw up this operation. Now we'll let Benjamin tell us his story."

Whitley, shaken by the confrontation, was sweating profusely.

Henry, with a look of disgust, said, "Excuse yourself, Benjamin, then come back and brief us."

Whitley left quickly and the room fell silent. Spencer glared at Henry. Skip avoided Spencer by looking around the room and at the ceiling. Henry ignored Baldwin and amused himself by watching Fitzgerald, then Chambers, who sat quietly with a smug look on his face. Whitley returned and nervously cleared his throat.

"I'd like to remind you of Director Henry's words of caution before I begin."

Henry smirked and glanced at Baldwin.

"What's been proposed is a plan that'll help us turn the tide of the war we've been fighting against drugs. From the beginning, we've been unable to stop or even slow down the flow of drugs into the United States. It's time to take action, bold action, to turn the odds into our favor."

"For God's sake, Ben, what in the hell are you talking about?" interrupted Skip. "You're knitting a damn flag. What's the plan?"

Whitley looked at him like a teacher with an inept student.

"We're going into business with the drug smugglers and form a partnership."

That was all Spencer could stand.

"You're out of your damn minds," he said, standing and raising his voice.

The Secret Service agents moved to protect their boss, but Spencer didn't back down.

"Now I know why you don't want an arrest; you're going to be on the take."

Henry burst out laughing, surprising the room.

"Quite the contrary, Detective Baldwin, we're going to seize jurisdiction, as you put it, but not over your investigation. We're going to take over the smuggling operations, discreetly of course, to control the routes into the country. In return, for allowing drugs into the country unhindered, we'll control quantity and quality by negotiating with the drug cartels. They get limited access and will not have to go to as much trouble to smuggle their goods into the country. We artificially create a shortage by controlling supply, which due to simple economics drives up prices so they're happy. We'll also dictate quality, by not allowing this stuff cut with poison onto the streets and demanding reduced potencies."

"What's in it for you?" asked Spencer angrily.

"Nothing but the satisfaction of a job well done, and the country wins in the end. We can start putting the money we've been wasting to better use."

"This is absolutely crazy. What kind of a guarantee are you going to get that you can trust from drug dealers?" said Spencer. "Even if you do strike a deal through the smugglers, you can't be sure the cartels will play by the rules."

"Oh, they will, detective. They'll police themselves to be sure that no one messes up the deal for the rest of them. If they do, I'll promise them and their country a military reprisal they won't recover from for decades."

Skip's jaw dropped open as Spencer finally sat down with disbelief. Whitley started to sweat profusely, and his drink spilled over as his hands started to shake. Chambers had heard it all before and remained smug in his chair.

"You misunderstand me, gentleman. I'm not talking about a nuclear strike though the option was discussed. We would however level everything with a significantly large cruise missile strike. The poor economies of their countries would put the cartels back in the dark ages. It would take them a very long time to rebuild their organizations."

"What about the United Nations and our allies?" Skip asked.

"Fuck them. We've let them play diplomatic games that have affected our national security long enough. Who is going to take on the United States? The fucking world can't blow its nose without our help. Nobody is going to do anything but cry foul, if that. Who's going to support drug dealers or a country that does little or nothing to stop them? Believe me, Agent Fitzgerald, we will make it work. The Snowman will be our first recruit."

"What makes you think he'll cooperate?" Spencer asked sarcastically.

Henry, with an evil smile on his face, puffed his cigar and drained the last of the brandy from his glass.

"He will, Detective. As they say, I'll make him an offer he can't refuse."

Skip and Spencer were silent on the ride back to the hotel after the incredible meeting with Isaac Henry. On the elevator, Spencer looked straight ahead, still seething. Skip cleared his throat, which brought an involuntary glance from Spencer, and he made eye contact.

"Spencer, I swear I didn't know anything about this crazy plan of theirs."

Spencer looked at him and looked away again. The elevator doors opened, and he stalked out. Skip, realizing it was useless to try to talk to him, followed in silence. He was surprised when Spencer whirled around suddenly and faced him stopping in his tracks.

With determination he said, "They won't get away with this."

"Exactly, what aren't you going to let them get away with, Spencer?"

"Seizing jurisdiction," Spencer spat as he said it. "I'm not going to let them take this from me, much less smuggle drugs in the name of God and country. You can be sure of that." Then he entered his room and closed the door with a bang.

Skip sighed heavily and went to his room. He flipped the lock, then went to the bar and found the ice had melted in the bucket. He shrugged his shoulders, said "Screw it," and poured it neat into a glass and walked to the window. He sipped the liquor and looked out trying to clear his brain. He needed help. He needed somebody on his side. This was crazy, it was wrong, and he had to do something. Whitley was obviously scared of Henry. That smug son of a bitch Chambers had just sat there, and Spencer was too mad and definitely didn't trust him now. He needed someone on the inside, someone he could trust. He drained the glass, and a thought occurred to him.

"Damn, it just might work."

He went through the numbers on his cell phone until he found it. He fixed another drink, dialed the number and sat in the chair looking out the window.

He heard the familiar voice on the phone and without introduction said, "I need your help again."

~~~~

Once Spencer was in his room with nowhere to go, he paced like a caged tiger. He noticed there was a message light on his phone. He took off his shirt, kicked off his shoes, and sat down heavily on the end of the bed. Expecting to hear Skip's voice, he was shocked to hear Alisheen. "Spencer, this is Al. Meadors told me you are in D.C. Please call me when you get home. I want to see you and we need to talk. I love you." Her voice trailed as if she was trying to think of something else to say and then she hung up.

"Crap, just what I needed with everything else going on."

He stared at the ceiling for a long time and checked the time on the bedside clock. An hour had passed. With frustration, he threw the covers off and sat up. He called his office to check his voicemail.

Isaac Henry and Clifton Chambers remained in the study after everyone had gone. Henry looked at Chambers.

"You were very quiet tonight."

Chambers smiled. "I thought you handled Baldwin beautifully, although for a minute, I thought he was going to risk getting shot in an effort to get to you."

"Yes, it seems our Detective Baldwin is a brave sort and possibly on the rash side in his reactions, which makes him very dangerous."

Chambers gestured with his empty glass toward the decanter and said, "May I?"

"Of course." Henry watched Chambers as he walked to the small table that held the brandy.

"I think I may've underestimated your value, Clifton. I've always held the opinion that you were a bureaucratic, by the book asshole, but I see you're a much lower form of bureaucrat. You're closer to my own level. You're a sneaky bastard who'd sell out his own mother for power and what it brings. Am I right?"

Chambers flushed at the candidness of Henry's definition of his character, but he lifted his glass in affirmation and smiled wanly.

Henry smiled. "I thought so. I watched you sizing up Baldwin and Fitzgerald. Do you think they'll work with each other or work against each other, and who do you think might collaborate with us?"

Chambers sat down, sniffed the delicate blend of the brandy, and took a sip.

"I think, sir," he said with deliberation, "that Fitzgerald will follow orders and try to convince Baldwin to cooperate, but he'll come to a critical junction of duty, career, and right or wrong, and make a judgment call. I'm guessing he'll do the honorable thing in the end and try to make an arrest despite his orders and to hell with his career. Baldwin is trying to figure out how to bring you down at this very moment."

He sipped the brandy again and looked at Henry.

"I think you're right. We must be prepared to take them both out of the picture at the right time. We'll need our own team in place to seize the Snowman to deliver him into our safekeeping."

"What're you going to do about Fitzgerald and Baldwin?"

"After we have the Snowman out of reach, we'll arrange for Fitzgerald to move to another location, higher up of course, with a lot of exposure. If this does blow up and go public, he'll be in a position of such distinction that he'll be unable, or unwilling if you prefer, to corroborate any of it. Whitley will be the fall guy. He'll retire out of the agency but with more than enough money under the table to buy his silence. Baldwin is a different matter. I don't think a promotion or money would sway him from his path. I think he'll attempt to do his duty."

Henry drained his glass. "Of course, if he's killed in the line of duty it would be a tragedy."

Clifton Chamber's lack of reaction to this revelation brought a chuckle from Henry.

"I knew I was right about you."

He stood up and put his glass on the silver tray.

"Good night, Clifton," and walked out of the room.

Chambers eyes followed him.

He toasted the direction that Henry had gone, drained his glass, and called for Amos to summon his car and driver.

# Chapter 15

"WHAT'S THE PLAN, Jack?" asked Bridges, who checked his watch as he drove.

Jack took a bite of biscuit and sipped his coffee.

"You get to hang out with the pretty girls in the library. I want you to look at yearbooks, newspapers, anything that covers the time-period those two were here that might give us a clue as to why Guilford has it in for Powers. I'm going to meet with the Registrar and look at their student files."

Bridges grinned and returned his eyes to the road.

They arrived at the campus of the University of Georgia, found their way to the administration building, and Bridges parked the car. They got out, stretched, and surveyed their surroundings.

Cooley said, "I'll be a couple of hours at least. I'll meet you at the library."

Bridges nodded, got into the car, and drove off. Cooley went up the massive steps of the administration building and followed the signs to the registrar's office. He found the office on the second floor, and a secretary pleasantly greeted him.

"May I help you?"

"I'm Detective Cooley from Savannah. I've an appointment with Mr. Hendrix this morning."

The secretary checked her computer and then offered him a seat.

"I'll tell him you're here, Detective." She disappeared and reappeared in a few minutes.

"He's on the phone right now, but as soon as he's done, he'll be out."

She resumed her activity at the desk, and Cooley browsed the décor of the office while he waited. Soon a well-dressed man, small in stature, appeared and introduced himself as Mr. Hendrix, the Registrar. He motioned for Cooley to follow, and he led him to a large corner office with a grand view of the campus. Offering Cooley a seat, Hendrix addressed him with arrogance.

"Detective Cooley, I gave you this appointment to discuss Mr. Powers because you said it was a serious matter, but there must be some sort of misunderstanding. Mr. Powers is one of our more famous and successful graduates and a generous benefactor of the school. I find it hard to believe he is part of something illegal."

His attitude pissed Cooley off.

"Mr. Hendrix, I never said Mr. Powers is involved in anything illegal. You're making an assumption. Mr. Powers and Mr. Guilford are connected to an investigation, but we didn't want to subpoena their records to avoid causing them any embarrassment. If I were you, I wouldn't tell them we examined their student records. Mr. Powers might get offended and stop donating money to the school. I'd hate to be the person responsible for that." Cooley was smiling on the inside as the man squirmed with discomfort.

Hendrix's attitude changed noticeably. "Of course, I'll be glad to help with your research, Detective."

The registrar led Cooley to the archives in the basement and consulted a computer screen. "I'll be right back."

He returned with two reels of film, handed them to Cooley, pointed, and said, "The view boxes are over there. I'll be upstairs in my office if you need anything else," then he left.

Cooley found the desk with the film readers and threaded the first film through the viewfinder. He flipped on the light and began to read. Powers had been a stellar student. High grade-point average, second team All-American at running back, honor clubs, a popular fraternity on campus, Powers was into everything and good at it all.

"Damn near makes you sick," muttered Cooley.

Not finding anything unusual, Cooley took Powers' record out and threaded the student record of A.J. Guilford. He focused on the first page and as he began to read, he unconsciously pursed his lips together, puzzled.

A.J Guilford barely graduated. His grade-point average was minimal; the evaluations from the professors reflected his poor academic record and there was reference to a student disciplinary hearing and probationary punishment but no explanation. The oddest thing of all was that Guilford was in the same fraternity as Powers.

"How in the hell did a guy like Guilford get into a fraternity with a record like that?" Cooley rubbed his temples, trying to squeeze an explanation out of his head.

He scanned the rest of the record, returning to the page that referred to the disciplinary action. He made some notes, returned the film to the canisters, and left them on the desk. He went back upstairs, walked past the secretary into the Registrar's office, and sat down, flipping open his notepad.

Hendrix, irritated by the interruption, said, "Yes, Detective?"

"Mr. Hendrix, can you tell me what Guilford did to warrant a student hearing and probation?"

"No, I can't."

"Does that mean you can't, or won't?"

The registrar was unruffled this time.

"It means I can't, Detective. I can't give you any information because I wasn't involved. You'll need to talk to the Dean of Student Affairs at that time, Dean Fredericks. He would've been directly in charge of the inquiry."

Cooley jotted the information down in his notebook.

"Can you arrange for me to meet with him this afternoon?"

Hendrix checked his watch. "I'll see if he's still on campus. If he is, I can get you an appointment."

Cooley stood.

"Thank you. I'll be sure to note how cooperative you've been when I file my report."

The registrar flushed with pleasure. "Happy to be of service, Detective."

Bridges entered the library and approached the desk, where a beautiful blonde with a deep tan was on duty. With a smile, he asked her how she got so tan working in the library.

The girl laughed. "Spring Break was last week. You're obviously not a student if you didn't know that. Can I help you find something?"

Bridges blushed. "I need to look at old newspapers and yearbooks for the school. Where can I find them?"

"Downstairs in the reference section," she said, coming around the desk. "I'll have to take you there or you'll never find them. It's pretty confusing if you don't know your way around the stacks."

Bridges admired her with his eyes as he followed her down the stairs. She took him to a remote corner, pointed out the yearbook collection, and then showed him how to access the old newspapers on file with the computer.

"Can I help you find something in particular?" she asked hopefully.

"No, I'm just doing some research."

She looked disappointed but smiled warmly.

"Well, if you need anything, I'll be here until two," then she went back upstairs.

Bridges watched her disappear, then browsed the yearbooks, pulling out the years that Guilford and Powers had attended school. Their senior year was the most revealing since it had their senior bios with the pictures. Powers's was incredibly long and his accomplishments were outstanding. Guilford's, on the other hand, was very short with no notable achievements. Bridges then pulled up campus newspapers on the computer for the same year and began to read. He found nothing interesting in the first couple of issues.

In the third newspaper, there was a small headline out of the ordinary, noting a rape on campus. He read the article then moved on to the next issue. There was another rape headlined on the inside page and information about how female students should protect themselves. His interest peaked as he checked the next few issues. The next three reported more rapes on campus, requested information and help, and detailed prevention tips. The sixth issue, oddly enough, didn't say anything about them, and there was no other coverage, except for the five papers he'd reviewed. He wrote the dates down and pulled up the local newspapers from the same time period to see if the rapes on campus had gotten any local press.

He found nothing at first, then uncovered an article that mentioned the rapes on campus in the middle of a larger story about college crime. There was nothing else. It was damn peculiar, but there were a couple of interesting facts. They were all in the spring of Guilford and Powers' senior year. While Bridges was making notes Cooley appeared with a bag, sat down, and pulled out two Cokes and two packs of crackers.

"Well, Junior, what've you found so far?"

Bridges sat back and popped a Coke.

"Not much, but I did find something weird."

He reviewed his discovery and research of the rapes.

When Bridges finished Cooley said, "You may have found out more than you know. I went through the student records and found out a couple of things. Powers had high marks and achievements in everything, including one of the best fraternities on campus. Guilford, on the other hand, was a misfit, academically and socially, except for one thing."

He paused and left Bridges hanging.

"Come on Jack, give, what did you find?"

"Guilford and Powers were in the same fraternity."

"You're kidding."

"That's exactly what I thought. Guilford was also the subject of a disciplinary hearing that put him on probation."

"When?" asked Bridges.

"Spring of their senior year."

They sat quietly for a minute then Bridges said, "Let's find a fraternity picture."

He got up, and pulling the yearbook off the shelf, flipped through the pages.

"Here it is. Guilford does not look like a happy camper."

Cooley looked over his shoulder. It was a typical fraternity picture with half of the group being serious and the other half hamming it up for the camera. Powers had a big smile on his face and looked like the All-American he was supposed to be. His arm was around a sullen looking Guilford, who looked like a nerd at a jock party.

They left the library, drove to a classroom building, and Cooley parked.

"I've got a meeting with Dean Fredericks. You'll have to wait in the car."

Bridges yawned. "No problem, I'll just catch a nap. I'm bushed."

Cooley left Bridges settling in for his siesta, and he entered the small classroom building. He found Dean Fredericks' office on the first floor. He was a tall man, with a balding head, wire-rim glasses, and the stem of a Sherlock Holmes style pipe in his mouth. The broad room was filled with shelves of books, and the fresh smell of maple and apple flavored pipe tobacco filled the air. Fredericks stood up as Cooley knocked on the doorjamb and gestured for him to enter.

"Detective Cooley I presume," said Fredericks, crossing the room with his hand out-stretched in a warm greeting.

"Yes sir," said Cooley, surprising himself by saying sir.

"Come in, come in, and have a seat. Do you care for a drink? I have some fine sherry in the decanter."

Cooley declined, but Fredericks ignored him, poured two small glasses, and handed one to him as he sat down behind the antique walnut desk. He tamped his pipe, lit it, took a generous sip of sherry, and fixed his gaze on Jack, who shifted in his seat like a student in trouble.

"Detective, you shouldn't have threatened Hendrix like you did. Though he's competent as a registrar, I find his arrogance irritating, as I'm sure you did. I'll be happy to oblige you if I can. I remember Carl Powers of course. I've fond memories of him, and he occasionally stops in to see me when he's here. Mr. Guilford I also remember, but I can't say it's with fondness, more like disappointment."

He scowled and touching another match to his pipe, leaned back in his chair.

"Now Detective, suppose you tell me what exactly it is you're after."

Cooley shifted in his seat again.

"Well, sir, I need to know what you can tell me about the disciplinary action taken against Guilford. I can only assume it was related to the rapes on campus."

Dean Fredericks slowly pulled a file out of his desk drawer shaking his head.

"I was afraid someone would dredge this up again. We tried for the sake of Mr. Guilford to keep it quiet and provided restitution to the families, hoping it would remain buried. Why are you here, Detective?"

The strong personality of the Dean was beginning to have less of an effect on Cooley.

"Mr. Powers and Guilford are related to an ongoing investigation."

Cooley steadily returned the gaze of the Dean.

"Detective, I'm nearing retirement. I've devoted my life to this school and have a good pension. I don't want to do or say anything that will jeopardize either one. Therefore, I can only hope and ask that you keep the school and me out of this, and promise you'll use this information discreetly. Too many women long since married with families would be ruined by this information."

"I promise," Cooley said.

With a sigh of resignation, Fredericks handed the folder over to Cooley. After surrendering the file, Dean Fredericks refilled his sherry and pipe and began to speak.

"It began at the end of the fall semester during exams. Two women students reported rapes two days apart. We knew it was the same person or persons because they were identical in methodology, or M.O. as you call it. We didn't report it locally and kept it out of the newspaper because the victims' families requested we keep it confidential, and there weren't any clues beyond what little they could remember. Within two weeks of school resuming the following spring semester, there was another rape identical to the first two. We assumed that a student or teacher was preying upon the female students. After the third rape in as many weeks, we asked the local authorities for help, but quietly, to keep a panic from spreading and to preserve as best we could the reputation of the school. We published discrete articles in the school's newspaper about the rapes and a lot of information about how the girls should take precautions to protect themselves. We only had a couple of consistent facts. All the girls were raped in the same manner, and they all had ties to a single fraternity on campus."

"Powers's and Guilford's fraternity," Jack said.

"You are correct of course. At first, we thought it was too obvious and that someone was trying to discredit one of the finest fraternities on campus, but soon we realized that was a little far-fetched. Continued investigation led us to believe that the rapist was big and strong since he was able to overpower the girls so easily. The police thought they had a suspect, Carl Powers. He had dated them all and was the last one to see two of the four girls before they were attacked."

"Sounds like a pretty good start to me."

Fredericks nodded in agreement.

"We thought so too until we got a search warrant for the fraternity house. The police searched Powers' room thoroughly and found nothing. When they checked other rooms, Guilford's in particular, they found some things that'd been hidden but not quite good enough."

"Tell me," was all Cooley said.

Fredericks stood up and began walking around the room stoking his pipe.

"The victims' accounts said they were hit in the back of the head, and a heavy blackjack was found. They also found several rolls of duct tape. One was half gone, and the clincher was they found their panties in a plastic bag."

"So," said Jack.

"So, Detective Cooley, you're not reading the file."

"I like your version better."

Fredericks sat back down.

"All of the victims were hit from behind with a heavy instrument, then bound, gagged, and blindfolded with duct tape, raped, sometimes sodomized, and badly beaten. When the attacker was finished, he took their underwear, and used more duct tape to secure their legs. We found all of this in Guilford's room and concluded he was a prime suspect. Especially since he couldn't account for his whereabouts during the time periods the rapes took place, nor could he explain how the evidence got into his room."

"That's the most circumstantial case I've ever heard," Cooley said accusingly.

"You're right of course. We never had anything more than a circumstantial case against Mr. Guilford. However, the rapes did stop. What little reputation Guilford had was ruined of course, but Powers was exonerated as far as the school and I were concerned. At the faculty hearing, Powers even intervened on Guilford's behalf. He made a very good case for leniency, and Guilford was put on probation."

"What about the victims?"

Fredericks blew a cloud of fragrant pipe smoke into the air.

"Since we had no clear evidence against Mr. Guilford beyond circumstantial, and the school wanted it kept quiet, as well as the girl's families, they were given the best medical care and counseling money could buy, and they all agreed to a substantial settlement."

Cooley looked at the Dean with disgust.

"When you say the school wanted to keep it quiet, you mean you don't you?"

Fredericks shrugged his shoulders. "It's the same thing, Detective. I was the representative of the school, and they were well taken care of."

"You mean you bought them off," Cooley said with sarcasm.

"You can call it what you wish, Detective, but I prefer to think of it as an agreement not to publicly humiliate the school and the girls."

The Dean picked up his glass of sherry, and Cooley stood up.

"What did Guilford have to say?"

"He pleaded innocent and that he was framed of course."

"Why did Powers intervene for Guilford?"

"Guilford asked him to. It was also a function of his job as the Chairman of the Student Disciplinary Committee for the Greek Council."

Cooley leaned on the desk and stared down at the Dean.

"Didn't it occur to you that Guilford was telling the truth? After all, Guilford is not exactly a physical specimen, now, is he?"

Fredericks said defiantly, "Of course we did, but with the element of surprise and the use of the blackjack, we concluded that Guilford was capable of raping the girls. With the victim stunned it would have been easy to overpower them, and helplessly bound, even a small person could deliver a severe beating."

"I have one last question."

"Yes?"

"I noticed you're the faculty advisor for the fraternity that Powers and Guilford were in."

"Yes?"

"How did Guilford get into one of the best fraternities on campus?"

"Powers campaigned for him. They were friends, though I never could figure out why."

"When did Guilford join?"

"It was the spring semester, that same semester as a matter of fact."

"Didn't it seem strange that Guilford was joining a fraternity right before he was to finish school? I mean he never bothered with it before, why then?"

"No, it didn't," stated Fredericks proudly. "It's one of the best fraternities on campus, and Mr. Guilford would have benefited greatly from the opportunity."

Cooley tossed the file on the desk with disgust and left the office.

He woke Bridges up as he slammed the car door.

"I take it things didn't go to well with the Dean?"

"Too good, Junior, too good. We need to see the Chief of Police before we leave."

At the local police station, they met with the Chief of Police in his office.

"What can I do for you boys?"

Cooley and Bridges sat down in the chairs offered.

"We're doing some background work on a case we're working in Savannah. Do you remember the rapes on campus a long time ago, and can you tell us anything about them?"

The Chief flipped a switch on the intercom.

"Mollie, pull the file marked Guilford / Powers out of the unsolved crimes files please and make a copy for our visitors."

Bridges and Cooley were stunned.

"I remember it because it left a bad taste in my mouth."

"How so?" asked Cooley.

"It was a cover-up from the beginning by some powerful people. We never had any hard evidence, but we had some basic facts. The M.O. was always the same, but I guess you know that already. But there were no prints, no voices, and no physical evidence to help identify their attacker."

"What about semen samples?" interrupted Bridges.

"Wasn't any, the rapist used a condom. Usually, a jogger would find the victim in the morning, in the bushes next to a path or sidewalk. Besides some bad bruises, cuts, scratches, and a big headache, they were unharmed otherwise, except for the rape itself. Physically they recovered, but mentally, who knows. We thought we had a suspect until we found evidence in another room."

"Guilford's you mean," said Cooley.

"Yeah," said the Chief.

"Was the first suspect Powers?"

"Yes, to that question also. Like I said the evidence was in Guilford's room, but it was circumstantial, anybody could have put it there. The local D.A. wouldn't touch the case. One of the victim's fathers, a powerful senator; I won't tell you who so don't ask, intervened. He came off being interested in protecting his daughter's reputation, but he was more interested in protecting the school than her."

"I can see why this case bothers you, Chief," Cooley said wryly.

"We thought it was Powers for sure, but it didn't fit. He was screwing them all anyway, so why rape them? Guilford was a loner, no friends, no girls; no one had much of anything to do with him. He was virtually invisible except for the relationship he had with Powers."

"What's your take on that, Chief?" asked Bridges.

"I don't really have one. It was strange though. Powers and Guilford were damn near inseparable after the investigation."

"Powers was keeping tabs on Guilford," guessed Cooley.

"It's a good bet. The school and the politics made Powers untouchable. He was a school hero, Bulldog football darling."

"Why do you think Powers did it?" asked Cooley.

"He'd dated them all, was definitely strong enough to overpower them from behind, especially with a blackjack, and the beatings were on the brutal, physical side. Like someone with strong arms and big fists, someone built like Powers, not Guilford. Powers also had a big fight at a fraternity party with two of the victims a few weeks before. The story was he'd asked them both to the same party with the intent of having three-way sex. The girls didn't like that idea too much, and it ended in a shouting match with Powers being slapped. That's not much, but it did give him a possible motive to get even. He always had an alibi though, except for one of the rapes, but we still didn't have anything to go on. To sum it up, we had diddly."

"Just a couple of more questions Chief?" Cooley said.

"Sure, fire away."

"How many girls were raped in total?"

"Seven that we know of for sure, two before the break at the end of the fall semester and the five after the spring semester started. The rapes stopped after the evidence was found in Guilford's room."

"That was convenient. Where can we pick up the file?" asked Cooley, standing and motioning for Bridges to do the same.

"Mollie will have it ready for you at the desk," said the Chief, rising also.

Bridges said, "You never really said why you thought Powers and Guilford were in it together."

"Guilford told me he helped Powers do it."

"He told you they did it together?" Cooley said astonished.

"Before the senator got involved, I questioned Guilford. He told me that Powers attacked the girls and beat them, and then forced him to rape the girls while he watched. Guilford was scared to death of Powers, who threatened to blackmail him. Once he'd helped with the first girl, he was in it and Powers had him under his control."

"Why didn't all of this come out during the investigation?" asked Cooley still flabbergasted.

"I told you," said the Chief. "It all went away after the senator got involved. There was no one to press charges, and the fact that Guilford was trying to blame the very person sticking up for him during the investigation, didn't fly with anyone but me."

Bridges asked, "Did Guilford say why Powers did it?"

The Chief nodded.

"Guilford's story was that for him to get into the fraternity, Powers told him he had to have been laid, and he hadn't. Powers offered to help him out. They went out together under the ruse of visiting a girl that Powers knew. Next thing you know, Powers has Guilford hiding in the bushes and he jumps the girl, drags her off into the bushes, and she's a victim. He forced Guilford to rape her while he watched. He said no one would believe A.J. had been laid if he didn't swear to it. A.J. was as much a victim as the girl. I'm surprised he even got it up under the circumstances."

"That explains why Powers worked so hard to keep Guilford in school and the fraternity," said Cooley. "He knew that if Guilford got put away or questioned long enough, the truth would come out. That's why they were together all the time. He didn't trust him to keep quiet, and so he kept him under his watchful eye."

"What did Powers do while these girls were being raped?" asked Bridges.

"Evidently, as we say in the country," said the Chief, "Powers did all of this out of 'pure meanness'. I say that because he did absolutely nothing but watch. It happened for no other reason than to commit a violent crime against another human being, to be in control. Guilford said Powers described it to him like taking a hit of speed. It gave him a rush to have that much power over somebody else."

They were quiet until they were out of Athens and headed for Savannah. Bridges finally spoke.

"I guess we know now what's motivating Guilford to get Carl Powers. I can't believe they were able to sweep that whole affair under the rug."

"Junior, money can buy anything. In this case it bought Powers freedom and put Guilford in virtual slavery to him for life until he decided to get even."

"What're we going to do with what we know?" asked Bridges.

"We give it to Spencer and Fitzgerald and let them decide. Who knows?"

They exited the two-lane road onto the interstate ramp and headed south toward Savannah.

"I'll be glad to get home," said Bridges.

"Me too, Junior, me too."

Cooley and Bridges arrived back in Savannah just before midnight and went their separate ways. Jack decided to check his messages before going home so he went to the squad room, checked his box, and checked his voicemail. The light was on in Spencer's office. As he reached in to turn it off, the phone rang. Without thinking, he picked it up, not giving a thought to the late hour.

"Hello?"

"Jack?" asked Spencer, "What're you doing there so late? How was Athens?"

"We just got back a little while ago. I was checking my messages and turning out the lights. Are you still in Washington?"

"Yes. I couldn't sleep so I was checking my voicemail. I didn't expect to get an answer."

"So, how's Washington?"

Spencer snorted with disgust on the other end of the line.

"Whoa, it isn't that bad is it?"

Spencer was quiet for a moment then said, "Jack, you've no idea."

"What happened?" Jack asked.

Spencer changed the subject.

"What did you find out in Athens?"

Cooley noticed but let it go. "You won't believe it. It's unreal."

Spencer laughed, "Try me anyway."

"We think we found out what's motivating A.J. Guilford."

"If you're not in a hurry, let's have it now."

Jack said, "Hold on a minute, let me get my notes."

He got his notes and returned to the chair at Spencer's desk. He outlined the information they'd gotten from the library and the student records, his interview with Dean Fredericks, and the more incredible interview with the Chief of Police. Spencer listened without interruption.

Jack finished, "What do we do now?"

Spencer looked at his watch, then out the window. It was past one in the morning, and he could see the outlines of the Memorials on the Potomac. He spoke with determination.

"I'm going to make Guilford confess so loud and long, to so many people, that Powers is a drug smuggler, that even if it doesn't stick, he'll be ruined."

Cooley was surprised by Spencer's tone.

"Why would we want to ruin Powers with accusations if we can't make an arrest? Spencer, what in the hell is going on?"

"For now, let's just say there are other players in this investigation that are forcing me to make choices. This includes Carol by the way. I'm not sure where she stands in this mess, but for now, I'm not willing to tell her anything. Jack, this needs to be between us for the time being."

Cooley was confused and scratched his chin, and then suddenly he jerked erect in the chair.

"We've been taken off the case, haven't we? They seized jurisdiction, didn't they?"

Spencer smiled as he remembered saying something along those lines.

"Let's just say that their plan is different from mine."

Cooley noted Spencer didn't deny it. "I guess I'll see you sometime tomorrow then?"

"No, I won't be back until tomorrow afternoon, and then I'll need some time to get my mind wrapped around it all. Let them know we talked, and we'll all meet Thursday morning."

"OK, Spencer, you're the boss," said Jack and he hung up.

Spencer remained at the window for a while and watched the lights of the city twinkle in the early morning hour. He thought of Alisheen and sighed. With all this crap going on between them, he couldn't just show up at the restaurant. He'd call her and arrange to meet her somewhere private and vowed to call her the first thing after he got back. Deciding to try to sleep again, he went to the door to be sure it was locked and saw the note on the floor. Curious, he picked it up, opened it, read it, and then crumpled the note into a ball, tossing it into the trashcan.

"Meet you for breakfast my ass."

~~~~

Carl had avoided the office and Jeanette for the rest of Tuesday to let things cool down a bit. He thought about Alisheen as he drove and frowned. He hadn't seen her since they'd gotten back from the plantation because he'd been preoccupied with Jeanette. He decided he'd remedy that and go to the She Crab for lunch. As he pulled into the parking lot Wednesday morning, he noticed several construction vehicles.

He was surprised as he entered. The entire first floor was undergoing a facelift. He made his way to the second floor and entered what had once been the large open area. It was now newly framed walled space. He found Jeanette standing in the middle of a future spacious office examining paint and wallpaper samples. She noticed Carl and smiled at him broadly, obviously excited by the activity.

"Carl, I decided to make some small changes to this old office, I hope you don't mind. I'm redoing your office as well so don't feel left out."

Before Powers could answer Jeanette said, "I decided to improve the way the employees downstairs are organized, so I have redesigned their space. I also decided to take this open space and give myself a private office and create another small conference room for upstairs meetings. I'm also paneling your office to give it a masculine look. All I need for you to do is pick out a new chair from the samples in your office."

Carl said without looking at her, "I suppose we can afford all of this?"

Jeanette looked at him with a sweet smile. "Of course, Carl dear, I wouldn't ever do anything we couldn't afford," with the emphasis on the "we."

She took him to his office to pick out a chair while she was called away to attend to details. Powers was annoyed and amused at the same time. Jeannette was definitely not wasting any time moving ahead with her new position. He decided it was best for now to give her enough rope to kill herself. He noticed the light blinking on his private voicemail and answered it. It was Ian, and Powers listened intently to the message. Jeanette came in a few minutes later and caught him staring out the window.

"Really, Carl, I thought you were in here picking out a chair, not day-dreaming and looking out the window."

"I returned a phone call."

"Well, have you decided on a chair?"

He turned and without expression nodded his head. He looked at her then spoke with an even tone.

"Jeanette, I suggest from now on you move a bit more cautiously with your rise to power. I will expect you to inform me of what you're planning to do. I want to be sure you don't get yourself into a situation you might regret later."

He stared at her evenly, and she returned his gaze without flinching.

"I assure you I'll check with you in the future Carl, when necessary. Have you picked a chair?"

Powers rose and said, "I like the one I'm in."

Then he walked past her and out of the building. Jeanette went to the window and watched him get into his car and drive out of the parking lot.

She smiled with mirth and malice at the same time. "Soon, you'll never walk out on me again."

Powers drove to the interstate loop that went around Savannah, exited on the south side of town, and drove to the riverfront. He parked and followed the sidewalk in Riverfront Park, bordered on one side by the seawall at the river. He spotted Ian sitting on a bench, and he walked slightly past and stopped, turning to look out at the river as one of the tourist riverboats went by. He spoke without looking at Ian, who was continuing to gaze out at the water.

"Have you already notified A.J. about the need for a shipment?"

"Yes, I've already done that," Ian said. "If the feds show when I spring the trap, I'll know he's the leak."

"If he is, you know he's being watched. How do you propose to get him away from them?"

Ian chuckled lightly. "I'll kidnap him from the office and get a friend of mine to drive us out in a truck from under their noses. He'll be on ice before they know what's happened to him, and he can't warn them off. Depending on how it goes at the fake drop site will determine the rest."

"Ian, are you sure it's A.J.?" asked Powers, looking at him directly for the first time.

"I'm sure. I hope I'm wrong, but I doubt it."

Carl turned his back on Ian and put his hands in his pockets.

"We'll have to lay low for a while after they lose their rat. We'd both better make plans to go on extended vacations for a while. When we come back, we can get new routes and networks established, and we'll be back in business."

Ian got up, stood beside Powers, and flipped his cigarette into the water.

"I'll see you around."

Ian walked away into the park, and Carl retrieved his car from the parking lot and headed toward the She Crab. Alisheen saw him come in the door. She leaned against the counter for support, her legs turning into jelly, and waved at him weakly. His smile turned into a frown as he approached, and he could see something was wrong.

"What's the matter, Alisheen? I haven't seen you since we got back, and you greet me like I have the plague."

She quickly recovered and gave a weak laugh.

"Oh, it's nothing to do with you, Carl. I'm sorry. I've just had a bad day, and I'm very tired."

Mentally, Alisheen was a wreck, but she gathered her courage.

"I'm glad to see you though. Are you going to eat lunch?"

"That's what I'm here for. I've been craving a plate of fried shrimp since we got back."

"Well follow me, and I'll get you a booth and we can talk too."

Alisheen led Carl through the restaurant to a booth in the back. She got him seated, took his order into the kitchen, and was met by Emily who had a look of panic on her face.

"Are you crazy?" Emily hissed at her.

"What do want me to do, Emily?" she asked with sarcasm. "Go off screaming into the street? The best thing I can do is to act as natural as possible, and I'm still not convinced this isn't a bunch of crap cooked up by Spencer just to keep me away from Carl."

"Even so, you better be careful because if Meadors wasn't lying to you, you could get into a lot of trouble."

"I'll act natural and keep him at arm's length. Now take him a pitcher of tea and his hushpuppy basket while I turn this order in."

Emily left and Alisheen spotted Mickey coming into the kitchen. They'd hardly spoken since Alisheen had told him off in the office. She'd apologized and he'd accepted, but they'd remained distant. She caught Mickey's eyes as he went to the ice bin, and he looked at her curiously.

With anxiety on her face, she mouthed the words, "He's here, what should I do?"

He understood instantly, nodded reassuringly, and mouthed back to, "Stay cool and it'll be all right."

Mickey went back to the bar, and Alisheen returned to Carl's booth. Emily had delivered the tea and hushpuppies, and Carl was munching away.

"Damn, I swear these are the best I've ever had. That Emily is a real sweetheart. You better keep her."

Alisheen smiled at him. "Yes, she is. She's so good I've made her permanent manager to help ease some of my load and give me some more free time."

Alisheen slid into the booth opposite Carl and sipped a glass of water.

"Carl, I'm glad you stopped by today. I want to talk to you."

"About what?" asked Carl as he picked up another hushpuppy and popped it into his mouth.

"Well, first I want to thank you for the wonderful trip again. It was so relaxing and needed, and the plantation is fabulous. I'm just sorry about that night. I know you didn't do it for that reason, but I just feel like, well, that you might've been disappointed the night we came so close, and I lost it."

Powers took a big gulp of tea. "Alisheen, look at me."

She looked at him, and he was looking at her with a hint of anger.

"I'll be honest with you. I was disappointed that night. I'd like nothing better than to make love to you. I'd love to do my best to give you the most satisfying sexual experience you've ever had, and if that day comes, so be it. In the meantime, forget about it."

Alisheen, surprised by the abruptness of his answer didn't have anything to say as a result. The food mercifully appeared, and Carl focused on eating.

She finally said, "There is something else I want to talk to you about Carl."

He continued to eat so she went ahead.

"I need some time to decide, to determine where I am in my relationship with Spencer. I don't know if it's over, or if we're just having a bad time, but I need to give it a chance."

Carl wiped his lips and put his napkin back into his lap. He picked up his glass, noticed it was almost empty, and filled it from the pitcher on the table.

"So you don't want to see me any more until you make a decision?"

"No!" Alisheen exclaimed quickly and immediately regretted her hastiness.

"I do want to see you; I'm just saying to give me some time and space to talk to Spencer and figure things out. I don't want to go any farther until I know how I feel."

Carl said with a bored tone, "Alisheen, I told you before I'll wait for the verdict and that there won't be any pressure from me. OK?"

She smiled at him then slid out of the booth. "You're an enigma, Carl, I'll give you that."

She hesitated for a minute then said, "Well, I got customers I'm neglecting. I'd better get around to them. How was your lunch by the way?"

"Excellent as usual," he smiled.

She leaned into the booth to kiss him on the cheek, but instead he held her face and kissed her with passion. Alisheen, surprised at first, immediately relented and returned the kiss. Carl broke the kiss off, and she pulled away and stood up.

"I'll be around, Miss Delaney," and he popped a shrimp into his mouth with a smile and turned his attention to his plate.

Alisheen, flushed from the passion of the kiss and confused by the conversation, made a beeline for her office. She closed the door, sat down, and absently picked up the bottled water on her desk.

~~~~

Ian had a good plan to trap A.J. The biggest problem was separating him from the feds. He picked up the phone and called an unlisted number leaving a message. He needed a redneck.

The phone rang back shortly afterwards. "I figured since you killed Jake that our deal was over."

Ian replied, "You knew the procedure and so did Jake. Anybody talks to cops, they're eliminated. His death protects us all, you too, although I know you've been talking to the cops yourself."

The voice on the other end was silent so Ian continued.

"I know you haven't said anything so you're not in danger from me, but I wonder what would happen if Vincent found out why you were late the night Jake got killed."

Ian could tell the breathing had changed to a quicker rhythm.

"What do you want?"

"I have another contract, and I need a driver."

"I'll do it, but I don't want to be in this anymore. I want out. I'm getting out of town after this."

"Suit yourself, I don't care what in the hell you do afterwards. Just be at the warehouse next Monday. I'll let you know when."

There was an affirmative grunt, and the phone went dead.

Ian smiled. "Vernon, you'll be laying lower than you think very soon."

The plan was simple. Ian would show up early on Monday afternoon, telling A.J. that the schedule had changed, and stay with him to keep him from making any phone calls. When it was time, Ian and A.J. would get in the sleeper of a truck, and Vernon would drive them out of the yard right from under the cops' noses. Anyone watching would think A.J. was still inside and no one would be the wiser. He'd put A.J. on ice at the cabin while he went to the fake drop at the Fenster farm. If the feds showed, Baxter would know the truth. Depending on what happened at the farm would determine A.J.'s fate. He'd take care of Vernon afterwards at the cabin.

~~~~

Clifton Chambers spent Wednesday trying to figure out how to cover his ass if all hell broke loose. He was the new kid on the block, and he didn't have many friends or options in Washington. Henry would set Whitley up as the fall guy, Fitzgerald was a team player although unpredictable, and Baldwin was definitely the enemy. Chambers browsed the editorial pages and noticed the name of someone he'd met at a dinner party. It turned out they'd a lot in common and became friends. He didn't see Saul Levy too much but knew he could trust him. He called the newspaper and asked for the editorial desk.

"Saul Levy please?"

"He won't be back until tomorrow morning sir, but I can leave a message on his desk for you."

Chambers hung up.

# Chapter 16

JEANETTE GREETED THURSDAY with excitement, dressing carefully and paying attention to every detail. She drove the BMW to work to match her new status, and after a quick stop at the post office, she arrived at the Coastal offices precisely at 7:30 a.m. Like a queen to her court, she waved at everyone as she went to her spacious new office. Carl wasn't in but that was typical. It's a wonder, she thought, how he managed without me.

She fantasized briefly about the life they'd share before making the phone call. She retrieved the post-it note with the number on it from her purse and closed the door to the office. She took out the prepaid cell phone and dialed the number, timing the call on her watch so they couldn't trace it. The D.E.A. office in Atlanta routed the call to Benjamin Whitley after she identified the purpose of the call.

"Hello?"

"Have you considered my offer on the Snowman?"

"I have, but I can't help wondering why've you waited so long to come forward?"

"I needed to take steps to protect myself. Safeguards had to be in place."

"I understand. How would you like to proceed?"

"That's simple. I'm willing to identify the Snowman if you agree to meet my terms, which I'll detail later."

"Let me be sure I understand. I have to agree to the terms before you'll tell me what they are?"

"Yes," said Jeanette.

"I can't agree to anything unless I've some sort of proof that your information is legitimate. If you can provide something like that, we'll meet your terms whatever they are."

"Of course, I anticipated this. I mailed to you, this morning, a diskette that contains enough information to prove that I'm legitimate. However, key pieces are missing so you'll need my help to make an arrest. I'll give you some time to review the information, and I'll be back in touch."

Jeanette checked the clock. It was time to disconnect.

"Goodbye!" she said with a lilting laugh.

Thursday morning, Spencer rolled over and knocked the alarm clock off the nightstand in response to the annoying ring. He was hungry by the time he was ready for work and decided to go to the Dixie. Dixie greeted him with his usual homosexual flair and escorted him to a booth. He brought coffee and a cup for himself and asked if he could sit. Spencer waved Dixie into the booth and watched him wedge his large frame into the seat.

"So how have you been, Spencer? You look terrible, and where is Alisheen this morning?"

Spencer rolled his eyes.

"Dixie, how do you manage to piss me off every time I come in here with your questions?"

"It's a gift, a talent that I developed as a defense mechanism years ago when I decided to be a flaming queer. You look like you need a friend this morning."

Spencer grunted, "You're right about that."

"So how can I help? I'm a good listener, and believe it or not, I keep secrets better than anybody you know."

Spencer said quietly, "I think I've lost Alisheen."

Dixie's eyes flew wide open, and he gasped at Spencer, "What happened?"

Spencer sipped his coffee, ignoring the question.

"I bet I can guess. You had a fight because you won't marry her."

Spencer scowled at him.

"Spencer, I've watched you two. You think I'm just a queer who can cook, and you don't have much respect for me, but I've noticed a few things."

Spencer tried to deny the allegation, but Dixie cut him off.

"Don't bother trying to deny it, you'll just insult me. For your information, I'm quite educated and have a Ph.D. in Clinical Psychology. I had a flourishing practice before the storied lives of the people I treated started to give me nightmares. When I no longer wanted to bear their burdens, my own issues were enough, I opened the diner. Anyway, I know people and I know you two. For instance, I know you've got a secret that has something to do with children."

Spencer looked away.

"It's true because I've seen you watch the children in the park across the street with sadness when you're here with Alisheen. I can only guess that your childhood was sad for some reason, which is why you won't marry her. You're afraid your own children might suffer the same fate. Am I right?"

Spencer ignored the question and drained his coffee cup.

Dixie refilled it.

"You need to give yourself and Alisheen a chance, Spencer. You must face whatever is troubling you and let her help. She loves you, and she'll deal with the problem with grace, just like she does everything else."

Spencer, continuing to look out the window, said huskily, "You're righter than you know," and looked at Dixie.

"I can't believe what I'm going to tell you because I've never told anyone else but growing up without my Dad was miserable. He died when I was young, and I still remember the pain I felt at his funeral. My daddy was dead, and the feelings he'd given me when we were together were now gone forever. I felt so many things that day that I couldn't even describe them at that age. All I could do was cry in my mother's arms. My Mom did her best, but she never could fill the void. As I got older, I guess I coped with the loss by being mad at him for leaving me, and the feelings of loss turned into feelings of desertion and abandonment."

Spencer's confession took his voice for a moment, and then he continued through clenched teeth.

"I can't risk getting killed and leaving a child fatherless. I won't do it."

Dixie said simply, "Is your father really dead Spencer?"

Spencer became angry. "What in the hell do you think I just said, damn it? I told you he died when I was young."

"Spencer, you need to recognize something which is so corny you won't believe it's a reality, but as long as you keep the memories, good and bad, of your father like you do in your mind, he's alive."

Spencer looked at Dixie like he was crazy.

"That's crap."

"Is it? Think about it. Do you still have pictures of your Dad? Do you remember the good times; a special memory, a favorite bedtime story, or even something bad about him that makes him a whole person? If so, then you've kept him alive in your mind and in your heart. I'm willing to bet you talk to him. I bet you still curse him for leaving you. I'll bet you ask him for help, for strength, or just say to him, *Hello Dad, I hope I made you proud of me.*"

Dixie stopped talking. Spencer was weeping softly and openly.

He whispered, "I do, Dixie, all of it." Spencer wiped his face with a napkin.

"Spencer, you need to reflect on who you are. Examine your life and decide what impact your father had on you. What role has your knowledge of him played in making you who you are, and how did it shape your character? The hardest part of all will be to admit to yourself your shortcomings and failures. Where did you miss the mark, so to speak, in trying to be what you think your father wanted you to be?"

"What if I don't like what I find?"

Dixie smiled at him with understanding.

"You'll find out you're human. Besides, if Alisheen, who I think is absolutely the greatest person in the world, can find something about you to love you like she does, you can't be all bad. And, for the record, I like you too."

Dixie flashed Spencer a big toothy smile and struggling out of the booth stood next to the table.

Spencer said, "Dixie, I don't know how to thank you."

"That's easy too. Marry the girl, you damn fool, and be sure I get the catering job for the wedding. I guarantee no one will do as good a job as me."

Spencer laughed, threw a twenty on the tabletop, and hurried out of the diner with a new outlook and a lot to think about.

~~~~

Thursday morning, Saul Levy lit a cigarette before answering the phone. He took a deep drag, then exhaled and laughed at the "No Smoking" sign on the wall.

"This is Saul Levy; how can I help you?"

"Saul, this is Clifton Chambers."

Saul replied, "Hello, Clifton. I haven't seen you around. What can I do for you?"

Chambers replied, "I need to talk to you but not over the phone. We need to meet."

Saul was a little surprised but didn't think much of it. "OK, how about Harold's downtown for lunch?"

"No, Saul," Chambers said quickly. "You don't understand. This has to be private and confidential."

Saul became more alert. "Clifton, are you in trouble?"

"No, but I do need to speak to you. It's urgent."

Saul asked, "Got a pencil and paper?"

Chambers replied, "Hold on a minute. Yes, go ahead, I'm ready."

"Head out of D.C. on the Expressway toward Arlington. If you watch the signs, you'll see the exit for Harper's Ferry National Park. It's about an hour and a half from here, but it's private and no one from around here will see us if that's what you're trying for."

Chambers said, "How about tomorrow afternoon at four o'clock?"

Saul checked his calendar. "It works for me. Park in the main lot and walk the nature trail. It's a short loop. I'll meet you somewhere on the trail."

"I'll be there," Chambers replied, and he broke the connection.

Saul hung up and stared at the cradled receiver.

"I wonder what in the hell is going on at D.E.A.?"

Spencer had left Dixie's with a new perspective, and by the time he reached the station, he had decided to tell Alisheen everything and see where the chips fell. He was still angry about the way she disappeared and turned up on Carl Power's plantation in a police investigation. She'd have to explain that to him, but he knew he loved her and didn't want to lose her. He wasn't sure Powers becoming acquainted with her during the investigation was a coincidence anyway. It seemed unlikely that Powers could know about the investigation, but there was a nagging doubt in Spencer's mind. With the plan on how to reconcile with Alisheen evolving in his mind, his thoughts turned to Isaac Henry.

Guilford was the key to his defeat. Spencer was hoping to convince him to put Powers away by getting him to testify publicly about his crimes. A confession to authorities in another city like Jacksonville or Charleston would do the trick and humiliate Powers. The more people that knew about him, the harder it'd be for Henry to keep it quiet and put his ridiculous plan into action.

Guilford would be safer in another city anyway, and in exchange for witness protection, he could confess to somebody else. It'd be difficult, but if he could convince Guilford to turn himself in, it'd be possible. Spencer arrived at the station and entering the squad room noticed that Carol was the only one in, but she wasn't at her desk. Spencer was sure he couldn't trust her with anything he was planning.

Carol entered the room about the time he reached this conclusion and greeted him with a smile. "We missed you yesterday. How was your trip?"

"Not too bad, I'll tell you all about it this morning."

With a wave, she moved on to her desk, sat down, and began to look through the stacks of paper on top. Spencer heard the voices of the others as they came into the room through his open door and walked into the squad room.

"OK, everybody, since I was out yesterday, tell me where we are this morning."

Spencer gave a quick look at Cooley as if to confirm their agreement and then went around the room. When he got to Cooley and Bridges he said, "OK, what did you two find out in Athens?"

Jack looked at Bridges. "I'll go first."

"The floor is yours," said Bridges with a smile.

Jack described his meeting with the Registrar, and they laughed as he detailed his reaction to the possibility of the money source drying up. He moved on to the library and let Bridges detail the newspaper accounts, the yearbook findings, and their conclusions. Jack took up the story again recounting the interview with Dean Fredericks. There were looks of disgust as Jack described the indifference of Fredericks regarding the ruination of

A.J. Guilford, and they were shocked into silence as he related the conversation with the Chief of Police.

"You've got to be kidding," said Meadors.

"I wish I was," said Jack, "but Guilford fingered Powers and was hung out to dry by some powerful alumni with money. I'm guessing Guilford figures he'd go down for the smuggling by himself and Powers would go free again if he tried to accuse him again, so the best way was to turn the cops on to him as an informer."

Spencer said, "I think Jack is right, and I'll share this information with Skip when I see him."

"What happened in Washington?" was the question that came from Meadors.

"It was very interesting, and Mr. Isaac Henry is everything you've heard and more. We agreed to continue to collaborate with the feds, and we are, as before, not to make an arrest."

"You mean to say you flew up there for nothing?" Meadors said disgusted.

Spencer just smiled. "OK, let's get to it!"

The abrupt ending to the meeting surprised them as Spencer got up and went into his office, closing the door. The group looked around at each other for a minute, then shrugged their shoulders and went about their assignments. Spencer sat down at his desk and began to make some notes. He wanted to have everything he was going to say to Alisheen straight in his mind before he called her.

Skip had flown to Atlanta the day after their meeting with Henry to catch up on his paperwork in the office. He drove back to Savannah Friday morning and called Carol as soon as he was in his hotel room.

"Carol, it's Skip, I'm back. What's going on and where is our boy?"

Carol said, "OK, here goes. Meadors is continuing background work on Powers and Coastal Seafood. He's getting deeper into things like financial reports, phone records, credit records, stuff like that, and trying not to alert Powers or his friends at the same time. He has influence everywhere. Meadors is also coordinating uniform patrols and unmarked cars keeping them on the lookout for Ian Baxter.

"Jack and Bridges got back from their research trip to Athens, and it was a doozy. Guilford and Powers seem to have been quite a pair in school, but it's a long story. You want that now?"

"Just a quick brief," said Skip.

"Guilford has a great motive for bringing down Powers. It seems they did a few rapes together in college, but Powers made sure Guilford got all the credit."

"Son-of-a-bitch, well that explains everything except why Guilford just didn't turn him in and ask for witness protection."

Carol said, "We think Guilford's scared to death of Powers, and he's afraid he'd take the rap again if he tried. He probably figured that a covert attempt to get him caught was the best way to get even. What kicked it all off we might never know. Guilford might even have hoped to take over later. Who knows what the little weasel was thinking."

"What else?"

"Jack and Bridges have become permanently attached to each other and are working the docks. They are scouting around for Benny and keeping their ear to the ground to see if the Klan pops up. Cooper is doing background on Miss Jeanette LaCrosse. She is the barracuda that ate Meadors' and Cooper's lunch the day they tried to see personnel files. She has been there since the start-up of Coastal but that's all we know so far. She may be involved but had such a low profile until recently no one knows much."

"Had?" Skip asked.

"She's made a sudden splash in the business world. For years, she's been Powers' Executive Assistant, but in the business section of the paper yesterday, there was a small blurb naming her as the Chief Operating Officer for Coastal Seafood. The business contacts we talked with say that's not a surprise because she's been running the Coastal operation for a while now on a daily basis. Could be she knows something, or maybe it's just a long overdue promotion. Anyway, Cooper is pulling her information together. He seems to have a knack for finding lost souls.

"I'm continuing to work on Vincent Sweet to pump him for information, but I haven't heard from him since the Klan meeting," Carol lied.

Skip said, "I thought you offered him a deal."

"I did. I offered him a head start on his brother's killer in exchange for information, but Spencer squelched it, and I told Vincent the deal was off. I haven't heard from him since."

"Carol, I got to side with Spencer on that," Skip said. "We can't make deals with people's lives. You know better than that."

Skip couldn't see the scowl on Carol's face, and she held it out of her voice.

"You're right. I was just anxious to make a deal that would get us eyes and ears on the docks."

"It's OK, let's move on to Spencer."

"He didn't come in at all Wednesday, and I didn't see much of him yesterday. He left after our briefing this morning, and I haven't seen him since."

"What did he say? How did he act?"

"For Spencer it wasn't too different. He was in a good mood and handed out the assignments after the meeting. He made a phone call or two, and then he was gone."

Fitzgerald was quiet for a moment. "Carol are you sure you read him right, his mood I mean. He didn't say anything about the trip to Washington?"

"Nothing earth shaking, just that we'll continue to work closely with the feds and we're still under orders not to make an arrest. He was his usual self and gave no indication that anything out of the ordinary had happened."

"Damn," Skip swore. "I'll bet he thinks he's come up with a way to beat Henry and bust Powers. He was mad as a hell Tuesday night. You haven't seen him since this morning?"

"Not even a glimpse," Carol said.

Skip was worried.

"Carol, keep me posted and find him if you can. I need to talk to him."

"I'll see what I can do. Where will you be?"

"Just call my cell. Carol, thanks for watching Spencer for me. I need to keep him from crossing Henry until I can find a way to help him. If not—he's going to go down and there won't be anything I can do."

Carol frowned. She didn't like being a spy again and wouldn't have considered it except to help Skip protect Spencer.

"I will. I don't want Spencer to get into trouble with the likes of Henry. I'll call you as soon as I know something."

Skip said goodbye and hung up. Carol sipped her water and smirked. "Talk about breaking the law." Vincent was supposed to call an hour ago, and he was late.

Skip's gut told him Spencer was up to something, given the remarkable attitude change since Tuesday. He had to convince him that he wanted to help, but they had to do it the right way. He decided to call Bo. Maybe he knew where Spencer was. He waited impatiently for an answer, but it rolled over to his voicemail.

"Bo, call me the minute you get this message. I need to know what Spencer is up to."

Skip hung up and noticed the suitcase sitting on the bed, still unopened. He checked his watch and began to unpack, keeping an ear tuned for the phone.

Jeanette breezed into the office on Friday as if she owned the world. After her phone call to Atlanta, she knew she had the upper hand. If Carl refused her demands, she'd threaten to turn him over to the police. She checked the mail in Carl's box and found the invitation to the Savannah Treasury Charity Ball with its gleaming gold lettering. She put it with her mail and went into her office, closing the door. She'd been expecting it. She'd gotten what she wanted so far. Jeanette was surprised Carl had given in so easily, but she knew he was preoccupied with the woman from the trip. His flings never lasted long though and when this one ended, she'd be ready to offer him her love. It was time for step two.

The Charity Ball for the Savannah Treasury was next week, and Carl was going to be her date. He just didn't know it yet. She had everything she needed to persuade him. She'd suspected something was up with the strange truck maintenance schedules and odd hour runs. Jeanette thought that idiot A.J. was using the trucks for a sideline hauling business and kept her eyes on manifests and truck schedules, but soon she realized it was more than just the odd truck or two.

It was a big operation, and only Carl could put something together on that scale. She figured out the trucks were being dispatched short on their orders but weighing out full. What was taking the place of the seafood they were supposed to be shipping? Her watchful eye and sharp business mind led her to the conclusion that Carl was smuggling. The key to the puzzle was in the Atlanta newspaper. A feature story about the supply of drugs into the east coast had identified Savannah as one of the key spots. It was then that she knew what he was smuggling.

She'd found out he was the Snowman by accident. He'd gotten a call that she'd transferred to his private line. After he finished, she realized the voicemail system had activated and recorded the call. The caller referred to him as Snowman when the conversation began, and Carl had berated the man for calling him at the office. It was a mistake, but it gave her another piece of the puzzle. Her plan had hatched over time as she collected the information. She didn't want Coastal ruined, after all; she'd built it, but it was time to force Carl to stop taking risks, marry her, and live happily ever after.

It was a key part of her plan for Carl to escort her to the Charity Ball. Now that she had a respectable title and they were on a first name basis, it seemed only reasonable that they should go out together socially. She sat in her newly upholstered chair and eyed the intricately engraved invitation. Her mind wandered into a dream as she envisioned herself with Carl, dancing and being the "Belle of the Ball."

"I think it's time Cinderella had a new dress for the ball!"

She hurried by the new secretary, saying she had some shopping to do and she'd be back before noon. She was in such a hurry she didn't notice Ian Baxter drive by in a rental car.

Ian waited in his rental car for Powers to arrive. He finally arrived and parked by the back steps. He noticed Ian sitting in the unfamiliar blue Taurus but didn't acknowledge him. He proceeded up the outside stairs and entered the building. Emerging from the back hallway, he overheard the new secretary telling Mr. Jenkins with Sun Diesel that he didn't have an appointment, and that she didn't know when Mr. Powers would be in.

"I'll see him. It's alright."

Carl paused, searching for her name, realizing he had no idea what it was.

"It's Jennifer, Mr. Powers. I just started a couple of days ago."

Carl flashed a quick smile.

"Its fine, Jennifer, Mr. Jenkins often stops in to see how things are going. Just give me a minute."

"Yes, sir," she said with the air of authority given to her, and she asked Mr. Jenkins to take a seat and offered him coffee. Carl went into his office and settled into his chair.

He buzzed Jennifer. "Send Mr. Jenkins in." She escorted Ian into the office and exited, closing the door behind her.

"What in the hell is going on, Mr. Powers?"

"Nothing to worry about, but Jeanette, as I've agreed to call her now, has decided to make a few changes."

"Do I need to take care of anything?"

"No, not yet. I want to find out what she's up to and what she knows before we do anything. I'm guessing she has finally caught on to my extra activities and has decided to use it for her benefit. If it becomes necessary to make a change, I'll let you know."

Ian smiled smugly and nodded in understanding.

"What about our current situation?"

"I'll know the full story Monday night when we see who shows up to play."

Carl said, "If things go as you expect, I'll want to personally handle the final phase."

"I'll contact you as soon as I know something. It will be late though," said Ian.

Powers waved it off and pointed his finger at Ian. "You just make damn sure I'm included before it goes too far."

"I understand."

Ian left and Jennifer knocked a few minutes later, appearing at the door with a steaming mug of coffee in her hand.

"Miss LaCrosse said to be sure you get your coffee every morning, and she was very specific about how to make it."

"Come in."

With a broad smile, she finished the distance from the doorway to the desk. She deposited the morning mail and paper on the desk, and then put the coffee down turning the handle toward Powers. Powers was inwardly amused at her efforts to please her new boss.

"Thanks, Jennifer," said Carl as he sipped the coffee.

She was obviously waiting for him to tell her if it was OK, and he nodded in the affirmative and said, "Where is Miss La Crosse this morning?"

Jennifer looked apprehensive, then said with tattletale's guilt, "She said something about going shopping, sir, but that she'd be back before noon."

Powers smile relieved her look of apprehension.

"That's fine, Jennifer. Miss LaCrosse doesn't report to anyone but herself. Her schedule is her own, and I don't worry about it. Thanks."

Carl waved her to her desk, and as she closed the door he sipped the coffee again, symbolizing it was indeed to his taste. He looked at the mail, glanced at the front page of the paper, and noticed the piece on the upcoming Charity Ball next weekend. It was Savannah's biggest fundraising event of the year and engraved invitations were mailed to the big donors. The rest of the world could buy a ticket at two hundred dollars a pop and that was just to get in the door. He wondered vaguely where his invitation was. He decided to call Alisheen and ask her to go with him.

~~~~

Alisheen picked up the phone casually when it rang in her office, thinking it was a routine sales call.

"She Crab, this is Alisheen, how can I help you?"

"Well for starters you can agree to see me today so we can talk," said Spencer.

Alisheen was surprised, excited, and a bit mad when she realized that it was finally Spencer. She didn't answer, and Spencer thought she'd hung up on him.

"Al, you still there?" said Spencer nervously.

"Yes, I'm still here. I'm really glad you called, but I'm still upset."

"I know. I figured you were. I was too and started to call you several times yesterday, but I honestly chickened out. I didn't know what I was going to say or how, so I took some time to figure it out. We need to meet in private. We have a lot to tell each other, don't you think?"

Alisheen sighed. "You're right. Frankly, I've been wondering what I was going to say to you too. I think it's a good idea."

"Great, how about if we go to the beach this afternoon? I can pick you up."

"No, I don't want to go there. I don't want you to pick me up either. How about meeting me at River Front Park at the fountain around 3:00 o'clock?"

Spencer was disappointed and she heard it in his voice. "OK, if that's the way you want it."

Alisheen decided to soften the mood. "Spencer, I'm really glad you called."

He brightened. "Me too, Al, I'll see you this afternoon."

"Bye, Spencer, I'll see you there."

Her heart was beating faster, and her eyes had misted with tears. She was glad he'd finally called. His voice was comforting to her. She loved him, but he had to trust her or she was going to have to end their relationship. She thought of the trip, the plantation, Carl, and everything that had happened.

"Damn," she swore as the phone rang again.

She was annoyed at the interruption. "She Crab, how can I help you?"

"Alisheen, this is Carl. It's always a pleasure to hear your cheerful voice," he said with humor and a light touch of sarcasm.

"Oh, Carl, I'm sorry! I was on the phone with a vendor, and he wasn't too cooperative so I'm a little grumpy."

She surprised herself with the ease of the lie. She wasn't accustomed to telling fibs, but lately, it seemed to be a habit.

"I was hoping we could have dinner tonight?"

"Carl, I'm going to meet with Spencer this afternoon, and I don't know what's going to happen. Besides, I thought you agreed to give me time and space to figure out things."

"I did, so I'm just making sure you knew I was around. I was really calling to ask you to go with me as a friend," he said with emphasis, "to the Charity Ball next weekend. I hate going alone, with all of those gorgeous women following me around all night, hoping to catch a rich husband. It's so boring."

"Poor fellow, what will you do?" Alisheen said with a laugh. "I really wish I could answer you right now, but I need to talk with Spencer first. I'm not on firm ground anymore, and I need the time."

"I understand," Carl said. "I enjoyed our time together."

"I did too, Carl."

"Goodbye, Alisheen, if you change your mind and want to go that'd be great. I'm not going to call anyone else so the invitation will stand."

"Bye, Carl," she said.

She bit her lip apprehensively and looked up to find Emily standing in the doorway.

"Emily, what am I going to do?"

"I don't know, Alisheen, but you must stay away from Carl if he really is trouble."

"I know, it just seems so unreal. I'm getting the hell out of here before anyone else calls, and I won't be back."

"Where are you going?" asked Emily.

"I'm going to meet Spencer this afternoon, and I need to get my act together. I'm so crazy right now I can't think straight."

Mickey appeared in the doorway of the office with a funny look on his face but didn't say anything. Emily and Alisheen both looked at him with questioning looks, waiting for him to tell them what was so funny.

Alisheen, exasperated, said, "Are you going to tell us what's so funny?"

"I was wondering if you needed a bottle of Tequila this afternoon!"

She turned red remembering Mickey's advice at the bar, and Emily shrieked at him, "Get out! You are an idiot."

Mickey laughed and Alisheen stuck her tongue out at him, gave him the finger, and stood up. "I'm outta here."

"Good luck," they said together.

A.J. was scared and knew his life was hanging in the balance, but he'd waited a long time for his revenge for what Powers had done to him and the humiliation he'd endured his entire adult life. He often wondered how different things might've been if he hadn't fallen into his hands.

*"Screw it. All he could do was kill him, and that'd be a relief. My life isn't worth crap anyway."*

He looked at the card Fitzgerald had given him in the bar. The number was a local number, so he figured they were watching him. That didn't make him feel safer, but at least he had a better chance of staying alive. He picked up his cell and Fitzgerald answered after one ring. He'd been expecting Bo's call and answered with aggravation.

"It's about damn time. What in the hell took you so long?"

A.J. was nervous and the gruffness of Skip's voice made matters worse. He almost hung up.

He stammered, "I, I, didn't know you were waiting for me to call."

Skip was shocked realizing it was Guilford.

"A.J., is that you? Are you alright?"

"Yeah, it's me."

His voice sounded more in control but still very much on edge.

"I decided to give you a call."

"A.J., I got people close by. You're under surveillance. You can come in if you want, and you can tell the whole story."

"I figured you were watching me. I called to tell you there might be a good chance to bust the Snowman Monday night. There's a shipment coming in. I'm supposed to help pick it up. He's supposed to be there to handle the money part of the deal."

Skip hadn't anticipated this. They had to follow A.J. to protect him. The thought occurred to him it could be a set-up.

"A.J., did it cross your mind that this could be a trap?"

"Yeah, I thought of that which is why I was hoping you were watching me. You just catch the bastard, and I'll have my satisfaction."

"OK, A.J., what's the plan?"

"Baxter will pick me up Monday after work at my house, and then we're going to drive out to a small farm off Springer Road. It's a county road toward the Carolina state line. The farm belongs to a man named Fenster. We've used it as a drop before, and Fenster gets paid big bucks to stay out of the way."

"OK, I got it. We'll cover you all the way," Skip said. He was quiet for a minute and then said, "A.J., is Carl Powers the Snowman?"

A.J. didn't answer, but Skip heard his breathing quicken.

"We know what happened in college, A.J."

A.J. hung up.

~~~~

Jeanette LaCrosse returned to the office full of joy with thoughts of Carl looking at her with desire. She'd found the perfect dress and accessories for the Charity Ball and was glad to see he was in the office. She was happier than she'd been in a long time now that her plans were under way. She'd make the other women jealous with Carl on her arm, and she was going to show him that she was just as desirable and alluring as any of those other women. She hoped it wouldn't get ugly and she wouldn't have to use the information she had to force Carl into it. It was in his best interest anyway.

"Silly man, I'm the best thing that could happen to him and he doesn't even know it yet." She breezed into his office unannounced, closing the door behind her as she waltzed in with the new dress in the bag over her arm. She sat down in front of his desk, crossing her legs demurely, making sure her high heel was visible to accentuate the sexy look of her leg.

Powers watched her enter and sit without expression and didn't speak. Jeanette wasn't about to play a waiting game now, so she opened the conversation.

"Good afternoon, Carl. I hope you don't mind, but the gorgeous spring morning got to me, and I had to get out and do some shopping."

"So, I found out from what's her name out there. I'm surprised. I've never known you to be taken by a beautiful day and feel the urge to shop."

"Oh, Carl, don't be silly. Everybody gets spring fever, even me. There's a lot about me you don't know, but I hope to rectify that soon. Her name is Jennifer by the way."

With impatience Carl said, "What do you want? I'm busy."

Jeanette's mood darkened briefly then brightened again.

"The invitation to the Savannah Treasury Charity Ball came in the mail today. I was so excited I opened it, and then I had to go and buy a new dress for the occasion. I wanted to show it to you that's all. After all, I want to look my absolute best that night."

Without waiting for an answer, she stood and unzipped the clothes bag, revealing the short black beaded sheath she'd bought.

"Isn't it fabulous?" she said excitedly.

"Yes, it's very nice. I didn't realize you were going to the Ball. Who're you going with?"

"Well, Carl dear, I assumed you and I would go together since we'd agreed to make some changes in our relationship."

Powers spoke to her in a dangerous tone.

"I'm not taking you to the Ball, Miss LaCrosse," he said with the emphasis on the Miss. "I've already made plans and our agreement didn't include a date."

Her face instantly drained of emotion, and her tone matched his.

"You'd better be careful, Mr. Powers. I know things about you that could turn out to be quite embarrassing if it got out."

She zipped up the clothes bag and sat down. They stared at each other across the desk.

"Well, it's all on the table now, isn't it? I play by your rules, or you make a vain attempt to destroy me. I'm surprised at you, Jeanette. You're usually so prepared, but you've obviously miscalculated this time. Any attempt to blackmail me into doing as you see fit will be no match for the wealth and influence I can bring to bear on you! I could fire you today, and you wouldn't be able to get a job mopping floors in this town."

"Anything you say would be a lie, something made up to get back at me. You could also be just as guilty as I am of whatever you think you know. You are the COO now, and you've been working here for years. How could you not have known what was going on? You drive a nice car, have a nice house with a pool, and buy expensive clothes. Who is to say you haven't been in on things from the beginning?

"No, Jeanette, I can erase you from this company and this town with a single stroke of the pen, a word to a few friends, and a whisper of rumor to the press. Without me, there is no Coastal Seafood. You don't have what it takes to make the connections to run a successful business. I built Coastal Seafood. You've been useful, but you can be replaced."

The anger was apparent on her face as Jeanette stood. She was now truly a woman scorned, and she looked at Powers with hate in her eyes.

With venom in her voice she said, "Don't underestimate me, Carl. I know all about your activities, and you're wrong about many things. I'll do whatever it takes for us to be together, and I won't let anyone, or anything stand in the way."

She walked toward the door, paused, and looked back at him.

"I'll kill her if I have to."

Powers said, "Not if I kill you first."

With calm defiance she said, "Please be on time Friday night and use the limo. I don't want to risk getting my hair ruined in the Jag."

She turned and opened the door to the outer office. In a bright and cheery voice she said, "See you later, Mr. Powers."

~~~~

Alisheen shopped all morning, buying new clothes and other things she needed before grabbing lunch and going home. She took a quick shower and putting on some fresh make-up brightened her mood. She changed clothes several times before deciding on an old pair of jeans and a new top she'd bought that morning. She didn't want to appear too anxious. After all, she was still mad at him, and he needed to apologize for being an asshole. She did a last-minute check in the full-length mirror, glanced at her wristwatch, and grabbed her purse as she went out the door.

Driving the short distance to the park, she thought about what she was going to say to him and what she hoped he'd say to her. She walked down the shaded path to the large fountain in the middle of the park. It was a pretty spot. The spring flowers were beginning to bloom, and the spray from the fountain carried by the light breeze drifted onto her face as she walked around it. She sat on a bench that looked at the river and waited for Spencer, closing her eyes to listen to the sounds around her and to feel the warm sun on her face.

"Excuse me, ma'am, but you're so beautiful sitting there that you take my breath away."

Alisheen's eyes flew open with surprise, and she laughed brightly. Spencer stood there looking sheepish with a wry grin on his face. He sat on the opposite end of the bench, averting his eyes, looking at the river.

"You do look great, Al. I was hoping to get here before you, so I'd be waiting on you for a change. I hope you haven't been here too long."

"No," she said not looking directly at him either. "I just got here and I'm early, so you're on time and even a bit early yourself. It's nice to see you, too, by the way."

Spencer reddened, and they both shifted uneasily on the bench like school kids on a date.

He said, "Alisheen, I'm sorry about what happened, and I've been doing some thinking."

Spencer paused and grinned, "Sounds like a movie, doesn't it?"

"Yes, it does, but it doesn't matter and I'm listening. Go on." urged Alisheen with a hint of anxiety.

"OK, well anyway, I had a talk with someone who made sense to me, and it got me thinking about things that I guess, in the back of my mind, were always there to hinder my relationship with you. So, I want to tell you where I've been coming from on this marriage thing we keep fighting about."

"That's wonderful, Spencer, but I'm not sure I like the way you phrased our problem as a marriage thing."

Spencer made a bad attempt at a smile.

"Yeah, I guess that didn't come out the way I meant it too, but anyway, you know what I mean."

Spencer continued before he lost his nerve.

"It goes back to when I was a little kid."

"Spencer, I don't understand," interrupted Alisheen. "Your mother is perfectly lovely and obviously adores you. You had a good loving home. What is the big deep dark secret?" asked Alisheen with a plea and a sense of frustration.

She grabbed Spencer's hand and held it tight.

"I'll tell you if you hush and quit interrupting," Spencer said with growing tension in his voice. "This is very hard for me, and I've never told anyone the whole story except for …" Spencer paused.

"Who did you tell?"

"Dixie," Spencer blurted out.

Alisheen reacted immediately and pulled her hand away.

"Good grief, Spencer! You can tell someone like Dixie this deep dark secret, and yet you couldn't tell me?"

Alisheen was incredulous and angry at the same time.

"I guess I know where I stand now!"

"No, Alisheen, listen to me. You don't understand," pleaded Spencer. "I was in the diner, thinking about you and everything that's happened, and Dixie came over and sat down and started talking to me about you. I know it sounds crazy, but he just started talking, and before I knew it, I was telling him things I've suppressed for years. Fears, shame, blame, and all sorts of things just came out. Did you know he has a Ph.D. in Psychology and used to be in practice?"

"No, I didn't," said Alisheen holding back tears.

"So, he got you to pour your heart out. Is that what you're saying to me? That Dixie was able to get you to confide in him?"

Alisheen leaned forward and put her elbows on her knees and her face in her hands. Spencer got up and paced, then turned and looked at her.

"Alisheen, this isn't coming out or going the way I'd planned. Everything is getting all twisted and confused and you're not helping any."

She looked up and fired back, "Well, excuse the hell out of me, Spencer Baldwin. I've been your girlfriend and lover for over five years, and I've been trying to get you to trust me and tell me why you're having trouble dealing with a commitment to me. Now I find out that Dixie of all people has analyzed and convinced you, in the course of a meal, that you need to open up and share your feelings with me. I just find it a little hard to take that's all."

Spencer sat back down on the bench. He put his arms around her and hugged her. She didn't resist and slumped into him putting her head on his chest.

"I'm sorry, Alisheen," he said into her hair. It smelled wonderful, and the softness of her body and the scent of her perfume assaulted him, and he knew he loved her so he hugged her tighter. She sniffed and lifted her head, then wiped her face with a Kleenex from her purse.

She smiled wanly. "I guess maybe I should be thankful he convinced you to tell me anyway. Who knew? I never knew he was a doctor."

They both chuckled and their moods lifted slightly. They sat close together for a while longer, and then Alisheen sat up straight, separating herself from his arms and cleared her throat.

"OK, I think I've recovered enough from that shock enough to get to the next one. What happened in your childhood?"

Spencer hung his head in shame, and Alisheen touched his arm in assurance.

"Well, you know my Dad died when I was young," he paused. "I've never gotten over the void it left in my life and after my analysis," he said sheepishly, "I'm sure it affected me in more ways than one. I knew for sure one reason I didn't want to get married, but there are some other issues I also need to deal with to make it all work out."

"Spencer, enough already, what is it?"

"I was … am afraid, that if we get married and have children that I might get killed in the line of duty, and my children would be without a father. I hated him for leaving us, and I've suffered with that feeling for a long time. I've tried to reconcile these feelings, but I just can't get over it. Don't get me wrong! Mom did a great job, but I missed and needed my Dad. He wasn't there for me, and I never forgave him. I don't want that to happen to any children of mine. I don't want to be remembered for leaving them. I'd rather be remembered for something else."

Alisheen looked at him with a mix of sadness, anger, and disbelief, and spoke to him with a firm tone.

"I'm not sure what to say, Spencer. My first thought is to be mad as hell. It's so simple we could've worked it out a long time ago. I'd never let any child of ours brood over your death and your mother didn't let you either, and shame on you for even suggesting such a thing. She gave you the best and always reminded you of the good things your father did and what kind of a man he was. Look at you! You're a successful, honest, and decent man!"

Alisheen raised her voice in frustration and anger.

"All the times I've sweated blood and cried tears over your work and worrying if you were going to come home or not! You didn't think about how I'd feel if you were killed? I cringe every time the phone rings, thinking its Meadors or somebody else to tell me something's happened, and you're worried about a child we don't even have?"

Spencer was angry and stood up.

"Alisheen, I'm trying to give you the reasons for the way I am, not excuses, and you know damn good and well that I love you and worry about you. I didn't know what to think when I saw you in that skinny bathing suit with Carl Powers of all people."

She flinched, but Spencer didn't notice.

"And while I'm at it, you owe me an explanation!"

"For what?" yelled Alisheen, standing.

"For what?" Spencer said with disbelief. "How about you just taking off and going to New York and doing who knows what, and with someone you supposedly didn't know very well. What were you two doing together all that time? I doubt seriously it was just a sight-seeing tour. Come on, Alisheen, I'm not that big a fool."

That was all Alisheen could stand. She slapped him and screamed, "How dare you?"

Spencer was stunned. His emotions instantly drained. Alisheen stood there angry and sobbing. Her breath coming in short heaves.

The pain of Spencer's words, the guilt she'd been dealing with, and the reality of the physical act she'd just committed overwhelmed her, and she cried out, "I'm sorry, Spencer, for the both of us," and she ran away.

Spencer watched her leave then slumped down on the bench, putting his head in his hands and crying quietly, oblivious to the stares of the on-lookers that had witnessed it.

"I'm sorry too, Alisheen."

# Chapter 17

ARRIVING AT THE Corner Mart where he'd arranged to meet Vernon, Ian cursed as he viewed his condition. Vernon was leaning against the store wall, smoking a cigarette, and a bit drunk. He drove past the store into the adjacent parking lot of a closed strip mall. Vernon casually walked over and caught up to Ian as he walked down the sidewalk feigning window-shopping.

"Anything wrong?"

"I'd kill your useless ass right now if it wasn't daylight, you drunken fool," Ian hissed.

"I'm not drunk. I've just had a couple of beers, that's all," Vernon pleaded nervously.

"Listen to me, you stupid redneck, you'd better show up sober at the warehouse on Monday. Be there by 5:30 or else. You'd better not cross me, Vernon, or I'll gut you like a fish and watch you bleed to death on the floor. You understand me?"

Ian slapped him with the back of his hand, splitting his lip and bruising his cheek. Vernon reeled against the shop window grabbing his cheek as blood trickled down his chin.

Cringing with fear in his eyes and hate in his heart, Vernon whined, "I'll be there, I swear, but remember, you promised me this was the last time, and I can get out of here after this."

Ian sneered. "I remember. Just don't screw this up or your name will be dropped to Vincent, and you'll be dead before the sun rises."

Vernon's head shrunk into his body like a turtle in danger, and he retreated from Ian and walked back across the parking lot to the Corner Mart. He went inside wiping the blood from his mouth, bought another beer, and walked off down the street in the other direction. Ian looked around and was satisfied that no one had witnessed the exchange. He got into the car and sped off. He wanted to scout the terrain at the farm during the night.

~~~~

Skip went into high gear the minute A.J. hung up, calling everybody he could think of but no one answered the phone. Frustrated, he went to the police station and paced the floor until Meadors walked in.

"Where in the hell is everybody? We got a crisis on our hands, and no one is working!"

He was almost yelling now.

"Find them, every damn one of them, and get their butts in here, now!"

Meadors didn't ask any questions. He jumped on the phone and the radio and began to assemble the task force. Skip called Bo again.

"It's about damn time," Skip said when Bo finally answered.

"Get your butt down to the police station and pull everyone in except the people that are watching Guilford. Double up on him and be extra careful that they don't lose them," then, without saying good bye, he hung up.

Meadors looked at Fitzgerald. "Everyone is on the way in. The only one I can't find is Spencer."

"Son-of-a-bitch," Skip said. "OK, we'll just have to catch him up later. I need a detailed map of the county that shows every dirt road in it. I'm going to go talk to the Captain. Keep trying to find Spencer, and then find someone to be sure we got food and drink for a long session. We got a long night."

Meadors nodded his head. "What's going on?"

"I hope we can save a man's life."

~~~~

Alisheen ran back to the car with everything in a blur. She reached the car, fumbled the keys into the lock, and slammed the door. She beat the steering wheel with fury and screamed then backed out of the space quickly without looking and almost wrecked. She hit the brakes hard, and the jolt brought her emotions in check enough to realize she needed to be careful. On the way back to the loft she was dazed and confused, and she wondered what in the hell had gone wrong. It wasn't supposed to have gone like that. She arrived home with sorrow and anger boiling inside her.

She went inside and locked the door in an effort to lock the world out of her life. She climbed into bed and arranged the pillows and covers in the best imitation of a hug she could manage and begin to cry from her broken heart. Exhausted, she finally dropped off into a deep sleep.

~~~~

Most of the group had arrived and seated themselves by the time Carol walked in and sat down.

Fitzgerald stopped pacing and said, "Where in the hell is Spencer?"

Carol, surprised by the terseness of the question, replied in an even tone.

"I don't have the slightest idea. I haven't seen him since early this morning."

He shook his head with frustration and continued to pace. He looked up expectantly when Meadors walked in, but the negative nod increased the anxiety in the room. Skip glanced at his watch then went to the board and uncapped a marker.

"I can't wait any longer. We're going to lose A.J. Guilford and the best chance we have of confirming what we think we know already that Carl Powers is the Snowman. He called me today and described an exchange that will take place on Monday night. We can't afford not to be there and pass up a chance to identify the Snowman on our own. On the other hand, it's probably a trap designed to identify A.J. as an informer. If we're within twenty miles of the place, he'll be a target for sure if he's not already. We need to decide what to do. I'm open to suggestions."

The room was quiet, and everyone shuffled papers and checked pens and pencils, acting like children in a classroom afraid that the teacher might call on one of them to go to the board. Skip capped the marker and put it down.

"Somebody want to tell me what's going on?"

Meadors spoke up.

"I don't think anyone is interested in doing much planning without Spencer here. He is the lead investigator."

Skip placed the marker back into the tray and then sat down at the head of the table.

"I wish things were different but they're not. I need Spencer here because I know the plan would be better with his input. I appreciate your loyalty to Spencer; however, unless you can find him, we have to go ahead without him because a man's life is at stake and this investigation is at risk. We must work together."

Skip picked up the marker.

"Now, anybody got any ideas?"

Looks were exchanged, heads nodded, and hands went up. Skip pointed at Cooper.

"OK, what you got?"

~~~~

Chambers followed the directions and found Harper's Ferry Park without trouble. It was deserted except for the elderly group wearing binoculars around their necks, peering at the treetops and exclaiming every once in a while, for the group to look in a particular direction. Chambers pulled his coat around him against the cool breeze and spotted the head of the trail.

Soon, he saw Saul sitting on a bench with his eyes closed as if he was sleeping. His eyes opened as he approached, and he stood up, turned, and walked down the path slowly to let him catch up. When he got close, Saul spoke.

"Let's keep walking and enjoy nature. I need the exercise anyway."

Saul pulled a pack of cigarettes out of his pocket and lit one.

He inhaled deeply, coughed, and laughed. "I love the fresh air, makes me feel better."

Chambers laughed nervously at the bad joke.

"What's the scoop, Clifton? That joke always gets a sarcastic comment, and you barely blinked an eye. What in the hell is going on?"

"Are you taping me?" asked Chambers nervously.

"No, but I'm prepared to tape it if you want me to … this sounds serious, Clifton. What's going on?" Saul asked with concern.

"I really can't tell you, but I need you to do me a favor."

"Wait a damn minute. I drove all of the way out here for a secret meeting, and you can't tell me anything, and you ask me for a favor? This sounds like its illegal Clifton. I don't want to end up in jail."

"I don't think jail is what you need to worry about, Saul," Clifton said evenly, and he stopped walking and faced him. "I need you for insurance to keep me alive in case something goes terribly wrong." Chambers held up a small gold key ring with a single shiny gold key. "If I end up dead, you go to the bank and open my safe deposit box. You'll have to sign this signature card in my pocket so you can have access without going to the police because you won't know whom to trust. That's all I can tell you."

"Bullshit!" said Levy. "I'm not going to risk my life for a secret I don't know about. You're out of your mind."

Chambers grabbed his arm with force.

"Damn it, Saul, listen to me. If they think you know what I know, you can end up dead."

Saul shot back.

"It sounds like I can be killed just because we've talked. They won't know if you told me anything or not, so I'm taking a risk either way."

They stood there looking hard at each other and finally Chambers said, "You're probably right, but you'll have to trust me on this."

They began walking again.

"You have to give me something. I just can't do it otherwise."

Chambers finally said, "A new policy that will deal specifically with the drug cartels is about to be implemented."

Saul stopped and lit another cigarette as he mulled over the information with obvious intensity. He resumed walking and put his hand out. "You'd better give me that key and let me sign the card."

He accepted the key, signed the card, and handed it back to Chambers. They continued walking while Clifton gave Saul the bare bones of the plan. They stopped at the end of the trail short of the parking lot.

Saul said, "This is absolutely crazy. You're talking about the United States government attempting to manage the drug trade through a deal that is undoubtedly illegal and dangerous to boot."

The fact that Chambers didn't deny it was enough to convince Levy he was right.

Clifton said, "Saul, I'll admit that this new policy is very radical, but it just might work. If it goes bad, however, I don't want to be a statistical suicide when the tracks get covered up."

"I can't believe you think this is going to work, Clifton. I can't believe I'm agreeing to be your insurance policy! I'm as crazy as the rest of you and now, damn it, just as guilty as the rest of you. I need a drink!"

"Get some more fresh air, Saul," said Chambers with a genuine laugh as he walked back toward the parking lot.

Saul watched Clifton drive away then sat on a bench, reached into his pocket for cigarettes and a light, and felt the key chain. He fingered the key for a moment and with a sigh, pulled out the pack and lighter. He shook one out, lit it and returned them back to his pocket once again feeling the key.

"Son-of-a-bitch!"

~~~~

"I think we should get a wire on him somehow, and then we can monitor the drop," said Cooper.

"That won't work," said Meadors. "They'll search him especially if it's a set-up."

"There's no way to get to him either," Skip said.

"What if you go in as a sales type on Monday morning? Whoever is watching him doesn't know us by sight," said Jack.

"That's not a bad idea," said Meadors, "but wired or not, we'd still have to be close enough to cover him and not be spotted."

"We're talking about being out on a farm. A large group of people would be noticed," countered Fitzgerald.

"Not a swat team that could hike in and stake out from surrounding cover," said Meadors. "Our swat team has done it before on this farm in particular on a drug bust. They scared the hell out of them looking like James

Bond ninjas coming out of the ground. It was over before they could react. It was a good bust too."

"Maybe that's why they chose it," said Bridges. "They know the area and how you covered it last time."

"Too risky," said Skip.

"Not necessarily," countered Meadors, "not if it's a small team—five, six guys tops. They could hike in and set-up before dark, way before the supposed meeting time. We got some very good ex-recon types who could get in there without being seen and be ready to deal with any situation that develops."

"I don't like it, but it's a better option than trying to cover him with a wire," said Skip. "We'd need back-up to block roads out of the area if necessary. There are only a couple roads in and out. Unless somebody objects or has a better idea, we'll cover it with a small team. I only hope Spencer shows soon. We need his input. Let's get the team picked and up here ASAP so we can get the plan together. Meadors, I'll depend on you to command the team. Are there any questions?"

Cooper's hand went up, and the eyes in the room turned to look at him. "Yes?"

"To be honest, I'm not exactly sure what we're supposed to do. I understand we're trying to keep Guilford alive, but what if the information is real, and it is a drug drop. If the Snowman is there, are we supposed to make an arrest?"

Skip said, "We let it go down and make no arrest regardless of who is there. Our only job will be to protect Guilford."

~~~~

Spencer sat on the bench for a long time before driving to the beach. He walked down the beach and stopped at the dunes where they'd last made love. With sadness, he sat on the sand and watched the waves, ignoring the time. It was after ten when Spencer finally got back to his apartment. He'd driven around for a while, resisting the temptation to go to Alisheen's loft and try to talk to her. The machine was blinking frantically with multiple messages and his cell phone was on the kitchen counter. He realized he'd better find out what in the hell was going on. He still had a job to do. He grabbed a beer from the fridge and sat down on the couch hitting the play button.

He heard Carol's voice filled with urgency, "Spencer, where are you? You're not answering your phone. We have an emergency. A.J. phoned Skip about a drug drop Monday night, and we have to try to cover him. We need you here ASAP!"

He put the unopened beer on the table, picked up his keys, and headed for the station.

Carol, Skip, and Meadors were sitting in the office when Spencer walked in.

Skip smiled grimly. "I'm glad you're here."

Spencer looked at him and said, "This doesn't change how I feel about things you know."

"I know, but we can worry about that later if he lives."

Skip began to explain the details of the current plan to Spencer as he looked at the map.

"Where is A.J. now?"

"He's at home."

Spencer was quiet and continued to study the map.

"A swat team in early is a good move, especially if someone is watching to see if we show up. We could grab A.J. after the bust and hide him away."

Skip looked around the room. "Guys, will you give us some privacy so Spencer and I can discuss this some more?"

They filed out with suspicion on their faces looking at Fitzgerald. He closed the door behind them.

"Spencer, what are you thinking? If the Snowman is there and we bust him, Henry will have your ass and mine too for not stopping you. I know their plan is crazy, but we have to follow orders. Our careers are at stake here."

"Skip, I have two choices. One is to follow orders and ignore the law. The other is to figure out how to circumvent those orders without making an arrest. I figure it this way. If I can get Guilford to sing loud and long, even if we don't arrest Powers, his reputation will suffer. He'll be soiled goods. No drug dealer will trust him again."

Skip said, "You might be on the right track, but let's compromise. I won't stand in your way if you can convince A.J. to finger Powers on his own. However, if we positively identify Powers as the Snowman, he's mine and I give him to Henry. That way we follow the rules, make no arrest, our careers survive, and Powers goes down either way. Powers will be out of business or under Henry's thumb. Either way it won't be pleasant for him."

Skip extended his hand and Spencer shook it.

"You got a deal."

~~~~

It was dark by the time Saul got back to his office, but the newspaper never sleeps, and people were working to get things wrapped up for Saturday morning's edition. Opening his desk drawer, he pulled out a large set of keys that went to a variety of doors and files. Except for the new finish, the key didn't look too different from the rest. He shrugged his shoulders, took the key off the gold ring, and placed it on the larger ring with the others. He held it in the air and shook them, the key blended in nicely. Happy with himself, he placed the key ring back in the drawer.

He lit a cigarette, opened another drawer, and pulled out a half-empty bottle of scotch. He found a paper cup with some dregs of coffee in it, dumped it out into the trashcan, and using an old napkin, wiped it out. He poured the cup half full, took a large drink, and a drag off the cigarette. He turned on the computer, paused, and looked at the Memorials outside the window, worrying about what Clifton had told him and the repercussions of an action like this. He wondered if it went as high as the White House. He cursed and began to write his column for the morning edition.

Alisheen woke-up with a migraine, rolled over, and looked at the ceiling. Then she turned her head toward the window avoiding looking at the alarm clock on purpose, but her bladder dictated, and she went to the bathroom. She put her robe on over her naked body and went to the window pulling the curtains back. It was dark, but not as late as she'd guessed.

"*Damn*," she thought. She'd better call the restaurant and let Emily know what was going on. She sat on the bed and dialed. Emily answered the phone with a pleasant voice.

"She Crab Restaurant, may I help you? This is Emily speaking."

"Emily, this is Alisheen."

Emily asked in a rush of words, "Alisheen, are you OK? You don't sound too good. Are you with Spencer?"

"No, no I'm not. Things didn't go too well this afternoon. I'm at home, and I don't feel well so I'll see you tomorrow."

"Alisheen, what happened?" Emily asked, worried.

"I'm OK, don't worry. I just have a migraine. I'll call you tomorrow."

She hung up before Emily could ask any more questions. Alisheen went into the kitchen, decided she was hungry, and pulled a frozen pizza from the freezer. There was the better half of a bottle of wine in the fridge and she poured a glass. She sipped the wine and absent-mindedly walked around the apartment.

The timer dinged on the oven signaling it was ready. She turned off the oven and took the pizza out, leaving it on the stovetop to cool. She picked up the wine glass in one hand, the bottle with the other, and went onto the deck. She sat in the rocker, pulled her knees up to her chin, and watched a freighter as it headed out to sea.

Alisheen finished the wine in a quick couple of gulps and poured another. She put her head back and closed her eyes; the memories of the day clouded her mind. She cried softly and then sobbed deeply with her heart broken. She was angry and considered finding that bastard and shooting him. She smiled and laughed as a mental picture of her standing in front of Spencer and threatening to shoot him came to her mind. She was startled from her thoughts by the phone.

The machine picked up after five rings, and she heard the machine play the message and the beep. The voice on the machine caused her to catch her breath.

"Alisheen, this is Carl. I tried the restaurant, but Emily said you were ill. I hope you're OK and feeling better soon. I called to see if you've changed your mind about going with me to the Ball next Friday. I know I said I'd leave you alone, but I wish you'd reconsider. Hope you feel better soon. Bye."

She sat in a daze and pursed her lips.

"I guess that option is the best thing I have going now."

She drained the wine glass again, filled it, and went to the kitchen to throw the now empty bottle in the trash and eat some of the pizza. She cut it into slices with vengeance, ate standing, and washed it down with the last of the wine. She went back into the bedroom, opened the sliding door, and let the breeze blow in. She turned on the ceiling fan, dropped the robe to the floor, and got into bed. The cool sheets and the breeze from the fan felt good on her nude body and face. She closed her eyes, and remembering it all over again, began to cry.

Now that Spencer and Skip seemed to have reached a truce, the energy in the room reached a new level, and it carried them through the night and into the early morning.

"Man, I could use some coffee," yawned Fitzgerald. Spencer nodded in agreement and said, "Let's go see if Eddie's Coffee Wagon is here yet. We might be in luck."

Fitzgerald followed Spencer and soon they were on the street and approaching a small coffee wagon. Eddie served them the "best damn coffee in Savannah" and a still warm pastry from his wife's oven. They chatted with him for a few minutes and got a free refill before going back inside.

Back in Spencer's office Fitzgerald said, "What's next?"

"We wait out the weekend and get back together on Monday as usual. Then we cover A.J. and hope for the best."

Fitzgerald yawned again. "In that case, I'm going to the hotel and get some sleep. I have a feeling we're going to need it."

He finished his coffee and dropped the cup into the trashcan.

"I'll see you Monday."

"Bright and early," said Spencer.

Fitzgerald arrived back at the hotel and promptly went to bed. He woke late in the day and decided to review the preparations they'd made for Monday night. He was hungry and ordered room service. The food arrived after about a thirty-minute wait, but it was hot and tasty for hotel food. He ate and worked, trying to put his finger on what was missing. He took a bathroom break, tried to call Carol, but got no answer. He resumed working and diagramed the connections of everybody in the case on paper. He finished it and began to write notes under it all. He checked his watch; it was after five. He stood up and stretched and walked around the room then came back to the desk. He stood over the desk and looking down saw it for the first time.

"*Holy smoke.* How did we miss this?"

~~~~

Alisheen spent Saturday in bed. The hurt she felt and the quick turn of the conversation that led to accusations and ending with the slap had put her into shock. Her emotions spent, she called Emily.

Emily answered with her usual cheerful voice and then asked quickly when she heard Alisheen's voice, "Are you alright?"

"No, not really. I could use a friend. Are you available?"

"I'll be there in an hour."

Alisheen hung up and curled back up on the bed. She felt better having talked to a friendly voice she knew she could count on. Soon there was a knock on the door and Alisheen answered it. She looked through the peephole and was relieved to see Emily standing there with a large grocery bag and Chinese takeout.

She opened the door and before she could speak, Emily pushed through the door and went to the kitchen. Alisheen had barely managed to close the door and turn around before Emily was back, guiding her to the bedroom and sitting her on the bed. She hung her head while Emily stood in front of her like a mother getting ready to lecture her child.

"Now Alisheen, I don't know what the hell is going on, but we're going to get to the bottom of it together. I want you to take a shower. You look terrible. We'll eat and have a beer while I listen to the whole, and I mean the whole story. Then we're going to eat an entire quart of double chocolate chip ice cream, and you're going to sleep at my place tonight."

Alisheen lifted her head and looked at Emily.

Tears were streaming down her face and almost yelling at Emily, she said, "It's over, Emily. It's over and it's all my fault!"

Emily grabbed her by the shoulders.

"Alisheen, we'll talk about this later but first things first."

She pulled her off the bed, got behind her, and pushed her toward the bathroom. She sat her down on the small chair in the corner and reaching into the shower started the water.

She pulled her up and said, "I love you dear, but I'm not taking a shower with you. I'll be in the kitchen when you're done."

Her face wet from tears, Alisheen hugged Emily with a half laugh, half sob and said, "I love you too."

Emily exited as Alisheen got into the shower and went into the kitchen. She put a couple of beers in the freezer to get them cold faster and found the dishes and silverware. She set the table, put the food in the microwave to heat it back up, and opened a beer. She leaned against the counter. "Girl, what in the hell has happened to you?"

~~~~

Alisheen woke up in a nightgown she didn't recognize in a room that was bright with sunshine even through the closed blinds. The light filtered around them and filled the room. She was comfortable and didn't want to get up. She surveyed the room and remembered the night before. She'd eaten Chinese with Emily and cried for a long time after she told the story of the scene in the park. She remembered Emily saying that it wasn't her fault even though she raised her hand to cover her mouth when she told Emily she'd slapped Spencer.

Alisheen rolled over onto her side, flipped the covers off, went to the bathroom, and got back into the bed. As she was making herself comfortable, Emily knocked on the door and entered with a smile. She was carrying a glass of orange juice and a cup of coffee.

"Good morning, sleepyhead. I heard the bathroom and figured you were at least awake. Want some juice and coffee?"

Alisheen nodded in the affirmative and sat up. Emily placed the juice and coffee on the side table and left the room. She returned with another cup of coffee and a muffin on a plate. She handed Alisheen a napkin and the muffin then sat down on the edge of the bed.

"How are you feeling this morning?"

"Let's review," said Alisheen. "I've ruined a relationship I've invested several years in. My boyfriend helped ruin that relationship by confessing his deepest fears to Dixie of all people. I slapped said boyfriend so hard that he probably has to sip his meals through a straw. I haven't worked for days. I'm in a strange bed in a borrowed nightgown, although both are very comfortable, thank you, and the events I have just described to you are reality and not a bad dream. So that's how I'm feeling."

Emily with a wry grin said, "Well, at least you still have your health. Drink up, we got stuff to do today."

"Like what?" Alisheen asked surprised.

"Stuff, so get your butt moving and get dressed."

Emily left the room. Alisheen finished her muffin, drank her juice, and took her coffee into the bathroom as she got ready to take a shower. After she wrapped her hair in a towel, she looked at herself in the mirror.

"OK, Alisheen Delaney, it's time to get your act together."

~~~~

Carl had gone to the plantation for the weekend to figure out what to do about Jeanette. He couldn't just have her killed. For her to go missing now, after being named the COO of Coastal, would be big news, and he admitted it was a bit of genius on her part. Ian was going to have to arrange an accident to get her out of the way. It was definitely a smart move.

Carl passed through the den, went out onto the patio, and looked at the sky. It was a gorgeous day, and he decided to go fishing. He kept a boat at the marina where they maintained it for him. He hadn't fished in a while and rumor had it that the Spanish mackerel were starting their spring run. He went into the house, changed clothes, and found Rupert in the kitchen.

"Annie will be here this afternoon to fix you some supper."

Powers shook his head.

"Call her and tell her not to bother, Rupert. I've decided to go fishing this afternoon. I don't know when I'll get back. Do you want to go?"

"Oh no, sir, I've some things to do here and there ain't no one to tend to the dogs. So I'll just watch television and make sure they're fed."

Carl smiled, "Well suit yourself, but I got a feeling the mackerel are running. It might be a busy afternoon."

"Yes, sir," said Rupert. "I heard in town that it might have started, but I'll just stay here. I think it's too early yet for them to be running this close to shore. They're still way out past the first buoy of the river. If you catch some though bring'em here straight away and I'll get to cleaning them and putting them in the freezer while you go back to the marina."

Carl grabbed the keys to the old Jeep he kept for trips like this off the key rack by the door and headed for the marina. He bypassed the store and went to the boat first. The owner came out shortly after he spotted Powers walking down the secured section of the pier.

"Can I help you, sir?" he asked a little bit leery.

"How about some bait to catch mackerel, Hank?" said Powers, turning around with a grin.

"Hey, Mr. Powers, long time no see," exclaimed Hank. "Mackerel huh?"

"Yeah, Hank, I hear they're running out by the jetty. My boat ready?"

"Yes, sir," said Hank. "I just ran it the other day. The battery is good, and I just tuned the outboards last week. Lights, radio and radar are working, and all the other electronics cued up like they were supposed to. Oh, I also changed the zincs last month. All you need is gas. Your rods and stuff are in the storage shed, and I can fix you a cooler of drinks and some snacks if you want while you get your stuff."

"That will be nice of you, Hank. Thanks. By the way, is this going to be a wasted trip or are they running? You never did answer me."

"Yeah, they're running. Most of the scuttlebutt says small silver spoons, with a slow shallow troll. And you heard right. They're out by the jetty."

"Excellent," said Carl. "I'll get my gear and meet you at the gas dock."

As Carl approached the fuel dock, Hank put down the cooler he was carrying and grabbed the bow rail, stopping the boat as Powers cut the engines. Hank flipped the pump on and passed the gas nozzle over to Powers. After filling up, Powers screwed the cap onto the filler tube and handed the nozzle back to Hank.

"OK, Mr. Powers, you're all set. It's almost high tide so you should be able to get across the sandbars with no problem. Just be careful coming back.

If the tide changes, you'll have to come back the long way around by the creeks."

"Thanks for the reminder," said Carl. "If I get some fish, I'll go to Blue Creek before I come back to the marina."

"I'll be here until at least ten, Mr. Powers. There'll be no problem bringing the boat back late if you want, or you could leave it at the house, and I'll pick it up tomorrow."

"Next time you get the chance, swing through the store. I got a picture of a fish you need to see. Don't see many that big."

"OK, I will," said Powers as he started the engines and headed for an afternoon of fishing.

Carl had good success fishing Saturday, and Sunday was another gorgeous day. He'd contemplated fishing again but decided to watch the baseball game instead. As he watched the game he thought, maybe it was time to get out of the business. Unexpectedly, he'd developed feelings for Alisheen. Perhaps it was a sign. He still needed to get rid of LaCrosse, but Ian could handle that. He got another beer from the fridge and sat back down.

Rupert walked through the room. "Do you need anything, Mr. Carl?"

Carl smiled. "No, thanks," and held up the beer. "I got it already. Why don't you get one for yourself and watch the baseball game with me?"

Rupert grinned. "Don't mind if I do, Mr. Carl." He went to the bar and pulled out a bottle of bourbon, filled a water glass half full, dropped in some ice cubes, and sat down on the leather couch. He told the dogs to sit, and they curled up on the floor. He toasted Carl and took a drink.

"Yes sirree, Mr. Carl, mighty fine whiskey, mighty fine."

Carl laughed. "I guess it does beat that moonshine you usually drink."

Rupert looked at Carl with a straight face. "Mr. Carl, I don't drink moonshine. I drink your bourbon because it's free, and you let me stock it whenever it gets low."

He smiled a big smile full of teeth and took another drink.

Carl burst out laughing. "I wondered why I was buying bourbon all the time when I don't drink it."

They laughed together.

After the laughter subsided, Rupert said, "Who is winning, Mr. Carl? I don't follow the new baseball teams too much."

"Then how come you always win our bets?"

"It's a feeling, Mr. Carl. I just get a gut feeling sometime about the way a game is going to turn out, that's all."

Carl laughed again. "Well, next time I make a bet with my bookie, I'll call you before I do because I'm losing today."

"Yes, sir, I'll be glad to help you with things. You know you can always count on me Mr. Carl."

Powers said, "I know I can Rupert, and thank you for that."

Rupert nodded and they watched the game in silence.

"Mr. Carl?"

"Yes?"

"Mr. Carl, do you trust me?"

Carl looked at him with surprise and sat up putting his feet on the floor. "Of course, I do, Rupert."

Rupert steadied his gaze at Carl.

"I'm glad to hear that, Mr. Carl. I think right highly of you, like you was one of my own sometimes."

Carl was silent.

"Mr. Carl, I think it's time you quit sneaking drugs around, hurting people, and get on with your life. Live decently and marry that pretty Miss Alisheen. You too good a man for all of that."

Rupert drained his glass and stood up.

"Mr. Carl, I told you I use my gut. Well, I got a feeling things are going to go bad real soon. I feel it, Mr. Carl, I do. You just promise you'll think about what I said. I'm going to watch some television in my room and go to bed early. Come on dogs, let's go outside."

The dogs jumped up and except for the jingle of their collars didn't make a sound as they followed Rupert out of the room. Carl was in shock and couldn't put any kind of thought together that made sense. His brain was on fire. He recovered when he heard the front door close as the dogs returned and followed Rupert down the hall to his bedroom.

Carl pushed himself backward in the recliner but immediately put his feet on the floor, sitting back up. He lit a cigar and took his empty beer bottle to the bar. Instead of another beer, he poured a scotch and went outside to the patio. He walked to the pier and boarded the sailboat, sitting in the stern and running his fingers over the teak wheel. It was smooth as a baby's butt from the years of sailing. He drained the scotch and threw the glass into the water with a curse, followed by the cigar. He put his head down on the wheel and listened to the water gently lapping the side of the boat with Rupert's words roaring in his brain.

~~~~

Spencer woke up Sunday morning rested despite everything that had happened. He frowned as he rubbed his sore jaw. She did pack a wallop. He tried to call Alisheen several times during the day but got no answer. He decided to drive by her loft on his way to meet Skip for dinner. Her car was there, but she didn't answer the door. He decided to run the risk of bodily harm and used his key to open the door. The chain wasn't on, so that was a good indication she wasn't there. He went inside and looked around. There were empty Chinese containers and beer bottles in the trash, so she'd had company. Emily probably, Spencer thought to himself, and he just hoped to hell that it was Emily, and not Carl Powers.

# Chapter 18

THE MONDAY MORNING gathering in the squad room held an impending air of doom. They all felt the tension of the upcoming night. The room fell silent when Spencer walked in with Skip, followed by the recon team that was going to carry out the evening's plan.

"Are you ready?" asked Meadors.

"Yes, sir," said the young sergeant leading the group. "We'll be in place by 1400 hours this afternoon. We'll hike in from the south side and recon the area before we take up positions. There will be three, two-man teams, and we understand that we're not to take action unless the subject is in extreme danger."

Meadors nodded in affirmation and looked at Spencer.

Spencer said, "Just be sure that if you have to shoot, you shoot to kill, and be damn sure our man is about to be killed before you do."

The team leader nodded.

"We'll protect him."

Spencer said, "Meadors will be your direct contact in a rolling vehicle on the perimeter, which will be secured with three hidden surveillance teams on the roads in. They will also be your backup in case something goes wrong. Once they're inside the perimeter, Meadors will contact you and let you know they're inbound. After that it will be up to you."

The sergeant said, "Yes, sir. We'll do a radio check after we're in position. Is there anything else?"

Spencer half smiled and said, "Nope, just good luck."

The team leader shook Spencer's hand and they left with Meadors following. Spencer looked around the room and noted the group's mood, but his matched it so there wasn't much use trying to change it.

"OK, we'll meet in the conference room to review the plan in half an hour. Any questions?"

They collectively shook their heads and dispersed.

Spencer looked at Skip. "You're damn quiet this morning."

"You said it all. Let's go get some coffee."

The team reconvened and spread out around the table and Spencer stood at the front by the whiteboard.

"OK, let's detail our plan on the board so that we have a clear picture of what we think is going to happen tonight."

Spencer uncapped a marker and began to write. "We have the three roads in covered by hidden surveillance teams. Meadors will be on the perimeter as the relay contact. The recon team goes in early and takes up positions around the field. They are only to act if A.J. is threatened."

With a quick look at Skip, Spencer said, "We're in agreement that no arrest is made regardless. They're there to observe and protect A.J. We have to assume it's a set up to trap A.J. as an informer so we can't give him away. That's all I've got. That's why we're in here now, to look for flaws."

Bridges raised his hand.

"Yes?"

"What if A.J. doesn't show?"

"What do you mean?" asked Spencer puzzled.

"I mean what if he doesn't show? What if it's a move just to get us to tighten up security on him? I mean we're watching the farm. What if he doesn't come to the farm? They could have someone watching A.J. too. Maybe we're being too cute. If they spot surveillance on A.J., it might be all they need to draw their own conclusion."

The room was in stunned silence.

Jack whistled. "Damn, Junior, I knew you could be a good cop. I didn't know you already were."

Bridges flushed and just nodded.

Skip banged the tabletop.

"He's right, damn it. If A.J moves and they spot a tail on him, he's dead."

He looked at Bridges.

"I wish you'd thought about this earlier son, but nice catch. Now what. The clock is running and we're going to be out of time soon."

Spencer said, "We'll have to keep surveillance on Guilford. There's nothing else we can do. If he stays in the city, we can't afford not to go with him. If he goes to the farm, then we'll let him go and hope the on-site team can protect him. We'll have to be extra cautious, regardless."

Meadors came back into the room. "The recon team will be leaving soon."

He noticed the looks on the faces in the room. "What's wrong?"

"Meadors, how good is the surveillance team on Guilford now?" asked Skip.

"The best, why?"

"Well, Bridges has made a good point, and we have to make a decision."

"What decision?"

"What do we do if A.J. sits tight and doesn't even show at the farm? What if it's a diversion to get us to tighten security on him? If they spot a tail or surveillance, he'll be just as dead."

Meadors said, "You're right, but we got a very good team watching him. Maybe we can *street it up* a little. I think the cars around the warehouse are OK. They won't stand out parked down there."

"What do you mean by *street it up*?" asked Cooper.

"You know, man," said Meadors smiling, "Plain clothes, street bum, average Joe walking a dog, a real cop on patrol, a jogger, anything that fits a neighborhood."

"Oh," said Cooper sheepishly, "I hadn't heard it put like that before."

"We'll take the neighborhood and *street it up*, as you put it," he said smiling at Cooper.

"Bo's team will cover the docks."

"We'll still need Meadors for a relay at the farm," said Carol.

Meadors said, "I've borrowed a truck from a friend of mine and will be in the area riding around. I'll take some caps and jackets with me and mix up the look. It's an average looking truck so it should be alright."

Spencer looked at the board.

"Anything we missed?"

With murmurs and silent nods, they agreed the plan could work, but it was going to take a lot of luck.

By two o'clock, they were in the conference room, listening to the radio. The recon team was on its way into the farm and soon would be in position. At three o'clock, they radioed in. They'd surveyed the area, found it clear, and had taken up positions. The waiting had begun.

Spencer said to Meadors, "Any word from the teams on Guilford?"

"He's still at the office. We got the street covered and the car on the warehouse is sitting in a used car lot. The backup is on a side street a couple of blocks away. I think we're in good shape."

Over the next two hours nothing new had developed.

"Meadors?" asked Carol. "Has there been any activity at the warehouse?"

"Nothing but the truck traffic in and out. A couple of cars, that's it."

"Strange."

"What's strange, Carol?" asked Skip.

"I'm wondering why Guilford is still there. It's after six and he's still working."

"Maybe he's waiting on a phone call to tell him it's time," Skip said.

"Maybe," Carol said, uncertain.

Carol sat tapping her fingernails on the table and watching the clock.

Skip watched her for a few minutes. "OK, Carol, out with it. I've seen that look before."

Carol looked at him with alarm.

"I think I know what we've missed."

~~~~

Ian snapped his eyes open with the beeps of his watch alarm. He found the stem of the watch and pushed it in to stop the beep. He rested for a few minutes as he brought his brain to full speed. He stood up, went to the bathroom, washed his face to clear the sleep from his eyes, and went to the kitchen. He ate the sandwich and energy bar he'd put in the fridge earlier and washed it all down with a sports drink. He wanted to be ready for a long night. He hoisted the knapsack and grabbed the car keys to the rented Taurus.

He looked out the window and checked the parking lot for anything out of the ordinary. It was time.

Ian drove carefully through the traffic, arriving at Coastal. He looked around for a surveillance vehicle. If they were watching, they weren't obvious. He circled the block and turned into the gate, driving past the main building and parking in the truck driver lot.

He sat in the car checking to be sure no one followed him. Satisfied, he grabbed the knapsack and went in the driver's entrance that accessed A.J.'s office area. He slipped into the bathroom where he waited in the stall with his feet up and checked his watch. It was almost five and time for the secretary to leave. His timing was perfect so far, if only that idiot Vernon doesn't screw it up.

After a few minutes, he heard someone coming down the hall and the door to the ladies' room open, then the toilet flushed, and the sink ran.

He heard the secretary say goodbye, and he gave her a few minutes to get down the stairs and into her car. When he felt sure she was gone, he opened the door and walked down the hall. He heard A.J. on the phone and waited until he hung up, then he appeared in the doorway casually and scared the hell out of him.

"Son-of-a-bitch Ian," yelled A.J., going pale white and looking as if he was going to pass out. "You scared the hell out of me."

Ian smiled slyly. "Sorry A.J., I didn't mean to scare you, but it's time."

"I thought you were going to pick me up at the house. What happened? Why didn't you call me?"

"Change of plans at the last minute. You know how it is."

A.J. nodded and looked around and out the window.

"You got an appointment or something, A.J.?"

"Uh, no, no, I was looking to see how dark it was. I'll be ready to go in just a few minutes."

A.J. fiddled with some files on his desk, checked his voicemail, and slowly a look of dread and defeat came onto his face.

Ian said, "Let's go, A.J. We got a long night ahead of us."

A.J. preceded him out of the office and turned to go out the front.

Baxter said, "Wrong way, A.J. We're going out through the maintenance building."

A.J. shrugged his shoulders and went through the door that connected directly to the maintenance warehouse. It was empty as planned since the employees in maintenance typically left at four. There were several of the bright red Coastal cabs, and they walked to the last one in line. A.J. removed the note from the door that said "parts ordered" with his initials on it and opened the door. He heard the gun click and turned around pretending to be surprised, but Ian wasn't buying.

"Let's wait until my driver gets here. We got a new plan tonight."

A.J., without a word, sat down on the running board of the truck with the look of a dead man.

The taxi stopped at the gates of the Coastal complex, and the cops on duty watched with interest as the man got out. He looked around after paying the driver, then skulked around the entrance for a minute or two before going through the gates. He walked to the first warehouse and went in. Vernon was sweating like a pig by the time he got inside the warehouse door. He found A.J. looking dejected and Baxter watching him with half closed eyes.

Vernon, with a smirk on his face, started to speak, but Baxter cut him off. "Just get in the truck and drive. A.J., we're going to ride in the sleeper. Let's go."

Ian forced A.J. face down onto the floor while he sat on the bed, putting his feet on A.J.'s neck and back. Vernon cranked up the diesel and headed out the entrance. The cops watched the big truck roll out and checked the driver carefully as they took pictures.

Vernon said, "Where to?"

"Drop me off first, then take A.J. to the cabin. Stay there and keep him on ice, until it's time to pick me up, and don't be late. Understand?"

Vernon gulped, nodded, and was damn glad he wasn't the one on the floor. A.J. heard Baxter tell him to put his hands behind his back. Ian taped them together, then his feet. He climbed over him and into the front seat.

"If they don't show up A.J., I'll apologize and buy you a whore." After riding in silence for a while Ian said, "Take this exit and let me off at the top. Pick me up here later and remember what I said about being late."

Vernon nodded in agreement, and Ian got out of the cab and closed the door. Vernon headed down the ramp, shifting gears and accelerating as he entered the interstate traffic. A.J. knew Vernon was too scared of Ian to help him so he resigned himself to the slim hope that Fitzgerald didn't show up at the farm or he was following the truck. After a while, A.J. felt the truck turning onto a rough road and bounced around on the floor. They were at the cabin after a short twisting ride.

Vernon cut the tape on his feet and got him out of the truck by pushing him out onto the ground. He held a gun on him and prodded him to the cabin where, once inside, he pushed him again from behind and A.J. hit the floor hard, stunning him. Vernon taped his feet again and left him alone in the dark bedroom. He heard the sound of a television and a chair scraping the floor as Vernon got comfortable. A.J. tried to free himself, but the tape was too strong and he soon tired. Exhausted he began to cry silently in the dark and fell asleep.

Ian watched the truck as it picked up speed down the ramp and entered the traffic, and then he looked around and determined he was alone. With another glance around, he started down the secondary road at a jog, checked his watch, and then slowed to a walk. He had plenty of time. He entered the woods at the path he'd marked earlier with engineering tape. After a few yards into the woods, he heard a car coming down the road. He stopped and took cover until they passed. He quickened his pace and followed the colored tape through the woods. He reached a spot on the trail that enabled him to look out with binoculars and survey the field and the small buildings at the other end. Hooding the lenses to keep them from reflecting sunlight, he studied the area. Seeing nothing, he moved on to the deer stand he'd found earlier and climbed up the ladder.

Hidden in the upper branches of a tall oak tree, he had a great view of the area. He sat in the padded chair and looked out the small hole of the stand. He loved rednecks. The deer stand was perfect and since it was a common sight, not suspicious. Checking his watch and looking at the sinking sun, he was satisfied that all had gone as planned, and he settled in to wait.

~~~~

"What is it?" asked Skip with dread.

"I'm willing to bet A.J. left in a truck," said Carol.

"Why would he sneak out and leave his protection behind?" asked Bridges.

"There's another option we haven't thought of," said Carol. "He's been kidnapped out from under our noses in one of the trucks. If so, and if anything goes wrong, he is a dead man."

"Damn! Why didn't we think of that?" Skip swore. "We need to confirm he's not in the office because we know he's not at the house."

Spencer said, "The team is in place to watch, right?"

Cooley checked his watch. "They've been in there since 3:00."

Spencer asked, "We got radio contact I assume?"

"Yes," said Cooley. "Meadors is in the area as the relay."

"Tell them that we think A.J has been kidnapped. If they see him on site, they are to let us know and stick to the plan."

Cooley called Meadors to inform him so he could relay the information to the recon team.

"Now what?" Bridges asked.

"We wait it out and pray we find A.J. in the meantime," said Spencer.

It was late and Ian was beginning to doze. He checked his watch. It was time to go. The trap hadn't worked. He had no real solid evidence to prove that A.J. was the informer. As he prepared to climb down the tree, he thought he heard a noise. Pausing, he listened intently then heard it again, but he couldn't identify the sound. He became very still and concentrated on breathing and listening to the darkness with every sense tuned into the surroundings.

He concentrated harder by holding his breath and listening. The noise was getting louder. After a few minutes, he knew the sound. It was an earpiece turned up too loud. He listened and didn't dare twitch as he heard the sounds of two-way communication. He heard a whispered, "all clear," and the faintest sound of footsteps below him.

If they hadn't moved, he would have left the airfield unconvinced that A.J. was guilty. Now he knew. The voices in the earpiece grew fainter, and then it was quiet. He descended silently and, with stealth, began to move away from the direction the voice had gone. He spotted the first ribbon bathed in moonlight and quickly followed the trail to the interstate ramp.

The truck was there and after he climbed into the cab, he looked into the sleeper to see A.J. on the floor bound with duct tape. His eye was swollen, and his lip was bleeding. Ian backhanded Vernon sending him reeling against the truck window, bloodying his nose and splitting his lip. Vernon, cowered and whimpering, wiped his face on his sleeve.

"I told you to watch him not beat him up. You better not have hurt him, Vernon, or I'm going to kick your ass. It's up to the Snowman now. Drive, you stupid redneck."

"Where?" asked a trembling Vernon.

"Back to the cabin."

~~~~

They waited in silence through the midnight hours hoping for the best. Spencer sipped hot coffee, Carol watched the phone, and Skip paced.

At 5:00 a.m., Meadors announced, "The team is back."

They quickly moved to the conference room, and the team members filed in.

The team leader looked at Spencer. "I'm not sure if what I have to say is good or bad. We arrived and secured the perimeter at 1500 hours and took up positions. We waited, watched, and never saw anything or anybody. At 0200, we skirted the perimeter on a search and secure recon, found nothing, and took up positions again. We saw no activity and pulled out at 0400. So in essence, we have no news, good or bad, to report. We didn't see or hear anything."

In the silence of the room, they heard it. The earpiece of one of the men against the wall sounded like thunder as a radio call went out. The team leader stood up quickly in shock. The realization of how loud the little earpiece sounded in the quiet of the conference room shocked them.

"Son of a bitch," Meadors said.

Spencer looked at the young man standing against the wall with horror on his face.

Spencer said, "Did you skirt the perimeter with that thing on?"

He nodded in affirmation.

Spencer looked at Skip. "If A.J. isn't already dead he will be soon. We got to have a warrant for the Coastal Seafood warehouses now."

~~~~

Carl Powers checked his watch and noted it was almost dawn. He sipped his Stoli, went to the kitchen, opened the freezer, and poured some more into the glass. He went back to the large living area, checked his watch again, and wondered where Ian was. The sun was beginning to rise when his cell phone rang. It was Ian.

"I caught something. I'll keep it on ice until you're ready."

"I'll call you later."

Carl drained his glass and went to bed.

~~~~

A.J. was awake, but he didn't open his eyes. He wanted to continue to listen to the voices in the other room and pretend he was still unconscious. He probably couldn't open his eyes if he wanted to. He was in a lot of pain, and his face felt like a hammer hit him. It hurt to breathe too, so he probably had a couple of broken ribs. Vernon, that damn coward, had beaten and kicked him in spite of Ian's orders not to touch him as he lay bound on the floor.

A.J. took satisfaction in the fact that Vernon probably didn't look much better than he did. Ian had smacked Vernon around when they got back to the cabin for not following orders. A.J. knew he was going to die. He hoped it would be painless and quick at least. He thought the cops might rescue him, but Ian had played it smart, and they didn't have a clue where he was. A.J. decided to open his eyes.

His face was very swollen so there was a good chance his cheekbones were broken. The pain at the effort to open his eyes and move his jaw made him gasp as the pain hit him from the effort, and he stopped trying. After a minute, he decided to try again, and he braced himself. With effort, he suppressed the pain and finally managed to open his right eye and his left eye to a slit. He was in the same room.

He checked his muscles to see if he could move anything else. He realized his legs and feet were free and that he could probably roll over if he wanted to. His hands were still behind him but not as tight. A short piece of rope tied them together. He made the effort to move his head to look around. There was a bed, a ratty looking chair, and an old scarred up chest of drawers. He was on a threadbare looped rug, which padded the floor beneath him. He suddenly realized it was the next morning when he noticed the sun was beginning to shine on the dirty window. He closed his eyes quickly as he heard footsteps approaching. He felt someone kneel behind him, and then his hands were free.

"Hey, A.J., it's time to wake up man."

Ian rolled A.J. over, and he gasped from the pain.

"Man, you look like hell."

A.J. tried to lick his lips, but his mouth was dry. Ian lifted him up into a sitting position. He groaned with the surge of pain, but Ian didn't stop his effort to move him. He pulled A.J. across the floor and propped him up against the bed. A.J. started to fall over, but Ian propped him back up.

"Here, man, take a sip of water," said Ian squatting down and holding a cup to A.J.'s lips.

A.J. took a small sip. The water was cold, and it felt wonderful going down his throat.

"Have some more," urged Ian, and he continued to hold the cup for A.J. until it was empty. "Do you want some more?"

A.J. shook his head.

"I need to piss."

"OK, but I ain't going to hold it for ya."

A.J. managed a weak smile, and Ian helped him sit on the bed while A.J. caught his breath. After a few moments, Ian helped him to his feet and guided him to the bathroom, holding his arm while A.J. urinated, then walked him back to the bed where he lay down. Ian locked a steel cuff around A.J.'s ankle and then looped the other cuff through the footboard and locked it around the chain.

A.J. said, "Why the special treatment?"

"I've got to take you to see Powers soon. He wants to talk to you. I need you in relatively good condition so you can talk back. By the way, I kicked Vernon's ass for you."

"I know. Thanks, I guess. I think my cheekbones are broken from when he kicked me in the face. I think a rib is busted too."

Ian said, "I got some painkillers and a bottle. You want them?"

A.J. nodded.

Ian left for a few minutes and came back with a bottle of vodka and a medicine bottle.

"Here, take these," he said handing the bottle to A.J.

"There are only a few in there, so don't think you can kill yourself."

Ian poured a paper cup full of booze and set it on the small table next to the bed. A.J looked into the bottle, dumped a couple of pills into his hand, and then popped them into his mouth. He took a drink of the vodka, coughed a little, and then settled back onto the bed. Ian left again and returned a few minutes later holding a paper plate with a sandwich on it and a cup of soup in his other hand. He pulled a cold Coke out of his pocket after giving A.J. the food and set it on the table next to the cup of vodka.

"Eat and get some sleep. You might as well be comfortable and enjoy a good buzz. I got a joint, you want that too?"

A.J. nodded and Ian put a thick joint and a lighter on the table.

"It's good stuff."

Ian started to leave and said, "A.J., don't start a fire. If you do, I'll let you burn to death. It would be quite painful and slow torture. Believe me, Powers will be quick and merciful if it comes to that. Who knows, you might be able to weasel your ass out of this mess."

Ian walked over to the table and picked up the joint. He lit it, took a big hit, and put it between A.J.'s lips.

"See you later," and he walked out and closed the door.

A.J. suffered some pain with his effort to take a big hit off the joint and hold it. He coughed as he exhaled the smoke and his injured ribs and swollen face hurt. He reached over and carefully stubbed out the joint on the tabletop. He decided to try and drink the soup and sipped it slowly with Ian's words echoing in his brain.

*"Who knows, you might be able to weasel your ass out of this mess."*

*"Damn, it could be a real possibility,"* thought A.J. After all, he never gave Carl's name to anyone so technically he never snitched. Powers had lost a lot of money though. Maybe A.J. could figure out how to pay him back over time or something. He could work for free and do extra runs to pay it off, whatever it took.

He finished the soup and picked up a sandwich. He ate half of it and was full. The prospect of talking Powers out of killing him was remote, but at least it was a slim chance. He picked up the cup of Vodka and took a large gulp. He lit the joint again and took a small hit, not wanting to cough again. He alternated between the vodka and taking small hits off the joint. The combination of the pills, booze, and marijuana began to have its effect. He put the empty cup on the table and stubbed out the rest of the joint. He tenderly moved into a prone position and closed his eyes. He felt his entire body relax and the pain in his face and side began to diminish. He moved his feet and felt the leg cuff around his ankle, reminding him of his plight and almost certain future before he fell asleep.

~~~~

Emily dropped Alisheen off at her loft Tuesday morning only after Alisheen promised she'd come to work later. She went to the bedroom, entered the walk-in closet, flipped on the lights, and browsed her clothes. She owned nothing suitable for the Charity Ball even if she did decide to go and frowned at the thought. *After all, what could happen if she went with Carl? Emily would have her committed, that's what.*

Alisheen was intrigued but knew it was crazy.

"I can't afford it anyway."

As if somebody was controlling her actions, she went to the kitchen, opened her laptop, and checked her credit card balance.

"Not too bad."

If she decided to go, a new dress and shoes would be necessary. She left the kitchen with the laptop in her hand and sat on the sofa to begin a search for dress shops. She didn't buy stuff like this routinely, so she needed to know where to shop instead of just going out and hoping to find something suitable. Alisheen laughed a little, thinking it was just like Atlanta, and then she remembered how she ended up in Atlanta in the first place.

She slammed the laptop closed and shoved it onto the floor with anger. Imagine that son-of-a-bitch telling Dixie, of all people, what the problem was, and he convinces Spencer to share his feelings. She'd considered talking to Dixie to find out more about what Spencer had told him but decided that'd be a bad idea. Her emotions burned with feelings she couldn't identify. She wasn't sure if it was shame, anger, guilt, or a combination of them all that overwhelmed her. How did Dixie get Spencer to tell him his fears and reasons for not wanting to commit to her when she couldn't? What did he say to him?

"*What?*" she yelled in anger.

"*Then on top of all that,*" she yelled again, "*He says he doesn't want me to have to raise our children without a father. Who in hell does he think he is? How dare he make a decision about my life like that when we aren't even married?*"

Alisheen broke down in tears and buried her face in her hands. The phone rang and she ignored it, not wanting to talk to anyone, especially Spencer. The machine answered and Alisheen, expecting the caller to hang up, was surprised to hear Carl's voice leaving a message.

She picked up quickly and with as much enthusiasm as she could muster said, "Hello, Carl!"

"Well, there you are. I was beginning to worry about you. You haven't been at work and, up until now, you haven't answered your cell. Where've you been?"

"I wanted to ask again if you'll go with me Friday."

Alisheen was quiet and Carl said, "Well, what do you say?"

"I accept," she said. "Call me later with the details, OK?"

She glanced at the clock and realized it was past ten.

"Carl, I have to go now. I'm running late."

"Alisheen, this is great. I'm happy you're going. I'll call you soon, OK?"

"That's fine, Carl, goodbye for now."

"Goodbye," and he hung up.

"Oh crap!" she said.

She decided to go to work, delve into the kitchen, and cook. She wanted to try some new recipes and update the menu. With Emily handling the business, she was going to focus on cooking and use it as therapy to get over her anger. The staff noticed her attitude and avoided her as she moved about the kitchen with a curse on her lips every time she couldn't find what she wanted. The first creative attempt didn't go well, and she threw it into the garbage can.

Emily finally had enough of her terrorizing the kitchen. She corralled her by the arm and led her into the office. Once inside, Alisheen broke down and tearfully recapped her morning's thoughts.

Emily said, "Well, is it over between the two of you now?"

Alisheen looked up in surprise. The magnitude of the question voiced by somebody other than her sounded horrible, and she didn't know the answer.

"I don't really know where we stand anymore. Damn it, Emily, I don't know if it's over or not. I don't know if Spencer will forgive me for slapping him. I don't know if I can forgive him for spilling his guts to Dixie when it should have been me. I just don't know anymore."

She began to tear up again and Emily sat down next to her on the couch.

"Alisheen, it's time to consider at the least moving on to the next step, whatever that is. If you and Spencer are meant to be then you'll survive. If not, then whatever is going to happen will happen."

She said, "I think I'm going to find out pretty soon then. I took that step this morning."

# Chapter 19

"WHAT DO YOU mean you've already taken the first step?" asked Emily. "Alisheen, you're scaring me. What've you done?"

"I told Carl Powers I'd go to the Savannah Treasury Charity Ball with him," she said looking down at the floor.

Emily was exasperated. "Are you out of your mind? Did you forget that's exactly what got you into this mess to begin with? What're you thinking?"

Emily leaned back on the couch with a heavy thud. Alisheen's ego burned at the scathing words.

"Just so you know, I haven't forgotten how I got into this mess but apparently you have. I went away with Carl because Spencer didn't love me enough to share his secret, until Dixie of all people urged him to share his feelings. I accepted Carl's invitation as a friend. If I'm going to have the future I want, then maybe he's the man I need to be with."

"You're leaving out one small detail. Carl Powers is under investigation for goodness sake! Have you forgotten that?"

Alisheen folded her arms in defiance. "I haven't forgotten. I also know Spencer may have cooked it up to keep me away from him because he's just jealous."

"Oh, that's a load of crap and you know it." Emily said raising her voice. "Spencer wouldn't do that, and besides, if I remember correctly this was all your fault yesterday."

Emily got up and faced her.

"You know in your heart that Spencer loves you. I think you're trying to get back at him for his confession to Dixie. You're being childish. I'd think you'd be glad he finally told you and now that you know what it is, you can deal with it."

Alisheen glared at Emily.

"I want to be happy, Emily, and Carl makes me happy. If it's the only way to know for sure, then so be it. I've made my decision, and I don't care about Spencer's accusations."

Emily put her hands on her hips and said, "Alisheen, we're best friends and I'll support you, but mark my words I think you're making a huge mistake." Emily left, closing the door. Defiantly, she went and sat down at her desk with a huff. She picked up some paperwork, then in disgust threw it onto the desktop with anger. She put her apron on the hook and left the office.

She found Emily out front and spoke to her with a superior tone. "I'm going shopping. Call my cell phone if you need anything."

Emily, angered by Alisheen's rudeness, said curtly, "Yes, ma'am."

Alisheen ignored her and walked out. She went to the mall, heading for the smaller dress shops that specialized in evening wear. As she began to browse through the racks, she noticed a woman near her because she seemed to be looking at her more than the clothes. Thinking she was probably store security, she didn't pay her much attention.

She was surprised when the woman appeared at her elbow and introduced herself.

"Hello, I'm Jeanette LaCrosse."

Alisheen, taken aback, nodded in greeting and began to introduce herself when the woman cut her off.

"Alisheen Delaney, yes, I know. You own the She Crab correct?"

"Why, yes, how did you know?"

"I've eaten in your establishment quite a few times. Anybody that has eaten there more than once knows who you are. You're quite famous from that perspective."

Alisheen was flustered.

"Well, thank you, Jeanette, for the compliment."

Jeanette smiled.

"I see you're shopping for an evening dress. It wouldn't be for the big Charity Ball this Friday, would it?"

"Well, yes, it is," she said. "I'm going with a friend. Are you going to the Ball too?"

Jeanette smiled slyly. "Oh, yes, I'm definitely going."

She checked her watch, claimed she was running late, and left quickly. Alisheen was glad she was gone. She'd been nosy and made her very uncomfortable. After browsing through several stores, Alisheen settled on a sapphire blue strapless evening dress. She thought Carl would like it, and she surprised herself with the thought. She couldn't remember buying anything with Spencer in mind, and she'd thought of Carl's reaction in a sensual way. As for Spencer, she was usually trying to get his attention.

"Damn him," said Alisheen.

~~~~

Jeanette LaCrosse was fuming when she got to her car. She'd followed the bitch to the mall and watched her while she shopped. She was looking at evening gowns, and there was only one reason for that. She was going to the Ball. It had to be Carl. She was going to have to make him believe that she'd kill her if she got in the way. One way or the other he was going to be hers, and she wasn't going to let Alisheen Delaney stand in her way.

~~~~

It was noon Tuesday before word came there wouldn't be a warrant.

"Damn it, Captain," yelled Spencer with anger. "We've lost A.J. Guilford. We've got to look for him, and the only place we know to start is Coastal."

"Spencer, I understand your displeasure," Drake said with sarcasm, "but that isn't a good enough reason. We're damn lucky the judge would even hear our request, given the fact we got no proof, and as he reminded me, Carl Powers was a friend. He also said if we came back again, we better have more than speculation."

"Speculation!" exclaimed Skip.

"What do we need, his body? It'll be too damn late then."

Drake said, "Here's the deal plain and simple. Nobody has reported him missing yet, and you got no proof that he didn't manage to lose your surveillance on his own. Unless you can come up with something concrete you guys are S.O.L."

Spencer sat down and rubbed his face with his hands.

"Captain, there must be something we can do. A.J. is going to be dead within the next 24 hours if he isn't already."

"I'm sorry, Spencer," said Drake, "But unless you've got substantial proof, there is nothing I can do and there's no way I can go back to the judge. Go back to the farm; find something that suggests Guilford is in peril. For all you know he gave you the slip because he got scared and he's on his way to Mexico."

Drake surveyed the room then left.

"Anybody got any ideas?" asked Cooley.

"Yeah," said Spencer. "The Captain is right; we don't have squat. Cooley, I want you and Bridges to go with the recon team back to the farm. Find something that indicates somebody was there besides us. After that, find Benny and see what he knows.

"Meadors, you and Carol go through the surveillance photos from the warehouse. Some of the officers were new and all they knew to look for was A.J. Now that I think about it that was short sighted on our part. Maybe somebody they didn't know who to look for came to the warehouse. Maybe Powers himself, who knows?

"Cooper, I want Ian Baxter found. He's the security for the Snowman, per Benny. I want you to find his ass. He has to be in Savannah somewhere. If he's using the name Jenkins, we should be able to get a credit card slip or something we can use to get an address. It's time he got our full attention.

"Skip, you and I are going to focus on Jeanette LaCrosse. Let's see if she's a player or not."

The room was quiet, and Spencer said loudly, "OK, let's go. We need answers now."

The group scattered, except for Skip, who remained in Spencer's office.

Spencer said, "Let's talk about LaCrosse."

Skip said, "I was putting all we know out on paper last night, and I think LaCrosse is the second informer."

Spencer pursed his lips and waited for him to continue.

"Look, Spencer, it makes sense," said Skip as he spread out his notes on the desk. "She has access to everything, and for years she's been his Executive Assistant. Now, out of the blue after all this time, she's all of a sudden, the COO? I'm willing to bet she figured it out. She probably doesn't know about A.J. or vice versa. Each one has their own motive. A.J. wants revenge, she wants power. She probably confronted him about it recently which explains the promotion. She gets what she wants, or she tells the feds."

Spencer said, "Makes sense. You could be right. Let's stay on her and see what else we can find out."

As Carol and Meadors were getting ready to go through the photos, her phone rang. It was Vincent.

"I haven't heard from you, Detective."

Carol said, "Hold on a minute."

She covered the receiver and mouthed the words, "It's Vincent," to Meadors and held up five fingers. Meadors signaled understanding and began to spread out the pictures.

"I could say the same thing for you," said Carol. "I was hoping you'd given me something by now."

"I swear, Detective, I got nothing. It's been damn quiet."

"Come on, Vincent. You expect me to believe they haven't heard a thing since Jake was killed? Somebody knows something somewhere."

"If they do, they aint' talking about it. No drugs have moved since Jake was killed and the boats are just out there shrimping. It's gotten real cozy and quiet."

"That in itself says something, but I'm not sure what," Carol said.

"Maybe they're just lying low," said Vincent.

"Maybe, but it doesn't seem likely. We need to talk. Either we aren't looking in the right place or asking the right questions. Let's meet at the cabin later."

"OK," said Vincent and the phone went dead.

Meadors looked up and said, "Vincent have any news?"

"Nope, he says it's all quiet, and I find that hard to believe. I'm going to meet him at the cabin instead. If it's OK with you."

"No problem, I'll give you a call if we find something. Be careful."

Carol said, "Thanks, I'll be back later."

Meadors began browsing the surveillance photos when Spencer and Skip split up.

"I think this is Baxter," said Meadors as Spencer walked up. "It's fuzzy, but I think it's him." He picked up the folder with Baxter's picture in it and compared them. "Yep, that's him, I'm sure."

Spencer came and looked over his shoulder.

"I think you're right," and sat down to help. "Where's Carol?"

"Gone to meet with Vincent."

They were down to the last few when Spencer said with a muted tone, "I'll be a son-of-a-bitch."

"What is it?" asked Meadors.

"Recognize anybody we know?" said Spencer, handing the picture to him.

"Vernon Faris," said Meadors. "What in the hell is he doing there?"

"I don't know, but there's a cab in the background so maybe they picked him up and dropped him off. Let's get the log for that cab and find out."

"You got it," said Meadors.

They began going through another stack of photos.

"Not much here," said Meadors. "No other sign of Baxter or Vernon for that matter. They could've been missed. The guys on duty might have figured they already had them going in, so they didn't take a picture of them going out."

"I hope not," said Spencer. "Every detail is important at this point, and these photos have a time stamp on them so a timeline would be useful."

Suddenly Meadors sat up straight with some excitement.

"Spencer, look at this!"

Spencer took the photograph.

"Look who's driving."

Spencer got the magnifying glass and looked closer then whistled softly.

"Vernon Faris again. I wonder if he drives routinely or if he's doing something special?"

"Spencer?" asked Meadors. "Do you think A.J. and Baxter were in the truck with Vernon?"

"It's a safe bet."

Cooley and Bridges returned from the farm with the recon team. Meadors frowned when the team leader shook his head in the negative.

"Did you find anything?" asked Spencer.

"No, sir, nothing that leads anywhere. We scouted the perimeter the same way we did the other night. There is only one spot somebody could have been in that we wouldn't have seen him. Other than that, there is no way we would've missed anybody."

"What's the one spot?" asked Spencer.

"A deer stand sir."

"A what?" asked Spencer with skepticism.

"A deer stand. There was one at the end of the field in a tree. Somebody could've been in it, and if they were really quiet we wouldn't have known they were above us."

Meadors said, "Why didn't you check it when you searched the perimeter the first time?"

"We didn't see it before and almost didn't see it today. The stand was built into the tree like a tree house and was well hidden. There was a chair that'd been moved around because there were drag marks and footprints, but there's no way to tell who made them or when."

Spencer sighed. "Anything else?"

"There was one thing out of place which makes me think that someone used the stand."

"What?" asked Spencer.

"We found some engineering tape."

"So," said Spencer.

Bridges broke in.

"Hunters use it to mark a trail they can follow in the dark Spencer. It's reflective. They can move through the woods by spotting the tape with a flashlight or moonlight if it's bright enough."

"Exactly," said the team leader. "This tape was new. It had no stains or fading and marked the path to the deer stand. We followed the tape backward until we came to a road. From there it was only a quarter mile to the interstate.

Anybody could have come and gone from there unseen. Once in the deer stand, all they had to do was be quiet and still. Then they could slip out when the coast was clear."

"Which is most likely what happened," stated Spencer.

"It's highly probable, sir," said the team leader with defeat.

"You think it's over with A.J. being caught and the Snowman won't take any more chances?" asked Cooley.

Spencer thought this possibility over.

"No, I doubt it," he said. "This guy has a great setup. With the informer gone, his odds got better. All he has to do is wait it out for a while, make some changes, and he's back in business."

"I agree," said Meadors. "His odds are improving."

Spencer said to them, "We got some interesting surveillance pictures from Coastal," and he handed out copies.

"The one in the sunglasses is Ian Baxter, Snowman security. The man in the photo marked number two is Vernon Faris. We'd arrested him earlier when we had Jake Sweet and others in custody. You all know the rest of the story from that point. The third photograph is the most interesting one; take a good look at the driver."

"Damn, its Vernon driving the truck," said Cooley.

"You are correct, which means an educated guess says," Bridges said, "Vernon drove A.J. and Baxter out from under our noses."

"It's an excellent possibility," said Spencer.

Cooley threw the photographs onto the desk in disgust.

"Crap!"

"I think that about sums it up," said Spencer.

Cooper burst into the room and came up short as he saw the look on everyone's face.

"I've got something that will cheer you up," he said with a smile. "We found Ian Baxter's apartment through his alias Jenkins. The credit card search had the same address but different names. I guess Baxter likes to keep his credit rating up. We showed some pictures around to merchants that had processed the cards, same man, different name. Then we faxed a picture to Sun Diesel. They identified him as Jenkins, their account rep to Coastal Seafood. They said Mr. Powers had personally vouched for Jenkins and requested him for the Coastal account, and it's his only account. There had never been any problems and Coastal was quite satisfied. Jenkins met all of his quotas and then some, so he made good money."

Cooper finished with a big smile on his face.

"That's too big to be a coincidence, don't you think?" asked Meadors.

"Definitely," said Spencer. He looked at Cooper with disappointment. "I can't believe you've left out the most important detail."

Cooper's face fell quickly.

"What's that, sir?"

"The address, man. We need the address."

The group laughed at Spencer's joke and Cooper smiled. "Only if I get dibs on the first surveillance team."

"You got it, you earned it," said Spencer.

Skip came into the squad room as the group was laughing.

"What've I missed?"

"A good bit. Some good, some bad, but the best news is that Cooper has found Baxter."

"That's great, what now?"

"You and I are going to scope out the neighborhood where LaCrosse lives and get the lay of the land," said Spencer. "Then we're going to Coastal and question employees off the premises. We need information, and we'll just to have to be sneaky about it."

"I've got Bo putting together background information on LaCrosse," said Skip.

"That's a good idea," said Spencer. "We need to drill down and go deep."

They drove to the neighborhood and went by the house from both directions, checking intersecting streets. It was an upscale neighborhood but not over the top.

"Not much here," said Spencer, "Let's go to Coastal and catch some employees getting off work."

"OK," said Skip, "Let's split up when we get there. We can cover more ground and be less intimidating flashing badges around."

"That's a good idea," said Spencer.

They parked down the street from the entrance to the office building, split up and talked to the employees as they came out of the building. When they convened in the car, they compared notes.

"Well, that was very revealing," said Spencer.

"What did you find out?" asked Skip.

"You first."

"OK," said Skip, "If it'll make you feel better. It turns out the best-kept secret that everybody knows is that Jeanette LaCrosse has had a thing for Powers for years. Only thing is he's the only one that doesn't know, or if he does, he doesn't care. She pretty much runs the business now, but Powers is the moneyman and the one with the connections."

Spencer interjected, "He has done very well I'd say."

Skip nodded. "Yep, but everybody was surprised with the sudden recognition of LaCrosse and they're wondering what happened. Powers has never acknowledged her before so it's all a big mystery and water cooler discussion. Your turn."

Spencer said, "I got the story about LaCrosse having the hots for Powers but with a different twist. Seems she came in the other day and announced to the staff that she and 'Carl' were beginning a new relationship and he'd turned over completely the operation of the business to her. Everything from that day forward was to go through her and no business at all was to be brought to Powers without her approval."

"Wow," said Skip, "That's quite a statement."

"You're right, and it blew those guys away. They're unsure about what's going on, so you're right, it's definitely water cooler discussion. And there's one more thing you didn't mention that I found out."

"What?"

"It turns out that none of them like A.J. He's a prick, and Powers only keeps him around as a whipping boy. He brought him in and made him trucking manager over some people who were much more experienced, and he's constantly messing things up. Trucks aren't serviced on time, out at odd hours, and running late on simple routes. They occasionally get complaints about loads being short, and Powers covers it with money and discounts to keep his customers from bailing. LaCrosse has been pitching a fit to get rid of him but Powers refuses. What do you think of that?"

"Sounds to me like A.J. was using the trucks to deliver things other than seafood and on somebody else's time frame," said Skip. "That way A.J. takes the heat for being an incompetent boob, and all of the deliveries get done under the guise of him being an idiot."

"I think this proves you're right," said Spencer, "LaCrosse put two and two together."

"If that's true, Spencer, then that backs up our theory that she's the other informer. She might've used that information to get her new position by using that age old method called blackmail."

~~~~

Carol had gotten the call from Meadors with the new information from the photographs while in route to the cabin. She knew she shouldn't tell Vincent about Vernon, but this is what she needed to trade for information on the Snowman.

"How does Vernon know Baxter, Vincent?"

"I don't know how they know each other. I guess they met through Jake. You might be right. Baxter could've recruited him to spy, seems likely. Vernon is a weasel, but I never figured him to betray Jake."

"So what's next?" asked Carol.

"I'm going to find Vernon and get some answers," Vincent said threateningly.

"Listen, Vincent, I've got my ass out on a limb. I told you about the picture of Vernon driving the truck to trade for information, not to give you a green light to kill him. It's my turn now. What about Baxter; is he Snowman security?"

"He always seemed to be around, and every time I went out with Jake he was there, so he's involved somehow. It makes sense."

"You got to give me more, Vincent. We made a deal."

"Don't worry, Detective," drawled Vincent. "I'll find out what Vincent knows before I take care of him, but he's not going to tell you anything you don't already know."

"What's that?" asked Carol warily.

"That Powers is the Snowman," Vincent laughed slyly.

"Vincent, you bastard," yelled Carol standing up with fury. "You could've saved us a lot of damn time and effort and maybe even A.J.'s life if you'd told me earlier. Damn, I knew you were holding out on me. Shit!"

Vincent replied with anger, "Don't give me that crap. I kept my end, detective. You didn't have anything until now and I told you what I knew. That was the deal, trading information."

Carol said with a threatening tone, "You better bring Vernon to me, or I'll put your ass in a sling. You find him. I talk to him first. I'll see you here tomorrow night."

With that she walked out, got in her car, and left.

Vincent dialed his cell phone.

When it was answered he said grimly, "Find Vernon and bring him to my cabin."

The voice on the other end said, "You got it," and hung up.

Vincent went outside, lit a cigarette, looked up at the night sky then looked down at the ground, and laughed with a shrug of his shoulders. "I'll get even Jake. I'll get even."

~~~~

The surveillance at Baxter's apartment had turned up nothing so far, but Spencer was hopeful. He and Skip were discussing their next move when Bo came into the office.

"I've got zip on Coastal. I've got guys digging as deep, some legal and some not so legal, as we can go, but so far it's all very clean and above board."

Spencer stood up and paced.

"It's Tuesday and no one has turned in a missing person's report?" Spencer asked.

"Nothing from Coastal and it's too soon for the neighbors to get suspicious," said Bo. "I doubt seriously if he'll be missed any time soon. In the neighborhood, nobody seemed to know much about him or cared. He wasn't well known or liked by those that did know him."

Skip spoke, "I think Bo needs to go back to Coastal and check on his job application."

"What application?" asked Spencer puzzled.

"The one he put in the day he found A.J. He can go in the warehouse office on the pretense of checking on the application. While he's there he can ask a few questions, harmless stuff on the surface, but it might give us a clue as to what's going on regarding A.J."

Skip turned to Bo, "What do you think?"

"It'll be easy enough to do. The girl that works in the front is talkative. If she's there, it'd be easy to get her started with a couple of questions."

Skip looked at Spencer. "You OK with it?"

Spencer nodded and Skip said, "OK. Come back here as soon as you're through. Good luck."

Bo nodded and quickly left.

Spencer said, "I hope this little trick gets us something we can use."

"Me too," said Skip.

Bo entered the trucking office and was relieved to see the same girl behind the desk. Her face broadened into a smile as she recognized him from his earlier visit.

"Why, hello there," she said pleasantly.

"Hello," Bo said, with his best southern charm. "I was checking on the application I put in a couple of weeks ago."

"Oh, I'm sorry," she said, "I wouldn't know anything about that here. I sent it to the main office. They would've contacted you for an interview. You haven't heard anything?"

"No, I haven't. I guess that means they aren't interested," Bo said disappointed.

"Oh, cheer up" said the girl, "It takes things awhile to get through the big office. I see it all the time."

Bo brightened up.

"Really?"

"Oh, yes. They have to process it and then Mr. Guilford has to review it. I tell you what, as soon as he gets back, I'll have Mr. Guilford call and check on it."

"When do you expect Mr. Guilford back?" Bo asked, grateful for the perfect opening to the question he needed to ask.

"He's out of town. The office got a call from him over the weekend saying he had a family emergency and he'd be in touch. I expected him to call in by now, but so far he hasn't."

"Is that unusual?" asked Bo innocently.

"Well, kind of. A.J., I mean Mr. Guilford is rarely gone except when he's driving or subbing for a driver, and he usually calls in when he's out on the road. I've never heard him speak about any family before, but it is odd he hasn't called in."

Bo said, "I'll give you my name and number, and when he comes back you can call me and let me know. Maybe I can come over and catch him in the office."

"Well, I'm not supposed to do stuff like that," she said.

Bo slowly folded a twenty-dollar bill in half and halved it again, then placed it on the counter along with his number and smiled at her. She picked them up and put it in her pocket.

"As soon as I hear from Mr. Guilford," she said smiling.

Bo thanked her and went straight back to the station. Spencer and Skip looked at him with anticipation as he walked in.

"Don't get your hopes up. The story is he called in over the weekend saying he had a family emergency. The girl in the office said he'd never spoken of family and didn't know where his family was. She said he was sometimes gone overnight on trips as a driver, but that he usually called in from the road, so it was strange not to have heard from him."

Skip said, "At least we got that."

~~~~

Benny drank the last of his iced tea and stood up, smacking his lips with satisfaction. He picked up his tray, dumped it into the big garbage can, and put the empty tray on the stack by the door. He refilled his cup from the tea canister, went outside, and sat down to have a smoke. Father Simmons came around the corner and spotted Benny.

"Did you get enough to eat Benny?"

Benny nodded and turned his head exhaling his smoke to keep it out of the pastor's face.

"Yes sir, I sure did. I do like Tuesday night's fried chicken. It's as good as St. Josephs on Thursday."

Father Simmons laughed heartily.

"Well, I'll have to tell Father Wilson that we're giving him some competition."

Benny smiled. He liked the preacher. Father Simmons sat down next to Benny.

"Have you given any more thought to what I said about letting me help you get off the street and find a job so you can make your own way in life?"

Benny smiled slightly.

"Yes, I have, padre. I figure the good Lord is taking care of me anyway, so I'm all right."

"Benny, you know prayer and faith can change a man. If you truly want to change, you can with help from God."

"You know, padre, I tried praying once, and it didn't help me much."

"What did you pray for, Benny?"

"I asked him to save my mama from dying of cancer when I was a teenager. She died anyway so it didn't do me much good. Daddy left after she died, so I been on my own since then. I reckon God is looking after me though, like I said before."

Father Simmons patted Benny on the knee. "Benny, sometimes the answer is no from God. Maybe he wanted her more than you did."

Benny's voice reflected his despair.

"God didn't do me right taking my mama. She was all I had, and I ain't had nobody since. He took away the only person that ever said they loved me. She was the only person I've ever loved, so he took love out of my life. I figure he owes me for that. I guess that's why he keeps taking care of me on the street. He knows he made a mistake. I'm not holding a grudge or nothing. I just figure he did me wrong and he needs to look after me."

Father Simmons, deeply moved by Benny's confession, looked away. He looked back after a few moments.

"You might be right, Benny, after all. The Lord does work in many ways."

Benny left the church and was soon walking along the fence at Coastal. He perked up a bit with the hope that Joseph might be working. Benny was in luck. He saw Joseph walking along the fence ahead, stopping to check a gate now and then. Benny waited until Joseph was close and called out to him.

"Hey, Joseph, howzit going man? I ain't seen you in a while."

Joseph pushed his cap back a little on his head and greeted Benny with a wave.

"Hello there, Benny, I took off a couple of days. I was staying with my daughter and the grandchildren out on Tybee while they were here on vacation. I don't get to see them much except when they come down to the beach. They went back home yesterday so I'm back at work. How've you been getting along?"

"Not too bad, I guess. Is there a truck I could sleep in tonight?"

"No, not tonight, Benny. I'm sorry."

Benny's disappointment was obvious.

"According to the schedule, I'm supposed to have one coming in tomorrow that is due for maintenance. It's going to be down for a couple of days," said Joseph with kindness.

"Come by tomorrow. I'm on the night shift again. If I can sneak you in, I will."

"That'd be great. I'd appreciate it."

"You come back tomorrow, and I'll see what I can do. I got to get moving and finish my rounds now. Take care!"

Joseph continued in his original direction.

Benny called out, "You're a good friend, Joseph."

Joseph stopped, turned around, and waved to Benny. Then continued his rounds.

Benny walked to the docks. Tugboats were pushing a large container ship into place, and he decided to watch them finish the docking ritual. He found a large crate, climbed on top, and leaned back against the wall, pulling out his bottle. He closed his eyes listening to the sounds of the dock.

Benny opened his eyes and looked at the clear sky above him that was beginning to fade from twilight to black. A few early stars were evident, and he picked out the brightest one.

"Don't forget we got a deal."

He took another sip of the booze and decided to spend the night on top of the crate. He spread out and cushioning his head with his arm, closed his eyes and fell asleep.

~~~~

Vernon listened intently, sipping a beer, while Ian finished his cell phone conversation with Powers. Looking past Ian, he could see A.J. chained to the bed in the other room sleeping on his back. He heard Ian finishing the call, and Vernon turned his attention back to him. Ian hung up and promptly kicked Vernon's feet off the coffee table as he walked by.

"Fix us some food."

Vernon started to complain, but the look from Ian silenced him.

Ian walked into the bedroom. "You can quit faking it now, I know you're awake."

A.J. opened his eyes and sat up stiffly on the bed. He'd been listening to Ian's conversation trying to glean something about his fate.

"How do you feel?" asked Ian.

"Sore," said A.J. "So, what now?"

"Powers said to keep you comfy until tomorrow night. He wants me to bring you to the warehouse before midnight. I hope you got a good story ready A.J."

"I've been working on one," A.J. said with a half-smile.

"Well, boy, it had better be a good one if you want to save your life," Ian said flatly.

"I sure could use another joint and some pain pills. My ribs and face are hurting pretty good."

"Sure, no problem."

Ian left the room and came back with the bottle of pills in his hand and a bag of dope. He tossed the bag onto the bed and handed A.J. the pills.

"This should do you for a while, but you're going to have to roll your own, and while you're at it, roll one for me too. I'll go and get the booze."

Ian left and returned a few minutes later with a new bottle of vodka. He opened it, poured some into a paper cup, handed the cup to A.J., and took a drink from the bottle. A.J. finished rolling the second joint and gave it to Ian.

He tucked it into his shirt pocket. Vernon appeared with a tray of sandwiches and a big bag of chips under his arm.

"Just put it on the bed," A.J said with a smirk.

Vernon gave him a dirty look and walked out of the room. A.J. picked up a sandwich and began to eat.

Spencer, Skip, and Bo met in the hotel room that evening to discuss where they were with the search for A.J.

"We've gotten nowhere in 24 hours," said Bo.

"I know it," said Skip. "We've tried everything we can think of to get information and still have nothing."

Spencer said, "But we're better off than we were yesterday."

"How do you figure?" asked Skip.

"Well, we know somebody has made up a cover story for A.J.'s absence, although we don't know who. If he'd taken off on his own, there wouldn't be a story about his absence. Given that information, I think we've confirmed that A.J. has been taken and is being held somewhere."

"How do you know he's not dead already?" Bo asked.

"I just got a gut feeling," said Spencer. "A.J.'s body will be one we find."

"Why?" asked Skip.

"I think the Snowman will want to send a loud and clear message how he deals with traitors. He'll use A.J. as an example. I'm betting we'll find his body when the time comes. That's why I think for now A.J. is still alive. Let's shift our focus to Jeanette LaCrosse. What do we know about her?"

Bo said, "There's not much information out there on her. Until a few weeks ago, she was virtually unknown."

"Meaning?" asked Spencer.

"Exactly what I said," said Bo with emphasis. "She was a nobody. Very few people outside of the company knew who she was or what she did. The company people knew she handled most of the daily business and personally kept Powers' schedule, but she'd never gotten any recognition, at least until a week ago, and then boom. She had a title, everything was out in public, and she was the number two person in the company."

"That gels with what we found out snooping around the Coastal site," said Skip.

"What about her background?" asked Spencer.

"She grew up in Savannah, her parents are dead, and she has no siblings. She attended Savannah public schools and graduated from a local community college. She's older than Powers by a few years, started working for him not long after he started Coastal Seafood, and she's been there ever since."

Spencer said, "Skip," he hesitated and looked at Bo. "Should we let him in on our discovery?"

Skip nodded. "I think it's a good idea under the circumstances."

Spencer said, "Bo, we think LaCrosse is the second informer." He held up his hand to silence his questions. "Skip can tell you how we got there later. I think we try a voice print match between LaCrosse and our second informer. If they match, we can go from there."

~~~~

Emily had been upset all day. Ever since Alisheen had walked out so rudely, she didn't know what to, but she had to do something. Finally, she reached a decision. It was the right thing to do even though she was betraying Alisheen's trust, but she had to protect her. She tried to call Spencer and tell him Alisheen was going with Carl Powers to the Charity Ball on Friday, but she had been unable to contact him. She'd put off talking to Mickey as a last resort but finally decided she needed his help.

She found him in the bar stocking the cooler. "Mickey, I need some help." Mickey stopped working and tapped a glass of water.

"Sure, Emily," he said taking a sip. "You got some stuff out back that needs unloading? I thought everything came in already?"

"Not exactly, why don't you meet me in the office when you get a chance? I've got something I need to talk to you about."

"Whoa, this sounds like I'm in trouble. I haven't done anything, have I?" asked Mickey with a worried tone.

"No, no, nothing like that," she said reassuringly. "I just need to talk to you about a little problem I have, and well quite frankly, I wasn't going to talk to you about it at all, but I seem to have run out of options."

"Well, I'm not sure that's a compliment or not," said Mickey with a laugh, "But I'll be glad to help if I can."

"Good, just come see me in the office when you get a chance."

"I'm almost through here. I'll be there in a few minutes."

She said, "Thank you," and turned to go, but he stopped her.

"Emily, is this about Alisheen?" Emily nodded in the affirmative.

They met in the office and Emily told Mickey everything that'd happened between them, including the decision by Alisheen to go to the Charity Ball with Powers.

"Has she lost her mind?" Mickey exclaimed.

"Please keep your voice down," said Emily. "We need to be calm about this and figure out how to stop her."

"Well, it's a bit late now. All we can do is hope she doesn't get hurt. Didn't you try and talk her out of it?" he said sarcastically.

"Of course, I did," Emily snapped. "She just got more obstinate and ruder."

Mickey frowned. "Well, what do we do then?"

"You need to try and talk some sense into her," said Emily. "Maybe she'll listen to you?"

Mickey shook his head. "She won't listen to me if she's already tuned you out."

"We can't give up," said Emily. "We need to keep trying."

Mickey said, "I'm not giving up. You keep trying to call Spencer. I've another number I'm going to try. In the meantime, I'll try to watch her back. I'll see you later."

"Where are you going?" asked Emily.

"Don't ask," said Mickey and he left abruptly.

Mickey drove to his apartment. Once inside, he rummaged through the papers and the mail on the kitchen table until he found what he was looking for. He dialed Agent Fitzgerald's number and left a message for him to call. It was urgent. Mickey then went to the dresser and opened the top drawer. He pulled out the gun, checked it to be sure it was loaded, and sat down with the gun in his lap as he turned on the television. He would meet with Powers personally and convince him to stay away from Alisheen.

~~~~

Carl was feeling satisfied regarding the news about A.J. He didn't know what had prompted him to snitch and was surprised he'd grown the balls, but it didn't matter. Life was good. Alisheen had agreed to go with him to the Charity Ball and A.J. was on ice until tomorrow. Coastal business was booming, and soon the smuggling would be back on track. He couldn't ask for more. His private cell phone rang and, assuming it was Ian, he answered casually.

"What did you forget?"

"I didn't forget anything," said Jeanette.

"How did you get this number?"

"Oh, Carl," laughed Jeanette. "I told you I know everything about you and your little sideline. You have no secrets from me."

"Is that a fact?" he said coldly.

"Oh, yes, Carl dear. I met your little girlfriend Alisheen today as well, shopping in the mall. Really, Carl, she is cute, but I'm thinking she's not mature enough for you. She seemed somewhat flighty to me this afternoon."

"I suggest you stay away from Alisheen, Jeanette. I would hate for something to happen to you," Carl said with menace.

"Don't think you can frighten me, Carl. I've done what I need to do to protect myself. Besides, I've already told you I'm not looking to ruin your little sideline. I just think it's time we get on with our lives, together."

"You must be joking."

"Oh, not at all, I'll kill her if necessary, Carl."

He was growing tired of her game.

"Why did you call, Jeanette?"

"I called to remind you not to be late Friday night for our date to the Ball, Carl dear."

"I told you I'm not taking you to the Ball."

"I was close enough to kill her today. Don't be late Friday," and she hung up.

Carl hung up and went through his private contacts. He found Ian's number and hit the send button.

"Hello?"

"I've got a job for you as soon as we're done with A.J. LaCrosse needs to be taken care of by the weekend."

"OK," said Ian and he hung up.

# Chapter 20

WEDNESDAY AFTERNOON JEANETTE sat demurely on the edge of the chair and sipped her champagne. She was listening to her wedding reception music and practicing holding her bouquet with one hand while she drank with the other. She'd positioned her dress, train, and veil neatly around her and was imagining greeting the many guests and well-wishers. She practiced with more frequency now that Carl was almost hers, but she was distracted. Alisheen Delaney was on her mind. Usually when she practiced her wedding day and fantasized about her wedding night with Carl, she was content, but today was different. That woman was ruining everything. She stood up, admired her image in the full-length mirror, and watched as she sipped her champagne.

"*She isn't in my league.*"

She put down the glass and lifted her dress, admiring her stocking-clad legs and the garter.

"Carl, you'll never be sorry. That I promise you."

She picked up her glass, walked to the stereo, and started the wedding music over. She decided it was too soon to kill Alisheen, and she would wait and see. If Carl takes her to the Ball, Alisheen lives; if he takes her, she dies. Then he'd have to learn the hard way that she was serious about her love for him. She pulled the champagne out of the silver ice bucket, refilled her glass, and drained it. She filled it again and placed the bottle back in the bucket. She picked up the Charity Ball invitation from the table and rubbed her fingertips across the raised lettering.

"If Carl does take her to the Ball, I could kill her there. It'll be a huge crowd, so it'd be easy to slip in, kill her, and slip out in the noisy crowd, and there are so many ways to do it."

She smiled with the malicious thought and noted the time. She called Carl's cell phone again and didn't get an answer, so she left him another voicemail. She put down her glass of champagne, turned up the music, and waltzed around the room thinking of Carl.

~~~~

A.J. woke up to see Vernon leaning against the doorway staring at him.

When he saw A.J. was awake, he said coldly, "You going to die tonight, boy."

A.J. didn't respond but looked around to see if Ian was back.

"He ain't back yet. I seen Powers kill before." Vernon paused for effect. "He's a mean son-of-a bitch. I watched him beat the hell out of a couple of people for fun until he got tired and then he shot them. It was gruesome too. He just splattered them all over the place, very messy."

A.J, wary of Vernon, shifted his weight on the bed without taking his eyes off him.

Vernon sneered.

"What's the matter, A.J.? You usually got some kind of smart-ass remark to make."

Ian returned and A.J was relieved and delighted when Ian came in and caught Vernon standing there. Ian walked over to the table and put the groceries down as Vernon slinked away from the door and A.J.

"Start getting supper ready, and don't screw up the steaks. I went a long way to get good ones so A.J can have a decent last meal."

Vernon glared with venom at Baxter but didn't say anything, and he began to take the groceries out of the bags. He opened a beer and began preparing the steak dinner under Ian's watchful stare. Ian laughed silently then turned to A.J.

"Powers wants me to bring you to the warehouse tonight."

Ian looked at A.J. intently.

"Why, A.J.?"

"Revenge," A.J. whispered hoarsely. "Powers befriended me, then tricked me, humiliated me, and virtually made me his slave. He took my dignity and self-respect. He took everything from me, and I just wanted to get something of myself back."

A.J. stood up and walked toward Ian. The rattling of the chain around his ankle brought him to a stop and back to reality.

"Powers took away every dream I ever had."

He lay down on the bed and rolled over facing the wall.

Ian noticed he was shaking. "You owe him A.J. I understand that, but this time it's your life he'll take away, not your dignity or self-respect."

A.J. rolled over and looked at Ian. His eyes were misty.

"He took that away from me too, a long time ago."

He rolled back over and faced the wall.

~~~~

Benny finished his dinner and casually poured another glass of tea. He looked at the clock on the wall in the gym. There was plenty of time to meet Joseph at the fence. He watched his back for a couple of blocks to be sure no one was following him and when he was satisfied, he made a beeline for Coastal. He sat on the curb to wait and smoked. He finally heard Joseph's whistle, and he hurried to meet him.

"Is everything on for tonight?" Benny asked anxiously.

"Sure, sure, Benny, no problem," replied Joseph with an assuring tone. "The truck is down for maintenance like the schedule says in warehouse number seven. You come by after nine and I'll let you in and get you in the morning before I get off. OK?"

"It sounds great. I'll be back after nine, and thanks."

"It's OK, Benny. I'm glad to help you out when I can."

Joseph sauntered off down the fence and Benny sat on the curb and smoked another cigarette. He checked his pockets and decided he was going to need another pack of smokes and a bottle. He hoped the truck connected to the electrical system. If so, he'd be able to run the sleeper's air conditioning and the satellite television. Benny walked away from the docks to buy his booze and cigarettes. He heard Cooley's voice behind him as he came out of the convenience store.

"You're pretty far away from your territory, Benny."

Benny turned around and saw Cooley and Bridges walking toward him. He knew it was useless to run so he waited until they caught up to him.

"OK, Benny, let's walk," said Cooley as he guided Benny by the elbow.

"What's the deal? Why are you so far away from the docks?"

Benny said with sarcasm, "I'm just trying to get away from it all, Jack."

Cooley gripped Benny's elbow harder causing him to wince with pain.

"I can't stand a smart-ass. It pisses me off. What's the deal?"

"Honest, Cooley, I'm just trying to buy some stuff so the bums on the docks won't be mooching off me. They'll bum it all if they know I got it. I'm just trying to save it for me, man. Come on, give me a break."

Cooley stopped Benny and faced him.

"You got anything for us?"

"I told you there ain't nothing going on. It's quiet on the street, man, I swear."

Cooley said, "If you're holding out on me, I'm going to make you regret it."

Benny whined. "Cooley, we got a deal. If I knew anything I'd tell ya."

Cooley began to walk away and motioned to Bridges, who threw him a pack of cigarettes with money in it.

"I'll be in touch, Benny."

"Yeah, I hear you, Jack." Then louder he said, "I can't wait until the next time. You're always such a fun guy!"

~~~~

Vincent straddled the chair facing the small group of men.

"No sign of him?"

One of the men spoke up.

"We checked his house, the bars, and where he works. Nobody has seen him."

There was a knock on the door and Vincent checked his watch.

"That will be Detective Naster. Let her in."

One of the men by the door opened it, and Carol strolled into the room and found an empty seat.

She lit a cigarette and exhaled. "Have you found him yet?"

"Hell no," said Vincent. "It's like he's just pulled stakes and left. No one has seen him. I think he's gone. They know where all of the hidey-holes are and checked them all; if Vernon was around, he'd be in one of them."

Carol said, "If he's with Baxter they're somewhere you don't know about. I'm guessing he's still around."

"What makes you so sure?" asked one of the men in the group.

Carol said, "We're convinced Guilford is going to be made an example of as a warning to the people who deal with the Snowman. He hasn't shown up dead yet so he's still alive. If he's alive he's being guarded, and I'm betting he's being guarded by Vernon and Baxter."

Carol stood up and paced.

"Do any of you know of any connection Vernon might've had with Baxter?"

Vincent said, "I already answered that question, Detective. Like I said, I don't know of any connection between those two except through Jake."

Carol said, "There must be something else. I'm guessing Vernon knows more about Jake's murder than he's telling."

The same man spoke again.

"How do you know that?"

"Simple," Carol said. "He was Jake's back up plan at the rest stop. He didn't back him up. Now he's disappeared at the same time Baxter and A.J. have disappeared. I think it's pretty clear he's working with Baxter."

Vincent broke in. "I told y'all earlier the Detective thinks he might've been spying on us the whole time he was working with Jake."

Carol said, "He was probably passing information to Baxter. He may have been looking out for potential problems and letting Baxter know on the side."

The room was silent. Carol finished her cigarette and got up to leave.

She looked at Vincent. "I've given you all I can. You're going to have to give me something I can use before I can do anything else."

Vincent said, "What else do you want? I told you Powers is the Snowman."

Carol said, "I'll overlook the fact you held that information from me the whole time, because you were waiting on me to give you something you could use to find Jake's killer. But now you've left me hanging, and I got nothing unless I get something else from you."

"What?" asked Vincent warily.

"I need you and others in this room to testify that Powers is the Snowman in court. Either that or you find Vernon for me so I can question him, and he testifies."

Carol threw her cigarette onto the floor, stepped on it, and walked out of the cabin.

~~~~

Spencer had gotten Emily's message to come and see her. The message, in conjunction with the one from Mickey relayed through Fitzgerald, created a sense of urgency. He was sure Alisheen had done something rash to get back at him, and now she was in danger. They wouldn't have gone to the trouble otherwise. He arrived at the She Crab, feeling like a stranger. Spencer girded himself and went through the front door, spotting Emily at the cash register. She waved at him and signaled for him to hold on a minute. He waited, shifting his feet and looking slightly embarrassed until she was free.

She gave him a big hug. "Boy, am I glad to see you."

Spencer felt awkward. "Thanks, Emily."

Emily didn't hesitate. "Spencer, I need to talk to you about Alisheen."

"Is she alright?" he asked with concern.

"She's fine," said Emily quickly, "but I'm afraid she's done something terribly stupid to get back at you."

"Oh crap," said Spencer. "Don't tell me she's going out with Powers again."

Emily nodded her head in the affirmative.

"Spencer, let's go to the office so we can talk more privately."

She led Spencer to the office and closed the door.

Spencer sat down on the couch. "Emily, what's going on? Where is Alisheen? I've tried to call her, but I finally gave up."

"Spencer, she was really doing OK for a while," Emily said, "But then she started thinking about whatever you told Dixie, and she totally changed. I don't know what you said to her, but she was devastated."

"I know, I know," said Spencer exasperated. "It all just came out wrong, and things went from bad to worse in record time. We both said things we shouldn't have, and all hell broke loose." Emily touched his shoulder and sat down next to him.

"Spencer, I tried to talk her out of going with Powers to the Charity Ball Friday, but she isn't listening to me. I hope you can talk some sense into her."

Spencer shrugged his shoulders. "What do you want me to do?"

"You're going to have to try and talk to her and get her to agree to see you."

"That'll be a neat trick since so far she hasn't seen fit to return a phone call," said Spencer sourly.

"Well, either way, when you do talk to her, you can't lose your temper. You have to plead your case calmly and convince her to meet with you so you can talk this through. She isn't thinking right now."

Emily held his hands. "You have to convince her to give you the chance you both deserve."

The door opened suddenly and Alisheen walked in. Emily stood up and looked at her.

"I told him everything, Alisheen. It's for your own good. Please talk to him."

Emily walked past her and firmly closed the door leaving them alone. Spencer stood up, walked to her, and without hesitation put his arms around her and gave her a hug. She responded in kind and for a few moments, they held each other as if there was nothing wrong between them. Spencer finally broke the hug and moved away from her.

"Emily tells me you're going to the Charity Ball with Powers on Friday. Is that true?"

She averted her eyes briefly and then looked at Spencer.

"Emily is a tattletale and has big mouth to boot."

"She's your friend and is concerned about you. She thinks we need to give ourselves a decent chance and not just throw it away on hysterics."

"Hysterics," she said flatly. "Maybe she's right, but I'm not sure about us anymore."

"Why, Alisheen? We've been together a long time. We owe ourselves another chance."

"That's just it Spencer," said Alisheen heatedly. "We've been together a long time and it all came down to the fact that you didn't trust me enough to share your fears with me."

"OK, I understand that. It all went sideways when I tried to tell you what I was feeling. I was wrong, I admit that, but why Powers of all people? Do you seriously think I'd make up something like this just to keep you away from him? I'm not going to accuse somebody of serious crimes like that just to keep you from dating him."

"No, you probably wouldn't do something like that," she said caustically.

Spencer didn't rise to the bait.

"You still haven't told me why."

Alisheen said, "There are a lot of reasons. He makes me feel special; he makes sure my needs are met; we have a good time together; like I said, lots of reasons."

She was silent for a moment then said, "He trusts me."

"Alisheen, I love you."

She shook her head.

"I used to think that Spencer, but I just don't know any more. I need to resolve this on my own terms and spend some time with Carl. I'm not saying we're totally through, but I've got to give myself a chance with him to see where it goes."

Spencer pleaded with emotion, "Alisheen, listen to me please, Powers is a criminal!"

"You don't know that" she yelled. "You can't prove it."

"I can," said Spencer, raising his voice to match hers. "He's a drug smuggler and a murderer. I have enough evidence to prove it."

"That's a lie," she said. "You'd have arrested him if you had proof."

"No, I haven't, but there are good reasons why. The time will come when the walls will come down around him, and I don't want you caught in the rubble."

"Oh crap, Spencer," yelled Alisheen, "That's so cliché I can't even believe you said it."

"Cliché or not, it's the truth. Take it or leave it," said Spencer defiantly.

"I'll leave it. Until you arrest him, or he gives me a reason otherwise to mistrust him, I will continue to see him."

"I've done all I can." Spencer said quietly, defeated by her words. "I'll be going now."

He looked at her with sadness and left the restaurant, passing Emily at the cash register. She could tell by his expression that things didn't go well. She quickly went to the office and found Alisheen sitting on the couch with her head in her hands and her face stained with tears.

"He won't even fight for me, Emily. He just gave up and walked out."

~~~~

Baxter poked A.J. awake. "You might want to hear this."

A.J. noticed that vodka and a joint were on the table. He picked up the joint, lit it and took a drag, held it, then exhaled. He sipped vodka from the bottle and watched Ian call Powers.

Carl checked the number before answering. Jeanette had been calling and leaving messages. He recognized Ian's number and picked up.

"Powers."

"What time tonight?"

Carl said, "I'll be there after midnight; you get there first and wait. I don't want too much activity in and out of the yard late at night."

"Which warehouse?" asked Ian.

"Number seven. There isn't anything going on in that warehouse, so we won't be disturbed."

"We'll be there," said Ian and he hung up. "OK, A.J. we'll meet him after midnight. You feeling better?"

A.J. nodded. "Yeah, I'm just sore. You got some more pills?"

"Yeah, sure," said Ian. He left and returned a few minutes later with the pills and tossed them onto the bed. A.J. nodded and popped the pills followed by a swig of vodka. He settled back onto the bed, lit the joint again, and contemplated the upcoming night. He just hoped he had a plan that'd keep him alive. He closed his eyes as the buzz kicked in, and he relaxed.

~~~~

Carl settled into a chair and looked out the window. He picked up his drink, took a sip, and flipped on the television, watching the news without interest as he pondered the night ahead. He was going to kill A.J. He'd made up his mind already, but he wanted to talk to him first. What A.J. told him would determine how much pain he inflicted. He also wanted the body found. as a warning to anyone that might try to double-cross him in the future. Ian could take it somewhere and leave it where somebody would find it later. Then they'd wait a few months and start again. He watched the news for a few minutes, and then decided to call Alisheen at the restaurant.

"Hello, Carl," she said pleasantly.

"I was wondering when I was going to talk to you again. I've called and left messages at the loft, but either you're not there or you're not answering your phone. Which is it?"

"I'm sorry," said Alisheen. "I've been avoiding the telephone unless I know for sure who it is."

"Oh, I was getting nervous about Friday since I hadn't heard from you."

She laughed. "I can't imagine you being nervous. I think I'm the one that should be nervous. I've never been to anything like this before. I'm excited about going."

Carl was thrilled with her enthusiasm. "I'm glad you decided to go with me. I'll call you tomorrow and let you know what time I'll pick you up. Will that be OK?"

"That will be fine," said Alisheen. "Just call me here or leave a message on my cell and I'll call you back, and Carl …"

"Yes,"

"I am looking forward to going."

"Great! Me too. Goodbye, Alisheen."

"Goodbye."

She hung up and pursed her lips, reflecting on her decision. She went out into the kitchen and looked around for Emily. Not seeing her, she went into the dining room and spotted her behind the cash register. Alisheen bit her lip, made up her mind, and walked toward her. Emily looked up as she approached and watched her cross the dining room. She stopped and looked down through the glass countertop, tapping her fingers on the top as if she was counting the items in the case.

Without looking up she said, "Emily, I was so rude to you the other day. I feel just horrible. I've wanted to talk to you, but I wasn't sure if you'd talk to me or not since I was so awful to you."

Emily came around the counter, hugged her and said, "You were awful, but I understand. I'm sorry too, for everything."

Alisheen laughed and stepped back from Emily with despair on her face. "I really need your help."

Emily hugged her again. "I guessed that. You're a crazy woman, but somebody is going to have to try and keep you straight."

"Then you'll help me?" she asked. "Because I'm scared to death, and I don't have a clue about what to do."

"Of course, I'll help you," said Emily. "We'll go to my place after work and figure it all out, OK?"

"That'd be great," said Alisheen, wiping a tear from her cheek.

~~~~

Mickey checked his watch. It was risky, but he'd decided to confront Powers and force him to leave Alisheen alone with a threat. He looked around the basement garage of the apartment tower where Powers lived. He still knew some old tricks, so it'd been easy to get past the lift gate and into the garage. He'd spotted the Jag easy enough with the arrogant *Shrimp1* license tag, and he backed into a shadowed space that gave him a full view of the elevator doors and the car.

He desperately wanted to smoke but knew the smell of a cigarette in the air might give him away, so he resisted the urge. He sipped on a bottle of tequila to help keep his nerves fortified and exhaled in an effort to relax and checked his watch again. It was nine. He hoped the bastard would show soon. He couldn't keep a vigil in the garage for too long. Eventually somebody would spot him, and he'd have to leave, but for the moment he was determined to stay and confront Powers. He had to keep him away from Alisheen.

~~~~

Benny heard the church bell ring and counted the strikes. It was nine o'clock, time to meet Joseph.

When he reached the fence, there was no sign of Joseph, so he sat on the curb and waited. Soon he heard Joseph's cheerful whistle getting closer as he made his rounds.

"Is that you, Joseph?"

Joseph chuckled. "Yep, it's me, Benny. You weren't expecting anybody else, were you?"

Benny grinned. "Is it time?"

"No, not yet, the other guard is still here, but don't worry. Everything is OK, just hang around. I'll come and get you as soon as he's gone."

"Ok, I'll stay close by."

"Good," said Joseph, "See you in a bit."

Joseph resumed whistling his tune as he walked away, and Benny crossed the street and sat on some steps to wait. After a short wait, Benny saw the beam of a flashlight, and he heard Joseph's voice.

"Benny?" asked the old man.

"Yes, sir," said Benny.

"Good, the other guard is gone so it's all clear now. Turn around and go down to the next gate."

Benny was so excited he almost ran. Reaching the gate, he looked around furtively. Soon Joseph appeared and unlocked it.

"Don't worry now, son," said Joseph, "I'm the only guard on tonight. No one else is around."

Benny flipped the gate latch up as Joseph pulled the lock free. He opened the gate and walked in, then flipped the latch back down so Joseph could lock it back.

"Follow me."

They cut across the grounds to the warehouse.

"Here it is, number seven," said Joseph.

His keys jingled as he searched through them to find the door key. As they entered the warehouse, the overhead night light offered a dim view of the inside. There were three trucks and two empty service bays. Two of the three trucks looked ready to roll, but the third was hooked up to the warehouse electrical service.

"OK, Benny, there it is. The other two are due to go out in the morning. I'll come and get you early and let you out."

Joseph grinned as Benny looked at the truck.

"You're in luck; it's still plugged in. They must've needed the electrical to run while they worked on it. That means you got satellite and air."

Benny grinned from ear to ear.

"I was hoping I'd get lucky. Thanks, Joseph, you're a great friend."

Benny hugged Joseph and held him for a second.

The old man patted him on the back, and with a chuckle said, "Sleep well."

Benny climbed into the truck, closed the door behind him, and then crawled into the sleeper of the cab. He took out his bottle, snacks, and smokes, and arranged it all neatly on the small shelf that served as a side table for the bed. He reached up to the overhead console and flipped on the air conditioning, feeling the cool air on his face. He turned on the television, confirmed the satellite was working, and tuned into the cartoon channel. He propped up on the bed, lit a cigarette, and opened the bottle. Then remembered to open the top hatch of the sleeper to let the smoke out.

~~~~

"It's time, A.J.," announced Ian.

A.J. sat up and swung his feet over the side of the bed. Ian unlocked the cuff and A.J. stretched carefully and stood up testing his balance.

Ian said, "A.J., I'll beat the crap out of you if you try anything."

"I won't. Don't worry." A.J. shook his head.

He knew he didn't have a chance anyway so to try would be useless. Vernon sneered at him as he walked by, preceding Ian outside.

"What about the truck?" asked Vernon.

Ian shook his head.

"Later, right now we need to deliver A.J."

Ian checked his watch. It was after 10:00.

"We got a couple of hours. So, we can stop and pick up some beer on the way to help pass the time."

Vernon grinned delighted at the prospect.

Ian opened the trunk of the Taurus. "Get in, A.J."

A.J didn't say anything, but complied, easing himself into the trunk and laid down.

"Put your hands behind your back," Ian said simply.

A.J. repositioned himself and put his hands behind him. Ian wrapped duct tape around his hands and then his ankles.

He said, "Sorry, A.J.," and he forced a rag into A.J.'s mouth securing it in place with duct tape. Ian closed the trunk, then turned to Vernon and said, "Let's go."

A.J. heard the engine start, felt the car lurch into gear, and began to roll. He could hear their voices coming from the inside of the car, and then the radio began to play ending his ability to hear what they were saying. He tried to look around the trunk, but he couldn't see anything other than the faint glow of red from the taillights. He shifted to make himself comfortable and focused on breathing. He was on his way to die.

~~~~

Mickey was half-asleep when he heard the elevator doors open. He quickly grabbed his ski mask and scrunched down to hide. It was Powers! He put the ski mask on and grabbed the gun off the seat. He quietly opened the door and panicked when the dome light went off; he'd forgotten to turn off the switch. He quickly slid out of the car and pushed the door closed until the light went out. He stood in the dark, hoping Powers hadn't seen the light and watched him walk to his car. Now was the time!

Powers had his back to him as he opened the car door.

Mickey moved forward quickly and spoke loudly, "Hold It!"

Before Mickey could react, Powers backhanded him with a closed fist. Too late, Mickey realized he'd gotten too close. Powers had noticed the light go on and off in the shadows as he approached his car out of the corner of his eye. He moved the mirror on the Jag by opening the door so he could watch behind him. He saw the mugger coming and was ready.

The backhand knocked Mickey down and Powers moved quickly kicking him in the head and gut, disabling him and knocking the air out of his lungs. Mickey groaned on the floor, and Powers kicked the gun from his hand. Then he walked over to it, picked it up, and put it in his pocket. He delivered a few more kicks to the mugger's face and body and then spit on him.

"Get out of here, bad boy, before I kill you."

Powers got into the Jag, backed out of the space, and put it into gear accelerating with a squeal of the tires. Mickey rolled over to keep Powers from running over him as he drove by and left the garage. He lay on the floor in pain, bleeding and could barely breathe. He was sure the kicks from Powers had broken some of his ribs and probably his nose. The fact that it had been so easy for Powers to overcome him and the total humiliation he felt overwhelmed him, and he vomited. He finally made it to his knees, crawled to his car, and got in. He took off the ski mask soaked with the vomit and blood. He grabbed some napkins from the console and pressed them in a wad to his bleeding face and nose. He drained the bottle of tequila and threw it onto the floor of the car, started the engine, and managed to drive home. With Powers' laughter ringing in his ears, he shed a tear. He'd failed Alisheen.

# Chapter 21

BENNY WOKE WITH a start. *"What was that noise?"* He got to his knees and quickly cut off the air and lights and sat in the dark. He heard it again. It was the warehouse garage door opening. *"He was going to get caught. What'd happened to Joseph?"* In a few minutes, he heard an engine.

The engine grew louder, stopping in the empty bay next to the truck. It wasn't another truck though; it was a car. Benny's curiosity made him throw caution to the wind, and he slid the curtain of the sleeper to the side and looked out. It was a car all right. He lay on his belly propped up with pillows to watch. When he recognized Vernon Faris in the gloom, Benny got excited.

He was thinking how much Cooley would pay for this information. He hated Vernon. This must be a drug deal going down, and he had a front row seat. He'd been right about being on a lucky streak. Benny almost yelped in fear when Ian Baxter walked into view.

He was scared. If Baxter caught him, he was dead. He withdrew from the window, wiped his brow, and took a drink.

*"What should I do?"* he wondered, *"Try and sneak out. No, you damn fool, you'll get caught, just stay put,"* he argued with himself. He could hear them talking through the open vent in the roof.

"You going to leave him in there?" Vernon said.

"Yeah, that way we don't have to watch him," Baxter replied.

"What were they talking about?" Curious he looked back out the window. They went into the shop, and the light came on spilling through the doorway onto the ground. He heard a television and smelled cigarette smoke. They'd gotten comfortable. After a few minutes, Vernon appeared with a large roll of plastic under his arm. He spread it out over the floor, and placed a chair in the middle, before disappearing into the shop again. Benny watched with growing fear and curiosity.

*"What in the hell was going on?"*

Vernon returned to his seat on the counter, envying the comfortable chair Baxter was in.

"I rolled the plastic out and put the chair on it, now what?"

Ian popped a beer and looked at his watch. "We wait."

~~~~

Powers laughed as he drove past the mugger on the ground. He could've swerved to run over him, but he didn't want to have to explain anything, especially tonight. It'd be on the camera, and somebody might ask him about it later. He'd decided to go to the plantation in case he needed an alibi after dealing with A.J., so he bought gas and food to establish the time he was supposedly leaving and drove to the warehouse. They'd have to prove he hung around and killed A.J. and that'd be impossible, especially after Ian dumped the body.

Carl arrived at the gate closest to the number seven warehouse and opened it. He drove in, stopped, and put the lock through the latch not bothering to lock it back. He didn't plan to be long. He drove to the warehouse, used his key to open the door, and stepped inside. He let his eyes adjust to the dim light before walking to the tool room. Ian was watching the door.

"I thought I heard a car door."

Carl gave Vernon a hard look.

"He works for me," Ian said.

Carl said, "Where is he?"

Ian nodded toward the garage, "In the trunk."

"Let's go," said Carl.

A.J was sweating and breathing heavily in an effort to get air through his nose. He heard voices as they got louder and realized they were coming. He blinked rapidly when the trunk opened even though the light was dim.

He heard Powers' voice, "Put him in the chair." A.J. felt someone grab his wrist and ankles and cut them loose, and Ian gently pulled the tape from his mouth. A.J. spit out the rag.

"Help me," Ian said, and Vernon leaned into the trunk grabbing A.J.'s arm.

They escorted him to the chair. Vernon pulled his hands behind him, and Ian taped them together. A.J. looked up into the light. He blinked again trying to focus his eyes and looked around the warehouse. Vernon was beside him and Ian was standing off to the side. He then focused on Powers leaning against the Taurus.

"A.J., you've cost me a lot of money." Powers' tone sent chills down A.J.'s spine.

"Before I decide what to do with you, I need to know why."

A.J. looked at Powers. "You know why. You humiliated me and took my life away. You took everything and left me with nothing. I wanted some of it back, and maybe I could pick up the business and run it myself."

The laughter from Powers hit A.J. with force, and he hung his head in shame.

"A.J., A.J.," said Powers. "You don't have the brains or the balls to run an operation like this."

Powers walked over to A.J. and lifted his head with his hand. The tears in A.J.'s eyes glistened.

"You're weak, A.J. You're crying like a baby. You can't kill anybody that gets in your way. You weren't even a good snitch."

Powers walked away, then walked back to face A.J. "You did cost me lot of money though."

A.J perked up. "Listen, Carl, I've been thinking about that."

"Oh yeah, just what've you been thinking?"

"I could pay you back," he said with a hint of hope in his voice.

"How?" asked Powers.

A.J. decided it was now or never.

"You don't have to cut me in any more on the action, you know. I work for free."

"Well, that's a start, but it would take a long time to pay me back. Maybe I don't want to wait."

"I could do extra stuff," blurted out A.J.

"How do I know you won't run when you get the chance?"

"Ian can watch me," said A.J. "And besides, I got nowhere else to go and nothing to run on. I'm broke."

Powers rubbed his chin as if he were thinking about it and then he hit A.J. with his fist so hard he almost knocked the chair over before Vernon caught it. A.J.'s mouth and nose were bleeding freely, and he was reeling with pain.

"That was for the first load you lost me," said Powers calmly, and then he hit him again. "That was for the second one."

A.J. began to fall and Vernon caught him, propped him up from behind, and supported him until he was steady again.

Powers hit A.J. twice more and said with the fourth punch, "That was for the fourth load you cost me, A.J."

A.J. was on the verge of unconsciousness. He felt cold water on his head and face. He managed to look through his swollen eyes to see Vernon holding a sponge. Vernon was wiping him down like a boxer to revive him.

Powers said, "You know, A.J., you might have a point. I might need a fall guy in the future, especially if I decide to get out of this business. You did such a great job in college you might be worth keeping around at that. If you were killed during a drug deal, it would be a sure way to get me in the clear."

Benny watched in horror through the sleeper cab window. When Powers appeared, his curiosity abandoned him, and his fear rose to a level that caused him to wet his pants. He was terrified and could barely draw a breath. If they discovered him, his death would be certain. In spite of it all, the scene held him captive. He watched in pure terror through his fingers, like a child watching a horror movie. Benny watched Baxter open a beer and take a drink with indifference to A.J.'s plight. Powers with a smile on his face, was watching Vernon try to revive A.J. He was having fun.

~~~~

When Joseph got to the gate closest to the warehouse number seven, he put the beam of his light on the lock and was surprised to find it open.

*"That's odd,"* mused Joseph, *"I'm sure I locked that after I let Benny in."*

He rubbed his chin and looked around, directing the beam of his light at the warehouse. The glint on the parked car surprised him. He hurried over to the car, and the *Shrimp1* license tag reflected in the beam of the flashlight.

"That's Mr. Powers' Jaguar," Joseph thought. "Oh gosh, I hope he didn't find Benny in the truck. I'll lose my job."

As Joseph opened the door to the warehouse, he briefly wondered why Mr. Powers was here at this time of night. It certainly was odd. He entered the warehouse uneasy, pulled his pistol, and held it nervously in front of him. Joseph heard voices as he rounded the corner and saw the scene before him. A man was sitting in a chair bleeding badly and there was somebody standing behind him and in front. He didn't recognize the man in the back, but he did recognize Mr. Powers.

He dropped his gun down to his side with surprise and said with a questioningly look on his face, "Mr. Powers?"

Benny's stifled scream was lost in the loud echo of the shots bouncing off the walls of the warehouse. He screamed into his sleeve and cried, rocking with terror. Joseph hadn't seen Baxter standing off to the side. Without hesitation, he shot Joseph in the chest three times as he lowered his gun. The kindly old man, who had a family and grandchildren, was dead in an instant. Benny had frozen with terror. He watched Ian grab Joseph under the arms and quickly drag him to the plastic and dump him on the ground.

"I don't want his blood all over the floor," he said, "Too hard to clean up." A.J. was unable to move, but the fear was evident even on his battered face.

Powers said, "Damn, Ian, now we got a mess." Powers pulled the pistol he'd taken from the mugger out of his pocket and shot A.J. in the chest twice, and he added one between the eyes. A.J. slumped over dead and fell to the plastic. Vernon cowered in fear and acted as if he was going to run away.

Ian said, "Stay put," pointing his gun at Vernon. "OK, Mr. Powers, now what?"

"Simple, we fake a robbery."

"It will go like this. You had A.J. call in and say he was going to be gone awhile, right?"

"Yes," said Ian as he looked down at the blood pool slowly growing under A.J.'s body.

"Then it's easy. He came back tonight unexpectedly and interrupted a robbery in progress with the security guard."

"So, what do we do?" asked Ian.

"Lift them up and get that plastic out from underneath them as fast as we can. We need blood all over the floor."

Ian motioned to Vernon to help him move the bodies off the plastic.

"What next?"

"I'll go bust the gate and the door lock with a crowbar. You start throwing tools and anything else worth stealing into the trunk of the car. Put the plastic and the chair in there too."

Carl looked at Vernon. "You, clean the tape residue off his wrists and ankles, and get his face too. They'll eventually figure it out, but I don't want it obvious he was bound. We need to slow them down as much as we can, understand?"

Vernon, pale at the sudden turn of events, nodded quickly, and Carl looked at him with disgust. He walked into the tool room, grabbed a crowbar, went outside, and crossed the grounds to the gate. He locked the gate, and then he broke the latch with ease. He went to the warehouse door, closed and locked it shut. It took him a few minutes, but he was finally able to use enough force to bend the doorframe enough for the door to pop open. He went back into the warehouse and saw Ian throwing tools into the trunk of the car, and that idiot with him was rubbing A.J.'s wrists with some kind of cleaner.

"Did you get his face?" asked Carl harshly.

Vernon looked up and nodded, too scared to speak.

Carl, satisfied, said to Ian, "I busted the gate and the door, the rest is up to you. Clean this place out. Then take the car down to the docks and put it in a container for one of our sea tugs to dump in the ocean. Make sure they know to dump it deep."

Ian nodded. "OK. Where will you be tomorrow when they find this mess?"

"The plantation. I'll have Rupert call in the morning to let them know I came to Beaufort last night. As soon as possible, take care of LaCrosse."

Ian nodded. "I will, but I'm leaving town after I do her. It's going to be hot around here, and I'm getting scarce."

"Good," said Carl, "Just call when you get back. Let's say three months?"

Ian nodded and Carl looked at the scene. The two bodies had a good bit of blood under them now, and they looked they'd been shot and fell where they were. The ransacked tool room looked professional. Carl took the mugger's gun he used on A.J. out of his pocket and carefully wiped it clean removing his fingerprints. Ian and Vernon watched him with curiosity. Carl walked over to A.J.'s body, dropped the gun on the ground, and grinned at Ian.

"A trail for them to follow," he said with a smile and left.

Ian told Vernon to get in the car, and he surveyed the scene one more time. It looked like a robbery with two bodies that'd ended up in the wrong place at the wrong time. He grabbed the rag Powers used on the gun, opened the warehouse garage door, and motioned for Vernon to drive. Ian closed it, then exited through the broken door and walked across the grounds to the gate where Vernon had stopped to wait. Ian got in the car and said, "Let's go."

Benny had remained frozen in place. He watched with fascination as they arranged the bodies and put the tools and equipment, the plastic, and the chair A.J. had been sitting in, into the trunk of the car. He watched Powers wipe the gun down and drop it on the floor next to A.J. Benny waited for a long time making sure they were gone.

He cautiously climbed out of the cab, listening briefly before he moved again. He ran over to A.J.'s body and then he went to Joseph's. The look of surprise and the question on his lips were frozen on his face. He knelt next to the kindly old man and cried as he closed his eyes with his fingers. He went into the tool room and saw the damage that Ian and Vernon had done in their attempt to make it look like a robbery. He saw a greasy pad of paper on the desk, quickly wrote a note, folded it, and wrote Cooley's name on the outside. Benny went back to Joseph's body and put the note into his shirt pocket. He said a solemn prayer, looked at heaven, said, "Amen" and ran.

~~~~

Vernon drove to the container docks where the moored sea tugs Powers owned for shipping by barge were located. Ian found an empty container and motioned for Vernon to pull in. Vernon got out and together they closed the doors.

"Wait here," Ian said.

He returned sometime later with a scared looking captain in tow and a lock in his hand. Ian locked the door, put the key in his pocket and turned to the captain.

"Get this thing on your barge and out of here now."

The captain disappeared, came back shortly with several men, and they quickly rigged the container for lifting. Within minutes, the barge crane swung over and down and picked up the container putting it onto the barge.

Ian said, "Take it out to deep water and dump it. We don't need to find it again either. The usual appreciation will be left for you and the crew."

The captain smiled, gave a half of a salute, and boarded the tug. Within minutes, the tug was pushing the barge out to sea. They watched it disappear and Ian noticed the sun was coming up.

"Come on, we got to get out of here." They walked for several blocks until Ian felt they were far enough away and hailed a cab.

~~~~

Benny ran until his fear took over again and he stopped, fell to his knees, and puked. He was shaking and wet with urine. He had to clean up and get out of town. Once that note got into the cops' hands, they'd know who put it there. He got up and hurried to the abandoned warehouse.

He entered cautiously and went up to the second floor, making his way to the small office at the end of the floor that he'd claimed as his. He stuffed his few belongings into a backpack he'd scrounged from the garbage some time ago, and then walked to the corner of the room and found the loose brick at the bottom of the wall. He pulled the brick out, reached in and looked around before pulling a wad of cash out of the hole that he'd squirreled away. It was almost $500. That'd get him far enough away, so he'd be safe. Benny gave his surroundings a last look and headed for the mission. He was going to be on the first bus out of town.

"Hey there, Benny," said the night attendant. "You're too early for breakfast. You look rough, bad night?"

"I was wondering if I could get a shower and shave," Benny said ignoring him. "I'm going to visit my sister, and I need to get cleaned up."

The surprised attendant looked at Benny.

"Sure, man, sure. You know where the gym is?"

"Yep."

The attendant said, "Wait here," and disappeared.

He came back in a few minutes with a small soap, disposable razor, shaving cream, and a towel.

"Keep the soap and shaving stuff, Benny, but leave the towel in the bin, OK?"

Benny nodded and hurried to the gym where he took a hot shower and shaved. He put on clean clothes, put the other clothes in a trash-bag, tied it up tight, and dumped it. He was at the bus station when it opened.

"When is the first bus out of town?" Benny asked as the ticket agent opened the window.

The agent glanced at the clock on the wall. "In about thirty minutes. The bus from Miami to New York will be here to make a stop."

"I'll take it."

As the sun rose over the river, Benny was on his way out of Savannah. He hoped the note in Joseph's pocket would be enough. It was all he could do. He settled into his seat, pulled the shade against the sunrise, and went to sleep.

~~~~

The cab dropped them off at an interchange. Ian held a $100 bill in his hand.

"That's to forget where you let us out if anybody asks." The cabbie took the money from Ian and stuffed it in his shirt pocket.

"I ain't ever seen you guys," and sped off. They walked to the nearest hotel, and Ian went in and got two rooms.

He handed a key to Vernon. "Don't try to sneak out on me. We need to get back to the cabin and lay low. You can drive the truck back in a few days and disappear. It should be clear by then."

"What if it's not?" said Vernon.

"Then we wait," said Ian.

Ian followed Vernon to his room and stood outside the door until he heard the chain latch and the door bolt as Vernon locked himself in, then he went to his room. He washed his hands and face and realized he was tired. It's been a busy night. Poor A.J. He might've made it except for the old geezer security guard walking in on them. Ian put the "Do Not Disturb" sign on the doorknob, then chained and locked his door. He picked up the phone and dialed the front desk.

The desk clerk answered. "You keep your eyes on my partner for me and call me if he tries to leave."

"Right, yes sir," said the desk clerk, "You paid me extra to watch him, and I'll watch him."

Ian without responding hung up, lay down on the bed, and closed his eyes.

~~~~

After leaving Vincent, Carol went home instead of going back to the station that night. She knew she was without options, and she needed some time to think. That lying bastard Vincent. He'd known Powers was the Snowman the whole time, but it wouldn't do her any good if she didn't find Vernon and get him to testify; because whatever in the hell Henry was using to hold them back had them stopped cold anyway. The next morning came too soon. She was tired.

The squad room was empty when she arrived. She checked her watch and scanned the chalkboard to see if anybody had checked in and gone back out. She was sipping her coffee and going through the papers on her desk when Skip walked in. The look of relief on his face was obvious, and she smiled at him.

Skip said, "Where did you disappear to yesterday?"

"I was so tired I went home and crashed after meeting with Vincent. I figured you would've called me if anything major had happened."

"I called but you didn't answer. If you hadn't been here this morning, I was going to come find you."

Carol smiled. "Thanks for thinking of me."

He blushed and said somewhat embarrassed, "I always notice when you're not around. I worry about you."

Carol started to answer but didn't get the chance. Cooley entered the room, followed by Bridges and a few minutes later, Meadors and Spencer. The squad was complete except for Cooper, who soon appeared looking as if he'd been up all night.

Spencer said, "Anything at the apartment?"

"Nope," said Cooper. "Nobody came near the car or the apartment."

"OK, get out of here and go get some sleep. Be back by six and check in here first to be sure nothing has changed."

"OK," said Cooper and with a wave he left.

Spencer started quickly, "Skip, brief everyone on our findings yesterday."

"We had Bo go back to the Coastal office and check on his application. The girl in the office told him A.J. had called in and reported he was going to be out of town for a while, so they aren't missing him yet. Bo bribed her, and she'll call him if she hears something."

"Carol, what happened when you met with Vincent?"

Carol's expression changed immediately.

"Well, he never has much of anything to share. I asked him about a possible connection between Baxter and Vernon, but he didn't know of one. He said Jake was the point person and if Baxter had something going on with Vernon, Jake didn't know about it."

Carol decided to go out on a limb.

"He's decided, since I asked, that Vernon is working with Baxter and probably had something to do with Jake's death. He's looking for him. If he finds him, he'll kill him."

"Damn it, Carol," said Spencer in anger. "I told you no deals."

"I didn't make a deal," Carol lied defiantly. "I asked if he knew of a connection since we saw Baxter go in, but not out of the Coastal yard, and we had a picture of Vernon driving a Coastal truck. He guessed the rest."

Spencer was angry, but the ringing phone on Carol's desk interrupted the conversation.

She answered, "Detective Naster."

She waved them quiet, and they watched her intently.

She looked at her watch. "We'll be there in thirty minutes," and hung up. "We got a break but its bad news. They found A.J. dead this morning in a warehouse at Coastal, along with a security guard. It looks like a robbery."

She pointed at Cooley. "Let's go, Jack." Bridges looked at her with a question on his face. "OK, you too, Junior," said Carol. They all grinned slightly as the three departed.

Spencer said, "Meadors, find Captain Drake. He must be able to get warrants for Coastal now with two homicides on the property."

Skip said, "I'll call Whitley."

Spencer couldn't tell if he was happy or not about the news of A.J.'s death, but something was different.

"Skip, you better find Bo and catch him up as soon as possible, and let's get together before you leave."

They went into Spencer's office, and he closed the door.

Spencer said, "What're you thinking? I could see it on your face when you said you were going to call Whitley."

"I think I'm going to enjoy telling him their informer is dead. I know it sounds bad, but with A.J. gone, they can't very well do what they're planning can they?"

"I don't know," said Spencer. "They still have the advantage. If they find out LaCrosse is the second informer, they'll pull her in."

Skip scowled.

"We didn't think of that. I think things may've just gotten worse. What're you going to do?"

Spencer said, "I'm going to see Carl Powers, you get Jeanette LaCrosse on tape."

~~~~

Carol, Cooley, and Bridges arrived on scene and passed through the police barricades. Carol spotted Doc Fenton and halted Cooley and Bridges.

"Jack, talk to the first officers on the scene and get their impressions. You know, what they found, what they saw, when they got here. Junior, investigate the site outside of the perimeter. Look at the grounds, fencing, gates, everything outside the police line. I'll go meet with Doc Fenton, then we'll compare notes."

"What's the scoop, Doc?"

Fenton looked at Carol with the bored look he got when you asked him an obvious question.

"Two dead bodies," he said sarcastically, "but there's a twist."

"Oh really?" said Carol.

"Yes, really, Detective, two different guns meaning there were probably two shooters."

That raised Carol's eyebrows.

"I thought that might interest you," Fenton said with a grin. "The guard was shot with something like a .45 or a hi-powered 9 mm. He has three big ugly chest wounds. The shots were close range, and all of them went through the body. We're looking for the slugs now. They shouldn't be too hard to find."

Carol looked at the body of A.J. Guilford, exhaled loudly, and looked at Fenton.

"This one was shot at close range, too, but with a smaller caliber gun, a .38 to be exact."

"And you know that how already?"

Doc Fenton held up the clear plastic evidence bag with the gun in it and smiled.

"We found it next to the body."

"Very funny Doc. What else is there?"

Fenton handed the gun to an assistant. "Get this down to the lab and run it. It's a priority. OK, Detective, if you'll follow me, I'll show you some of the things that make all of this unusual."

"Unusual?" said Carol, "Like what?"

She followed him to the tool room and peeked inside after he stopped at the door.

"The tool room is cleaned out and the adjoining office ransacked. It's supposed to look like a robbery."

"It's not?" asked Carol with a half-smile. Fenton looked at her again with that bored look. "Hell no, it's not."

"You going to tell me why, or do I have to guess?"

He walked over and pointed at the security guard. "He was hammered three times with big slugs. There isn't enough blood on the ground for wounds like that, and the blood pool is all wrong."

"You mean he wasn't killed here?" Carol asked surprised.

"That's not what I said. Look at this." Doc knelt and pointed at the blood pool. "This guy bled out from those three slugs, I mean they tore up his insides. There should be twice as much blood on the ground and there's not. I'm thinking he was on top of something at first, like a plastic sheet or a tarp or something and placed here. He looks natural enough lying there with the blood underneath him, but there isn't enough of it."

"Anything else?" Carol asked now genuinely interested.

"Yes, the second body at first glance also looks natural enough, but again not enough blood on the ground."

He gave Carol an *I dare you look* and continued. "Also, somebody beat the crap out of him before he was shot and more than once. He's got new bruises on top of older ones." He raised his hand to stop Carol's question. "The short explanation is the coloring of the skin. That's how I know some are older. I felt his rib cage around the entry wounds and there are some badly cracked ribs, and his eye is swollen shut. He was hit hard before he was killed. There are veins under the skin that were broken while he was alive. I'll know more once I get him on the table and can do a full examination, but he was in bad shape. I'm guessing he has some broken cheekbones too. The body is actually pretty ordinary except for the clincher that convinced me all is not as it seems."

Carol didn't say anything this time and Fenton continued. "He has abrasions around his wrists, ankles and lips. I'm guessing somebody beat him while he was secured with duct tape since there are no defensive wounds, and they pulled it off after he was shot. The funny thing is his skin smells. Somebody tried to clean the tape residue off his skin with some kind of cleaner. We're looking for it now."

Carol said, "Why clean his skin?"

Fenton said, "Because they stupidly believed they could hide the fact he was bound, but he's got abrasions on his wrist and face, and then I smelled him. He smells like pine cleaner."

"Is there anything else you can tell me?" asked Carol.

"Yes, but you aren't going to believe it."

"What?" said Carol.

"You had a witness. That was really the best clue I had to tell me it wasn't a robbery."

"You're right. I don't believe you," she said with sarcasm.

"I'm not kidding. You had a witness. They left a note in the pocket of the security guard, and it's got Cooley's name on it."

Carol looked at him in utter disbelief and Doc said, "Do you know anyone named Benny?"

~~~~

Alisheen woke up to familiar surroundings, but they weren't hers. She'd spent the night at Emily's again after their reconciliation the night before. She got up, put on her robe, and walked down the hallway to the kitchen where she found Tom, Emily's fiancé, browsing the paper.

"Hi, Alisheen," said Tom with a sheepish grin.

"Do you want some coffee?"

"Yes, please," she said.

He put down his paper and got a cup from the cupboard, then poured her a mug and handed it to her. "Do you want anything in it?"

"No, thanks, this is fine. Where's Emily, still asleep?"

"Yep, still getting her much-needed beauty rest."

"I heard that," said Emily as she entered the kitchen with a yawn and headed for the coffee pot.

Tom and Alisheen looked at each other and smiled.

Emily said crossly, "Just what in the hell are you two smiling at?" then she looked at Alisheen. "You better get going red, if you're working today, or is the boss taking the day off?"

Alisheen looked at the clock on the wall and with a laugh said, "Nope, the boss is definitely working today."

They rode to work together, entered the kitchen through the back screen porch, and greeted everyone. Emily went to the dining room and Alisheen went into her office. She flipped on the computer, checked the bank accounts, the food inventory, and placed an order to replace some stock items. Then she went out into the kitchen putting on an apron. Emily came back from the front.

"Alisheen, Mickey called in sick this morning."

"That's unusual, he usually comes in sick as dog, and I have to make him go home. We'll check on him later. How does everything look out there?"

Emily said, "They're spreading the sawdust now, and the bar is stocked."

"Great," said Alisheen. "I'm going to do some cooking."

"I almost forgot. What do you want the lunch special to be today? Sidney wants to know."

Alisheen remembered Carl's lunch advice and smiled. "Big bacon cheeseburgers with fries and a drink."

Emily said, "Oh, come on, quit kidding around. We don't even have that on the menu."

"We do as of today," Alisheen said firmly.


~~~~


Back in his hotel room, Skip called Whitley but didn't get the reaction he expected.

"So, he's dead then, you're sure?" Whitley asked calmly.

Skip said, "We're sure."

Whitley said, "I'll call Mr. Chambers and call you back later," then he hung up and called Chambers.

"Mr. Chambers, I just received a call from Fitzgerald in Savannah. A.J. Guilford is dead."

"How?" asked Chambers.

"He was murdered, sir, kidnapped out from under them, and now he's dead."

Whitley called Fitzgerald back.

"Skip, Mr. Chambers said to continue to follow orders and don't make any arrests."

Skip lost it.

"Damn it, Ben, what in the hell is going on? You're too damn smug about this. Your star informer for your insane proposal is dead, and you tell me to keep working and do nothing. What gives?"

"Agent Fitzgerald, you've been told what to do," said Whitley sternly.

"Don't give me that crap" yelled Skip hotly. "The last time I got that directive was right before you told me about your plan, which leads me to question your sanity."

Whitley said with anger, "You got your orders," and hung up.

Skip slammed the receiver down with a curse and Whitley called Chambers back.

Chambers said, "Well?"

"He didn't like it, sir."

Chambers said with disdain, "I don't care if he likes it or not. You just be sure Blackwell knows to protect Jeanette LaCrosse. I'll want him to take her into custody and bring her here as soon as we've confirmed the voiceprint match and made arrangements so we can question her about Powers. Understand?"

"Yes, sir, I understand."

Chamber's response was a click and a dial tone.

# Chapter 22

JEANETTE HAD CALLED Carl early that morning to tell him the news. He had to admit her quick thinking suggesting A.J. may have been part of the whole thing was very good. Too bad he couldn't keep her around.

Carl said, "Let the attorneys know they'll be needed if the police ask more questions."

Their conversation seemed to be over when she said, "Carl, I hope you realize now how valuable I can be. I don't know what happened, but I'll bet you do. We can go a long way together if you'll give us a chance." Carl didn't respond. "Remember, don't be late Friday night or I'll carry out my threat. I'd hate for it to come out that A.J. was your drug errand boy. What happened, Carl? Was he getting greedy?"

Powers said, "you've told me all of this before, Jeanette. I'd think by now you'd know I can't be threatened."

"And you should know I don't hand out idle threats. You do it my way from now on, or the girl dies, and your little empire will go up in flames."

She hung up.

Carl said, "Soon, very soon."

~~~~

It was late afternoon when Ian rapped on the door and Vernon opened it.

"Come on, let's get going."

Their hotel and two others shared a large lot for overflow parking. They walked into the host of cars and chose a Camry. Ian had it running in less than a minute. They quickly exited the lot, hopped onto the interstate, and headed for the cabin. When they arrived, Ian stopped the car and told Vernon to get out.

"You stay here. I'll be back later. Understand?"

Vernon sullenly said, "Yeah, I got it. Just don't be too damn long. I got to get clear too. What do I do if somebody comes around and starts asking questions?"

"Tell them it's private property and to get the hell out of here. Now get out of the way."

Ian needed his bags to get out of town. He parked on a side street that bordered his apartment complex and waited for a while before making his move. He scaled the fence and dropped into the bushes, went to his building, and entered the apartment. He went to the window and cracked the curtain, scanning the parking lot but didn't see any surveillance. The BMW was where he'd left it, and the tarp seemed to be untouched. He took a small penlight from his pocket, hooded it with his hand, checked the apartment over one last time, and then placed the bags by the door. He peeked out the curtain a second time, and satisfied, opened the door. With his bags in hand, he closed the door, went down the steps and gained the shadows. He walked out the front entrance, went down the street to the Camry, and then drove back to the hotel. He entered the lot, backed into a space to hide the tag, and went to his room.

~~~~

Cooper was ecstatic; he'd found Baxter. The second peek out had tipped him off. From his spot under the trees bordering the parking lot, Cooper thought he'd seen the curtain pulled back through the binoculars, but he wasn't sure. He was watching the curtain when it moved for a second time. He had him. Cooper hurried to his car and pulled up to the main entrance as Baxter drove by. He followed, confident that Baxter hadn't picked him up. When he hit the interstate Cooper began to worry, but Baxter soon exited toward the city. He drove into a large parking lot shared by the hotels on the exit and backed into a space. He climbed the outside steps of the nearest hotel and entered a second story room. Cooper parked in a space that gave him a full view of the door and quickly placed a call to the station.

Spencer and Skip were there when Cooper called in with the news.

"Stay on him, he might lead us to Powers," said Spencer with excitement. "Oh, and Cooper," said Spencer quickly before he hung up.

"Yes, sir?" said Cooper.

"Great job man, great job."

~~~~

After Jeanette's call, Carl decided to fish as an explanation for arriving at the plantation in the middle of the night. Out fishing, he could avoid the inevitable phone calls and Rupert for the major part of the day. Rupert had tried to make light conversation while he fixed Carl's breakfast that morning in an obvious attempt to get Carl to tell him why he'd decided to show up in the middle of the night. It wasn't rare, because he'd done it before, but Carl was sure that Rupert suspected something bad had happened this time.

Under his suspicious stare, Carl left to go fishing. He'd decided to ask Alisheen to come back to the plantation after the Ball. He'd tell Rupert when he got back that afternoon. That'd cheer him up. He intended to be with Alisheen at the plantation when Ian did LaCrosse. Three deaths in a week were going to be hard to explain, especially hers, but Ian was smart. He'd make it look like an accident, and Alisheen would be the perfect alibi. In addition, he could protect her and make sure that LaCrosse didn't get the opportunity to carry out her threat before Ian killed her. With these thoughts in mind, Carl parked the Jeep in the marina's parking lot.

He noticed Sam Miller's patrol car. He hoped he hadn't heard any news from Savannah yet. He didn't want to answer any questions. Hank and Sam were watching the television and chatting idly when he walked in.

"Hey, Mr. Powers," said Hank in greeting as he stood up from leaning on the counter. "Do you want me to get the boat ready?"

"Yeah, Hank, I'd thought I'd try my luck with those mackerel again."

"OK," said Hank, and he grabbed a set of keys off the board behind him and headed for the dock.

Sheriff Miller said, "Morning, Mr. Powers."

"Good morning, Sam, how's everything going in town?"

"Oh, just fine, Mr. Powers, just fine. I can't complain. I sure am glad I don't have to deal with the kind of stuff going on in Savannah. That's some kind of bad luck that happened at your warehouse last night. Me and Hank were just watching it on the morning news."

Carl hid his surprise and spoke with remorse. "Yes, I know. I came over last night and found out this morning when I called my office. I decided to stay here, avoid the questions, and let my staff handle it."

"I understand," said the Sheriff. "A robbery and a double murder, and the news reports are saying that you went to school with one of the victims."

Carl's surprise that this much information was on the news already was obvious. Sheriff Miller interpreted the surprise differently.

"Oh, my gosh, Mr. Powers. I'm sorry, that was rude of me."

Carl recovered. "That's OK, Sam. Yes, it was quite a shock. Actually, A.J. and I were roommates at Georgia."

"I'm sure sorry to hear that, Mr. Powers. I apologize for bringing it up."

"No need to apologize, Sam, no need. You couldn't have known," Carl said, and changed the subject.

"I wonder if Hank has the boat ready."

About that time, Hank came back in announced the boat was fueled and ready to go.

"Thanks," said Carl, "What else is biting out there besides the mackerel?"

"Everything," said Hank. "It's spring now and there's a lot of bait in the water. Redfish, flounder, you name it."

Hank suddenly perked up as Carl turned to leave.

"Hey, Mr. Powers, did you ever see the picture of the fish I told you about?"

Carl didn't want to appear in a hurry to leave so he stopped, turned around, and said, "What picture?"

"The picture of the huge flounder that guy caught around here a couple of weeks ago. I told you about it the other day when you were here. That damn fish was so big I gave him a cooler to get it home."

Hank was excited. He quickly came around the counter and grabbed Powers by the elbow steering him.

"It's right over here on the bulletin board. It won't take but a second, come see."

Carl followed the pull by Hank with Sheriff Miller following. Stopping at the bulletin board, Hank pointed out the picture to Carl.

Sheriff Miller said, "Hey, I met that guy. I stopped him and he showed me the fish. It was a whopper all right. He came out of your driveway entrance Mr. Powers; said he'd been fishing and needed to take a leak. He was a nice guy."

Carl recognized him at once and knew the Sheriff finding the same man from the dock in his driveway that day was no coincidence.

Hank chimed in, "Yep, he was nice young fellow, said he worked in Savannah."

"When I pulled him, he said he was a cop," said the Sheriff. "He pulled out his badge to prove it to me."

"A cop," said Carl. "Well, how about that?"

Carl was calm on the outside, but he felt a cold chill run down his spine. They'd found him.

"Well, I need to get going. Thanks for showing me the fish, Hank. I'll call you later about the boat. See you around, Sam."

Powers turned on his heel and headed for the fuel dock. He got in, started it up, and ignoring the "No Wake" sign he sped out of the marina. Hank and Sam had followed Powers outside and watched him leave.

"Nice man," said Hank.

"Yep," said Sam.

As soon as Carl was out of sight of the marina, he pushed the throttles forward, jumping the boat to full speed. He made the main channel and headed for Blue Creek. He had to find Ian.

~~~~

After lunch, Emily and Alisheen took a break and met in the office. The new cheeseburger plate had been a huge success with the customers proclaiming it "the best cheeseburger in the city." The platter consisted of a half-pound cheeseburger with apple-wood smoked bacon, red onions, the special house cut fries, and dill pickles on the side. It was awesome. It was so awesome in fact that they made several emergency runs to the grocery store to buy more hamburger meat, cheese, and bacon.

"Who'd have thought a cheeseburger plate would be that big of a deal?" laughed Alisheen.

Emily said, "The Mister Crab Cheeseburger was a huge success because it was so different for us. I wouldn't have believed it if I hadn't seen it for myself."

"Wait a minute," laughed Alisheen. "Who named it the Mister Crab Cheeseburger?"

"I did," said Emily simply. "I figured the She Crab needed a counterpart. Cheeseburgers are man food, hence, Mister Crab's Cheeseburger."

"I like it," said Alisheen. "The Mister Crab it is."

They laughed and talked about the success of the special for a few minutes and then Alisheen suddenly said, "I forgot to call Mickey."

"We were so busy that I completely forgot about it. Let's try him now." She dialed Mickey's number and let it ring until his voicemail picked up.

"Mickey, it's me, Alisheen. Emily and I were checking on you. Please give us a call in the morning and let us know if you need anything and if you're OK. Bye, take care," and then she hung up. "I'm worried about him."

"He's probably asleep, especially if he feels bad," said Emily.

"Well, if we don't hear from him in the morning, I'm going over there. He may be really sick and need help," Alisheen said.

Emily dropped her off at her loft that afternoon. She entered, locked the door, and checking her messages, found one from Spencer urging her to call him so they could talk. She bit her lip and threw caution to the wind. He wasn't at his apartment, so she hung up and then called the station knowing that's where he'd be anyway. She learned that Spencer was in a special meeting and couldn't be disturbed, but they'd get him the message as soon as he came out. She hung up, thinking it was the same old story, and went into the bedroom, throwing her bag on the bed. She turned on the television and began to unpack. As she walked into the bathroom, they announced the breaking lead story. She heard the words murder and Coastal Seafood and rushed back to the bedroom. She watched in horror with Spencer's words echoing in her ears.

"That's ridiculous" she said to the television. "Carl had nothing to do with any of that." She opened her closet and spotted the dress she'd bought for tomorrow night. "Charity Ball, here I come."

~~~~

"It was a setup," Carol said. "It looks like a robbery, but Doc Fenton says otherwise. There wasn't enough blood on the ground to match the wounds on the victims, and there were other things too."

"Like what?" asked Spencer.

"There were two different guns, and one of them strangely enough was left behind. We should have the ballistics on the gun at the scene by morning. The security guard was killed with three shots at close range, from a 45 or a big powder 9 mil. He was a real mess."

"Hey, a 9 mil is the M.O. for Baxter according to his file," said Cooley breaking in.

"We have some good news in that regard," said Meadors. "Cooper found Baxter and has him under surveillance at a hotel off the interstate. We got back-up headed out there to cover Baxter so he can come in and report."

Carol interrupted the discussion.

"I got some more."

They fell silent and turned back to her.

"A.J. is a different story. Doc Fenton said he'd been bound with something like duct tape. He had pine cleaner on his skin where somebody tried to clean the residue from the tape off his skin in an attempt to hide that fact. While he was bound, he had the crap beat out of him. All of this was an educated guess until Doc found a piece of evidence that verified his conclusions. He found a note in the security guard's pocket."

"What do you mean a note!" Spencer exclaimed.

Carol exchanged looks with Cooley and Bridges, and then pulled a clear plastic evidence bag out of the manila envelope she was holding. Inside, there was a piece of paper from a Coastal note pad with grease smudges and a spot of blood. Carol handed it to Spencer.

He read aloud with a flat tone. "I saw Baxter kill Joseph and Powers kill A.J., Benny."

~~~~

Friday morning arrived, and Carl still hadn't heard from Ian.

"*He'd better still be around*," Carl thought while he ate breakfast. He frowned as Rupert's shadow passed outside the window. Rupert had avoided Carl since yesterday. He'd met Carl in the den the day before as he hurried into the house. He didn't say anything, and he didn't have to. Rupert looked like he'd just lost his best friend.

Carl didn't explain, he just said, "It had to be done."

Rupert had brightened some later when he told him Alisheen was coming for the weekend. However, beyond saying that he'd call Annie, Carl couldn't draw him out. It was late in the morning when Ian finally called.

"Where in the hell have you been?" asked Carl with frustration. "I've been trying to reach you since yesterday."

"I've been lying low," said Ian. "In case you haven't noticed, it's all over the news."

"I know it's on the news, damn it, but we've got a bigger problem."

"What?" said Ian.

"I killed A.J. too quickly. The cops are definitely on to us."

"How do you know?"

Powers recounted the fish story from the marina and the revelation by the Sheriff.

"We got to get out of here," Ian said anxiously.

"You do two things first. Take care of Vernon, and be sure LaCrosse has an accident. Today. Then you vanish."

"What about you? Where are you?" asked Ian.

"I'm driving into Savannah now and headed for the office. I can't leave just yet. That'd be an admission of guilt in some people's eyes. I'll stay here, act like nothing has happened, and go to the Charity Ball tonight as planned. The robbery, murders, and Jeanette's un-timely death will be tragedies and excuses I can use to my advantage later. You just take care of them."

"I think it's a bad idea. I say we get out now," Ian said worried.

"No. Vernon is a definite threat if they talk to him and LaCrosse knows everything, but hers is more personal."

"OK but be careful Mr. Powers. If they know as much as you think they do, they're watching you."

"I'm sure of it. That's why I can't leave. In a few weeks, after it's died down, I'll leave the country for a while."

Ian said, "I'm in a hotel off the interstate. I can do what I need to do from here. I'll take care of Vernon at the cabin, and you'll have to read about LaCrosse tomorrow in the papers. I'll be long gone by then. You just be sure you have an alibi."

"I've already taken care of that. I'll be in the company of a lady. Be careful Ian and don't take anything for granted. We don't know how much A.J. told them."

"I'm always careful," and the line went dead.

With two bodies in the morgue, they had the warrants by 10:30 Friday morning. Bo and Meadors would serve the subpoenas and organize the search through the personnel records and financial files.

"Follow the money," said Spencer, "and we'll get our answers."

Before they were even out the door, Captain Drake appeared and stopped them.

"Sorry, boys, we're dead in our tracks."

"What?" yelled Spencer, "How?"

Drake said, "Simple, it's called influence. The Coastal lawyers filed injunctions against the subpoenas with a judge who is friends with Carl Powers. They're claiming we're damaging Mr. Powers' business and reputation by asking for records that aren't germane to the case. Since its Friday, we can't see a judge until next week, and even then we'll be lucky. Coastal is very powerful and organized. We've got our work cut out for us."

"LaCrosse knew we'd go for those warrants and beat us to the punch," spat Meadors.

Spencer slumped back into his chair and threw the paperwork into the garbage can.

"Where is she now?" asked Spencer.

"She's at Coastal," said Meadors.

"I think it's time I take her head on," Spencer said pointedly. "Still no sign of Powers? I find it odd that there's a major crime on his property, two of his employees are dead, and he hasn't shown up yet. Don't you?" Spencer stood and surveyed the room.

"Carol, Cooley, and Bridges, you guys pour it on from the homicide perspective. We don't need warrants for evidence linked to the murders and the robbery. So press as hard as you can from that angle."

Carol said to Cooley and Bridges, "I'll drive and meet you there. I've got some things to do later."

She called Vincent from her car.

"Did you see the news?"

"Yeah," replied Vincent, "Too bad about that old man."

"Was there anything scheduled?"

"I knew you were going to ask so I did some checking around. Nobody I talked to knew anything about a delivery on Wednesday night, but I did find out something that'll interest you, although it's too damn late now."

"What?" Carol asked.

"A couple of my guys heard that Baxter and Vernon were on the docks very early Thursday morning. It seems they'd put something in a container. Baxter locked it and kept the key. He told the captain to put it on his barge, take it out to sea, dump it, and make damn sure it was in deep water."

Carol said furiously, "Why didn't you call me sooner? We might've had a chance to stop it."

"Because the guys on the boat didn't tell anyone until after they got back into port. It'd already been dumped at sea, and between the currents and the tides there's no way to find it again."

"They didn't know what was in it?"

"Nope," said Vincent. "Like I said, it was locked up before anyone saw it. Only Baxter and Vernon knew what was in there. They waited until it was loaded on the barge and watched the tug pull out. They were gone when the tug got back, and outside of the crew members no one else knows about it."

Carol said, "This certainly proves that Baxter and Vernon are working together."

"I'm still looking for Vernon. He knows what happened to Jake. If he tells me anything before he dies, I'll be sure and pass it on to you."

"Vincent, listen to me," Carol said with urgency. "I need to question him about what happened in the warehouse."

"No promises, Detective."

"Vincent, I need him."

Without a reply, he hung up.

Carol met Cooley and Bridges at the Coroner's office. In the morgue, Doc Fenton did his usual gross-out routine in an effort to make Jack sick, but it had no impact on Bridges who was fascinated by the autopsied body on the table.

Cooley said, "Looks like Junior is a ghoul too, Doc."

Fenton looked at Bridges and grinned, "You like this stuff, huh?"

Bridges nodded. "Awesome."

Doc grinned at him and turned to Cooley holding up a section of intestines.

"You know, Jack, this stuff in a pig is called chitlins."

Cooley turned one shade greener and at a fast walk headed for the bathroom. Doc laughed and grinned at Bridges and Carol, "Gets him every time."

After returning, Jack cursed him as always, calling him a "sick bastard with no respect for the dead." Doc ignored him as usual and went on.

"OK, Carol, here's my official report. Due to the amount of blood on the ground in comparison to the wounds to the bodies, one of which we're sure was bound and beaten, it's my finding there was some type of ground cloth—a tarp, or plastic sheeting—underneath them which was removed. The flow pattern of the blood pools and the small volume on the ground supports this conclusion. The pine cleaner from the bathroom was used in an attempt to clean the tape residue off the bound victim's skin. We have two weapons—a big powder 9 mil and a .38."

"Summary please, Doc," Carol said impatiently.

"The victims were murdered, and the robbery staged to try and hide that fact. One of them was committed by a person unknown. The other murder was carried out by ..." Doc paused, pulled his gloves off, threw them in the stainless-steel trashcan, and opened a file. "The other murder was carried out by a man named Mickey Springer."

"No way!" Bridges exclaimed. "I met him while I was undercover at the She Crab. He's the bar manager for goodness sake."

Doc looked over his glasses and down his nose at Bridges like a professor at an inept student.

"The evidence," he said sternly, "says otherwise. His fingerprints were on the empty casings and bullets left in the gun. There were smudged prints on the gun butt, so he wore gloves, or he wiped it down and forgot the bullets, but the gun is registered to him. So that is that, as they say. He has an arrest record for dealing drugs and got out on parole a couple of years ago."

They sat in stunned silence. Carol finally said, "OK, Doc, let's keep the details and official findings out of the press for now."

"Will do," said Doc. "I'll say we're still investigating the situation."

"Thanks," said Carol, and she looked at Cooley and Bridges. "You two find Benny."

Cooley said, "What about you?"

"I'm going to find Spencer and let him handle the She Crab mess."

~~~~

Spencer walked into the offices of Coastal Seafood, and after asking to see Miss LaCrosse, was shown to a conference room. She entered after a short wait and sat down.

Spencer took the offensive. "Do you have some coffee available? I haven't had my morning allotment yet."

She eyed him briefly, "Of course, my apologies," and picked up the phone. "Please bring us some coffee, thank you," and hung up.

Spencer was silent after explaining he wanted to wait on the coffee because he didn't want to be disturbed once they got started.

LaCrosse watched coolly while Spencer played with his cell phone, made a call, and paced until the coffee arrived. He poured a cup, sat down and took a sip.

"Nice," he said, "Is it gourmet?"

Jeanette said calmly, "Detective Baldwin, you aren't here for coffee or chit-chat so let's get down to business. I'm very busy."

"Very well," Spencer said. "That was a nice move with the attorneys."

She looked at him with a gleam of superiority and primly said, "Thank you."

"Still, it won't take long for us get around them," Spencer said leaning back in his chair. "No matter how many judge friends you have, they won't be able to ignore a public announcement that Coastal is not being cooperative in the investigation of a crime where the victims were employees. I'd think your organization would want the perpetrators brought to justice."

"Oh, but we do, Detective," she said pointedly. "We just need to be sure the rights of our employees and clients are protected while the police are carrying out their investigation. We must protect our reputation."

"Of course," said Spencer, "I understand. Where is Carl Powers?"

She straightened up notably. "He's still at his plantation in South Carolina. I informed him of the situation yesterday, and he'll be back today. As I told you earlier, I'll have him contact you when he returns. However, I do have the authority to represent the company."

At that moment, Powers walked in the door, stopped, and looked at Spencer.

"Detective Baldwin isn't it?" he asked politely extending his hand.

Before Spencer knew it, he was shaking hands and nodding.

"Good," Powers said with disarming warmth. "Let's go to my office; it's more private. Miss LaCrosse, will you please have somebody bring us more coffee? I could use some, and it looks like the detective can use a refill. Follow me, Detective."

Powers led them to his office. When they arrived, he said, "Thank you, Miss LaCrosse. I'm sure you have things to do that need your attention. I'll meet with the Detective privately."

Spencer could tell she was fuming at the rebuke, but she calmly said, "Yes, I do have other things to do," and left.

Carl escorted Spencer into his office. A girl brought a coffee tray, and Carl offered Spencer a refill which he accepted. The girl promptly fixed Carl's coffee, brought it to him, refilled Spencer's cup, and left. Spencer didn't waste any time.

"Mr. Powers, can you tell me anything about what's happened?"

"No, I can't. A.J. and I were roommates briefly at Georgia. We were in the same fraternity and when he joined, I had the only empty space in the house, so he lived with me until he got his own room. He got into some serious trouble at school and was an outsider in many ways. I felt sorry for him and took him 'under my wing' so to speak. He was a troubled young man, and I don't think he ever really came around. I hadn't seen or heard from him in over two years after school, but one day he showed up looking for a job. I hired him and later promoted him to trucking and warehouse manager. Frankly, he wasn't overly competent, but he was my friend, so I overlooked his performance. He wasn't a real go-getter if you know what I mean."

Spencer said, "May I have a copy of his personnel file?"

"Yes, of course," said Carl and he picked up the phone. "Make a copy of A.J.'s and poor Joseph's files and put them in an envelope for Detective Baldwin."

Spencer said, "Thank you. We're getting subpoenas ready for the rest of what we need."

"Why do you need subpoenas?"

"Let's just say Miss LaCrosse is an advocate for the legal system."

Carl smiled. "She is the COO of this company and has full authority to do what she deems necessary, but I'll see what I can do to help. However, if our legal consultants are advising we protect our personnel and financial records, then I'll have to go with their decision."

Spencer nodded. "Do you know a man named Ian Baxter?"

"No, should I?"

"Probably not," Spencer said casually. "I was just checking. He's an enforcer type. Our information says he's working in the area for someone known as the Snowman. We suspect he's a drug smuggler, but that's all we know."

Carl leaned back in his chair. "Was A.J. involved with this smuggler in some way?"

Spencer smiled. "Mr. Powers, you know I can't answer that question."

Carl smiled back. "Of course, I understand. My curiosity got the best of me."

"Mr. Powers, do you know why A.J. might've been murdered?"

"I thought he and Joseph interrupted a robbery?"

"Well, we're not sure. Robbers don't typically kill people. They usually tie them up and cut and run so it's all very unusual."

"I see."

Spencer continued.

"Did you know A.J. was absent for three days before he was found dead in the warehouse?"

"I was told he'd called in to say he was attending to some personal business, something to do with family. Is that not true?" Carl asked.

"We don't know. We'll contact his family once we have his file to see if his story checks out. Why would he be here in the middle of the night?"

"I don't know, he kept his own schedule," Carl said and sipped his coffee. "A truck might've been needed to pick up a load, and he was going to drive the truck himself. He often filled in when we were short on drivers so that'd be my guess. His being there at that time of night wasn't really out of the ordinary. Trucks come and go all night depending on the schedule and the season. I can check for you and see if there was something on the schedule. It's a real tragedy. We have insurance, but the tools certainly weren't worth their lives. I assumed they were killed trying to stop a robbery."

"Well, the verdict is still out on that," said Spencer. "Until we get the Coroner's official report, we won't know."

Spencer rose and extended his hand.

"Thanks for your time and help, Mr. Powers. We'll probably need to talk to you again at a later date."

Powers stood and shook Spencer's hand. "That'll be fine. You can contact Miss LaCrosse, and she'll schedule it."

Spencer left and picked up the envelope with the files on his way out. He got into the car and said, "It's on now."

Meadors arrived at the hotel and found Bridges sitting comfortably in his car.

"Where's our boy?" he asked, tapping on the roof.

Bridges said, "He's in room 211. There aren't any other exits, and I can see both stairs from here so I'm positive he's still in there."

Meadors said, "Go and get some sleep."

Bridges said, "Gladly," and Meadors relieved him and settled in.

After a short wait, Meadors saw the door to room 211 open. He picked up the binoculars and did a double take. He wasn't sure the man that came out of 211 was Baxter because his head was clean-shaved bald.

"*What in the hell was going on?*"

The man stepped out onto the second-floor balcony, looked up at the sky, then put on sunglasses and a Panama to keep the sun off his head. Meadors recognized him when he looked up into the sun. It was Baxter for sure, but he had shaved his head.

"Nice try," he thought.

He descended the stairs with a small bag and crossed the parking lot to a blue Mustang. If he hadn't been watching through binoculars, he'd never have seen it. With one deft motion, Baxter placed a slim-jim down inside the window well and opened the door as quickly as if he had a key. Within a minute, he was pulling out of the parking lot. Meadors put on sunglasses a baseball hat and followed him.

~~~~

Jeanette was miffed with the way Carl had dismissed her, but she wasn't going to be distracted from her task. She strode into Carl's office without knocking.

He looked up from his desk and said with a flat tone, "Can I help you, Jeanette?"

"Yes, Carl," she said briskly but pleasantly. "What time are you picking me up tonight?"

He smiled pleasantly as if reminded of something that he'd forgotten. "About 9:00, how does that sound?"

She looked at him warily. It wasn't what she'd expected.

He quickly said, "I don't like to get to these things too early. I find them extremely boring."

Jeanette guardedly said, "Well, I guess 9:00 would be OK. I'll admit I was hoping to go earlier. I was also expecting an argument from you. What changed your mind?"

Carl leaned back in his chair and folded his hands in his lap.

"I don't want Alisheen to get hurt. I think the best course of action for the time being is to be reasonable."

"What about Alisheen? You've told her you're going with me tonight?"

"Yes, of course," said Carl.

Jeanette still wary said, "I'll take that for now, and I promise you Carl, you'll have a great time with me. I'll see you at nine!"

She turned on her heels and walked out.

Carl watched her go. *"With luck you'll be dead by nine."*

Carl called Alisheen at the She Crab.

"Hello, Carl," said Alisheen, "I was wondering when I'd hear from you."

"I got back into town this morning and had to speak with the police about this tragedy at the warehouse first thing."

She said, "Oh, Carl, I was so sorry to hear about A.J. and that poor security guard. Is there anything I can do?"

"Oh, no, Alisheen, the police are handling it all, but thanks. I called to give you the details for tonight."

Alisheen said, "What time do I need to be ready?"

"I'll pick you up with the limo around 6:00. We'll eat dinner and go to the Ball."

Surprised, she said, "I thought they had food there?"

"They do, but its hotel food. It's good but not great. We'll eat someplace special, OK?"

"Ok," said Alisheen, still surprised.

"Alisheen, why don't you spend the weekend at the plantation? I've already told Rupert and Annie you're coming so you can't get out of it."

"That was awfully presumptuous of you, sir," Alisheen said laughing, "but it sounds like fun, and I'd like to see Rupert and Annie again. I can arrange it, and it'll be good to get away."

"Great, I'll see you tonight."

Alisheen left the office and found Emily out front.

"Carl is picking me up for dinner, and then we're going to the Ball. He's asked me to go to the plantation for the weekend. Can you do without me?"

Emily said, "Alisheen, I hope you know what you're doing."

"I have to give it a try, Emily, I know that. If I don't, then I'll never know."

Emily hugged her. "Have fun and be careful."

She hugged her back. "I will and thanks. Have you heard from Mickey?"

"No, I haven't. I tried to call him earlier this morning but didn't get an answer. Do you think he's alright?"

"I'll check on him later and take him some food. He's probably hungry."

"That's a good idea," Emily said.

~~~~

Carol found Spencer in the squad room after returning from the Coroner's office.

"I've got Cooley and Bridges searching for Benny," she said. "I'm betting he's scared to death and has flown the coop."

"You're probably right," Spencer said.

Carol continued, "Vincent finally had something interesting."

"It's about time."

Carol flinched at the sarcasm. "Baxter and Vernon were together on the docks early Thursday morning. They'd locked up a container, put it on a sea tug with a barge, and had it dumped in deep water."

"Damn," said Spencer exasperated. "Do they know what was in it?"

"No" said Carol. "It was locked up before anyone could see what was inside, and Baxter kept the key."

"Any chance of finding it with sonar?"

"I doubt it. They could've dumped it anywhere, and between the tides and the currents, it could be a mile or more off the mark where they dumped it. It was open water so even if the boat charted it, it'd be guesswork."

"I wonder what was in it," mused Spencer.

Carol said, "I'm guessing it was the tools missing from the warehouse and any other evidence from the crime scene. Doc Fenton has confirmed the robbery was staged in an attempt to cover up the murders, but we're not releasing any information for the moment."

Spencer was silent and Carol said, "Spencer, we got a problem that you need to deal with personally."

Spencer looked up from his thoughts. "Oh?"

"The .38 found at the scene belongs to Mickey Springer, who works the bar at the She Crab."

Spencer was in disbelief. "What?"

"I'm afraid so. The gun is registered to him, and his prints are on the bullets and empty casings. There are smudged prints on the butt, so he wore gloves, but there aren't any other prints on the gun."

Spencer collapsed into his desk chair.

"I can't believe he killed A.J. It doesn't make any sense. Mickey set A.J. up for Skip."

"I know," said Carol. "Maybe he had something going on the side with A.J. and had to kill him before we found out."

Spencer shook his head. "I doubt it. He's fiercely loyal to Alisheen. I can't imagine him being back in the business."

"I hope we can find Benny," said Carol shaking her head.

"That note we found is useless without him," said Spencer. "It may be Mickey's only chance."

Carol left and Spencer picked up the phone and called the desk Sergeant.

"I need some uniforms to pick up somebody, quietly."

"Yes, sir," said the sergeant.

"I'll give you an address. If he's not there, wait until he is. I don't want him picked up anywhere else."

"What's the charge, Detective?"

"Pick him up on gun possession for now. He's in violation of his parole for that anyway," said Spencer. "No cuffs, very quiet, and keep him isolated. He's a friend."

~~~~

Blackwell had followed LaCrosse from Coastal to her house Friday afternoon. Now that that A.J. loser was dead, he was going to be her guardian angel as opposed to her killer. He was sure from listening to Fitzgerald over the last few weeks that Powers was the Snowman and told Whitley so, but Whitley said they had to wait. The Snowman was important for some plans they'd made. Blackwell didn't give a damn about Whitley and his plans. His job now was to keep LaCrosse alive.

He'd chosen a position on the corner of the first side street. He had the frequency for her cell phone and a powerful directional microphone. Once he had her tuned in, he'd be able to hear her no matter where she was. He glanced through the binoculars making sure he had a clear view of the house and began to wait.

~~~~

Alisheen went to Mickey's apartment after lunch at the She Crab, stopping by the grocery store first to buy a few things so he wouldn't starve. She arrived at the apartment and knocked since there was no bell. Mickey opened the door peeking through the crack.

"What are you doing here, Alisheen? You shouldn't be here."

"I've brought you some food. Are you all right Mickey?"

"Yes, thanks, I appreciate it, but I really don't need anything. I'm just sick and need to rest."

He started to close the door. "Mickey, what's going on? You open this door."

Mickey gave up, shielded himself behind the door, opened it, let her inside, and quickly closed the door behind her. The apartment consisted of a single room with a Murphy bed, a kitchen area, and a bathroom. The sitting area, arranged neatly in a corner had a couch, recliner, and a flat-screen television on a small table.

"You're very neat, Mickey," Alisheen said, unloading the groceries.

"It's dark in here."

She flipped on the lights for the kitchen area and the apartment lit up. Mickey turned away and walked to the darker side of the room.

She followed him. "Please go, Alisheen. I don't want you to catch what I have."

Alisheen stopped, looked at him for a minute, and then kept coming. She gently grabbed his shoulder turning him around.

"Mickey," she pleaded softly, "look at me."

Mickey reluctantly turned around. Alisheen gasped, inhaling a quick breath. One eye was swollen shut and was black and blue. His cheek on the other side was heavily bruised and swollen. He held his ribs and wheezed with every breath. He was sweating and his skin was pale.

"Oh, my goodness, Mickey!" she exclaimed. "What happened?"

Mickey, through his swollen face, said, "I can't tell you."

Alisheen was alarmed.

"Mickey, please tell me you're not dealing again?"

"It's nothing like that, I swear. I just can't tell you."

"Well, you can forget that" she said sternly. "I'm not leaving until you do."

Mickey sat down gently on the couch holding his side.

"Oh come on, Alisheen. Just leave me alone, OK? I'm fine."

"You don't look fine," she said sitting next to him, "You need a doctor."

"Really, it looks worse than it is. I'm embarrassed to tell you, but if it'll get you to leave me alone I will. I was drunk the other night and got into a fight. Two guys jumped me and beat the crap out of me. Now are you satisfied?"

She was angry.

"Fight, my ass," she said.

Mickey sighed.

"The truth is I mouthed off, and two guys beat me up, end of story. It was just a parking lot fight between drunks."

"Mickey Springer, I don't believe that cock and bull story for one minute. I've seen you drink, and you haven't been drunk in the two years I've known you, and I know you don't get into drunken brawls. Tell me the truth."

"I've told you what happened. Now please just let me go back to bed."

"Well, I give up if you want to stick to your story, but I'm going to take you to the doctor."

"No, Alisheen, I'm OK, really. I promise, if I'm not better in a couple of days I'll go to the doctor. I swear."

She wasn't convinced.

Mickey said, "Thanks for caring and coming to see me. I'm OK, and I promise I'll go to the doctor if I'm not better soon."

Mickey got up and headed for the door, and Alisheen reluctantly followed.

"I'll leave on one condition," she said at the door. "You'll let me take you to the doctor if I'm not convinced that you're getting better."

"OK."

"Promise?" asked Alisheen.

"Promise," said Mickey.

As he reached to open the door, a loud knock sounded that made them both jump. "Now what?" asked Mickey.

He opened the door and was shocked to see two police officers.

"Mickey Springer?"

"Yes."

"You're wanted for questioning. Will you please come with us?"

Alisheen stepped between them. "What are the charges, and what is this all about?"

The officer said, "Ma'am, please step back and don't interfere. He's wanted for questioning for possession of a firearm."

Mickey said, "It's OK, Alisheen."

The officer gently moved her to the side and motioned for Mickey to step out.

The second officer went down the steps and opened the door. Mickey urged Alisheen out and said, "I need my keys."

She helped him down the steps to the car.

"No handcuffs?" Mickey asked surprised.

"No, sir. We were told you'd be very cooperative."

She hissed with anger, "Spencer."

"Alisheen, it's a misunderstanding. I'll get it straightened out, don't worry," and he got into the back of the car.

~~~~

Alisheen had fire in her eyes as she stormed into Spencer's office. He was writing on a legal pad when she crashed into his office and slammed the door.

"What the hell is going on, and why did you have Mickey arrested?" she demanded.

Spencer didn't react immediately. He put his pen down, leaned back in his chair, and said coldly, "How're you, Alisheen? Shouldn't you be getting ready for your big date tonight?"

"You asshole," Alisheen said hotly. "I want to know why Mickey was arrested."

Spencer glared at her. "It's none of your business. It's police business. You're not his lawyer, and I don't have to tell you a damn thing."

"Damn it, Spencer," yelled Alisheen frustrated, and she plopped down into a chair.

Spencer said calmly, "If you'll quit yelling at me and remain calm, I'll tell you what I can."

Alisheen forced herself to relax and looked at him with cool eyes.

"I'm calm now. Why was Mickey arrested?"

Spencer said, "Mickey's gun turned up in an investigation. I just want to talk to him."

Alisheen's eyes opened wide. "Spencer, this doesn't have anything to do with the Coastal robbery, does it? You know Mickey isn't involved in something like that. He just can't be."

Spencer said, "I know, Al. This is confidential, so please don't say anything to anyone. You know about the robbery at the Coastal warehouse then?"

"Yes," said Alisheen simply. "I saw it on television at home. Carl said it was a tragedy and he had no idea what happened."

Spencer frowned at the way Alisheen used Powers' name with familiarity.

"A.J. Guilford and the security guard were killed in the robbery attempt. Mickey's gun was found at the scene. It's registered to him, and his fingerprints are on it."

Alisheen shook her head in denial.

"Spencer, please help Mickey."

"I'll do all I can," he said simply. "I just hope he has a good excuse for the gun and how it ended up in the warehouse."

"He was in a bar fight that night," Alisheen said quickly. "They beat the hell out of him, and he hasn't been to work since Wednesday. He looks really bad."

Spencer's interest peaked.

"A bar fight?"

"Yes."

Spencer said, "Al, I'll talk to him in a little while. He's in a private cell, and I'll see that he's looked after."

She got up and went to Spencer. She hugged him and kissed him on the cheek, then quickly turned and left. Spencer followed her out and watched her go down the hall.

He said quietly, "I love you, Alisheen."

# Chapter 23

VERNON WAS TIRED of waiting for Baxter. He didn't trust him and decided to get the hell out of there. He walked down the logging road toward the interstate. As he made the road, he heard a car coming and quickly ducked into the bushes. A Mustang rounded the curve, and he relaxed, but he was wary and remained hidden. The car slowed down enabling him to get a good look at the driver. It wasn't Baxter. The driver was a bald man wearing sunglasses. The Mustang turned into the road that led to the cabin, and Vernon expected the car to stop and turn around, but it accelerated and disappeared. Vernon decided to be cautious and wait when he heard another car. A truck with a black man behind the wheel appeared around the curve and slowed down. Vernon could see the driver looking around frantically, and he cursed when he recognized the cop that roughed him up.

*"What in the hell is he doing here?"*

Quickly, the truck sped up and disappeared down the road. Vernon wondered if he'd been following the Mustang and got scared. He wanted to leave, but his fear held him in place. In a few minutes, the truck raced by, and headed back toward the interstate. The Mustang still hadn't come back from the cabin and that made no sense to him. Maybe Baldie had car trouble.

He thought about robbing the bald man and taking his car so he wouldn't have to walk. The possibility of obtaining easy cash and a car helped him forget his fear before distant yells from the direction of the cabin broke the late afternoon silence. He could've sworn the voice was calling his name. He cowered closer to the ground at the sound of gunfire and backed deeper into the woods. He pulled the gun from his waistband, sweating and scared.

Several minutes passed with no more yells or gunfire, so he moved closer to the road. The sun was setting, and the ground turned into dappled spots of shadow and sunlight. Vernon thought about going to the cabin to see what had happened when he saw headlights approaching through the woods. The car turned slowly onto the road heading toward the interstate. Vernon could see the driver scanning the woods on both sides of the road. He moved slightly to get a better look and, at the same time, the driver turned, looked in his direction, and stopped with a jerk.

In the dim light Vernon recognized the driver of the Mustang and froze as Ian stared in his direction. Ian's eyes fixed on him, and he pointed his gun. An approaching car's headlights illuminated the Mustang, and he quickly dropped his arm and looked away. Vernon didn't move and was relieved to see a County Sheriff's patrol car.

Ian put the Mustang in gear and accelerated as the Sheriff's car approached. The patrol car slowed down as it passed him but didn't stop. Vernon took the opportunity to crawl backward, keeping his eyes focused on the road, into a thicket of bushes, and he rolled over to his back. The fear and bile in his stomach turned into nausea that overwhelmed him, and he vomited. He lay there until the dusk had turned to dark and the woods were alive with the sounds of the crickets and tree frogs.

Vernon stood up, cleared his throat and nose, and spit. He brushed himself off, pocketed his gun, and emerging from the brush, began to walk. His plan was to thumb a ride to town, get his money, and hop the freight that ran by his house. He was picked up by an obliging trucker and got a ride the rest of the way down the road to the interchange closest to his house.

Vernon stayed in the woods until he reached his house. He stopped at the edge of the woods and looked around. If he was going to make the midnight train, he'd have to hurry. Crouching down he ran across the yard to the back porch, topped the steps, and leaned over the rail to get the key from the nail hammered into the tree. He went inside, closed the door, and stood in the kitchen, listening and letting his eyes adjust to the dim interior. The yard light in the front provided enough light through the shabby curtains to see.

He left the kitchen and went into the bedroom, grabbed a duffle bag out of the closet, and stuffed his clothes in. Kneeling beside the bed, he reached underneath it feeling with his hand until he found the small hole. He inserted his finger into the worn smooth hole and lifting up the loose floorboard, reached in and grabbed the roll of cash held tight by a rubber band. He tossed the cash into the bag and brought his head up quickly, tuning in to the sounds around him. He thought he heard a noise.

He pulled the gun and started sweating nervously. Was he hearing things? Deciding it was nothing, he went back to the kitchen, but he kept the gun in his hand. He looked at the creepy cat clock his mother had given him with the tail that swung back and forth and the eyes that looked side to side on the wall, and he heard the long whistle of the train. It was 11:30. The train was pulling out.

Vernon scanned the backyard through the window, then opened the door and closed it behind him, taking the time to put the key back on the nail. Then he ran into the woods towards the tracks. He heard the whistle again and could see the signal light through the trees. It was green, the track was clear. That meant the train would be heading out soon. He came out on the side of the tracks where they made a huge, curved turn before it went straight. The train pulling out of the yards always went slow until the length of the train cleared the curve. Then it picked up speed as it headed out of Savannah and the last set of switches that determined its final direction. It was on the curve that Vernon planned to catch the train.

The pulpwood cars were going to be the ones he was looking for; they were the easiest to get onto since their ladders were lower. The roaring engines approached and passed, and he stood up and moved out into the open. He saw the shape of the first pulpwood car as the train rolled by and he began to trot, then run beside the tracks, matching the speed and direction of the train. He was going to make it. He grabbed the side rail of the ladder and swung his foot onto the bottom rung. As he stepped up on the ladder, the train whistle blew loudly, and he felt something sting his side.

He realized he was losing his grip and beginning to fall. *What was happening?* He was getting away and he was going to start over! In an instant Vernon hit the ground hard, rolling over several times ending up in the tall grass beside the tracks face up. He could see the shadow of the train in the dark as it went by. He felt pain, his back was wet, and he couldn't move. It was hard to breathe, he couldn't focus his eyes, but he heard voices.

"You got the bastard, Vincent."

"I told you he'd go for the train. Thanks to that phone call from Baxter, I caught the son of a bitch." Vernon realized he was thirsty and wished for a beer, and then it all went black. He was dead.

~~~~

Ian exited onto the ramp from the interstate, and as he turned right at the top, he noticed a truck had followed him. To be safe, he gunned the Mustang, only slowing down to turn onto the dirt road that led to the cabin. He felt confident that if the truck was following him, he'd lost it. He drove slowly up to the cabin and stopped the car. He got out holding the pistol down by his side and partially hidden behind his leg. Ian expected Vernon to come out whining about how long he'd been there, but he didn't show.

He cautiously entered the cabin and quickly realized Vernon was gone. The redneck had double-crossed him. He went outside and looked around. With nothing to lose he called out Vernon's name several times hoping the damn fool would give himself away. He went back inside, and in frustration he fired several shots into the wall.

It was getting dark, and he needed to leave, but first, Ian called Vincent Sweet.

"I was wondering when you'd call. What do you want, Baxter?"

"I thought you should know that Vernon helped me kill Jake, and A.J. too for that matter," Ian said gloating.

"You know I'll kill you when I find you."

"I don't think that'll ever happen, but I know where you can find Vernon."

"Why tell me where he is?"

"He double-crossed me. I owe him. Vernon's flown the coop. I'm guessing you'll find him hitching a ride," and Ian hung up.

He exited the cabin and started the Mustang. The woods were dark enough for the headlights to come on automatically, so he turned the car around and headed for the road. There was just enough light left to see so Ian scanned the woods. Maybe Vernon was hiding somewhere, and Ian could spot him. He rolled slowly and suddenly he thought he saw something move, and he quickly stopped the car.

He wasn't sure, but he'd almost swear he was looking at Vernon in the dim light. He raised his pistol to take a shot. After all, if it was Vernon, he had him. If not, it was just a bullet into the woods. As he took aim, a car came around the curve and Baxter quickly dropped the gun to the seat. He accelerated the Mustang as the headlights beamed into the car. Baxter lifted a wave to the patrol car as it passed. He'd leave Vernon to take his chances with the brother of Jake Sweet.

~~~~

"Damn, damn, damn," yelled Meadors in the truck. When he turned right, the Mustang had obviously accelerated because by the time he got to the top of the exit, it was out of sight. He floored it to catch up and sped down the road. He went around a broad curve of the road and slowed down, looking right and left hoping for some sign of the Mustang, but it was gone. He hurried down the road hoping to catch up, but it was useless. He'd lost Baxter. Meadors pounded the steering wheel in frustration and, giving up, turned the truck around. He called Spencer.

In a tone that communicated his feelings, Meadors said, "Spencer, I'm sorry man, but I lost him."

Vincent called Carol to tell her Vernon was dead.

"I told you I needed him," she said angrily.

"He was getting away on the train. I didn't have a choice."

"If you find Baxter, you leave him to the police. Do you understand?"

"I understand," and he hung up.

Spencer had gone to his office to take the call from Meadors.

She entered his office and he said with frustration, "Meadors lost Baxter so we're back to square one. Let's go see Mickey."

As they walked, Spencer said, "What did Vincent say?"

Carol, with resignation, said, "He found Vernon. It's over."

Spencer whirled on her. "I'll arrest him if that's true."

"He doesn't care," Carol said indifferent. "All he wanted was revenge for Jake's death."

"I hope you didn't help him get it."

"I didn't," she said defiantly.

Spencer looked doubtful, then said, "Come on, we're wasting time."

Proceeding in silence, they found Mickey in the interrogation room.

"You OK, Mickey?" asked Spencer.

Mickey nodded. "Yeah, I'm OK."

"You look pretty bad. I'd say you need a doctor."

Mickey laughed and winced.

"That's what Alisheen said."

Spencer smiled briefly. "OK, Mickey, tell me about the gun, which you know is a parole violation."

"I can't."

Carol said skeptically, "You've no idea how your gun got into the Coastal warehouse and on top of that you didn't use it to murder A.J. Guilford?"

Mickey looked stunned.

Spencer said, "Did you need cash for a stake to start dealing again?"

Suddenly, Mickey stood up and exclaimed, "Hold on, you mean my gun was at Coastal? You found my gun at Coastal, and you think I killed A.J.?"

"Yes," said Spencer.

Mickey yelled, "Oh, man, no way. I swear. I didn't kill him."

"Then let's get back to the gun," said Carol. "It's registered to you, and it's got your fingerprints on it. How'd it get there?"

Mickey said, "Spencer, can I talk to you privately?"

"I'm afraid not. Detective Naster needs to be able to corroborate what you tell me, or it's no good as testimony. We have to have a witness."

Mickey looked at them and then blurted out, "I'm scared for Alisheen."

Carol said, "Why are you scared for Alisheen?"

Mickey leaned on the table for support.

"Powers is bad news. Believe me I know the type, and I've been around enough to know."

In an effort to calm Mickey down Spencer said, "I believe you, but what about the gun?"

"Spencer!" Mickey started to speak, but Spencer cut him off.

"I appreciate your concern, but Alisheen refuses to listen to me."

Mickey sighed, "Yeah, she's hard-headed."

They both smiled and Carol said impatiently, "The gun!"

Mickey took on a defeated look.

"I knew Alisheen was going to the Ball tonight. I thought if Powers didn't show up maybe she'd forget about him and go back to Spencer. I decided to threaten him to keep him away from her."

Spencer was floored, "You what?"

Carol said quickly, "Mickey, what exactly did you do?"

"I'm trying to tell you. I broke into the apartment garage of Powers' building Wednesday night and waited for him to show. I was drinking Tequila for my nerves, you know, I was scared."

Mickey lit a cigarette.

Carol prodded him, "So what happened?"

"Like I said, I was drinking tequila and I guess I had too much to drink. Powers came out and went to his Jag."

"What time was this?" Spencer asked.

"I don't know, 11:00, 11:30, could've been earlier. I'm not sure. Anyway, I came up behind him with a ski mask on. He turned and hit me with his fist, knocking me down, and kicked the gun out of my hand. He laughed and said he saw me coming in the mirror of the car, then he kicked me in the face and ribs several times, which is why I look the way I do."

"Why'd you tell Alisheen you were in a bar fight then?" Spencer asked, curious.

"Simple," said Mickey. "I didn't want her to know I tried to stop Powers from seeing her. She'd kill me."

"Or she'd do to you what Powers did," Spencer said with a wry grin.

Mickey laughed and winced again.

Spencer said, "What happened after he beat you up?"

"He picked up the gun, put it into his coat pocket, and left. If I hadn't rolled out of the way he'd have run over me."

Carol broke in.

"This sounds good, but how do we know you weren't getting even with A.J.? He was a jerk."

"I wouldn't kill him for that. He was a jerk with everybody. I wasn't special."

"That still doesn't prove anything," Carol said pointedly.

Mickey said, "Why do you think I wore a mask?"

"So, you wouldn't be recognized," she said irritated.

"Precisely, they got security cameras. I didn't want Powers or anybody else to recognize me, you know. I'm betting the whole thing is on camera."

Spencer looked at Carol, who said, "I'm on it," and she left in a hurry.

After she was gone, Spencer said, "Thanks for trying to help."

"No problem. Spencer, can I give you some advice?"

"Sure."

"You need to drink a bottle of tequila with Alisheen, get drunk together, and open your heart up man. That's all she wants."

Moved, Spencer said, "I hope I get another opportunity to do just that. I'll have them drive you to the hospital to be sure you're OK."

"No, I just want to go home, get back in bed with a bottle of tequila, and get some sleep."

Spencer laughed. "That's what got you into trouble in the first place."

They both laughed and Mickey winced, forgetting his face was bruised and swollen.

~~~~

Alisheen left Spencer in tears. She didn't know what made her feel worse, Mickey in jail or seeing Spencer again. She called Emily to tell her what happened to Mickey. Emily was incredulous and wanted to know what she could do to help.

Alisheen said, "Just check later to see if he's back home. I'll be at the plantation for the weekend, but I'll be back late Sunday afternoon. Hopefully by then all of this will be straightened out."

She glanced at the clock.

"I have to go, Emily. It's late and I haven't even started to get ready for tonight. Damn it, now I'm so confused. I'm not sure about anything anymore. After seeing Spencer today, everything got all jumbled up again."

Emily said, "Well, you better get it together girl. I say, just go ahead with your plans. Have a great time tonight and enjoy the luxurious lifestyle of the rich and famous on the plantation."

Alisheen laughed and felt better. "It should be a lot of fun."

Emily said, "That's the spirit. Have fun this weekend and talk to Spencer after you get back."

"You're right," said Alisheen. "I'm going crazy over nothing. I'll call you later and let you know how tonight went, OK?"

"OK, I can't wait to hear all about it, and be careful."

"I will, Emily, thanks."

"Goodbye," said Emily.

"Goodbye," said Alisheen and she hung up.

She checked the clock and jumped into the shower. She went with minimal make-up as usual and dressed quickly in the new gown she'd bought for the occasion. She decided to wear her hair up, and after a few minutes she had it brushed out and expertly arranged into a swirl updo. She fastened the clasp on a diamond necklace that Spencer had given her, then started to take it off, but changed her mind trying to be indifferent. She added a bracelet and drop earrings and was ready. She slipped on the shoes she had dyed to match the gown, and she grabbed a handbag and a wrap. She wasn't sure if she was going to need any of it, but she had them just in case. She checked the clock again and laughed when she decided to wait and have a drink in the limo.

"I'm sure getting used to 'high on the hog' living." She sat down and flipped on the cable to wait.

~~~~

Jeanette arrived home from work, nervous over the upcoming evening, and decided to take a nap. She smiled with a naughty look and shivered with anticipation. She'd need her rest since she was planning to stay up late with Carl. She woke up hungry, ate some cheese and crackers, and drank a glass of wine. She refilled the glass, lit some candles, and filled the bathtub, settling into the perfumed water. She bathed with the perfumed soap that matched the scent of the water and felt glorious when finished.

She carefully put on her make-up and the lingerie she'd bought just for this occasion, her first night with Carl. She felt so sexy in the all black lingerie, with the garter belt and seamed stockings. She was going to drive Carl wild with desire for her. She put on the dress she'd shown Carl in the office and slipped on her high heels. After touching up her hair and make-up, she was ready. She got her handbag from the closet and posed in front of the full-length mirror, admiring herself. She was beautiful. She sat down to wait for Carl.

~~~~

Precisely at 6:00, Alisheen's cell rang. She hesitated but quickly picked up when she saw it was Carl's number on the screen.

"Hey, I'm here," she said brightly.

"Good, I was beginning to wonder if you were going to stand me up."

"Oh, no," said Alisheen. "I wouldn't miss out on a free meal and drinks even if you were ugly."

Carl chuckled. "Well, I'm coming up the steps. I hope you're ready."

A moment later, she heard his knock on the door and there he was in a white dinner jacket with a red rose. He was very handsome.

"Not bad, not bad," she said and burst out laughing.

Carl smiled. "I was wondering. I thought I cleaned up pretty good."

"You look very dashing in your dinner jacket. I'll be honored to have you as an escort."

Carl took in her beauty and was overwhelmed.

"You are absolutely the most beautiful woman I've ever seen. Believe me when I say the honor is all mine."

Alisheen blushed and lied, "This dress is old and so are the shoes. It's nothing special."

"That may be, but I doubt it. You're special and I'm undone. I hope you don't mind if I just stare at you all night."

"Oh, stop it, you nut," laughed Alisheen. "I'm hungry and ready for a glass of wine." She cocked her head and with a haughty voice said, "I do hope there is something in the limo worth drinking."

They both laughed and Carl said, "Where's your bag for the weekend?"

"Oh gosh, I forgot with everything else going on this afternoon. I won't be a minute."

"I can wait. We're not in a hurry."

Alisheen handed Carl her things and rushed off to the bedroom. She returned a few minutes later with a small bag.

"I'm ready, let's go."

Carl traded her purse and wrap for her bag and led her down the stairs. The waiting chauffer hurried forward to relieve Carl of the bag and held it as he opened the door for Alisheen.

Carl walked around the car and got in.

The chauffer opened the trunk, put the bag in, and took his place behind the wheel.

He nodded at Alisheen in the mirror. "Hello, Miss, it's nice to see you again."

"Hello, Frankie, it's nice to see you again too."

Frankie blushed, pleased that Alisheen remembered his name. Carl opened the fridge and peeked inside.

"It seems all we have is some chilled white wine and a decent champagne. Which would you rather have?" he asked with a laugh.

Alisheen made a fake pout and said with a bored tone, "Oh how I must suffer. I guess the wine will have to do."

They laughed and Carl popped the cork, poured two glasses, and handed one to Alisheen. She leaned back into the seat with a comfortable sigh.

"What was the big sigh for?" asked Carl.

"I think it's the first time I've relaxed all day."

"What happened today?" Carl asked settling next to her on the seat.

Alisheen told him about Mickey's fight and arrest.

Carl was surprised. "Your bartender, Mickey, from the She Crab?" he repeated.

"Yes, I hope it all gets straightened out. I'm very fearful for him."

Carl said, "Is there anything I can do? I have a law firm at my disposal. I'm sure I can get him some help."

"Oh, I don't think that'll be necessary," and she changed the subject. "What's for dinner?"

"Steak," said Carl.

As they finished dinner, Carl said, "Are you about ready to go? We really should be getting on. I'm expected to make a reasonably early appearance so they can thank me for my generosity."

Alisheen said, "You make it sound like a chore."

"Oh, it's not that, I'd just rather they not make a big fuss like they do. I like doing it. If they didn't thank me at all I'd still do it."

"A noble sentiment," said Alisheen, "but they feel the need to show their appreciation, so you'll just have to endure it."

Carl laughed and placed his hand on her back as they walked. The warmth of her bare skin under his hand combined with her soft scent was powerful, and Carl felt wonderful.

~~~~

Jeanette looked at the clock and realized she'd gotten ready earlier than she thought. "Must be the excitement." She decided she had time to eat a small *Lean Cuisine,* so she slipped off her shoes, went to the kitchen, and covered herself with an apron. Following the directions precisely, she cooked the food, and ate it with a glass of water after deciding that she'd had enough wine for the moment. She cleaned up the small mess and went back to the living room; she looked out the window to be sure she hadn't missed a horn and sat back down on the couch.

It was 8:30. Carl would be here soon. She was so nervous she decided a little more wine would calm her down, so she poured another glass. She sat on the couch sipping the wine, listening to the television, and watching the clock. As it approached 9:00, she became more apprehensive. The hands finally reached their proper positions, and she stood up in anticipation. She picked up her bag, checked the window again, and waited by the front door. At 9:15, she was miffed that Carl was late and sat down on the sofa. By 10:00 she was a woman scorned, and she'd carry out her threat. She was going to kill Alisheen Delaney and take down Carl Powers. She looked down at herself and laughed on the verge of hysteria.

"That bastard tricked me, but I have the invitation, so I'll go by myself."

~~~~

When they arrived at the hotel, the valet opened the door as the limo came to a stop. Carl got out, told Frankie to stay put, and helped Alisheen exit the limo. As they entered, the crowd swallowed them up, greeting Carl and introducing themselves to Alisheen. An official-looking man appeared and escorted them through the crowd into the ballroom. It was a little embarrassing.

Alisheen whispered to Carl, "Why is everyone staring at us like that?"

"One, because I'm a huge sponsor; two, I never bring a date; and three, you're the best-looking woman in the room. In addition, you're not exactly unknown. There are lots of people in Savannah who know who you are."

A tuxedoed man greeted Carl and Alisheen and dismissed the man that had guided them through the crowd.

He extended his hand. "Carl, it's so good to see you."

"Thank you, John," said Carl returning the handshake. "I hope everything is going as planned."

The man beamed. "Splendid, just splendid. The items you donated are doing well of course."

Carl said, "John, I would like for you to meet Alisheen Delaney."

"Ah, the owner of the infamous She Crab, of course."

He reached out and kissed the back of Alisheen's hand.

"I'm honored to have you here with us tonight."

Carl smiled. "Alisheen, this is John Bowers. He's the Chair this year for the Ball."

Alisheen smiled and said, "Thank you, and it's very nice to meet you."

Bowers said, "Carl, my thanks to you for your generous donations again this year. If there is anything I can do for you, just call me."

Bowers left to speak to other guests, and Carl suddenly grabbed Alisheen and gave her a gentle hug, which she returned, but with surprise.

"What's that about?"

"I wanted to say thanks for being one of the best things that has ever happened to me."

Alisheen stood up on her toes and kissed him softly on the lips. "I think, Mr. Powers, the feeling is possibly mutual."

Carl, with pride, escorted Alisheen to the podium table where she handed her wrap and bag to an attendant.

"Would you like to dance?"

Alisheen agreed and they went into the adjacent ballroom where the band was playing. He took Alisheen into his arms and guided her effortlessly around the dance floor.

"How about a drink?" asked Carl as they finished the second dance.

"Perfect," said Alisheen, and they headed for one of the many bars in the room. Alisheen was at ease after the initial shock of the entrance and was having a great time. Carl excused himself to go to the restroom, and she continued to mingle and nodded to some faces she knew. She nibbled at the varied buffets and sipped an excellent white wine while she waited. She was contemplating going to the restroom, when she noticed a vaguely familiar woman moving through the crowd toward her.

Jeanette flashed her invitation with authority and entered the ballroom. She went to a bar, ordered a vodka martini, and politely greeted people who spoke to her because they obviously recognized her as an important person. It felt good to be a "power broker." She laughed inwardly at the thought and froze. There they were. Carl and that bitch.

She couldn't believe he'd actually brought that tramp instead of her, the two-timing bastard. Jeanette debated on what to do next. She couldn't decide whether to speak to them both and spoil the fun or to catch Carl alone. She'd be able to make Alisheen jealous; after all, she was just as pretty. She decided what to do when Carl left Alisheen for the bathroom.

"Well, hello there," Jeanette said brightly as she walked up quickly to Alisheen, looking her up and down.

"Uh, hello," said Alisheen unnerved by the woman's demeanor.

"We met the other day while shopping, remember?"

Alisheen haltingly said, "Yes, I do remember. We were both shopping for a dress for tonight, I believe. Is that right?"

Jeanette laughed and said, "That's right, we were. I'm Jeanette LaCrosse in case you don't remember."

Alisheen, wary, said, "Yes, I remember."

Jeanette looked around. "I thought you had a date tonight, but you appear to be alone."

Alisheen quickly said, "Oh, I'm not here by myself. My date had to be excused for a few minutes."

"I see," said Jeanette, as she watched for Carl's return.

"Do you have a date?" asked Alisheen politely.

"Oh, no, my dear," said Jeanette with a hint of anger. "My date stood me up tonight. He's a terrible bastard. I can't wait to get my hands on him. I'll kill him."

Alisheen wasn't sure how to take the comment the strange woman had made.

"That wasn't very nice of him."

"No, it wasn't, but I'm betting he'll come around to my way of thinking. Who is your date?" Jeanette demanded.

"Carl Powers," said Alisheen, taken back by her rudeness.

"Oh, him," said Jeanette, bored.

"Yes, do you know him?"

"Not very well really, but I know about him," she said with sarcasm. "He's quite the player. Dating all sorts of women and casting them off when he's done with them like toys. I hope you don't turn out to be one of them." Jeanette leaned closer to Alisheen and whispered harshly, "He's quite the devil."

The words carried a tone of evil that scared her. She was uncomfortable with the conversation and the woman.

Jeanette said, "Have you been here long?"

"I guess we got here a couple of hours ago," Alisheen said distractedly, wishing the woman would leave. "After we went out to dinner."

Something flashed in the woman's eyes and disappeared, but it scared Alisheen even more. She wished Carl would hurry. The woman seemed to be looking for Carl with as much intensity as she was.

*That son-of-a-bitch* thought Jeanette when she found out about dinner. *He told me nine to put me off until he could have her safely with him.*

"That sounds wonderful," said Jeanette.

"Oh, it was very good," said Alisheen trying to be dismissive. She was positive the woman was watching the door. She never took her gaze from it to look at her when she spoke.

Jeanette wanted Carl to see her with Alisheen so he'd know how close to death she'd been, and there was no way he could protect her all the time.

They saw him coming at the same time, and Alisheen said with relief, "Oh, here comes my date. Would you like to meet him?"

"Oh, no," said Jeanette hastily, "I must be going, goodbye, for now."

"Goodbye," said Alisheen, and she was lost in the crowd. That bit about "for now" bothered her for reasons she couldn't put her finger on, and she was glad when Carl reappeared with an apprehensive look.

"You, OK?"

"That was the strangest person I think I've ever met. Her name is Jeanette LaCrosse. Do you know her?"

"Jeanette works for me, and I'm frankly surprised to see her. What did she say?"

"She told me her date had stood her up, and she was going to kill him if he didn't see the error of his ways."

"What else?"

"She asked me about how long we'd been here, and I told her we went to dinner. She was very nosy and rude, especially when she talked about you. She told me you were a player. Then she said 'Goodbye, for now,' as if she was going to see us later. I was so glad you came back when you did."

Carl shook his head and said, "Well, don't worry, Jeanette tends to drink too much." He smiled at her with reassurance and changed the subject.

"Let's go look at the silent auctions. They might have something I want to bid on."

Alisheen smiled and took his arm. "OK, Mr. Player."

As they walked, her mood lightened, but Alisheen admitted to Carl that the possibility of encountering Jeanette LaCrosse again was not a pleasant thought.

After Jeanette left Alisheen, she got another martini from the bar and roamed the hall, keeping a distant vigil. She ate from the vast array of foods available until she was satisfied. She wasn't going to leave hungry anyway. She continued to watch them from a distance, had another martini, and finally decided to go home. As she walked out, she spotted Carl staring at her. She smiled at him demurely then casually slid her finger over her throat and disappeared. What in the hell had happened to Ian?

~~~~

When they came out of the hotel, Frankie was waiting. Alisheen leaned back in the seat and closed her eyes. She heard a clinking glass and opened them. Carl was pouring brandy into a snifter.

"Do you care for a nightcap?"

"No, thanks, I'm fine. I'm going to rest. It was a hectic day."

Carl settled beside her. Alisheen felt his presence and leaned against him, putting her head on his shoulder. Carl felt her warmth and inhaled her perfume. She snuggled a little closer and got more comfortable. Suddenly she sat up and kissed him on the lips.

"I forgot to say, thank you, for the wonderful time I had tonight."

Carl gently kissed her back.

"You're welcome."

She kissed him again with softness touching his cheek, then snuggled for the ride to the plantation by placing her head in his lap. Carl felt feelings he'd never known before. Was this what it felt like to be in love? He really didn't know. He'd never loved anybody before, especially someone like Alisheen. He wasn't sure what he was feeling, but he did know he felt great, and he remembered Rupert's words. Maybe it was time to get out and live right. He could definitely do it for Alisheen.

Carl topped off his brandy, turned off the cabin lights, and relaxed, lightly rubbing Alisheen's back. He loosened his bow tie and unbuttoned the top button on his shirt as the limo crossed the Savannah River Bridge headed for South Carolina. He was in love for the first time in his life.

# Chapter 24

COOLEY AND BRIDGES reported that Benny had flown the
coop. They'd searched all day, and after talking to the mission attendant, went
to the bus station. The ticket agent identified him as the purchaser of a ticket
for the bus to New York first thing that morning, and there was no guarantee
he was still on the bus. He could've gotten off anywhere, and the chance of
finding him was slim.

Mickey's revelation about the cameras in the garage was the only bright
spot. The problem was the ski mask. It'd be hard to prove he was the mugger
Powers kicked the crap out of and took the gun from, and Carol still hadn't
returned with the tape.

Spencer said, "Two days ago we caught a huge break, and so far, we've
gotten nowhere. We've got to get back on track."

Fitzgerald's cell phone rang.

"OK, I'm sending back-up. You sit tight. If he moves, follow him."

He hung up and looked at Spencer with excitement. "Bo has been
following LaCrosse tonight. He's sure someone else is too. He's seen him
several times."

"Is he sure it's not a coincidence?" asked Spencer, skeptical.

"I think he'd bet on it right now," Skip replied.

"Who could be tailing her and why?" asked Meadors.

Fitzgerald and Spencer exchanged knowing looks and nodded in
agreement.

"What're you thinking, Skip?"

"I'm thinking the same thing you are. I'm betting he's working for Whitley and setting up to grab LaCrosse. They'll take her to a safe house so Isaac Henry can get from her what he wants, and that's confirmation that Powers is the Snowman."

Meadors said, "What're you two talking about?"

Spencer said, "I can't give you details right now; suffice it to say, its bad news." He looked at Skip. "I think for the moment we let Bo watch the watcher until we can figure out what to do."

Skip agreed.

Carol entered the squad room holding a DVD in a plastic case.

"I looked at the video and made a DVD copy. It's identical to Mickey's story, but you can't identify him. A good lawyer would kill him on the stand."

Spencer said, "OK, put it on the computer screen so everyone can see it."

Carol selected the drive, pushed play, and turned the monitor around. As a group, they saw Powers come out of the elevator and approach the Jag. The mugger appeared wearing a ski mask and holding a gun leveled at Powers. It was obvious why Powers was an All-American athlete in his day. He turned so quickly, the poor bastard trying to mug him never had a chance. The backhanded fist sent the mugger sprawling. He fell to the concrete floor, his head hit the concrete with a snap, and Powers kicked the gun from his hand.

They watched him methodically place well-aimed kicks to the face and body. He was obviously enjoying himself. He finished his short but brutal assault on the unidentified man, spit on him and then, oddly enough, checked his watch, then stooped over, picked up the gun, and stuffed it into his coat pocket. Powers got into the Jag and backed out of his space, then accelerated toward the man on the ground, who barely rolled out of the way in time. Eventually, he got to his hands and knees, puked and crawled out of sight. The tape ended with snow.

"Mickey was lucky," Spencer said.

"If it was him," said Carol. "We don't have any evidence except that Mickey got the crap beat out of him like the guy on the ground, and his credibility is questionable. We have to prove that was Mickey in the ski mask."

"I know," said Spencer, "I just don't know how. Bring Mickey back here tonight so he can look at the tape. He might remember something. Maybe Powers said something to him. He checked his watch and decided it was time to go. He had to be somewhere, that's for sure."

Spencer reorganized the group. He put Cooley and Bridges back on Benny to find and stop the bus. The feds could arrest him, take him off and hold him.

"He's out on bail so he's a fugitive. We need him back. He's an eyewitness."

"What if he's not on the bus?" asked Cooley.

"Then we put an all-points out on his ass, but I want him found and back in Savannah. Right now, he's all we have."

It was a long shot but worth the gamble. Spencer put Carol at the apartments and Bridges back at the hotel on the slim chance Baxter might come back to one of them. Meadors would meet him at the warehouse, and they'd look around some more. He'd join him after he called Drake about the subpoenas. Maybe fresh eyes would find something everybody else missed. Fitzgerald was to contact Bo and determine who was watching LaCrosse.

Skip said, "Spencer, it's getting late, don't you think?"

"It's already too late for A.J., and I don't really care what time it is or who I piss off. We're running out of time."

~~~~

Bo watched the man in the car through the binoculars. He was sure he'd seen him before, and not only tonight. He'd seen him somewhere else but couldn't place him. He'd followed LaCrosse to the hotel and noticed him parking his car and going in. He came out later and left. Bo continued to wait on LaCrosse and didn't think any more about it. After following her home, Bo passed the house and saw the familiar car down the street at the corner. He turned onto the street, shining the headlights on the car, and got a good look at the driver smoking a cigarette before he turned away. It was the same person. Bo rounded the next corner, parked, and called Skip, who told him to sit tight and follow him if he moved. Bo snuck back around the corner and set up vigilance in the shadows of the trees. His phone vibrated with a call from Skip.

"Bo, its Skip, give me an update."

"He's just sitting there smoking and occasionally looking through a set of binoculars."

"Are you sure he's watching LaCrosse and he's not some private detective working for a wife or husband that suspects their spouse of cheating?"

"Maybe, but I doubt it. He's been everywhere I've been tonight following LaCrosse, and there's something else."

"What?"

"I've seen him before, but I just can't remember where."

"Well, if it comes to you, call me and let me know."

"Bo, I've got back-up on the way, so you've got help."

"OK, I'll keep an eye on him."

~~~~

Spencer met Meadors at the warehouse, but there was nothing new. Yellow tape barriers protected the blood pool evidence and the tape outlines of the bodies where they'd lain on the floor.

"I wonder where Benny was hiding?" asked Meadors.

"That's a good question," said Spencer. "Let's figure it out by putting ourselves in his place. He couldn't have been on the ground close by because there's no place to hide. It's wide open." Spencer walked to the shop and stood at the door. "He wasn't here because they would've seen him, so where else could he have been?"

Meadors pointed up.

"There's storage up there, but he'd have to hang over the edge to see below him. He wouldn't risk exposing himself and be caught. He'd have been too scared."

"Oh, crap," said Spencer.

"What?"

"I remembered something in Carol's report from Benny's interrogation. The security guard would sometimes let him sleep in a truck. I'll bet the old man let him in that night, and he was in a truck sleeper watching it go down—probably this one. It's in the photographs of the crime scene so it hasn't been touched." Spencer walked over to the truck and opened the door. It smelled like urine.

"Meadors, take up a position where the gun is marked on the floor and point toward the body."

Spencer climbed into the sleeper and pulled the curtain back.

He could see the entire scene from his elevated vantage point and Meadors was less than twenty feet away.

"Bingo," said Spencer through the vent.

He crawled out of the sleeper and hopped out of the truck.

"The crime lab missed the truck. It smells like urine in there. Benny was either trapped or so scared and shocked by what he saw, he peed in his pants. Either way, they should find his prints. It might be something we can use later."

Meadors said, "I'll get the night crew from the lab out here and have them start on the truck."

Spencer said, "OK, I'm going to watch the DVD and check with Drake. They're stalling, but he's getting ready to rock the boat. He's pissed off he's got a double homicide on his hands and can't get a single warrant."

Meadors laughed. "It's his town."

Spencer laughed at the imitation of Drake. "You better not let him catch you doing that."

While Spencer was in route back to the station, he got a call from Skip.

"Bo is watching this guy over at LaCrosse's. He's seen him somewhere but can't place him. I told him if he figured it out to let me know. Maybe he's working for Powers."

"That's a possibility," Spencer said, "but I doubt it, or she'd be dead by now too. Tell Bo to sit tight and to wait and see what he does. I'd like to see where this takes us, but I'm betting it's Whitley protecting his interests. If he thinks that LaCrosse is the second informer, he needs her to make his insane plan work since A.J. is dead."

"I wouldn't put it past him," said Skip. "They threatened us with jail and seizing jurisdiction. They'll protect their interests at all costs."

"Would they go as far as eliminating anybody in their way?" Spencer asked.

"They have ties to the C.I.A. and their own black ops units. They'd do it in a heartbeat."

"I changed my mind, arrest him," said Spencer.

"Are you sure?" cautioned Skip.

"Yes," said Spencer. "We don't know who he is or what he's doing. We plead ignorance and buy us some time."

"Whitley will go ballistic."

"Look at it this way, this guy appears out of nowhere. He makes no contact with you or us, so there's no way we can know to stay clear of him."

"OK then, I'll tell Bo to arrest him."

Spencer laughed lightly. "What about your career with D.E.A.?"

"I don't have the character flaws needed to be a lifer."

"I knew I liked you for some reason."

"Thanks for the vote of confidence. What do you want to do with our mystery man?"

"Hold him until we can find out what's going on."

"Will you be back soon?"

"I'm almost there now."

Spencer arrived and learned that Mickey was already there. He waited for Skip and Meadors to join him before bringing him to the squad room. Noticing Mickey's condition, they wished him a speedy recovery.

Spencer said, "Mickey, I wanted you to come back to be sure we aren't missing anything. Did Powers say anything you might've forgotten that'd be helpful?"

"I can't think of anything. He called me a bad boy and laughed at me, that's it."

Spencer said, "We got a copy of the video and it's on a DVD. We can't tell if it's you or not with the ski mask on. I need you to watch it and hopefully you'll remember something that'll help."

"No Problem, Spencer. Hell, I've already been through it, so it won't hurt to watch."

Mickey flinched a couple of times while watching, and when it was over, he touched his face.

"No wonder I look like raw meat. He kicked the shit out of me."

Meadors was staring at Mickey as if he was a ghost.

Mickey, uncomfortable, said, "What's the deal, Meadors?"

"Meadors," said Spencer, "what is it?"

Meadors grabbed Mickey's right hand and held it tight.

"Back up the DVD."

Spencer hit the rewind button and Meadors said almost immediately, "There, freeze it!"

Spencer hit the pause button and looked at the screen.

"Don't you see it? Look at the hand holding the gun."

Meadors held up Mickey's hand beside the screen.

Mickey grinned. "Well, I'll be damned."

Meadors said, "I thought I saw it when you pointed the gun at Powers but wasn't sure. I saw it the second time when you rolled out of the way and just now when you touched your face."

There was no mistake. On the back of Mickey's hand was a large tattoo of Mickey Mouse. Underneath it, written in red and yellow letters, was the word, Mickey. It was a match to the hand on the screen holding the gun.

Spencer asked, "You weren't wearing gloves?"

"No."

"Then your prints should've been all over it, and Powers' too since he picked it up with his bare hand. He used it on A.J. and wiped it clean. That's why only your prints were on the bullets and casings. You loaded it."

"We got him," said Meadors with determination.

~~~~

Jeanette arrived home and parked the BMW behind the house. Her vision was clear. She would go to the plantation tonight to kill that bitch and anyone else who got in her way. Even Carl if he tried to stop her. He'd lied to her, and she'd been delighted at the look on Carl's face when she drew her finger across her throat. She entered the house, locked the doors, and stared at the candelabras she'd practiced getting married with so many times. With purpose, she took every candle and broke it into pieces. Satisfied with the start of the purge, she went into the spare bedroom carrying scissors.

She took the wedding gown out of the closet, arranged it on the bed, and methodically cut it into shreds. The veil of lace and tulle followed, and then, with deliberation, she destroyed the bridal bouquet she'd made and preserved so carefully. Next, she opened the bottom drawer of the chest and took out her precious wedding day lingerie. She cut up the lace bustier and matching panties, and with her hands tore the sheer white stockings apart, dropping them to the floor with the remnants of the lingerie and wedding dress.

She grabbed the back of the dress she'd worn for Carl on what was to be their special night. She pulled and tore at the zipper until the fabric ripped, and it fell to the floor around her feet. She stepped out of it and ripped off the seamed stockings. The pieces left hooked to the garter belt she removed by cutting the delicate ribbon garters. She cut the lace belt off with one stroke, then the lace bra and panties. She stood naked in the midst of her shattered dreams, for a moment, then she calmly walked to the other bedroom and sat down at her dressing table. She methodically removed her jewelry, took off her make-up, brushed out her hair, and then dressed in old clothes.

Jeanette went to the kitchen and opened the bottle of champagne she'd been saving for a special occasion. This seemed to be a good time to open it. She drained the first glass in several swallows and poured another. She saw her reflection in the kitchen window and lifted her glass with a loud toast.

"Here's to your death, Alisheen Delaney."

She drained the glass and threw it at the window, breaking both. It was time to take care of business. Jeanette went to the bedroom and walked over the shredded clothes on the floor. She opened the top dresser drawer, pulled out a wooden box, and then carried it to the kitchen. She poured another glass of champagne but sipped it this time and sat down at the table, opening the box. The nickel-plated 9 mm gleamed under the kitchen light. She'd bought it for protection years ago when she began to live alone.

She knew gun owners most often were hurt because they didn't know enough about their weapon to be safe. Like everything else in her life, she wanted perfection and had taken shooting lessons. Her instructor had marveled at how quickly she'd progressed and had urged her to take up competitive shooting. But she declined so she could work for Carl. That was all a long time ago now.

She checked the chamber to verify it was empty, then loaded the gun but locked the slide open. There was no need for a live round yet. She checked the safety, picked up the loaded spare clips, and put two each into her back pockets. She put the gun in a shoulder purse along with her car keys, wallet, and cell phone, and finished the champagne. Shouldering the purse as she walked through the house, she looked at the destruction, laughed hysterically, and screamed with rage.

"I'm coming to kill you, Alisheen Delaney! Ready or not, here I come."

~~~~

Drake came into the squad room.

"Gentlemen, I got good news. You can serve your subpoenas in the morning. If they're uncooperative, the D.A. has a team standing by to help."

Spencer said, "Captain, we've got evidence that places the gun at the scene in Carl Power's possession the night of the murder at the warehouse."

Drake, exasperated, said, "How in the hell can you do that?"

Spencer explained Mickey's presence and showed Drake the DVD.

"Damn," said Drake when it was over. "If that's you, son, you took a beating, but like I said, if that's you," he said skeptically.

Meadors grinned.

"Oh, it's him Captain, look close."

They froze the video at the appropriate spot, gave Drake a magnifying glass, and showed him the back of Mickey's hand. He went back and forth several times.

"Son-of-a-bitch, I'll call the D.A. and get busy finding a judge that will issue an arrest warrant on suspicion of murder. Where is he now?"

"He's in South Carolina on his plantation," Spencer said.

"Then I'll have to find a federal judge, but with the D.E.A. in support, we can cross state lines."

Spencer said, "What about our directive?"

"We're talking about capital murder," sputtered Drake. "If Ben Whitley wants to come down here and seize jurisdiction of a murder case, I'd like to see him try. I'll stomp his ass on the courthouse lawn. He can complain to the Commissioner later. Sit tight until I have that warrant. Fitzgerald, have your team ready to go. I'll be back as soon as I can." He paused and looked at his watch, "Ten minutes until midnight. I'm going to call Ben and wake him up, just so I can piss him off."

~~~~

Bo could tell something had happened. His man had bolted upright and covered his ear.

*"He must have her bugged, who is this guy?"*

The taillights blinked on when the engine started.

He spoke into the radio, "Take him."

The screen quickly closed in around the suspect with lights flashing and agents with guns drawn. They ordered the suspect out of the car and onto the ground face down. He was yelling something trying to explain his presence, but they were having none of it.

"We got him in custody, where to?"

"Take him to Fitzgerald at the station. Does he have any ID on him?"

"Yeah, that's the weird part. He has D.E.A. ID, a gun, and some damn good listening equipment."

"What's the name?"

"John Blackwell."

"Damn," said Bo, "You better get him to Fitzgerald right away."

"Yes, sir."

Bo called Skip.

"What's happening?"

"We busted the watcher. He was gearing up to go. He's on the way in now."

Fitzgerald didn't like Bo's tone. "What's happened?"

"Remember how I said he looked familiar?"

"Yeah."

"It's Blackwell."

"Damn!"

"That's what I said."

~~~~

LaCrosse went out the back door and by-passed the BMW for her old car, a Chevy Cavalier. She'd abandon the car and report it stolen in the morning. Loud sirens and squealing tires erupted on the street, and she hurried to the front of the house. Two police cars went racing by, and she could see a car surrounded at the corner of the next street. She gave a huff of indignation thinking, *what was happening to her neighborhood,* and she returned to her car. It was after midnight. If she hurried, she'd be back in time for breakfast, and she accelerated to make up time. Soon she was on her way over the bridge and headed for the plantation.

Ian was satisfied Vincent would take care of Vernon. In case he wanted a little more revenge, he wasn't going to hang around, and he was out of the country as soon as he took care of LaCrosse. He turned onto her street and stopped dead; police cars were everywhere. Instantly, he decided he wasn't that loyal, not when it came to choosing between his skin or making a kill for Powers. She was Powers' problem anyway, not his, and he turned around in a driveway. He'd drive to Atlanta and catch a flight out of the country. Australia sounded good.

~~~~

Whitley was mad as hell after Drake's call, and to top it all off, Blackwell had called to say he was being detained. He hated to call Chambers and wake him, but it was an emergency. When he answered, Whitley told him about the warrant for Powers and Blackwell's predicament.

"We told them clearly, no arrests," said Chambers.

"It's a capital murder, sir," said Whitley with a plea. "The evidence puts Powers at the scene and identifies him as the shooter. He killed A.J. Guilford."

"I'll call Mr. Henry."

Chambers placed the call.

"What is it, Clifton? I'm busy and it's late."

"They've issued a warrant for Powers on suspicion of murder. The evidence indicates Powers killed our informer, and they can put the gun in his hand."

Henry was silent and Chambers knew better than to interrupt, so he waited.

"What's Blackwell's status?"

"Activated, but they're holding him too," said Chambers.

"I assume his team is in place?"

"Yes, sir. He's just waiting for a green light."

"Was Blackwell on the woman LaCrosse?"

"Yes, sir. Evidently, they had surveillance on her and saw Blackwell. When they couldn't figure out who he was, they arrested him."

"Call Whitley and green light Blackwell's team. From this point Blackwell has the authority to seize jurisdiction. He's to acquire Powers and bring him here. You're responsible for getting him into a safe house."

"What about LaCrosse?"

"Eliminate her. We don't need her if we have Powers. I don't want her appearing on the nightly news later telling the world about Carl Powers and his illegal activities. She needs to be removed."

"Sir, how do we know Powers is the Snowman?"

"Clifton don't be stupid. They're arresting Powers for killing Guilford. Let me know when Powers is in our hands. Good night, Clifton."

"Good night, sir," said Chambers, canceling the connection and immediately calling Whitley. "Hello?"

"I just talked to Mr. Henry. Call Blackwell and tell him to seize jurisdiction and order Fitzgerald and the Savannah police to stay out of their way. Blackwell is to arrest Powers and bring him to a safe house in Virginia, and he is to eliminate LaCrosse."

"What do you mean eliminate?"

"Exactly what you think it means, Benjamin." Whitley swallowed and said, "Yes, sir."

He hung up and called Blackwell's cell phone.

"It's about time. I've been cooling my heels long enough."

"You're to activate your team and seize jurisdiction by order of Director Henry. Arrest Powers and take him to Virginia to a safe house. Call Mr. Chambers when it's done."

"Anything else?" Blackwell asked.

"You're to eliminate LaCrosse."

"I understand."

Blackwell sat at the table and, looking at the mirror on the wall, dialed his cell phone.

"We're a go. Come get me at the police station ASAP. Bring our orders and the warrants."

The agent known as Tommy hung up and began to issue orders.

"We're a go. I'm going to go get Blackwell and will meet you at the airport. Have the equipment loaded and the choppers on the pad warmed up. Let's move it!"

Captain Drake walked into the room after Blackwell finished his phone call.

"Mr. Blackwell?"

Blackwell smiled. Drake nodded, left, and met Skip and Spencer in the hall.

"I just got a call from the Commissioner, who has talked to the Mayor, who has talked to all of our State Senators. We're to wait until Mr. Blackwell's assistant arrives."

Spencer started to speak, but Drake put up his hand. "Not now!"

They looked up at footsteps coming down the corridor. A uniformed officer was escorting a man in black paramilitary clothes.

He didn't say anything but, "Where's Blackwell?"

Drake said, "In here, follow me," and they filed into the room followed by Spencer and Skip.

"Finally," said Blackwell.

"Yes, sir."

"You got the papers?"

The man nodded, handed him a manila envelope, and stepped back.

Drake confronted Blackwell.

"Do you want to tell me what's going on? Several important people have cussed me out tonight, and I'm a little pissed-off."

Blackwell opened the envelope and pulled out the papers. He sorted through them and then handed one to Drake.

"This one says I have the authority to seize jurisdiction, and I'm now the senior officer of the investigation. It also seizes all evidence, files, police notebooks, and any other materials and resources that are part of this investigation. They are now the property of the D.E.A."

Blackwell separated two more pieces of paper, handing one to Skip and the other to Spencer.

"What in the hell is this?" asked Spencer with anger.

"These are injunctions ordering you both to *Cease and Desist* with your investigation. In plain English, you are ordered to stand down, Detective."

Blackwell handed the last pieces of paper to Drake.

"Captain, one is a copy of my federal warrant to arrest Powers. The other one, in a nutshell, says if you or your department fails to comply with the notice to seize jurisdiction, you'll be prosecuted for obstruction, interfering with a federal investigation, and anything else they can think of."

Blackwell looked at his assistant.

"Where's the team?"

"Savannah airport."

Blackwell got up, motioned for his assistant to follow, and they left. Spencer wadded up his paper and threw it into the garbage.

Skip said, "I knew this was coming. The minute I heard Blackwell was here. I knew it."

"Who in the hell is he?" asked Spencer still furious.

"He's D.E.A. or C.I.A., no one really knows. Hell, he's probably both. He's black ops and goes deeper than a sub. He's bad news and has the power behind him to do whatever the hell he deems necessary."

Drake walked over to the trashcan, dropping his papers in on top of Spencer's. "I don't really care what in the hell he said or who's behind it. I'm tired of this crap. You two get your butts in gear and get to Powers first." He pulled the warrant for Powers' arrest out of his pocket. "Here's my piece of paper. If they're going to the airport and fly, you can beat them there if you haul ass."

Spencer watched Skip as he walked over and dropped his paper into the trashcan with the others.

"I like Savannah. It just might be time to give up the Atlanta rat race; although, I'll need a job."

Spencer grinned and said, "You got one."

As they left the room, Bo met them in the hallway.

"Spencer, you got to come quick. I think Alisheen is in real danger."

They rushed up the stairs to the squad room and arriving out of breath, Bo said, "We got the tapes from Blackwell's car. I wanted to see what in the hell had motivated him to get ready to go so fast, so I started listening to the tapes. Listen to this."

Spencer's face went white with fear as he heard Jeanette LaCrosse screaming, she was going to kill Alisheen Delaney.

Skip said, "Where's LaCrosse now? Isn't she at home?"

"No," said Bo. "The white BMW is there, but she isn't. When we got to her house, there was no answer, but the door was open. The officers went in, and she was gone. They found a wedding dress and some clothes cut up with scissors, and torn lingerie in one bedroom. In the kitchen, there was a half-empty bottle of champagne and an empty box that obviously had held a gun and clips. One of the neighbors said they'd come outside to see what was going on, and they saw her leave after the sirens had gone by. When we asked about the white BMW, the neighbor said she had an old Chevy of some kind that she parked in the back. It was gone."

Skip grabbed Spencer. "Come on! We've got to go, now!" They bolted for the door and Drake yelled after them, "Take Fitzgerald's car with the fed plates on it. I'll coordinate everything from here."

Drake addressed Bo. "Don't just stand there. Get on the radio and the telephone. Call everybody you can find and get them in here now. Then call the South Carolina Highway Patrol and the Beaufort County Sheriff's department and let them know of the situation. Tell them it's a federal investigation, we'd appreciate their cooperation. Federal officers are in route, and they're to be escorted to their destination."

Bo said confused, "What about Blackwell?"

Drake replied with fury, "I don't give a damn about Blackwell. If we get to Powers first, then we have the ability to negotiate. I'm not letting anybody come in here and seize jurisdiction. I don't care who they are. Now get going."

"Yes, sir."

Cooley and Bridges arrived first, and Drake intercepted them.

"Follow me, you two," and Drake led them into the squad room. Drake looked at Bo.

"Well?"

"I spoke with the Highway Patrol and the Beaufort County Sheriff. They'll be waiting for them at the State and County lines."

Drake looked at Cooley and Bridges. Both wore puzzled looks.

"You two go with Bo and haul ass for his plantation in Beaufort," Drake said as he pointed to the location on the map. "Fitzgerald and Baldwin are going to need backup. Take Bo's car, another fed car will be a plus. He can fill you in on the way. Bridges, you establish radio contact with me as soon as you're on the bridge."

Bo said, "I'm out front."

Drake called Fitzgerald "The Beaufort County Sheriff and the Highway Patrol are expecting you. Cooley and Bridges are with Bo, and they're on the way for backup."

Fitzgerald acknowledged. "We're almost over the bridge now."

Shortly, Carol, Meadors, and Cooper arrived, and Drake pointed at chairs.

"Here it is in a nutshell. The feds have seized jurisdiction, and we're going to beat them to Powers."

Carol said sarcastically, "Is that all?"

"No," said Drake, admonishing her with his tone. "Fitzgerald and Spencer are on their way to the plantation. Bo, Cooley, and Bridges are not far behind them. LaCrosse is headed for the plantation to kill Alisheen Delaney, and the feds are flying by helicopter from the airport to arrest Powers."

Carol's hand flew to her mouth, and Meadors stood up quickly.

"I have to help Spencer."

Drake said, "You're too late. They're already over the bridge."

"I got a Marine buddy that pilots choppers for charter and he owes me. He can get me there in time."

"Then get the hell out of here because Spencer is going to need all the help he can get. Cooper, take my place on the radio. Carol, you used to be D.E.A. I need you to help me figure out how I'm going to handle this if we beat them to Powers."

Carol said, "I'll try."

"Good, what do you know about a man named Blackwell?"

"We're in deep trouble if Blackwell is here. Does he have a team activated?"

"Yes."

"Then it's too late. If he's active they'll do whatever it takes, and I mean whatever, to accomplish their mission. They're like missiles on target lock. They won't quit."

"Let's go to my office and talk some more. Cooper, what's their status?"

"They're already over the bridge with an escort and a clear road. They'll be in Beaufort County soon."

"Keep me posted," said Drake. He hooked a finger at Carol and said, "Let's go."

Meadors called Ivory, waking him up, and he wasn't happy.

"Damn, Meadors, do you know what time it is man? I got a charter tomorrow!"

"Ivory, this is life or death man. You know I wouldn't call you unless I really needed you."

"OK, OK, meet me at the hangar. I'll be there as soon as I can."

Meadors, assuming the D.E.A. was using the commercial airport for logistics, was hoping they didn't know about the smaller one. By the time they got through the traffic, he could be halfway there. Meadors arrived at the deserted airport, went through the gate that led to the hangars, and parked. Ivory arrived and hopped out of an open Jeep.

"This better be good. My girlfriend wasn't happy."

"Ivory, this is bad, dude. You know Alisheen Delaney?"

"Yeah, man, she runs the She Crab, doesn't she?"

"That's her. She's in danger, and so is my partner. I have to get there in a hurry, and you're my best shot."

"Where're we going?"

"Let's find a map."

"I got a big one on the wall in the office."

They entered and Ivory flipped on the light switch. Meadors walked to the map, scanned it, and then pointed with his finger.

"I've got to get here or as close I can get."

"What in the hell is going on at Blue Creek?"

"I don't have time to explain. I got to get there ASAP."

"You're still a lucky bastard," said Ivory. "I've picked Powers up there before. About two hundred yards south of his property, there's a fire tower station. They use it when it's dry as hell and they got a fire watch on. There's plenty of room to drop you, and then you follow the creek."

"Ivory, we have to beat some feds there too."

"Where're they flying from?"

"The big airport."

"Do they know the area?"

"I doubt it."

Ivory grinned and it was obvious where he got his name. He flashed a huge smile from ear to ear, full of white teeth.

"No sweat man. They have to get clearance, and then they must fly to a buoy to get a marker signal for a bearing. By the time they do that, you'll be on the ground and in the woods."

Meadors smiled and said, "I need some artillery. You got anything I can use besides this pistol?"

Ivory, opening a locker, took out a flight jacket and two sets of headphones. He opened the adjacent locker, pulled out an M-1, and handed a set of headphones and the rifle to Meadors.

"We better move out."

Ivory smiled at Meadors as they lifted off. "Just like the old days, Sarge."

~~~~

Jeanette drove slowly through Beaufort. A few miles outside of town, she looked for the entrance to the plantation and identified it easily enough. She'd driven by it hundreds of times wishing and pretending she'd been invited by Carl for the weekend. Checking her mirrors for other cars, she cut the lights off, left on the parking lights, and turned into the dirt road entrance. She smiled happily. That bitch was going to be out of the way, and Carl would belong to her.

She reached the gate and got out to punch in the security code she'd obtained from the bills and noticed the gate's lock hadn't reset. She smiled knowingly; this was in her favor. Whenever someone entered the code to open or lock the gate, a signal beep notified the house. Pushing it open, she drove through then closed it, but didn't enter the code to lock the gate. She didn't want the signal to be heard, and it'd be easier to leave after she was finished. Determined, she drove to the house.

Clearing the woods, she saw the front porch lights were on, and a few lights on inside the house. She stopped the car, parked on the lawn, picked up the gun, and got out. She jacked a round into the chamber and patted the extra clips in her pockets. As she walked toward the house, the dogs came around the corner of the house barking and heading for her at full speed. She raised her pistol, took aim, and shot the lead dog. It hit the ground rolling with yelps of pain. The other dog stopped, confused, and began to whine and lick its companion on the ground. She shot it dead. LaCrosse focused her attention on the house and screamed at the top of her lungs, "I'm going to kill you, bitch!"

~~~~

After Bo made the initial contact with the Sheriff's office, Cooper took over. They'd found Sheriff Miller at his home and roused him from bed. Cooper explained that D.E.A. agents, accompanied by Savannah police, were on their way and would need his department's cooperation.

"Sheriff Miller, we need these agents met at the County line and escorted to Blue Creek Plantation. They have arrest warrants for Mr. Carl Powers on suspicion of murder." Sam Miller had never moved so fast in his life. He dressed quickly, went to the jail, and roused the sleepy deputy.

"Activate every off-duty officer now and have them report in. This is an emergency. I'm going to meet federal agents at the County line. Call Jimmy Dugan with the Highway Patrol and have him call me on the radio. We'll need assistance keeping the road clear since they're moving at a high speed. Anyone on duty meets me at the line, the off-duty officers take up patrol. Got it?"

The deputy saluted and said, "Yes, sir."

Fitzgerald monitored the radio and Spencer drove because he knew the roads. At the end of the bridge, the Highway Patrol waved them through, and periodically they'd pass a checkpoint with an officer on the radio waving them on. Cooper relayed the Beaufort County Sheriff would be waiting for them at the county line.

Spencer said, "Tell Cooper to tell them we'll be there in about 10 minutes."

Skip relayed the message and asked, "Where is everyone else?"

Cooper replied, "Cooley, Bridges, and Bo are following you. Carol is with the Captain, planning a strategy if we get Powers first, and Meadors is getting a war buddy to fly him in by helicopter."

Spencer said, "Meadors will be a big help. I just hope he makes it in time."

Skip nodded. "Carol, hopefully, can think of a way to keep us out of jail for ignoring a 'Cease and Desist' order under a federal order to Seize Jurisdiction."

"What about Blackwell's team?" asked Spencer.

"I've only met Blackwell a couple of times, and I've never worked with him, but he's one of our best. He's half-crazy and very dangerous."

"Let's just hope we beat him there for Alisheen's sake. It's bad enough we got LaCrosse trying to kill her. We don't need Powers using her as a bargaining chip."

Skip said, "There are blue lights ahead, and they're in the road."

"I see them. It must be the Sheriff. I thought we were getting close to the line."

Spencer slowed down as he approached and confirmed it was a Sheriff's patrol car in the road. He pulled onto the shoulder to by-pass the car, but a man ran in front of the car, waving frantically, stopping them.

Spencer, furious, cursed, put the car into park, and left the motor running.

As he got out the Sheriff came up to him. "You need to hold it right there. I need to see some ID and talk to the federal agent, so I know he has the right to be in this state before we go any further."

~~~~

Blackwell and Tommy arrived at the airport after numerous traffic delays, and they impatiently went through the security process to get clearance to the hangar.

"At this rate," Blackwell said, "Powers will have a good night's sleep before we're even off the ground."

As they walked into the hangar, Blackwell said, "Tell me where we stand."

Tommy pointed at the choppers with rotors turning on the runway.

"I got two choppers, eight guys, and the usual compliment of equipment. It's overkill, but we're prepared for any situation."

Blackwell nodded.

"Good, let's get in the air. I got a gut feeling we're in a race for Powers, and you know I don't like to lose."

The team stood as they approached and Tommy said, "Maps!"

They instantly cleared the small table and the maps rolled out.

Blackwell said, "Talk to me."

One of the pilots tapped his finger on the map.

"It's somewhere on this creek, but I can't pinpoint it without a bearing. We could try to fly straight to it, but without a marker on the ground, we could fly right by it, especially if the target is dark. It'll take time but I suggest we fly out to this buoy, pick up its navigation signal, and ride that sucker right into the back yard."

Blackwell looked at the other pilot. "You agree with him?"

The pilot nodded in affirmative. "It's the long way, but he's right. We could miss it. We could try to identify the target from the air, but it'd take search time and low flying that'd alert them to our presence long before we got on the ground."

"I don't like it, but let's use the buoy," Blackwell said.

In minutes, they were airborne.

Blackwell said over the headset, "How long?"

Tommy tapped the pilot who held up three fingers and then a fist. "Thirty minutes."

Blackwell swore. The moonlight was bright, and the water glistened as the choppers made the coastline.

"At least we got plenty of light," said Tommy.

Blackwell nodded and said with sarcasm, "Yeah, it's beautiful."

Tommy said, "What's the deployment?"

"Two, four-man teams by chopper. I want a diamond pattern with rotation so we're covering each other and each team. Together, we'll work side by side across the grounds until we're in the house. Then we'll split into twos, with a point and a rear. Our orders are to secure Powers and eliminate LaCrosse."

"Then what?"

"We put Powers in the chopper and go back to the airport, get on the charter to DC, and Henry does the rest. I don't think we'll have any opposition, but if any locals show up and get in the way, shoot low. No dead cops. I also don't want to blow this place to hell and back for a single capture and hit, so pass the word. I don't want anybody trigger-happy."

Tommy nodded and passed the orders over the headsets.

~~~~

Spencer was livid.

"You stupid son-of-a-bitch, are you out of your mind? There're lives at stake."

Sheriff Miller said, "I understand, but I got to be sure we aren't breaking any laws here."

Spencer stood nose-to-nose. "Shoot me or get the hell out of my way."

The Sheriff, shaken by Spencer's fury, backed off and motioned to the deputy standing in front of Spencer's car.

"You heard him; this is an emergency. Lead them straight to Blue Creek and I'll follow."

"Follow me, sir," the deputy said to Spencer, pointing at a patrol car.

Biggers, Cooley, and Bridges could see the lights of another checkpoint as they approached. The patrol officer waved them through, and Bo kept up his speed. On the radio, they heard Fitzgerald calling them. Cooley acknowledged.

"Cooley, where are you?"

"We just passed the second checkpoint."

"Good, you're closing the gap. When you get to the County line, there'll be a Sheriff's car there to escort you straight to Blue Creek, understand?"

"I got it."

"If they give you any trouble just run over them like Spencer did." Cooley heard Spencer swear and call the Sheriff a moron in the background.

"I wonder what that's about," Cooley said to Bridges and Bo.

Bo could see the Sheriff's car on the side of the road as he approached the County line and began to slow down, but the deputy flashed his lights, pulled out, and accelerated.

Bo said, "I guess we follow him."

After they were through town, the patrol car in front of Spencer slowed down. Skip got a call on the radio from the Sheriff.

"The road is hard to find in the dark. It's not marked and it's dirt. He has to go slow to see it. Once we find it, I'll go in with you and leave him on the road as a marker for the others. They're not far behind."

The deputy's brake lights blinked on, and the car stopped. The Sheriff pulled out from behind and motioned for them to follow as he went by. They turned onto a dirt road and drove into the woods. The Sheriff's car stopped, and he got out. Spencer and Skip followed suit. In the headlights was a large iron gate.

Bo soon saw blue lights ahead on the side of the road. "That must be it, we're slowing down."

The deputy on the road signaled for them to turn into the dirt road. Bo did as directed and drove into the woods. Within minutes, they pulled up to the stopped cars and joined the group, stymied by the closed gate.

Spencer turned and said, "Glad you're here, any ideas?"

# Chapter 25

MEADORS SAT HUNCHED in the co-pilot seat, prepped the M-1, and then checked his pistol and spare clips. Ivory watched with concern.

"Meadors, what's going on, man?"

"We got to get to Blue Creek before the feds. Once they get there Alisheen will be in danger because they're after Carl Powers."

"Why?"

"He's a drug smuggler and murderer. He's responsible for the deaths of those two men murdered in his warehouse on Wednesday."

Ivory's lips formed a whistle that went unheard with the noise of the helicopter.

"I'm not going to get busted for flying your ass in there am I?"

"No way, man. They won't have any idea how I got there."

Ivory smiled in relief.

Meadors said, "Do you think we're ahead of them?"

"If they're flying those big choppers and using the buoy, yeah, we'll beat them there. Besides, you're forgetting who you're talking to."

Meadors gave a high-five and yelled, "Only the best damn chopper pilot in the whole damn desert!"

"You bet your ass!" yelled Ivory.

Meadors said, "Get the hell out of dodge after I'm on the ground. How much longer?"

Ivory checked his watch and looked out the window.

"Fifteen minutes. We're over the marsh, and the first thing on the other side is Blue Creek. We'll follow that, and the tower will be on our left. We should be coming up on the creek in about five minutes."

Meadors nodded. He could see the creek in the distance shining in the moon light. After they crossed the creek, they turned and paralleled the water.

Ivory said, "There's the tower, bro. I'll drop you in the yard by the guardhouse and point the chopper in the direction you need to go, but its due north just in case. It's about two-hundred yards through the trees from there."

Ivory put the chopper down with a feather touch and shook Meadors' hand.

"Good luck, man."

"Thanks, Ivory. I owe you one."

Meadors hopped to the ground, slung the rifle, and took off at a fast jog, checking the compass on his watchband as he entered the tree line. Ivory watched him disappear before he lifted off and turned for home.

Rupert had let the dogs out the back door and was standing on the pool deck when they began barking and running for the front yard.

"Must be a deer again."

He trotted through the house to get to the front and heard the first shot followed by the dog's yelp. He ran for the front door and heard the muffled boom of a second shot. Rupert turned on the ground lights, went out the door. He could see the dogs on the ground.

"Oh my God, some damn fool has shot these dogs!"

As Rupert started toward the animals, he glimpsed a figure on the lawn walking toward the house. He turned and hurried back inside the door, closing it behind him. He locked and bolted the door in a swift motion. He ran to the doors in the back, locked them as well, and hurried to the study, arousing Powers as he slept in the easy chair.

"Mr. Carl, you got to wake up."

Powers instantly woke at the panic in Rupert's voice and stood up.

"What's the matter?"

"Mr. Carl, there's somebody out there with a gun. They shot the dogs. They're coming toward the house right now."

Carl was in disbelief.

"What?"

Rupert grabbed his arm and pulled.

"We got no time to talk about it, Mr. Carl. I'll go get Miss Alisheen and take her out so she's safe. You go outside and hide, Mr. Carl. Maybe all they want to do is rob the house!"

Carl grabbed him by the shoulders and said calmly, "Did you see who it is?"

Rupert, impatient with Carl's demeanor said, "I don't know, Mr. Carl, but whoever it is, they is coming to the house! We got to get out of here!"

Carl walked over to the desk, opened the drawer, and pulled out a pistol.

"No more guns, Mr. Carl, please." He put the gun back in the drawer and closed it.

"OK, Rupert, calm down. Where're you going to take Alisheen?"

Rupert showed relief that Carl was beginning to cooperate.

"I'll take her out the old slave tunnel to the woods and put her on the path by the creek. She can run to the neighbor's house from there and call the police. I'll come back by the path after she's gone and meet you at the dock."

"OK, go get Alisheen."

As Carl went toward the back of the house, he heard loud knocks on the door. He froze in his tracks when the intruder screamed with a hysterical voice.

"I'm going to kill you, Alisheen Delaney!"

"Damn, it's Jeanette!"

Rupert was at the top of the stairs when he heard the enraged scream of the intruder. It was a woman, and she was going to kill Miss Alisheen. Suddenly, the sound of gunfire and the thud of bullets hitting the front door meant only one thing; the woman was trying to shoot the lock loose so she could get in. Rupert ran down the hall and met Alisheen coming out of her door. She was tying her robe and putting on slippers.

"Rupert, what's happening?" she said anxiously. "Do I hear shots and somebody screaming my name?"

Rupert grabbed her hand and pulled her with him.

"Miss Alisheen, you got to come right now."

Alisheen sensed the need for urgency and quickly followed. He led her down the hidden steps to the kitchen. At the bottom, he stopped and pushed the wall; it opened. As they entered the room behind the wall, the front door crashed open as the intruder finally succeeded breaking in.

Alisheen heard a voice call out loudly as if it was playing a game, "I'm going to kill you, Alisheen Delaney!"

Alisheen gasped, recognizing the voice. It was Jeanette LaCrosse.

"Come on, Miss, we got to get you out of here."

Rupert pulled her the rest of the way into the dark room, closed the door, and locked it from the inside. He turned on a flashlight, signaled for her to be quiet and to follow him. Across the room, he led her to a set of steps that went down into darkness. She held up the bottom of her gown and robe to keep from tripping, and she followed Rupert as he held the light for her to see the steps. At the bottom was a tunnel with a stone floor leading off into the dark.

Rupert held her hand and whispered an explanation. "This tunnel was used to help slaves escape long before, and even some after, the war. It runs out to a stone house on the property near the creek. They used it as a cold house back then."

They continued in silence until they reached a blank wall. Rupert pushed and it opened. "This is the back wall of the room they kept the cold goods in," he explained.

They entered a wooden framed room with a set of steps that led up to the ceiling. Rupert flashed his light and grinned at Alisheen.

"There it is."

He led her up the stairs and pushed on the ceiling. It gave easily and Rupert held it by the rope handle so it wouldn't fall over and make a noise. He closed the door after she climbed out.

"Come on, Miss."

He cut off the flashlight before they went outside.

"We got good moonlight to see by. We're almost a quarter mile from the house."

After a short walk through the woods, they were on the path that followed the bank of the creek.

"Miss Alisheen, that woman is here to kill you, so you got to get out of here."

Rupert pointed in the direction away from the house.

"You go that way and don't stop until you get to the neighbors. The people there are the Moore's. They're good people, and they'll help you. You can call for help from there too. I'm going back to find Mr. Carl. He's going to meet me at the dock, and then we're coming."

Alisheen started to protest, but Rupert shushed her.

"Now Miss Alisheen, you do as I say now and get out of here. Mr. Carl and me will be OK, and we'll be along in a little bit. Go on now."

Alisheen gave Rupert a hug and a peck on the cheek, then at a fast pace walked down the path toward the neighbors. Rupert watched her go and then hurried toward the dock. When Alisheen was sure she was out of sight, she stopped and checked her watch. She decided to wait for about twenty minutes. If they didn't come by then she was going back.

~~~~

Jeanette finally got through the door and went upstairs. She opened every door of every room, closet, and bathroom, hoping she'd find Alisheen hiding somewhere.

In her state of madness, she was calling out in singsong, "Come out, come out, wherever you are. I'm going to kill you."

Frustrated with her search, she began to scream Alisheen's name hysterically, proclaiming she was going to kill her. Unsuccessful upstairs, she went back downstairs and resumed her search. Every minute that went by without finding Alisheen or Carl increased her rage.

She stood in the entry hall and yelled.

"You can't hide from me forever bitch. I'm going to find you, and I'm going to kill you!"

With an evil smile, she took a new tact.

"I'm going to kill her, Carl. I told you I would! I just want what's mine, what I'm due. I love you; didn't you know? I'll be great for you. Together, we'd be unbeatable."

Her mental storm reached a state of calm that disguised her insanity. She realized the house was probably empty because they'd heard her coming. She went out the french doors onto the deck and fired a shot into the air. She laughed and yelled.

"I'm going to kill her Carl. You bastard, I'll kill her when I find her."

She went back into the house screaming and firing random shots into the walls and ceiling. She threw lamps and vases in anger, crashing them into the walls. From the dock, Carl could hear her, and his anger rose to a point that drove him back to the house. Rupert was coming up the path.

"Is she safe?"

Rupert nodded out of breath.

"Yes, sir. She's gone to the Moore's for help."

"Good, you go too. I'm going back to the house now that she's safe and stop this."

"Do you know who it is, Mr. Carl?"

Carl nodded. "It's Jeanette LaCrosse."

"Then I'm going with you."

"Rupert, it's too dangerous."

Rupert shook his head.

"I'm going and that's final. She's crazy, and you'll need my help."

Carl knew there was no chance of changing his mind. "OK. Go through the woods and around to the front to see if the dogs are dead or wounded. Then go to the gate and open it. When Alisheen gets to the Moore's she'll call the police and they'll need to be able to get through the gate."

Rupert nodded and said, "You be careful, Mr. Carl. That woman has lost her mind."

"I will, Rupert. You better get going now."

Carl watched him enter the woods and then walked calmly toward the house, crossing the lawn and stopping at the pool, keeping it between him and the house. He yelled loudly so she'd hear him inside.

"Here I am, Jeanette! Come and get what you deserve."

Jeanette LaCrosse was upstairs and stopped suddenly when she heard her name called. She heard it again and ran to the nearest window, looking out. Carl was standing by the pool still dressed in his clothes from the Ball, with his bow tie hanging loose around his neck.

For a brief moment, she thought, "How handsome he looked," but the moment of sanity snapped when he yelled out.

"She's gone, Jeanette, you missed your chance."

She screamed with rage, ran down the stairs and out the back through the french doors. She stopped on the other side of the pool and faced him.

"Carl, how could you do this to me? I love you!"

Then her demeanor changed.

"Where is she, Carl?"

Carl shifted his position slightly, moving toward the cabana bar at the end of the pool.

"Stop right there, Carl," Jeanette said with dangerous calm, pointing her gun.

"She's gone, Jeanette. It's just you and me now."

He moved toward the cabana again.

"Please stop, Carl, and tell me where she is. She's keeping us from being happy."

Carl moved again and she cocked the pistol. Jeanette started to cry from hysteria and rage, but the pistol didn't waver.

"I told you to stop, Carl. I don't want to kill you. I love you with all my heart. I've always loved you. Ever since the beginning when we first started working together. Don't you understand? It's our destiny. Together we built Coastal, but you never gave me any credit."

Her tone changed and she became more dangerous.

"You bastard, you never even thanked me by taking me out to dinner or buying me a gift. It was just a casual, 'Thank you, Miss LaCrosse,' or 'you do such a great job around here."

She laughed with increasing hysteria.

"Oh, this is my favorite, 'I don't know how I could've done it without you."

"Jeanette, I admitted I overlooked your contribution and the role you played in building Coastal. I conceded that. You got your title and the recognition you so dearly craved."

Jeanette screamed, "Overlooked, overlooked! You couldn't have done any of it without me."

Carl moved toward the cabana again, and she fired a warning shot.

"I told you to stop. I don't care about any of that now. I just want you to love me."

Her voice increased in pitch and volume.

"I dressed up for you in sexy shoes and clothes. I exercised and dieted to be beautiful, but you never even noticed until I forced you to pay attention to me. I even overlooked your dirty little secret of drug smuggling. I know you've killed people and made others disappear. I know everything, Carl. All of it, all of it, I was willing to ignore because I loved you, but you screwed it all up because you got the hots for that bitch."

Carl had used the time LaCrosse talked to edge closer to the cabana. She suddenly realized he was moving, and she fired. He'd managed to get close enough to the cabana to dive for cover. She fired several shots at the bottom of the building, knowing he was on the ground. She was raging again.

"I'm going to find her, Carl, and when I do, I'm going to kill her. I promise you. I'll shoot you if you interfere. You're mine, you bastard, and there's nowhere for you to go."

Rupert made his way through the woods and broke into the clear in the front when he heard the first shot. Torn between going back and doing what Mr. Carl had told him to do, he caught sight of the dogs on the lawn. With a tear in his eye, he hurried forward. One dog was dead, but the other was still alive. She'd shot the dog in the leg, breaking it, but the dog would live. He patted it on the head and the dog licked his arm in return with a slight whimper.

Rupert said affectionately, "I know boy, pretty soon we'll get you fixed up."

At the sound of another shot, he ran to her car, started it, and drove toward the gate. He could see lights twinkling off through the woods.

"It must be the police. Miss Alisheen made it!"

Rupert got to the gate, parked, and jumped out, yelling, "I'm coming. I'm coming."

Sheriff Miller yelled, "Rupert, open the gate."

Rupert was out of breath.

"There's a crazy woman at the house. She shot the dogs, and she's shooting up the house and talking about killing Miss Alisheen."

Spencer said in a panic, "Open this gate and tell me where Alisheen is."

Rupert looked at him and said, "I got her away. She's safe, Mister."

He went to punch in the code and said, "You damn fools, it ain't even locked."

"How could we be so stupid?" Spencer said with anger. "We didn't even try to open it."

They drove through the gate with Rupert in the lead car.

They stopped the cars on the lawn and Rupert said, "She's in the back."

~~~~

Alisheen waited twenty minutes and reversed her direction on the path, finally reaching the dock. The "Po Boy" rocked gently with the tide, but there was no one there. She looked toward the house and could see Carl and LaCrosse by the pool. Alisheen sensed danger but couldn't turn away if Carl and Rupert needed help. She took off her robe and hung it over the dock railing, then bent over and, with her teeth, made a tear in her long nightgown. She ripped off the bottom making it knee length. She kicked off her slippers, wishing she'd thought to put on her running shoes, but who knew what in the hell was going on at the time? She'd be much faster barefoot if she needed to run.

Alisheen crept toward the house, staying hidden in the edge of the trees. She was finally able to determine that Carl was on her side of the pool and LaCrosse on the other, pointing a gun. Undeterred, she kept moving. She could hear snippets of LaCrosse's tirade but not enough to know what was going on. Then Carl made a sudden leap for the cabana and LaCrosse fired. Alisheen could see Carl on the ground but couldn't tell if he was dead or not.

LaCrosse screamed as she fired additional shots at the cabana. Alisheen froze. Carl was crawling toward the dock, trying to keep the cabana between himself and LaCrosse. She began to walk around the pool toward Carl. Alisheen knew that if she saw him crawling on the ground, she'd kill him. She had no choice, and before she knew it, she was running across the lawn toward Carl when LaCrosse saw her.

"I'm going to kill you," she yelled and fired a quick shot in Alisheen's direction.

Alisheen turned and ran for the dock and path, hoping LaCrosse would follow her and bypass Carl. She planned to lose her in the woods until help arrived. Her diversion worked. LaCrosse ignored Carl on the ground and gave chase. Alisheen heard another bullet go by as LaCrosse fired again but didn't slow down. She knew her life depended on it.

~~~~

Spencer and Skip came around the corner of the house prepared to fire, but there was no one there. They heard the scream and the shot and saw a figure running for the woods with LaCrosse giving chase.

Spencer yelled, "That's Alisheen!"

Skip said, "We've got to hurry, or we'll lose them in the woods."

Suddenly, from off the ground in front of them, a figure lunged up and gave chase to the fleeing women. It was Powers, and he was still fast for a man his age because he was closing the gap on LaCrosse.

"Hurry," yelled Spencer, and he ran after them as they headed for the woods. As they reached the dock, they heard a shot, a loud scream, and then two more shots in the woods.

"That was Alisheen. *Oh God, please let her be all right,*" he prayed as they ran into the woods. Spencer yelled her name, but there was no answer. They slowed down to a trot on the path for the moonlight was partially blocked by the trees and it was harder to see. They held their guns ready. In the distance, they could hear shouts from the house. Going farther, they could see a body in the path trying to crawl down toward the water. It was Powers. He was alive but bleeding badly from wounds in the shoulder and the leg. Not far from him, lay LaCrosse sprawled on her back. She was dead from a headshot.

They heard Meadors calling, "Down here, I need some help, quick."

Spencer crashed the brush next to the path and, bursting through, found Meadors in the water up to his knees. He was holding Alisheen, and she was as limp as a rag doll in his arms. Spencer and Skip helped Meadors out of the water and steadied him as they made the path.

Spencer said with tears streaming down his face, "Give her to me."

He took off at as fast of a pace as he could toward the dock. The grounds were flooded with lights and people as Spencer made it to the dock and turned toward the grounds, on the run now that he could see better. He met the EMTs halfway between the dock and the pool. Alisheen was breathing but slow and very shallow. She was losing a lot of blood from a bullet wound in her back. They got it packed, put her on a stretcher, and hurried to a waiting ambulance. Spencer climbed in behind her and held her hand. He leaned over and spoke to her softly, hoping she could hear him.

"I love you, Al, please don't leave me. I need you. Please hold on. I love you."

Skip and Meadors appeared carrying Powers between them. He was still conscious and bleeding. At the dock, they eased him to the ground and made him comfortable.

Skip said, "Mr. Powers, before anything else happens, I need to inform you that you're under arrest."

Powers just smiled, winced with the pain, then passed out.

Meadors said, "I don't think he was surprised by your news."

Meadors waved at the paramedics urging them to hurry. They came quickly and attended to Powers' wounds.

Meadors looked at Skip and said, "Now what?"

Skip exclaimed, "To hell with that. How did you get here so fast, and what in the hell happened in the woods?"

Meadors smiled wryly. "I'd call it almost perfect timing."

Meadors explained his buddy, Ivory was an ex-Marine pilot and a friend from his Afghanistan tours. He knew the area well and had gotten him here in record time.

"Two-hundred yards south of here is an old fire tower station they use in the dry season. He knew about it, oddly enough, because he'd picked up Powers there a couple of times and flown him to the airport. He dropped me in the yard at the fire tower, and I hauled ass through the woods."

"I came out and saw Alisheen moving through the trees toward the house. I couldn't do anything but get to her side of the yard and into the trees so I could try to cover her. I didn't want to call out to her because that would've drawn LaCrosse's attention, and her fire, to Alisheen."

"Unfortunately, she did that on her own by running out into the open, distracting LaCrosse's attention from Powers on the ground. I watched her turn and run toward the dock, but then my angle was bad and I couldn't cover her. I could see LaCrosse running after her, and then I saw Powers get up and start chasing them. I cut through the woods hoping to get between Alisheen and LaCrosse, but I got there too late."

Meadors explained that as he broke out of the woods onto the path, Alisheen had already run past him. He saw LaCrosse aim and fire the pistol and Alisheen scream and turn, staggering into the woods. LaCrosse then turned and shot Powers running up behind her. She was oblivious to Meadors, who aimed, ordered her to drop her weapon, and put her hands behind her head.

"Everything went into slow motion from that point on. She turned around slowly and when she saw me, she just laughed and then smiled at me. I ordered her to drop her weapon and put her hands behind her head again. She just kept smiling at me and then she began to raise the gun. I ordered her to stop, but she kept going. I had to shoot her."

Meadors hung his head.

"I didn't want to, but she left me no choice. I had to kill her. If I wounded her, she'd still be too dangerous for me to approach."

Skip said, "I got it, Meadors. I understand."

Meadors picked his head up at Skip's words and cleared his throat.

"Anyway, I knew Alisheen was hit so I went into the woods after her. She was floating in the water face down. I jumped in and got her out as quick as I could. I heard you up on the path and yelled for help. You know the rest."

Blackwell's team approached from the water, and he wasn't happy. Their target was lit up like a Christmas tree and given the number of ambulances and people, it was already over.

"Crap," said Tommy over the headset. "We obviously took the long way."

Blackwell looked at him and with sarcasm said, "Did you figure that out all by yourself?"

"Put it down away from the buildings toward this end of the grounds. Pass the word onto the other team to get ready to deploy. We still might have to persuade them to give up Powers."

As Blackwell and Tommy hit the ground with their teams, he saw Fitzgerald waving at him from the ground.

"Over there."

Blackwell saw several people heading their direction in a hurry.

Blackwell said, "Keep those locals out of the way."

Tommy shouted orders and the team spread out and fired a couple of shots into the air. They yelled, "federal agents" and told everyone to "stay back."

The crowd stopped in their tracks, and the men had spread out effectively, creating a perimeter screen.

Blackwell walked up to Fitzgerald.

"Where is Powers? I hope for your sake that he's still here."

Skip said with contempt, "You're in luck, asshole. He's wounded, and I've been able to keep him isolated for you. The EMTs have him stabilized for now, but he's going to need a doctor if you're going to get him to Virginia alive."

Blackwell ignored Fitzgerald's tone.

"Where?"

"On the dock. The paramedics are with him, but they'll stand down with no problem."

"And LaCrosse?"

"Dead," said Skip, and he walked away.

"Nice guy," said Tommy wryly.

"Yeah, he's a real charmer," said Blackwell. "Pull two men with a stretcher and take Powers along with the EMTs to the airport the short way. Call and have a doctor meet us at the airport with whatever support he needs, whether it's people or supplies. Take the EMTs with us to Virginia if we have to."

"Will do."

He called out to a couple of men, gave orders, and they separated themselves from the perimeter group.

"Done. What's next?"

"As soon as Powers is out of here and on the way, we follow but not until he's clear."

Tommy again issued orders to the men on the ground, and two more broke away to help get Powers on the stretcher and into the chopper. The EMTs were protesting but weren't getting anywhere, and Powers was loaded onto the helicopter along with the EMTs. The doors closed and they were airborne. Tommy and Blackwell signaled for the rest of the team to back out, and they covered them from the chopper. They were on board and lifted off heading toward Savannah.

Skip watched them leave and when the twinkling lights of the choppers were gone, he turned toward the house. He went inside and found Cooley and Bridges.

"Where's the Sheriff?"

"Gone," said Cooley. "He took Rupert and the one dog that was still alive to the vet."

Skip laughed. "How about that? After all we went through tonight, it ends with the dog going to the vet. Ain't that a kick in the butt."

Bridges asked, "Where's Powers?"

Skip waved in the direction of the docks.

"They took him. He'll be exonerated and resume his wonderful life. We never had the evidence we needed anyway since we couldn't name him as the Snowman."

"What about the tattoo?" asked Cooley. "How can they make that go away?"

"They'll come up with a whole bunch of people that have that same tattoo, and since the gun had no prints there's really no way to actually put it in Powers' hand."

"But" said Bridges, "what about the video, and what happens to Mickey?"

"I'm sure something will happen to the disc, and it will be missing, edited, or ruined. One way or the other they want Powers exonerated and him to return to outstanding citizen status. As for Mickey, he'll be fine. The evidence will become circumstantial, and it'll all go away."

Bridges said, "How can they do something like that?"

Cooley looked at him.

"Junior, sometimes there are things in this world we just can't explain."

Bridges and Skip began to laugh, and they laughed together.

After they settled down, Cooley said, "What happened to LaCrosse?"

"Dead," said Fitzgerald. "Meadors shot her to keep her from shooting him."

"Meadors!" exclaimed Bridges. "How in the hell did he get here in time?"

Meadors came walking in through the door to the den.

"Did I hear my name?"

Skip laughed.

"I'll let you tell it. I'm still not sure how you pulled it off."

He felt his phone buzz in his pocket, and he left them standing there as Meadors began his tale. Skip went out to the pool deck and sat in one of the lounge chairs. He put his head back and answered his phone. It was Carol.

"What in the hell is going on? The police scanners are going crazy. Are you alright?"

A thought came to Skip.

"I'll tell you what. Why don't I come over and tell you in person?"

He paused and realized that the sun would be coming up in a couple of hours.

"Better yet, we can have breakfast at your place, and I'll tell you all about it. It'll be about that time by the time I get there anyway. Then I can take a nice long nap after breakfast. I've been up all night and I'm bushed."

Carol was silent for a moment, and Skip thought he'd gone too far.

Carol said with a teasing tone. "Are you sure you finally want to go there, Agent Fitzgerald?"

"Yes, I do. I'm even thinking about getting myself reassigned to Savannah with a raise, now that I have some leverage."

"How do you like your eggs?"

"Scrambled with cheese. I'll see you in a little while."

"I'll be waiting."

"We got a lot to talk about, don't we?"

Carol said with a sexy laugh that made Skip feel wonderful inside, "Eat first then talk. I'll see you later."

As he was about to hang up she quickly said, "Skip, wait, there's something I forgot to tell you."

"What is it?"

"They detained Benny in Newark. He was on the bus all right. What do you want me to tell them?"

"Tell them to turn him loose and send him on his way. It's a case of mistaken identity."

"OK, and hurry up, will you? I'm starving!"

Skip turned off his cell phone and put it in his pocket. He put his head back and closed his eyes. He heard footsteps and then the voices of Cooley and Bridges as they approached.

"If you want a ride with us, you better wake up. It's time to get out of here."

Skip didn't open his eyes but said, "Where is Meadors and what happened to Bo?"

"Meadors is out front, and the paramedics are trying to get him to go to the hospital," said Cooley.

Skip opened his eyes. "Why?"

"Evidently," laughed Bridges, "He took a pretty good tumble running through the woods and his shoulder is broken. They're trying to get him into the ambulance so they can take him to the hospital for x-rays and to set the shoulder. Bo is out front taunting him about being a baby."

Skip laughed lightly. "Let's go help them so we can go home."

Meadors finally gave in on the condition that Bo drive him so he could drive him back to Savannah because he wasn't going to stay in any hospital. Bo agreed, if Meadors would buy breakfast. It was a done deal, and they followed the ambulance to the hospital.

Skip said, "Let's go too, boys, I'm tired."

Cooley looked at Bridges, "Junior, you drive. The old men are tired."

Skip said, "Speak for yourself about the old part," and they all got into the car laughing and headed for Savannah.

As they hit the bridge and crested the top, the sun was rising. It was a bright fireball signaling the dawn of a new day.

"Man, that's beautiful, isn't it?" Bridges said.

"Absolutely," said Skip.

~~~~

Alisheen's eyes fluttered open, and she tried to shift positions but found she was bound with bandages and lying in a hospital bed. She turned her head with some effort and saw Spencer staring at her.

"You look tired Spencer, and you need a shave."

Spencer laughed, choked back a tear, and said with a raspy voice, "You look wonderful. How do you feel?"

Alisheen grimaced and smiled wryly. "I feel like I've been hit with a ton of bricks. What happened?"

Spencer stood up, walked over to the bed, and gently held her hand. "A lot has happened. Are you sure you want to know now?"

Alisheen shook her head and squeezed Spencer's hand.

"Jeanette Lacrosse shot you in the back on the path in the woods. You stumbled into the woods below the path and fell into the water. She also shot Powers. Meadors had to shoot her and she's dead. He rescued you from the water, and I carried you to the house. The paramedics stabilized you, and we put you in the ambulance. That was early Saturday morning."

"What day is it now?"

"It's Tuesday."

"I remember falling into the water, vaguely anyway. Meadors got me out?"

"Yep, he saved your life and Powers' too. If he hadn't been there to stop LaCrosse, she would have killed you both."

"Where am I?"

"St. Joe's in Savannah."

He stroked her hair and kissed her cheek.

"What happened to Rupert, is he all right?"

"Yes, he's fine. She killed one of the dogs, but they were able to save the other one. He was talking about getting a new puppy last time he was here to see you."

"That was sweet of him to come."

"He's a fan," said Spencer with a smile.

Alisheen struggled to sit up a bit and Spencer helped her and fluffed her pillows. "You said Carl was wounded, what else?"

"He's OK and in DC with the feds. They took him there because they need his help with something very important. They're looking after him. I expect he'll be back in Savannah in a few weeks and back to business as usual."

"I'm glad he's going to be OK."

She licked her lips and Spencer fed her some ice chips.

"Thanks, that tastes wonderful."

She looked around some more and noticed the room was full of flowers.

"Oh, the flowers are so pretty. Who are they from?"

Spencer laughed. "Everybody. The gang at the She Crab, lots of your friends, the guys at the police station, and me of course."

Spencer suddenly grabbed both her hands and held them gently. "Alisheen, this is all my fault. If I hadn't been such a jerk, this never would've happened. I'm so sorry. I love you."

She reached up and stopped the tear as it rolled down his cheek. "Spencer, come closer. I want to tell you something."

Spencer bent down closer to her.

"Put your ear closer to my lips so I can whisper."

He did as she requested, and she whispered in his ear with a gentle kiss on his earlobe.

"I love you too."

He looked at her, and his eyes flooded with tears. "Alisheen, will you marry me?"

She smiled and squeezed his hand. "I don't know. I might have to consult with Dixie first."

Spencer laughed and she smiled.

~~~~

"Mr. Powers?"

Carl turned his head as two men walked into his hospital room and closed the door.

"Where exactly am I?"

"You're in private room—on a private floor I might add, in Walter Reed hospital in D.C."

"I see."

"Let me introduce myself, Mr. Powers," said the older man. "I am Isaac Henry, the Director of the D.E.A. This is my associate, Ben Whitley."

Powers said with curiosity, "Am I under arrest?"

"Oh, no," said Whitley with a very nervous laugh.

Henry said, "We have a proposition for you Mr. Powers."

"I'm listening."

~~~~

Clifton Chambers sat in his new office as the Deputy Director of the D.E.A. and looked out at the much grander view than he had before. He picked up the phone and called Saul Levy, who answered with his usual less than enthusiastic, and very bored, "Hello?"

"Saul, Clifton Chambers, how're you doing these days?"

"You son-of-a-bitch, Clifton. I haven't heard from you in two weeks, and then the next thing I know, you're a Deputy Director. What happened? What in the hell is going on over there?"

"Saul, do you still have the key to the safe deposit box I gave you?"

"Yeah, I got it, what's going on Clifton?"

"Keep it! I'll call you for lunch one day soon and we'll catch up." Then he hung up.

Saul stared at the receiver for a moment and hung up. It suddenly dawned on him what Clifton had meant, and he laughed as he lit a cigarette.

"Well, I'll be damned."

He opened the drawer, took out his scotch, and poured a generous cupful. He raised it with a smile and a toast, "God Bless America!"

# About the Author

Jay is a retired Healthcare Administrator and Consultant. A graduate of Clemson University and the Medical University of South Carolina, he has always had an interest in writing and is looking forward to publishing his first book, Seizing Jurisdiction. He is already working on new projects and expects the next one to be available next year.

When not writing, Jay is enjoying his retirement and catching up on all the projects left undone while he was working and traveling. He lives with his wife in South Carolina, and they have three children and two grandchildren.

Made in the USA
Columbia, SC
05 March 2023

13353576R00264